To Terrance,

Hope you enjoy the READ.

Daniel Eugene

EMPIRES AND KINGDOMS

The
English Slave

David Eugene Andrews

ADAMO PRESS
Aliso Viejo, Calif.

Library of Congress Control Number: 2016958643

Cover design by John Deguzman.
Cover background art by Adèle Franklin.
Used with written permission.
Maps and photographs by David Eugene Andrews.
ISBN 978-0-9862471-2-5

Dedication

This book is dedicated to my nieces and nephews, since the next generation must write their own history, and to my son and daughter, whom I have always encouraged to "do the right thing."

Table of Contents

EMPIRES AND KINGDOMS

The
English Slave

Chapter 1 - Axiopolis Slave Auction

At Axiopolis they were all sold for slaves, like beasts in a marketplace, where every merchant, viewing their limbs and wounds, caused other slaves to struggle with them, to try their strength . . .

John Smith

Campsite, Wallachia, Southeastern Europe, Late Nov. 1602

"PRISONER! COME HERE!" The short captor tugged the rope.

The knot cut into Captain John Smith's wrist. His half-eaten biscuit slipped from his fingers, crumbling on the ground.

"Prisoner! Come here!" The scar on his captor's neck grew larger as he yanked the rope again—harder.

Like a bowstring drawn taut, his shoulders flung forward: Smith staggered to his feet.

His tormentor motioned to his two compatriots. Hurry up!

They hastened to their two-wheeled cart, filled with weapons and metal pillaged from the deadly battlefield miles away. One captor, his hair tangled and long, unhitched their bay horse and tied it to a tree. The last of the trio secured the cart, chocking rocks beneath its thick-spoked wheels, and picked up Smith's fancy saber and battered shield.

Retrieving Smith's favorite knife, the captor tucked it into his waistband. He killed the flames of their overnight campfire, kicking dirt onto the smoldering coals.

The short captor tugged the rope taut again and led Smith out of the thicket of trees. Leaving behind their transport and horse, safely hidden, the other two pushed Smith along the overgrown trail. "Keep up!"

The English captain lurched forward and regained his balance. The four weaved around the hill along the narrow path ending at a river.

Morning mist floated above the wide river, so large John knew it must be the Danube. He floundered along the muddy riverbanks. The thick haze, like a damp rag, clung to John's skin. At an outcrop of rocks, the four hikers scaled a boulder. Below, a waiting ferryman waved the cap-

1

tors and their prize forward. His flat-bottom boat, large enough to hold a family and wedged between two boulders, did not appear stable.

After negotiating a fare and handing the skipper a coin, the small captor led John onto the skiff. As soon as they and the other two escorts sat down, the crewman shoved off and the ferryman steered his less-than-steady craft into the current.

In the middle of the lower Danube, the border separating Ottoman-controlled territory from Wallachia, John peered back. A morning breeze kicked up along the Wallachian shore, pushing away the light fog and baring trees of their leaves. Beyond muddy riverbanks and the fruitful Wallachian plains, the Carpathian Mountains, separating Wallachia from Transylvania, rose high.

Still suffering from battle wounds, John turned his attention back toward the bow. The bright autumn sun behind the pillager's head reminded John of the day he was found. Sorely wounded and dying in a sea of departed friends, Smith had readied himself to meet his Maker when the man with the neck scar found him.

During the days following that terrible battle at the foot of the Carpathian Mountains north of Targoviste, the three captors had nursed the richly decorated captain back to health. Smith had recovered at their hidden lair nestled deep in the plains of Wallachia, disputed territory indirectly controlled by the Habsburg leader of the Holy Roman Emperor, Rudolph II.

The trio of captors escorted John from their lair to the hidden campsite. After his treatment that morning, one thing had become clear: the three were not his friends. They nursed him back to health only because they considered him worth more alive than dead. The care they had shown him during his recovery evaporated faster than morning mist.

In the middle of the Danube, John focused on several fishermen tossing nets from small vessels. Other fishermen cast lines from the far shore. Below a bluff where the Danube widened, the oars of an Ottoman slave galley hit the water. As it passed by the front of their skiff, the ferryman pointed to the knoll, topped by fortified walls and square towers. "Axiopolis!"

John had heard of the former Byzantine border town. He suspected his Gypsy or *Roma* captors—like the Midianites who had taken Joseph, the Biblical youngest son of Israel, and sold him in Egypt—planned to sell John into slavery.

The English Captain viewed the stone walls of Axiopolis for the first time. Nearly a dozen towers overlooked the right bank of the Danube and the town below. Cannons protruded from the stone towers, protecting the dark city from potential enemies, whether Cossacks from the Dnieper River or the armies of the Holy Roman Empire. Hoping against hope, knowing almost all of his friends had died, John looked around—a Christian army was nowhere to be found.

Axiopolis, Silistra Province, Ottoman Empire, Nov. 1602

THE HELMSMAN EASED his skiff to the busy dock. His crewman jumped out, secured the line, and pulled the stern straight. The captor with a scarred neck stepped out and tugged the rope tied to Captain John Smith. "Prisoner!"

Smith stepped onto the dock and the boat shifted. His foot caught the edge. Smith's bearded face headed toward weathered wood. Throbbing pangs raced through John's side. His wounded ribs ached beneath outstretched arms.

The second captor caught him just in time. The captor's neck tensed, his scar bulged.

He must not want his property damaged, John thought.

The last captor, carrying John's dented shield emblazoned with his Coat of Arms, disembarked.

The bound Englishman, his feet loosely tied, shuffled through the crowds on the busy dock. A local fisherman wrestled a basket of fish, brimmed full.

The captors stopped John and waited for a line of slaves with shouldered sacks of grain to pass. One slave stepped too close to the dock's edge and slipped. His knees slammed against the deck. The weakened wood cracked and a piece broke loose. His sack split open. Grain leaked onto the water mere feet below. A slave driver whipped the white slave.

"What's going on?" The loud voice reverberated down the dock.

The line of slaves stopped in mid-stride. Crowds pulled back. A large, turbaned guard stood at the end of the dock. Hands on his hips, the guard scowled and motioned to John and his three escorts. "Move!"

The slave scooped some of the grain back into the sack. Fish scavenged at the surface and birds swooped low.

Stepping off the dock onto dry land, John looked around. Three thick walls encircled the border town, ancient Axiopolis. Two older walls extended up the hill to his right. A third wall enclosed flatter terrain to his left.

The large tormentor shoved his captive. "Move!"

John squeezed between vendors manning their small booths. In the lower town, merchants and scores of local townsmen mingled. Some women wore veils, but many others, dressed in more colorful Bulgarian attire, did not.

The main road passed through a fortified gate in the middle of the second wall. To John's right, Ottoman sentries scrutinized incoming prisoners and exiting travelers.

At the guard station, an official collected taxes from merchants entering the city. With resignation on their faces, each paid. One merchant with a cartful of goods argued with the collector, but stopped when a sentry approached him.

Beyond the fortified gate, the busy main street of the center town teemed with activity. Townspeople emerged from numerous small wooden and stone houses that lined the side streets. Elderly women congregated by a priest in black garb by a small Byzantine Church built in the middle of the road.

Along the main road, a cart carrying lumber skirted around the church and moved further up the hill. High above, just before the gate in the first wall, the cart pulled to the side and abruptly stopped.

A Turkish rider, holding a standard, a pole eight feet tall, topped with a gold crescent and three horsetails, exited the upper gate. He yelled, "Make way! *Vizier Azem*!"

People parted for the Turkish leader wearing a massive turban and sporting a grey-streaked beard. An armed entourage followed.

Back at the bottom of the hill, the crowds hurried about their business.

"Keep moving!" The marauder with the scar shoved John once again—this time toward an arena just inside the third outer wall that encompassed the lower town.

On the left hand side, storage sheds for grain had been built. Open horse stalls also backed up against the outer wall. They extended from the docks all the way to the outer gate on the far side. Captain Smith, experienced in siege warfare, realized that the lower outer wall provided only minimal defense from infrequent attacks.

Slaves lugged more grain to the sheds, while attendants fed and groomed horses in the stalls. Directly in front of them, others secured saddles. They held the reins for Turkish riders, the *sipahi* cavalrymen, who had just exited nearby barracks.

Those cavalrymen quickly mounted. The Ottoman unit trotted past Smith through the outer gate. Just outside the gate, one lone tree quivered. Its dead, brown leaves swirled around its trunk when the riders' trot turned to a gallop. As they rode down an old Roman road that paralleled the Danube, the sky darkened.

Smith looked beyond the riders in the distance and saw several Tartar horsemen adorned in their traditional black sheepskin. The feared warriors—the direct descendants of Genghis Khan and the Mongols who had invaded Russia and Europe four centuries earlier—dragged several men behind them. The prisoners, dressed in the Slavic peasant attire of the borderlands, ran and struggled to keep pace with the small Tartar horses. After crossing the rolling open fields and reaching the road, the Tartar riders saluted the *sipahi* and approached the outer gate.

Arena, Lower Axiopolis, Ottoman Empire, Late Nov. 1602

INSIDE THE THIRD wall, morning fires dotted the perimeter of a large wooden corral. Smith and his captors walked toward a long corridor leading to the arena. As soon as they reached the chute, the captors handed the rope tied to his English prisoner to a Turkish guard.

Behind John, another prisoner wearing Italian attire entered the corridor. John asked him in Italian what was happening, *"Che cosa accadrà?"*

"Schiavo!" the Italian answered.

"They will auction us into slavery?"John asked.

"*Sì.* They call slaves *köle* in Turkish. After paying the Sultan's high tax, the slave merchants give money to the previous owners."

"*Banditi*, pillagers, and renegades."

"And soldiers," the Italian added. "That man takes money from successful bidders."

At a table behind the auctioneer, money changed hands.

John shook his head. "All cash in on the spoils of war." His suspicions about what was going to happen to him were confirmed.

"We will be sold into slavery, just like him." The Italian pointed to a man just purchased.

The news did not surprise John.

Although thankful he had survived the battle, John was uncertain what would happen next. He wore a uniform as fine as the coat of many colors that Biblical Israel gave to his favorite son Joseph. Like Joseph whose jealous brothers threw him into a pit, Captain John Smith could only trust God.

"Whatever you do, you don't want to be a galley slave," the Italian prisoner said. "Their fate is the worst. Most don't live long."

Captain Smith turned toward the dock. The tops of the masts of a slave galley slowed to a stop.

When the breeze picked up, the stifling smoke from nearby fires stung John's eyes. His throat was dry and irritated. He felt like coughing, but his ribs hurt too much.

"More prisoners!" The Italian gestured.

Just outside the fenced arena, dozens of guards watched scores of prisoners. Wooden cells held slaves not yet sold, but one cell was reserved for those just purchased.

The three captors reached the table manned by officials keeping accounts. The plunderers exchanged words with one of those seated and the small captor with the scar pointed to Smith.

The moneychanger marked the paper. He signaled the guard holding Smith's rope. The gate to the corridor opened and Smith entered.

The guard at the other end of the long chute motioned Smith forward. *"Buraya gel!"*

"*Buraya gel* means *venire qui*," the Italian translated.

Following the instructions, "Come here," Smith progressed down the corridor.

The first guard kicked the Englishman high on his upper thigh and yelled.

Pain shot up John's spine. He lurched forward and nearly fell. The memories of recovering wounds faded as quickly as new ones were inflicted.

The guard snapped his short whip. "Come here!"

Leaving the Italian prisoner behind, John stumbled down the narrow, fenced corridor and into a holding pen, more fit for cattle than for men.

One by one, the Italian and the other prisoners followed the English officer. The line of captives wove past the slave merchants.

A stream of sunlight caught the brown splotch on Smith's drab bandage. The nearby slave merchants looked at him intensely—like shoppers picking out and discarding meat at a butcher's stall: too tough, too red, or too lean.

One of them stepped closer to Smith and reached out towards the bandaged wound. The guard intervened and touched his sheathed scimitar, a curved sword. The startled merchant backed away.

Dressed in once sharp, but now torn, military attire, the captured Englishman entered the main arena. He stepped up onto a weathered boulder. Like a lone eagle on a perch, Smith scanned his surroundings. Both inside and outside the small, wooden fenced arena, numerous soldiers and hired mercenaries stood guard. They watched the waiting slaves, making certain none escaped.

Captain Smith noticed his three captors leaning against the fence. The largest one signaled the guard standing nearest the auctioneer and pointed to the Englishman's weaponry they had brought with them.

When the guard reached the fence, the second scavenger handed over John's curved saber with its finely engraved silver handle, the one John had received for three victories in single combat.

The third disheveled captor handed the guard John's dented shield, engraved with John's Coat of Arms.

John recalled when the noble Prince Sigismund Bathory of Transylvania, Wallachia, and Moldavia had rewarded him with that Coat of Arms—for valor on the battlefield. The upper center of the scratched shield featured a gray, closed helmet, framed by long feathers on either side. Below that, three separate turbaned heads were displayed in profile.

"Bring them!" The auctioneer directed the guard to show everything to the merchants, who had moved inside the arena. The guard carrying the items pointed directly at Captain Smith.

Smith recognized the distinctive dress of the slave merchants of the Ottoman Empire, including the Arab one from Alexandria. The merchants shifted their focus from Smith to other human merchandise further down the line—prisoners still waiting to be sold into slavery. John knew that the threatening sky of this November day did not dampen the need for shoppers to find a bargain.

Among the slave merchants, Smith recognized an important official—the one he had first seen riding down from the upper town. His entourage stood outside the simple wooden fence.

The man with the long mustache yelled at the auctioneer and pointed to several Greeks standing on the far side of the pen. "Test him!"

With pain returning to his side, John grew apprehensive with every shallow breath.

"Yes!" The other slave merchants echoed in unison. "Test him!"

A group of Greek slaves stood to the left of Smith's auction block and attempted to keep warm near one of the larger fires. Townspeople, visitors, and off-duty soldiers mingled near other fires. One local vendor sold food. Another offered thick Turkish coffee to the waiting crowd.

"You! Over there!" The auctioneer pointed at the Greek wrestlers. Garnering their attention, he motioned to the largest one. The auctioneer yelled words in Turkish.

John knew the guard had ordered the Greek to wrestle him, the newest slave.

The guard pushed the biggest one towards the waiting Englishman. The medium-sized and smaller ones continued their futile efforts to stay warm.

Not quite twenty-three years old, Captain Smith knew he must face his next challenge. Turning to the auctioneer, Smith blurted, "I knew you would choose him."

"Let me at him!" The biggest and strongest Greek stepped toward Smith.

From the steely glare and anxious tension of his new adversary, John figured that the guards must have promised him extra food. Almost everyone has a price, Smith thought, perhaps even my newest opponent.

Another guard unsheathed his scimitar sword. The rounded blade quickly cut the rope binding Smith's wrists. He swished it once more, slicing the rope between John's ankles.

Before putting his sword back into its sheath, the guard prodded Smith off the rock.

The two grapplers stood and faced each other. Guards held leather whips and appeared anxious to use them. It seemed a mismatch, wholly unfair: the Greek was a bear.

Eager spectators pressed against the fence. John's opponent motioned Smith to come towards him. The swarthy grappler bent over with his hands outstretched, his thick fingers urging him on. The crowd began to stir. Several whistled. Others screamed and shouted.

Smith, by contrast, displayed little interest. The captured officer just stood upright. He did not want to fight. With his arms hanging at his side, John voiced, "I don't want to participate in this charade."

The closest guard with the whip spat into Smith's face, screaming Turkish words John knew meant *fight, you fool, or you'll face a worse fate!*

With the back of his hand, John wiped the taste of spittle from his mouth. He looked with disgust at the guard. The foul, pungent taste of drool lingered on his lips. A drop clung to his brown beard.

The brass bell clanged, signaling the start of the match. The Greek slave charged and reached to grab Smith by the arm. Smith, knowing his own quickness and strength, used his opponent's momentum to trip him. He threw the Greek and smashed him facedown onto the ground.

Appearing somewhat amazed, the slave merchants nodded to one another. John Smith shrugged off the increase in his monetary value.

The Greek quickly pushed himself off the ground. He spat out the dirt caught between his gapped teeth. His eyes grew bigger and more intense. The wrestler focused his complete attention on the full-bearded Englishman.

Breathing deeply, the Greek approached Smith more slowly this time. Smith saw more determination in his opponent's eye. The Englishman put his hands out in front, mimicking his adversary. Smith realized he had fooled the Greek once, but probably would not be able to do so a second time.

With his teeth showing and his face reddening, the strong man—his joints slick with oil—stomped closer. Smith attempted to circle behind. The Captain consciously protected his left side, where bandages covered his wounded ribs.

Though physically large, the wrestler also displayed quickness. He blocked Smith's advance. With a slap, he grabbed his right arm. Smith tried to wriggle loose. He twisted his forearm from side to side and raised his arm up and down. He could not escape the Greek's firm grip.

With his left hand, the wrestler grabbed the back of Smith's neck. He placed downward pressure with the palm of his hand. Smith countered, cupping his opponent's neck with his own left hand. In like manner he pressed down, but while reaching up, the bandages pulled. His wound reopened. He could not hide the pain. His jaws tightened; his teeth clenched. He grimaced.

The two adversaries circled each other for almost a minute. The crowd jeered its disapproval. Each tried to get the advantage. Neither released his grip. The crowd yelled and hollered. Several young boys moved closer, seemingly mesmerized by the action.

The slaves in the holding cells watched the contest. The Italian prisoner, who waited for his turn to face one of the Greeks, shook his head.

More curious spectators—both men and women—arrived. They pressed against the wooden fence on all sides. Armed guards kept the crowds back. One guard snapped his whip. The onlookers initially stepped back, but they soon roared even louder. They pressed forward once more.

Using his superior strength, the bulky wrestler stepped behind Smith and slammed him down to his hands and knees. Smith held his body up on all four limbs. When he attempted to stand, the grappler pulled back Smith's left arm. With a thud, Smith's left jaw, cheek, and nose scraped the hard, dusty ground.

Many in the crowd grimaced at Smith's pain. Others screamed support for the Greek. All stared. As soon as Smith recovered, he haltingly rose to his feet. The Greek tightened his grip around Smith's waist.

Ignoring the shooting pain, the Captain peeled the Greek's fingers away from his hurting side. Smith dropped his body, stepped forward, pushed away, and escaped his opponent's strong grip. As soon as Smith turned around, the prisoners in the line voiced their approval.

Once more, Smith faced his opponent eye to eye, but this time, riled with anger, Smith was determined to fight. He stepped forward and the two men grabbed each other.

The bell clanged. It clanged again.

Guards rushed in, attempting to separate the two wrestlers. Not calming down, the Greek seemed more determined than ever to fight and win. He reached up for John's beard, but two guards held him back.

"Kole! Buraya gel!" the other guard yelled at John. Slave! Come here!

Stunned by being called 'slave', John hesitated, the words trapped in his mind.

"Kole! Buraya gel!" the guard yelled again,

Those words echoed in Captain John Smith's ears. Slave! Come here!

The guard with the scimitar sword prodded Smith.

"Slave!"

Breathing deeply, Smith wiped the dirt from his face and brushed the dust from his uniform. The hurting Englishman scanned his surroundings once more and noticed he had gained a wide audience. The guards bound the slave's feet and hands again.

Fresh redness permeated the cloth around the dark center splotch. Oozing blood seeped from the bandage wrapped around Captain Smith's side and dripped to the ground.

The slave merchants jostled to view the newest slave. Dust rose and dissipated at the edge of the auction block; the crowd peered at his reopened wound. John's saber, belt, and shield lay at his feet and the English slave stoically returned the glare. Tied and bound, Captain John Smith knew he had no chance to escape.

Glancing at the endless line of prisoners behind him, John empathized with them for what they would have to endure that day. The Italian captive stood at the gate in front of other prisoners of war. These Christian soldiers, destined to follow Smith to the auction block, waited in front of the more recent arrivals, the ones dressed in Slavic peasant clothes.

Exhausted from the match, Captain Smith prepared himself to be sold.

A full-bearded man wearing a huge, white turban stared.

Chapter 2 – The Grand Vizier

By his wit [Hasan the Fruiterer, later the Grand Vizier] remounted to so high an honor [Kaimakam], he will (in mine opinion) pass a great way further, if he lives . . .
The Ottoman [1597] by Lazaro Soranzo
Translated from Italian by Abraham Hartwell in 1603

The Sultan [Mehmet III] also, to recompense the Grand Vizier [Yemisci Hasan]....With a dower [kabin] of…gold ducats, the Sultana Aisha, widow of [Damat] Ibrahim [Pasha], whom he had reserved for him as an incitement and a prize of the campaign.
History of Turkey, Vol. III by Alphonse *de* Larartine
Translated from the French

He [Captain John Smith] fell to the share of Pasha Bogall [Begler-Beg / Beylerbey / Grand Vizier / Hasan the Fruiterer].
John Smith

Lower Town, Axiopolis, *Jumada II*, AH 1011 (Nov. AD 1602)

THREE HORSETAILS WAVED in the breeze. Secured beneath a golden crescent and attached to the top of a sturdy pole, the tails represented the power and authority of the Grand Vizier, the most powerful official in the Ottoman Empire.

Vizier Azem *Yemisci* Hasan *Pasha*, the Grand Vizier of the Ottoman Empire, monitored every movement of the slave on display.

The brown-bearded prisoner on the rock straightened his uniform.

"Auctioneer!" the Grand Vizier said, "You must start the bidding low."

The Alexandrian slave merchant, a personal representative of the current *Pasha* of Cairo agreed. "That wounded wrestler isn't worth anything."

The Grand Vizier disagreed, but wanted to keep his costs down. Even though he had not been allowed to examine the officer's wound, the slave possessed too much life. He had to be worth something. Besides, the

Grand Vizier told himself, I could have beaten this worthy foe in battle.

"You get a slave!" The auctioneer pointed to the items in front of the soldier. "And also his fine saber and shield!" The auctioneer acknowledged the three captors who had delivered the prisoner. "The items were found with this officer."

The Grand Vizier did not wholly trust the three and wondered whether the articles were truly the slave's.

"Let me see them!" A slave merchant from Kaffa in Crimea motioned.

As the guard brought the shield and saber closer, the Grand Vizier stepped in front of the other merchants. "I know silver."

Though as a youth he had been trained in the fruit business in *Stamboul*, *Yemisci*—meaning Fruiterer—Hasan had far exceeded his modest beginnings. By his own skills, he had risen to become Grand Vizier of the entire Ottoman Empire, a *Pasha* of Three Tails and current commander of the Sultan's army in Europe. Only the Sultan was more powerful than he. After the former Grand Vizier *Damat* Ibrahim *Pasha* died, Sultan Mehmet III had promised Ibrahim's young widow, the Sultan's Sister Aisha, to Hasan *the Fruiterer* in marriage.

The Alexandria slave merchant reached for the saber and examined the workmanship. "Italian design."

"Perhaps." The Grand Vizier outlined the design with his finger.

The finely crafted handle of the saber, as well as the shield with its engraved design, matched the attire and demeanor of the captured officer. The Grand Vizier decided he must bid.

The auctioneer gestured at the Christian officer. "A fine specimen, you can plainly see."

The important officer of the Holy Roman Empire did not look Italian. The prisoner must be a Bohemian Lord, the Grand Vizier reasoned. Afterall, the Holy Roman Emperor Rudolph II ruled his empire from Prague in the Kingdom of Bohemia. A Bohemian Lord like the one on the auction block must be worth much.

The Grand Vizier knew that without taking a risk, there would be no gain. Besides, that nobleman's family would certainly pay an ample ransom, easily covering any cost the Grand Vizier would consider paying.

The red circle surrounding the brown splotch on the bandage had ceased growing, but since the prisoner was wounded, the Grand Vizier thought he could use that his advantage—he could later boast to others that he had fought the officer in single combat.

The second guard grabbed the prisoner's brown hair at the nape of his neck. He snapped the slave's head back. "You bite, you die."

The guard stuck his dirty thumb into the corner of the slave's mouth. The prisoner twisted his neck and clenched his teeth.

Remarkably good, the Grand Vizier observed, not wanting to waste money. If the prisoner died before being ransomed to his family in Bohemia, the Grand Vizier would lose his investment. He knew negotiations oftentimes took months, if not years. A prudent buyer, he wanted only the best.

"A fine ransom this slave will bring," the auctioneer began. "Who will start the bidding at one hundred?"

The Grand Vizier pulled at the end of his graying beard. He gestured his bid of *Sultana*tes, gold coins.

"The Grand Vizier starts this bid at one hundred!" The auctioneer's cadence quickly hit its rhythm. In short staccato syllables, he asked, "Do I hear two hundred?"

A merchant from Baghdad raised the stakes. "Two hundred."

"The merchant from Baghdad bids two hundred," the auctioneer said. "Three hundred?"

The Grand Vizier considered the saber and gestured.

"The Grand Vizier bids three hundred! Four hundred?"

The other merchants glanced at each other and stared at the slave.

"Four hundred?" the auctioneer repeated.

The Grand Vizier could not believe his impending luck—he was about to get an officer at such a bargain price.

The merchant from Kaffa signaled.

"The merchant from Kaffa bids four hundred!" The auctioneer peered at the Grand Vizier. "Five hundred?"

The Grand Vizier did not want to go that high. A captain of two hundred and fifty horsemen could be hired for nearly two years at that rate. He glanced at the poorer slaves down the line, looked back at the auctioneer and signaled.

"Five hundred! Six hundred?"

No one else bid.

"Sold!" the auctioneer declared. "The slave goes to the Grand Vizier for five hundred *sultanates*."

The guard prodded the Grand Vizier's new purchase off the rock. The slave, breathing less deeply than before, wiped the last of the spittle from his beard. He did not cower when he walked away. Meanwhile, an Italian prisoner took his place on the weathered boulder.

The Grand Vizier smirked in triumph.

His able assistant congratulated him.

"Thank you," The Grand Vizier pointed to the first guard. "Retrieve my saber and shield."

The Grand Vizier reached the table where he would finalize his purchase. His assistant poured out five hundred *sultanates*.

After the Ottoman taxman took his share, the accountant distributed the bulk of the monies to the three captors who had brought him. The shorter captor with the scar on his neck scooped up and divided the new-found wealth with the other two.

Clearly ecstatic, the three men ignored the other waiting prisoners and headed toward the docks on the right bank of the Danube.

Back inside the arena, the auctioneer renewed his cadence. "Who will start the bidding on the newest slave?"

Satisfied with his purchase of the noble Bohemian, the Grand Vizier turned to his assistant. "The best of the lot."

"Are you going to ransom your slave?"

"I haven't decided." The Grand Vizier had plenty of money, power, and prestige, but something was missing. "I might give the slave to my promised bride."

"In *Stamboul*?" the assistant asked.

"She can use the ransom money more than I."

"Aisha will be happy."

"I know."

While two of his men escorted his newest purchase away from the arena, the Grand Vizier told his entourage, "We will soon return to Belgrade, so I can set in order the affairs of the frontier." He gestured to Wallachia, across the Danube. "When we recapture Wallachia, we will all be safer."

His purchase in tow, the Grand Vizier passed the Byzantine church and returned to the upper town.

They feasted and rested one more night in Axiopolis, the Danube village known to the Turks as *Bogazkoy*.

South Gate, Axiopolis, Ottoman Empire

KEEPING HIS CUSTOM, the Grand Vizier arose early the next morning. In the presence of numerous attendants, he prayed toward Mecca, the holiest city of Islam.

He pulled back the curtains of the upper window. Down in the courtyard below, two guards kept a close watch over his new slave, his hands bound in leather straps. An attendant fed grain to his favorite horse, a brown Arabian.

He turned and picked out one of his turbans lined on a shelf. With the help of his servant, he donned a comfortable one.

When he reached the courtyard, a guard handed him the reins of his favorite Arabian horse. The Grand Vizier told the guard, "I will take my newest slave with me to Silistra. I must see Khan *Ghazi* Giray II." The leader of the Crimean Tartars, the Ottoman Empire's closest ally, had been recovering with the army of Moldavia in Silistra.

The guard kept his eye on the Bohemian slave. The leather could cut into the slave's wrists, but his new owner did not care. Even if his chattel resisted, the Grand Vizier expected to make good progress on his journey.

Accompanied by mounted guards, the Grand Vizier rode on ahead to meet the rest of his escorts at the South Gate of Axiopolis.

Five hundred *janissaries*, the foot soldiers of the Ottoman Empire, joined them. The Grand Vizier urged his brown Arabian forward. Well-guarded, his bound slave walked behind. A second guard carried the slave's sword and shield.

Around midday, the sun finally broke through the scattered clouds, illuminating the Grand Vizier's standard. The gold crescent set atop the standard's long pike glistened brightly. Beneath his banner the three horsetails swayed in rhythm. Only the Sultan himself traveled with more horsetails than he, the Lieutenant General of the army of the Ottoman Empire, the world's largest and most powerful.

Silistra, *Vilayet* of Silistra, Bulgaria, Ottoman Empire

BY THE END of the next day, the Grand Vizier and his *janissary* escort arrived at the outskirts of Silistra, an even more important border town than Axiopolis. Further upstream was Belgrade, where the Grand Vizier had kept his headquarters for nearly two years.

Flags and a few banners flew above Silistra's fortified walls, but the two horsetails of its *Pasha* were nowhere in sight. A welcoming party of *janissaries* stood in formation outside the gate.

Mustafa *Agha*, the Grand Vizier's Lieutenant, exited the gate, galloped past his *janissaries*, and saluted the Grand Vizier. "The *Pasha* of Silistra awaits you at his palace inside Silistra. The Crimean Khan *Ghazi* Giray II left after he had defeated the Transylvanian Christians in Wallachia. He took his two sons and his Tartar army to Belgrade."

"We will summon use his help in the spring." The Grand Vizier pointed to the Tartar huts built on the meadows above the treelined Danube. "And those warriors?"

"Only the wounded remain."

Scores of Tartar warriors limped, others tended their bandaged arms. Days earlier, a heated battle across the Danube in Wallachia inflicted much harm.

Mustafa *Agha* and the Grand Vizier entered the outer gate and rose up to the palace. Townspeople stood and gazed as the Grand Vizier passed. Several groups of citizens followed him to the largest residence in the town.

The Grand Vizier dismounted at the Palace courtyard.

The *Pasha* of Silistra, waiting for him, bowed. "Grand Vizier, it is so good to see you. You will be pleased that everything is in order."

"That is not what I heard."

"Grand Vizier?" The *Pasha* of Silistra questioned. "You are right. Wallachia must be restored to the Sultan."

"And these citizens?" The Grand Vizier gestured.

"Many want to see you."

"Me? Silistra belongs to the Crimean Khan." And it had been ever since the fortress city had been transferred from the *Vilayet*, or province, of Rumelia to the Khan *Ghazi* Giray II, the Ottoman Empire's greatest ally.

"Yes," the *Pasha* of Silistra said, "but he has gone, but I could use your wisdom."

"Very well, I will help, but first I must take care of my horse." The Grand Vizier stroked the neck of his fine Arabian. He handed the reins to a waiting stable hand. "Check for rocks."

"Yes, Grand Vizier." The attendant bowed. "It shall be done."

The attendant led the horse towards the stables. Meanwhile, the guard with the Grand Vizier's new slave and the other guard, holding the slave's shield and saber, drew closer.

"I bought a slave in Axiopolis," the Grand Vizier said.

The "Bohemian" was still bound with leather straps.

"What use is a slave here on the frontier?" Mustafa *Agha* asked. "Will you resell him?"

"I have not yet decided."

The *Pasha* of Silistra motioned to the far side of the courtyard. "He can stay in the stables."

As the guards led the slave away, the Grand Vizier warned, "Do not allow anything happen to him."

In the middle of the courtyard, a recovering Tartar warrior pushed through the crowd of citizens and reached out at the slave. "You!"

"Stand back!" A guard touched his scimitar sword.

A growing number of citizens lined up at the main entrance of the small palace.

As they entered the inner gate, the *Pasha* of Silistra informed the Grand Vizier, "The treasurer from Edirne awaits you."

"The treasurer? Why did you not tell me sooner?"

"I thought we already informed you." The *Pasha* of Silistra glanced at Mustafa *Agha*.

The leaders entered the main reception room.

The treasurer rose and handed the Grand Vizier a letter. "The Sultan's Mother sends her greetings."

"Have you been waiting long?" The Grand Vizier unsealed the letter.

"I arrived at noon."

"Bad news?" the *Pasha* of Silistra asked.

"Nothing I cannot handle." The treasurer turned to Mustafa *Agha*. "The *devshirme* is behind schedule."

"I will collect it," Mustafa *Agha* said.

"I will personally see to it that it is done,"the Grand Vizier said. "Any word from Aisha?"

"The Sister of the Sultan looks forward to your return," the treasurer said.

"I am famished." The Grand Vizier turned. "*Pasha?*"

The *Pasha* of Silistra clapped his hands twice. "Bring drinks and food!"

The servants set a round table on a large oriental rug in the middle of the floor and the Grand Vizier sat down. When the interpreter and the other leaders joined him, the servants brought out *mezes*, Turkish appetizers.

"Thank you." The *dragoman*, the Grand Vizier's interpreter, sat crossed-legged like the others. Seated in a circle, all nibbled on the tasty pastries on the low table.

"I bought a slave in Axiopolis," The Grand Vizier told the treasurer.

"You already have many house slaves."

"This slave is different. I am going to give him to my future bride."

While the men relaxed, a few singers performed several old melodies. Instrumentalists later played more lively tunes.

The Long War seemed far away that evening, until the *Pasha* of Silistra asked, "Grand Vizier, what brings you to Silistra?"

"I must make certain the border with the Holy Roman Empire is secure. The threat continues."

"If the enemy General Giorgio Basta regroups and attacks," the *Pasha* of Silistra said, "his Christian army might again advance from *Transylvania* into Hungary."

"Not if the Crimean Tartars are there," the Grand Vizier said.

"Khan *Ghazi* Giray II lost many men across the Danube in Wallachia," the *Pasha* of Silistra said.

"The Ottoman Empire has other problems," Mustafa *Agha* said. "The rebellion continues in Anatolia."

"We need more *janissaries*," the treasurer said.

"And it takes years to train *janissaries*," the *Pasha* of Silistra said.

"It can be done." The Grand Vizier turned to his lieutenant. "First, we must collect the *devshirme*." He was referring to the routine collection, or tribute, of young boys from Christian families living within the Ottoman Empire who would later be trained as *janissaries* or Ottoman court officials.

"We have taken tribute from all around Silistra," the *Pasha* of Silistra said. "The Christian tenants working the lands of the *sipahi* have provided many young boys."

"We must all make sacrifices." The Grand Vizier peered directly at his Lieutenant. "Mustafa *Agha*, we must go to the mountains."

"When do we leave?"

"Tomorrow."

"Shall I return to *Stamboul* to advise the Sultan's Mother of your course of action?" the *dragoman* said.

"No, I will send another messenger. You know Bulgarian and can help us collect the *devshirme*." The Grand Vizier recalled the order Sultan Mehmet III had issued only two years earlier. He turned back to Mustafa *Agha*. "Remember, the Sultan's orders still stand."

"Kill anyone who resists."

"Yes."The Grand Vizier moved to a large chair placed at the far end of the room.

"Are you ready for the citizens?" The *Pasha* of Silistra sat next to him.

"Bring them in one by one."

When the first of two citizens entered, he pointed at the other one. "This man owes me money!"

"Is this true?" The Grand Vizier peered at the second man.

"The Grand Vizier?" The poor man bowed. "I can't pay."

"Then you must work for him until you pay your debt in full."

As soon as all of the citizen complaints were heard, the *Pasha* of Silistra said, "Your judgements are sound."

"They were simple, but now I must rest." The Grand Vizier rose and turned to the Mustafa *Agha*, "Tomorrow, you will come with me to collect the *devshirme*. We must show others how the tribute is gathered."

The Grand Vizier retired to the guest quarters and penned a letter to his betrothed, Aisha, Sister of the Sultan.

Chapter 3 - Blood Tribute in Bulgaria

The Household troops received their usual allowance; the feudatory troops received each man two pieces of money, and the foot soldiers one. The Agha of the Janissaries [Ali Agha] was permitted to return to Constantinople, and the feudatory troops were also allowed to retire.

Mustapha Naima, Annals of the Turkish Empire
Translated into English by Charles Fraser

Every seven years a Colonel of the Janissaries, out of the regiments of Yaya [or Piade, paid infantry troops], sets out with five or six hundred men for Rumelia [Turkey in Europe], to draft from all the villages, Albanese, Greek, Albanian, Serbian, and Bulgarian boys. The seven or eight thousand boys collected in that way, according to the institute of Sultan Orkhan [Son of Osman I, Orhan Ghazi], sanctified by the benediction of Haji Begtash, are dressed in the town of Uskub [Skopje, Macedonia], in jackets (Muwahadi) or red Aba, with a cleft on the shoulders, and with caps of red felt, which resemble the night-caps of Karagoz (the merry fellow in the Chinese shades).

Narrative of Travels in Europe, Asia, and Africa in the Seventeenth Century,
Vol. 1, Part 2 by Evliya *Effendi*
Translated from Turkish by Ritter Joseph von Hammer

Danubian Plains, *Vilayet* of Silistra, November 1602

BEYOND THE WALLS of Silistra, two guards rechecked the leather straps still binding wrists of Captain John Smith who wondered where they were taking him, as they journeyed south across the Danubian plain. The English slave only knew he was being taken much deeper into Ottoman-controlled territory.

His turbaned owner had taken him west, up the Danube. Passing by harvested fields separated by groves of evergreens, the number of men accompanying the important Ottoman leader had grown to more than a thousand. Ahead, two hundred mounted guards, more confident than other *sipahi* horsemen, rode in tight formation close to the Ottoman leader. Several hundred more *sipahi* riders divided into several companies rode behind.

A *janissary orta,* or regiment, marched, followed by mules and pack horses laden with supplies. Not wanting to be whipped, Smith trudged onward, keeping up as best as he could. He noticed a Bulgarian farmer standing at the side of the road. Along with his ox and cart, half-filled with hay, the old man waited for the contingent to pass.

A turbaned officer, an important Lieutenant of Smith's new owner, spurred his horse forward.

~ ~ ~

MUSTAFA *AGHA* CAUGHT up with Grand Vizier *Yemisci* Hasan *Pasha,* the General of all Ottoman forces in Europe. "The *Agha* of the *Janissaries* awaits your final instructions."

"At Shumen?" The Grand Vizier, who nearly a decade earlier commanded the *janissaries* himself, asked.

"Both *janissaries* and *sipahis* await their pay."

"Yes, it is due in two days."

"The *sipahis* are upset."

"Their *timars*?"

"The rebels have overtaken much of Anatolia. They forgave the tax and distributed the land to others."

"I must put an end to the rebellion in Asia, but before I can return to *Stamboul,* we must put everything in order along the frontier here in Europe."

After passing more fields, several *sipahis* saluted their *sanjak* and the Grand Vizier. Riding behind the *sanjak*'s banner, the *sipahi* horsemen had served at the command of their provincial governor and the Sultan.

Those riders, fully armed with scimitars and lances, battle axes and maces, as well as pistols and arquebuses, rode away, across empty fields to return to their *timars,* feudal land holdings. Every *timar* holder had earned his right to own land through service to the Sultan, but he had to provide at least one *sipahi* rider with supplies whenever the Sultan called upon him.

Larger *timars,* known as *ziamets* provided five or more men with horses to serve the Sultan for the duration of the fighting season. Although a *sanjak* could claim a small *timar* for his own son, other *timar* holders could not. Unlike the feudal lands of Christendom, *timars* were not inheritable.

Toward the end of the second day of his journey from Silistra, the *Sanjak* of Shumen dismissed several more *sipahis* and allowed them to return to their *timars.*

Ahead, the Plateau of Shumen rose above the plains. Nearly two centuries earlier, the Ottoman dynasty had defeated the Second Bulgarian Empire, capturing the large castle. About fifty years later, in the Christian year AD 1444, the Hungarian King led the Crusade of Varna against the Black Sea port about fifty miles to the east. The Battle of Varna turned when *janissaries*, the Sultan's chosen, mounted a decisive counterattack. Although the Christians of the Varna Crusade were defeated, the Fortress of Shumen was completely destroyed. With all of its homes burnt inside, only the stone foundations remained. Afterwards, the Turks rebuilt the town below the rocky plateau.

Smoke rose from the large Ottoman encampment on the outskirts of Shumen.

Shumen, *Vilayet* of Silistra, Bulgaria, Ottoman Empire

ALI *AGHA*, LEADER of all *janissaries*, wearing his off-white turban, greeted the Grand Vizier and the mounted leader of the *janissary* regiment. "We are ready to return to *Stamboul*."

"The *orta* accompanying me may return also."

"You do not need their service?" Ali *Agha* asked. Earlier in the year, the janissary leader had negotiated the terms of the marriage contract between the Grand Vizier and Aisha.

"Only my mounted guard shall accompany me to the Balkans."

The mounted guard of Hasan *the Fruiterer* was well-tested. Further south, beyond the Plateau of Shumen, the *Stara Planina*, or the old mountains, separated the Danube River Valley from ancient Thrace and Rumelia.

The leader of the *janissary orta* motioned for his men to keep marching.

All wearing long blue robes, the footmen soon reached the encampment. As soon as the mules and camels arrived, the footmen set down their muskets. For every ten soldiers, a mule had carried their personal luggage, identically wrapped

Agha of the Janissaries

packets. They unloaded their supplies. Each man carried his pack of warm clothes to the common tent site.

An elder *janissary* directed several young men to unload a camel. It had carried the common tent, large enough to hold twenty-five men. Ever since they had departed the barracks in *Stamboul* at the beginning of the season, the elder *janissary* had ensured order and obedience to all of the rules. None of the twenty-five soldiers under his charge in the common sleeping area could stir without his permission.

With the whole *orta* organized like a well-run kitchen, other *janissaries* started a campfire. The head cook brought out the cauldron, the large black pot carried at the head of the *orta*.

The Grand Vizier told Ali *Agha*, "Your *janissaries* need to be paid for their service in the campaign."

As soon as the quartermasters of the respective *orta*s arrived, the treasurer distributed the pay, writing down the monies and recording exact amounts. Each *janissary* received a coin, individually weighed. No *janissary* could ever accuse the Grand Vizier of having his pay clipped. Like usual, the *janissaries* were paid a day before it was due. There would be no cause for insurrection under Grand Vizier Hasan *the Fruiterer*'s watch.

While handing out the monies, the *sipahi* leaders approached.

"You finally decided to pay your respects to me?" the Grand Vizier asked.

"Our camp was not set up."

"But now you saw that you will be paid?"

"My men fought hard."

"The *janissaries* have been paid."

"The *sipahis* deserve more."

The Grand Vizier turned to the treasurer. "Pay each of the *sipahis* two coins."

"As you wish."

After everyone was paid, the *Sanjak Bey* of Shumen, the Governor of the town, invited the Grand Vizier to rest at the *caravanserai* inside.

"I will camp with the *janissaries*." The Grand Vizier meandered to a large campfire, where *sipahi* and *janissary* leaders discussed the recent campaign and the rebellion in Anatolia, Asia Minor. "No need to rise." The Grand Vizier sat on the largest stone.

"Something must be done about the administration of the empire," one *sipahi* leader said. "There is chaos everywhere."

"Szekesfehervar has been recovered," the Grand Vizier said.

"The ancient capital of Hungary should never have been lost."

"It happened before I arrived."

"And many of the *timar*s were lost near Ankara," the *sipahi* leader from Anatolia said. "My *sipahis* have no home to go to."

The Grand Vizier glanced over to that part of the encampment. Even though they had been paid, the *sipahi* horsemen did not appear happy. "I will see what can be done."

"It is best we take our leave."

The *sipahi* leaders returned to their men and horses.

The next morning the Grand Vizier *Yemisci* Hasan *Pasha* exited his large tent and noticed the *sipahis* had already departed. He told Mustafa *Pasha* and the *Agha* of the *Janissaries*, "They did not even bid me farewell."

"They departed before dawn," Ali *Agha* said. "Do you have further need for my service?"

"No, you may return to the Palace."

"In any case, my men are ready."

"As always." The Grand Vizier handed the *Agha* two letters. "Give my regards to the Sultan and his mother."

While the *Agha* checked with the officers supervising the packing of the mules and horses, a guard stepped forward. "Your slave?"

"Take the slave directly to Edirne, to the field east of the city."

Ali *Agha* and his officers rode at the head of the smartly dressed soldiers. In quick determined steps, three *orta*s of *janissaries* marched in quick determined steps towards the pass leading to Adrianople, the city of Edirne. The two guards and the Christian slave followed, but when the slave glanced back, the Grand Vizier turned to the *dragoman*. "He'll not escape."

"You're giving him to the Sultan's sister?"

"Aisha can ransom the slave back to his family."

"And me?"

"You shall accompany me."

The Grand Vizier and his 'Bohemian' slave parted paths.

Balkan Mountains, Bulgaria, Ottoman Empire

THE FOLLOWING MORNING after camping the night in the foothills of the *Stara Planina* or Balkans, the Grand Vizier halted his company of mounted soldiers. A fresh dusting of snow, as white as his turban and perhaps the first sign of another cold winter, capped the highest peaks.

"Mustafa *Agha*, we must collect the *devshirme*."

"The men are ready," Mustafa *Agha* said.

"I expect no problems."

"There'll be none."

The Grand Vizier motioned for his *dragoman*. "How well do you know Bulgarian?"

"Almost as well as my skills in Italian and Tartarian."

The Interpreter seemed confident.

"Stay close." The Grand Vizier brought his horse around.

With the wind at their backs, the Grand Vizier, the *dragoman*, and the escort advanced up the mountains, up an ever narrowing road. Ahead, a scout waited for the riders and their pack horses. The Grand Vizier and his standard bearer reached him first.

The scout pointed up the hill.

The Grand Vizier spied an old monastery nestled in the forest and turned to his trusted Lieutenant. "Mustafa *Agha*, surround it."

"Right away." His turbaned officer relayed the command.

The vanguard charged and galloped up the hill, quickly surrounding the small compound.

By the time the Grand Vizier rode into the church courtyard, a priest was standing in the doorway. Dressed in a flowing black robe, the Ortho-dox Christian cleric asked, "*Pasha*, what are you doing?"

"Collection time."

The *dragoman* translated from Bulgarian to Turkish.

"My congregation already gave. Our four villages paid the tithe and your double tax."

"You did not pay the other tribute," the Grand Vizier said.

"Two summers ago, your men took my grandson and killed his fa-ther."

"You did not pay this year and certainly not to me."

"God will judge!"

"Silence!"

The Grand Vizier needed to prevent the priest from warning four nearby villages. He turned to two young riders. "Guard him!"

The men dismounted and cornered the priest.

At the same time, their captain pointed up the steep incline behind the compound. "Look!"

A fleeting shadow wove through the deep woods. Like a surefooted doe, the fast runner with a brown cap escaped over a ridge.

The Grand Vizier maneuvered his horse around and his flagman mimicked his action. He dug in his heels and encouraged his horse up the narrow road. "Hurry!"

Mustafa *Agha* relayed the order.

Leaving the two guards with the priest, the galloping horsemen pressed forward. Dust rose and, like rolling thunder, pounding hooves roared through the narrowing valley.

Steep drop-offs on one side and high embankments on the other side did not bother the Ottoman leader. His fearless escorts were all loyal veterans, valiant in the fight. Personally picked and paid by the Sultan, most had survived battles where others would have died.

The Grand Vizier rounded a sharp bend. A crisp gust hit his face and the cold wind slapped his cheek. His eyes stung, but when he squinted, the fleeting shadow once more snared his attention.

Long legs traversed the hill. Wearing a woolen cap, the runner plowed through golden leaves, jumping over low stumps and hurdling fallen trees.

The Grand Vizier needed to go faster to intercept the fast sprinter. Rounding the next bend, he pulled the reins. A flock of sheep blocked his path.

His whole company halted. Horses neighed and bunched together.

Above the noise of bleating sheep, the Grand Vizier yelled, "Move!"

"I can't!" The shepherd pushed through to the front of his flock. His dog, a brown and white Karakachan, barked.

"Move!"

"No room!" The shepherd glanced down the foreboding cliff. "I must shelter them!"

"I shall not say it again!" The Grand Vizier forced the shepherd against the steep wall.

"No!"

The Grand Vizier signaled Mustafa *Agha* forward. The horsemen pushed through the flock. One horse trampled a ewe. Bleats turned to silence as many sheep disappeared down the deep ravine.

The Grand Vizier shouted at the shepherd. "Never slow me down again!"

"My sheep!" The shepherd picked up the injured ewe.

The dog still barked. The Grand Vizier spurred his Arabian forward.

At the outskirts of the mountain village, the Grand Vizier caught up with the rest of his men.

Villagers shouted and screamed. All ran into their homes. Doors slammed shut.

At the grassy area in the village center, Mustafa *Agha* divided the company who immediately surrounded nearby houses on opposite sides of the road.

The Grand Vizier, his Lieutenant, and the *dragoman* dismounted at the first house. "We're here to collect the *devshirme*." He kicked in the door. "Where are they?"

"*Pasha*! Not my children!" The mother backed up against a plain wall and stretched out her arms. "Don't take a blood tribute from us!"

"Blood tribute?"

Her husband stepped in front of the protective mother.

"Do as I say!" The Grand Vizier exclaimed. "Line them up!"

The frightened peasant and his weeping wife stood their four children in front of them. The children ranged in age from a young girl of three or four to a teen-age boy.

The Grand Vizier passed in front of them, turned back, and lifted the chin of the middle boy, about ten years of age. "This one will do."

"*Pasha*! No! I love him dearly." The mother reached for the middle son. Her husband held her back.

The Grand Vizier put both hands on the boy's shoulders. "Perhaps you only want me to take part of him?"

The father cried, "Don't maim him!"

The mother wept. "My favorite!" Tears flowed.

"No more resistance! The Sultan's order still stands."

"Pasha!"

"Quiet, woman!" The Grand Vizier handed off the boy to the nearest soldier and turned to the father. "Where's the money?"

"We have none; we're but poor farmers."

"I'll take the youngest." The Grand Vizier grabbed the boy's shirt.

"Son!"

"No resistance!"

"He's only nine."

The mother's sobs and pleas fell on deaf ears. The Grand Vizier refused to listen. "I said quiet!" He handed off the youngest boy. "Be happy. I left you your oldest son and your daughter."

"Burn in hell!"

"Don't worry. We'll take good care of him. It's an honor for the boys to become *janissaries*." Mustafa *Agha* added. "If they show talent, maybe they can become a vizier."

"Or Grand Vizier, like me." The Grand Vizier smirked.

"Can't I hold them one last time?" Tears flowed down her cheeks.

"No." The Grand Vizier motioned to the nearest soldiers. "Take the two boys to the yard." He followed them out the door. "They belong to the Sultan now."

Outside, most riders had dismounted. The men milled around the grassy area, some leaning on a fence.

"What are you doing?" the Grand Vizier demanded.

The men straightened to attention. "We await your orders."

"We have three more villages. I want a hundred boys." The Grand Vizier ordered. "Mount up and be back at the monastery in six hours."

His men galloped up the road.

Meanwhile, within the enclosed yard, the Grand Vizier's physician examined each boy for physical defects.

Once they passed the exam, the Grand Vizier commanded his scribe, "Write down who paid the *devshirme*."

"I'll record their ages and descriptions," the scribe said. "We'll discover their talents later."

A soldier brought a stack of folded clothes from a pack horse and distributed them to the *ghilman*, what the new boys would be called until they were properly trained into janissaries.

The Grand Vizier picked out two of the dark red robes. "All new *ghilman* must wear these." He tossed them to the two novice boys whom he had personally taken. While they put on their new garments, a movement up the hill captured the Grand Vizier's attention.

A shadow peeked around the corner of a house.

When the Grand Vizier recognized the brown cap, it removed all doubt. It was the runner. He turned to the older boy. "Who was that?"

The boy did not answer.

By the time the Grand Vizier turned back, a hand had pulled the shadow away.

"Men, surround that house!"

The soldiers rushed up the steep incline, the Grand Vizier followed.

At the next collection point, a peasant woman blocked the doorway.

The Grand Vizier pushed past her into the one-room shack. "Who are you hiding?"

A small altar with dying candles stood against the far wall.

"No one," the woman said. A young one peeped from behind her skirt.

"Do you have any more sons?"

"I've already given you two sons."

"Not this year." The Grand Vizier peered into the woman's eyes. "Where's your son with the brown cap?"

"No, *Pasha!*"

The Grand Vizier turned to his men. "Search everywhere."

Minutes later, his men had the long-legged youth with the brown hat.

"Where was he?" the Grand Vizier asked.

"Behind the shed, under tools and the woodpile."

"No more sons?"

Tears ran down the woman's cheeks.

The youth kept his head down.

"Let me take a good look." The Grand Vizier pulled the wool cap off.

Wavy hair fell down over the youth's shoulder.

"You warned the village."

"I had to."

"A spirited beauty she is." The Grand Vizier lifted the girl's chin and turned to the woman. "Very well. I'll leave your son." He turned to his soldier. "Take the daughter."

"Pasha!"

"Where's your husband?"

"Dead. Please, don't take my daughter."

"Do you want me to take your son, too?"

"No." The woman pulled her toddler closer.

"It's settled."

The guard escorted the girl out the door.

"Baby!" The mother reached out.

The girl twisted her arm, but couldn't escape. "Take care of brother."

Holding her young son's hand, the tearful mother followed the daughter down the incline.

Near the grassy knoll by the main road, frightened villagers, many sobbing, watched the gathering of youth. After the scribe finished writing down the physical descriptions of the tributes, the tall *dragoman* lifted up the frightened girl, setting her atop one of the horses.

The two brothers from the first house shared another horse. Other boys walked.

The Grand Vizier, his Lieutenant Mustafa *Agha*, the *dragoman*, the girl, and the *devshirme* returned down the road. When they passed by the sharp bend, they found the shepherd, who had corralled the remnant of his flock at a widening. Though he said nothing when the Grand Vizier passed, his dog growled and barked.

Monastery, Balkan Mountains, Bulgaria, Ottoman Empire

BY NIGHTFALL, THE rest of his company had returned to the church and the priest had been released. The Grand Vizier counted more than one hundred young boys, all dressed in dark red robes. "Good work."

"Only two locals resisted," the captain said.

"You took care of them?"

"They're dead."

His men had obeyed Sultan Mehmet III's command. He was pleased.

The next morning, the Grand Vizier told the *dragoman*. "Accompany the *devshirme* to the *janissary* school by Selimeye Mosque." He referred to one of the most beautiful mosques in the Ottoman Empire at Edirne. "Except for these two boys."

"What would you like me do with them?"

"Deliver them to the *Agha* of the *Janissaries*. He will be at the fields by the *Bayezit Kulliyesi*." The Grand Vizier spoke of the mosque, kitchen, and hospital complex built by Sultan Bayezit II, whose father was Mehmet *the Conqueror*. "He will know what to do."

The Grand Vizier handed the *dragoman* a letter. "Find my Bohemian slave at the fields and deliver him, along with this letter to Aisha to the Palace of Ibrahim *Pasha*."

"Yes, Grand Vizier."

"And the girl?"

"Take her to the Sultan's Mother at the Imperial Harem."

The *dragoman* bowed low and kissed the hem of the Grand Vizier's robe. "As you command."

Chapter 4 - Blacksmith of Edirne

Pasha Bogall [Beglerbeg or Beyler-Bey/Lord of Lords/ Grand Vizier, Hasan the Fruiterer]
  . . . sent him [Captain John Smith] forthwith to Adrianople [Edirne] . . .

John Smith

They do call themselves Musulmanni [Muslims], that is the Circumcised [submitted to
God], or as some do interpret it, the Right Believers. But they will not be call Turks, for
they account that name very reproachful, which in the Hebrew language, signifies
Banished men, or as some interpret it spoilers or wasters.

"The Turkish Empire" by Jodocus Hondius, Historia Mundi,
Atlas Minor by Gerardi Mercatoris (1634), translated from Latin

A little without the City [Edirne] Northward stands the Grand Seignior [The Sultan] his
Seraglio [Palace], with a Park walled, some three miles compass: The palace is very low,
all covered with lead rising up for a flat, into a sharp round, and seems but like a Garden-
House for pleasure: It is kept by this Acemi Oglan [Rookie/Cadets], to entertain, not only
the Grand Seignior but in his absence, any Pasha, or other principal minister.

A Voyage to the Levant [Begun in AD 1634] by Henry Blount

Outside Edirne, Ottoman Empire, Late November 1602

METAL STRUCK METAL, the clanging jarred John Smith awake. The English Captain sprung off the clammy ground, his wrists still leather-bound. Pained ribs kept John from rising wholly to his feet. His neck cringed and his back stiffened. Layers of fog, white and moving, obscured his view of a field filled with captive men.

John longed for a warm meal, but the smoky haze did not smell like food. Cold biscuits, his normal fare since sold into slavery at Axiopolis days earlier, were all he expected.

Within the mist, the outline of an open tent emerged. Next to it, a muscular blacksmith had set up shop. With every pump of the bellows, hot coals glowed brighter, flames leapt higher. Sure and steady, the black-smith picked up a hammer and raised his arm. When he powered it down, his hammerhead clamored against the anvil. Clangs pierced the calm and the harsh noise resounded across the rolling fields.

"Up!" Guards stirred the sleeping slaves. "Up!"

From the marshes at the low end of the field, geese flocked to the skies. In a 'V' formation they circled south. Below a few ducks flew above the water's edge. As dawn broke over the horizon across the Tundzha River, plumes of smoke snaked upward from the fortified, once Christian city of Adrianopolis, or what the Turks now called Edirne.

The guard pointed at John. "Rise, you're first."

John did not understand Turkish, but he had little doubt about the guard's meaning. His hands tied, John could neither resist nor escape.

The turbaned guard led John to the open tent and sat him down on a three-legged stool. He shoved the Englishman's chest, pinning John's back against a wooden table.

Once more, the blacksmith stirred the coals and stoked the fire. The heat should have felt good on this late autumn day, but its glow only served to remind Captain John Smith of his predicament. He wondered, *would I become a galley slave?* John longed for England, but his homeland was far away.

Dozens of brass rings and collars lined shelves near the fire. More brass items were piled high in baskets. The blacksmith grabbed one of the collars and slipped it around John's neck. He pushed John's head down next to the cold anvil fastened to the table. "*Kalmak!*"

John knew the blacksmith meant *stay*. Unprepared to challenge the blacksmith's strength or attentive guards armed with bladed pikes and curved swords, John held steady.

The blacksmith tightened the brass collar around the slave's neck and once more fanned the flames. He wiped the sweat from his brow with his sooty hand. Appearing like a warrior painted for battle, the huge man grabbed a pair of tongs, pinched an open ring from the shelf, and dropped it onto the hottest coals.

Blue flames rose, red metal glowed. The long tongs retrieved the ring. John raised his head, but the large Turk pressed John's forehead back down. "*Kalmak!*"

John watched the blacksmith's every move.

White heat swept by John's cheek. The blacksmith slipped the small ring through the hole in the collar. He backed John's neck against the cold anvil and gestured for him to hold still.

Frozen in position, John's eyes widened.

The blacksmith wrapped his thick fingers around the hammer's handle, raising it high and powering it down. The hammerhead gained momentum.

John flinched to the deafening sound. His shoulders shook. His ears rang. Shivers raced down his spine as the ring around his neck tightened.

The blacksmith raised his hammer and lowered it again. Sparks flew like miniature lightning bolts. Metal banged against metal. The noise thundered through his skull and reverberated through his bones.

The blacksmith pulled at the neck brace resting just above John's collarbone. Finding it securely locked and tight, he lifted John's head.

John stretched and twisted his neck, but he could no longer move freely. His disgust with the blacksmith grew.

The blacksmith dipped his tongs in a bucket. They sizzled in the cold water.

The guard yanked the English slave to his feet and escorted him past other slaves waiting their turn.

Another armed guard shoved the next slave down onto the wooden stool and the blacksmith wrapped a brass collar around the captive's neck. He held his head down.

The blacksmith grabbed the tongs and picked up another glowing ring. With military-like precision, metal clanged against metal. The link locked tight, the slave rose, and another took his place.

Scores of newly enslaved Christians, some like John descended from the Balkans, others from the west, lined up single file; more and more arrived by the hour.

The rumors that the Holy Roman Empire had suffered losses in the sieges of Buda and Pest in Hungary the previous season must have been true. Surviving prisoners, if not ransomed, became slaves. Both young and old faced the same fate.

Morning turned into the afternoon. The blacksmith's fire brightly burned; the line of waiting slaves gradually diminished.

The Italian officer John had spoken with in Axiopolis exited the tent. A guard sat him down on the ground close to John, a row away.

"Will they make us galley slaves?" asked John in Italian.

"Unlikely," the Italian replied, "they paid too much for us."

After guards led more slaves past, John gestured to the countryside along the river. "How can we escape?"

"Through a major Ottoman city?"The Italian threw his hands up.

After the Romans conquered the Thracian territory along the banks of the Tundzha, Roman Emperor Hadrian built a wall across northern England. He founded Adrianople in AD 125. Two centuries later, with the Roman Empire already divided in two halves, West Emperor Constantine sought to reunite them. With his army of twenty thousand Roman soldiers, he defeated East Emperor Licinius and his much larger army of thirty-five thousand in the Battle of Adrianople. However, a thousand years later, in AD 1362 the Turkish Ottoman Empire conquered Adrianople, renamed it Edirne, and made it the Ottoman's second capital.

"That's not what I meant." John huffed. "Why would we try to go through Adrianople?"

"Why not?" the Italian said. "Escape?" He shook his head and turned away. "God willing."

As John waited for more slaves to meet the blacksmith, he heard the Islamic call for prayer coming from the other side of the Tundzha River where on the hillside, four minarets stood next to a mosque.

Minutes later further up his side of the river, a line of young boys, all dressed in red robes, approached. John recognized the tall Turk accompanying them as the man who had been with his slave owner in Shumen, the town in Bulgaria where the Grand Vizier and John had parted paths.

The boys, their guards, a girl on a horse, and the tall Turk passed the slave encampment and headed east toward a rural palace, partially hidden by a forest.

Bayezid Külliye, **Edirne**, *Jumada II*, **AH 1011 (Nov. AD 1602)**

THE TALL *DRAGOMAN* observed the guards escorting the Bulgarian devshirme, the young boys gathered in and brought from the Balkans. On the northern outskirts of Edirne, they ambled by *Bayezid Külliye*—a mosque, school, kitchen, and hospital complex. Inside the hospital, sweet music and flowing water soothed the torments of anguished patients. Though some believed it good luck to be touched by such patients, the *dragoman* did not have time to stop.

After they passed the slave encampment, a wild-eyed man in a long robe, swirled to his feet, raised his arms and stopped the *dragoman's* horse. "You will travel far."

The *dragoman* motioned to the guard to put away his weapon. "He's a

Dervish priest."

"You will travel far." The priest twirled around.

Surprised at the saying, yet taking the prophecy to heart, the *dragoman* tossed a coin to the man, who swirled and sauntered away.

They reached the brick-and-stone walls of the *saray*, or palace, and at one of its seven gates, the Chief Gardener greeted the new arrivals. "*Dragoman*, your presence greatly honors us."

"No need to indulge me." The *dragoman* knew the Chief Gardener not only tended the vast palace grounds, but also commanded the palace guards, three thousand strong. An attendant grabbed his horse's reins and dismounted.

"The *devshirme*?" the Chief Gardener asked.

"The Grand Vizier showed his men how to collect them. They completed their task most efficiently."

"The Grand Vizier collected the tribute?"

"And set a standard," the *dragoman* said. "He insists this year's collection be done correctly."

"Most impressive. The Headmaster of the *janissary* school will be pleased with the arrival."

"He should be."

As the boys crossed the threshold, the guards lined them up in double rows along the walkway. The Headmaster of the *janissary* school, a building with a sloped roof made of lead, hurried over, bringing a *janissary* band with him.

Wearing long robes, the band members marched diagonally across the field to the beat of a martial tune. They welcomed the new arrivals with cymbals and drums, pipes and trumpets. When the band reached an interlude, the Headmaster inspected each of the new recruits, head to toe. "We have much work to do."

"There are one hundred *ghilmun*," the Chief Gardener said.

The older of the two boys personally collected by the Grand Vizier, nudged the *dragoman* to translate from Turkish to Bulgarian.

"There are 102 boys," the older youth corrected.

"What did he say?" the Chief Gardener asked.

The *dragoman* translated the boy's response into Turkish. "He said there are 102 boys."

"He's good in math." The Headmaster laughed. "You taught him numbers?

"Only a few," the *dragoman* said. "Do you have room for all of the Bulgarian boys?"

"The *janissary* school here can train up to three thousand *ghilman*. Besides the use of arms, each will learn a trade, like masonry or woodworking." The Headmaster gestured to young workers repairing the brick facade of the large *hamam* or bathhouse.

"Take them all," the *dragoman* said, "except these two brothers."

"And the girl?"

"She's under my protection."

"What will you do with the three?" the Headmaster asked.

"I'm taking them to the New Palace in *Stamboul* at the request of the Grand Vizier."

The Chief Gardener looked down at the boys. "If the boys are going to the New Palace, you should show them the gardens here. They should see some of the imperial riches."

Palace Gardens, North of Edirne, *Rumelia*,

AS SOON AS the hundred *ghilman* left across the field with their new *janissary* headmaster, the Chief Gardener led the *dragoman*, the two brothers and the girl through the Palace Gardens. "I hear the Grand Vizier will soon marry."

"The Sultan promised his sister, Aisha, in marriage to the Grand Vizier," the *dragoman* said.

"The widow of Ibrahim *Pasha* is beautiful, at least the last time I saw her."

"Aisha *Sultana* would like the gardens here." The *dragoman* translated from Turkish to Bulgarian.

"I like them," the Bulgarian girl said.

They followed the water route and strolled down the wide walkway.

Clear water streamed out of a fountain near one paved courtyard. The overflow from the large pool cut through shallow channels carved in marble slabs. Adorned with gold and silver etchings, wooden buildings stood next to the water route and the translucent slabs. At last, the pure stream emptied into a lower pool, smaller than the upper one.

Further away, other streams of fresh water flowed over waterwheels, watering the numerous gardens and fruit orchards, tended by a few *acemi oglan* or cadets learning how to trim. The vast palace gardens extended to the edge of the Tundzha. With no palace wall by the river, only the gardeners, who doubled as guards, provided protection.

One of the Bulgarian boys dipped his hand into the clear water. "Can we drink it?"

"The water is good." The Chief Gardener turned to the *dragoman*, "I can see why the Grand Vizier wanted to present them to the Sultan."

"Both boys are bright."

"And strong for their age."

"It looks like paradise," the older boy said.

"We strive to make this as beautiful as the Garden of Eden." The Chief Gardener pointed to a forest beyond the rows of fruit trees. "Both tame and wild animals roam the forest by the river. If you have time, *dragoman*, perhaps you could go hunting." He pointed to a falconer practicing his craft.

"We can't stay. I must deliver my report to the Deputy Grand Vizier."

"Will you see the Sultan's sister?" the Chief Gardener asked.

"The Grand Vizier wants me to help deliver his slave, but first I must take care of some business inside Edirne."

"You will say a good word for me to the Chief Gardener at the New Palace?" the Chief Gardener asked.

"Yes, and to the Sultan's Mother."

When a crane flew low, the falconer released his bird. It avoided the beak and brought down the crane, a difficult task.

As they returned towards the main gate, the younger boy stopped. "Can we watch?"

Two wrestlers soaked in oil to their waist faced each other. The first one screamed, charged, and grabbed a thigh. When the opponent slipped the first one's grip, he turned and counterattacked. Screaming even louder, the opponent tackled the first one, threw him to the ground, and pinned him.

The younger boy held his hands over his ears. "Do they always do that?"

"Always," the *dragoman* said.

"Those two are our best wrestlers. They'll compete in next summer's competition at the fields of *Kirkpinar*."

"*Kirkpinar*?" the older boy asked. "What does that mean?"

The *dragoman* translated. "*Kirkpinar* means Forty Springs, named in honor of forty Turkish soldiers who crossed the straits from Asia into Europe and captured a Byzantine fortress. After the victory, two of them wrestled with each other in a meadow further downstream, after the Tundzha empties into the Maritsa River. When neither won the first day, they resumed their match the next. It lasted into the night."

"Into the night?" the boy asked. "Who won?"

"Neither, both died of exhaustion."

"They died?" the girl asked.

"The other wrestlers buried them by a fig tree, but do you know what happened?" the *dragoman* asked. "The next year, springs appeared in the meadows around their grave sites, so late each spring the best wrestlers in the whole Empire compete in a tournament to honor them."

"Kirkpinar?"

"Yes, and within decades, Thrace was conquered and the Ottoman capital was moved from Bursa to Edirne."

Fatih Koprusu, *Saray*, Edirne, *Rumelia*, Ottoman Empire

THE *DRAGOMAN* ENJOYED hunting, but he needed to attend to business inside Edirne. Leading the youth to the middle of *Fatih Koprusu*, he asked, "Do you know why this bridge is called *Fatih*?"

The bridge spanned an arm of Tundzha. Further downstream, smoke rose from fires at the slave camp, where the *dragoman* knew guards watched The Grand Vizier's 'Bohemian' purchase.

"I don't even know what *Fatih* means," the older boy said.

"*Fatih* means Conqueror. About one hundred and fifty years ago, Sultan Mehmet II inherited his father's throne in Edirne, then capital of the Empire. The new Sultan led his army to and captured the Byzantine city of Constantinople. Ever since then, he has been known as Mehmet *the Conqueror*. This bridge is named for him."

"And what is that building?" The older boy gestured to a square tower rising in center of the island."

"*Adalet Kasri*, Justice Palace." The *dragoman* stopped the youth in front of the stone tower and pointed out two stones. "Do you know what these stones stand for?"

"How could we?" the younger boy asked.

"The first stone is where people petition the Sultan."

"And the other?" the older boy asked.

"For the heads of those advisors who give the Sultan bad advice. After you are trained, remember to never give the Sultan bad advice."

"We wouldn't want to do that." The older boy shook his head. "Where are you taking us?"

"To *Stamboul* and the best *janissary* school in the Empire," the *dragoman* said. "They will train you well and if you prove yourself, you can even become Grand Vizier, like Hasan *the Fruiterer*."

"I don't want to be a *janissary*," the younger boy said. "I want to go home."

"It's a great honor to become a *janissary*, to work for the Sultan." The *dragoman* proceeded to the far side of the island and crossed a longer, stone-arched bridge. Stopping in the middle the Saray Koprusu or Palace Bridge, the *dragoman* asked, "Have you heard of Noah?"

"Who hasn't?" the older boy asked. "He built the ark."

"Much bigger than that boat." The *dragoman* pointed downstream, to small boat drifting away from a landing built of solid marble. "When the Flood destroyed the whole earth, only Noah, his sons and their wives survived."

"And all of the animals," the girl added.

"You are right. One of Noah's three sons was named Japheth. After the ark landed on Mount Ararat on the far side of Anatolia, Japheth's wife gave birth to a son named Gomer, the progenitor of the Turk." The *dragoman* turned his attention back to the two boys. "Everyone knows what great fighters the Turks are."

The group reached the fortified walls of Edirne. They crossed over a moat and viewed the Macedonian Tower anchoring a corner.

"Sultan Murad I captured Edirne a little more than two centuries ago. He moved the capital of the Ottoman Empire from Bursa to Edirne."

"I thought Constantinople was the capital," the older boy said.

"Now it is, but instead of calling it Constantinople, we call it *Stamboul*."

To their left, on a hill outside the inner city walls, a beautiful mosque overlooked the narrow streets and bazaars of the crowded city, second only to *Stamboul* in size. The late afternoon sun illuminated four slim minarets with triple balconies and the large dome of Selimiye Mosque.

"What's that?" the older boy asked.

"Our destination—Rustem *Pasha Caravanserai*. Rustem *Pasha*, the Grand Vizier for Suleiman *the Magnificent*, had the inn built for travelers who frequented the city."

Rustem *Pasha Caravanserai*, Edirne, Ottoman Empire

"DRAGOMAN! WHAT A pleasure!" The keeper of Rustem *Pasha Cara-vanserai* welcomed the travelers with open arms. He led them into the central courtyard. Porches supported by columns surrounded the busy opening on all sides.

"You heard I was coming?" the *dragoman* asked.

"News travels fast." The keeper led the rest of the travelers into a private room. "Did you bring any fruit?"

"No," the *dragoman* said. "I am on business for the Grand Vizier."

"Oh, the collection. I heard." He let the *dragoman* enter the room first. "Well, I'm running low on fruit. It's been almost a year since you visited."

"A month."

The keeper motioned for the *dragoman* to sit and as soon as he did, he sat down too, crossed-legged. "I know you like coffee." The keeper signaled for servants to bring drinks.

"You have rooms?"

"It's been very crowded since the *sipahis* returned from the frontier."

"I can pay."

"My best room is available for you."

"I knew I would be treated well." The *dragoman* gestured to the two boys and the girl. "And for these three?"

The keeper told a servant. "Make rooms for the men, these two boys, and the girl."

"Watch over the girl. She is special."

"My second wife will personally take care of her."

When the veiled wife arrived at the door, the *dragoman* told the pensive girl, "Go with her."

"When you return I will serve you *cigeri*," the keeper said to the girl.

"Calf's liver with peppers and yogurt," the *dragoman* translated. The girl did not smile, but the *dragoman* did. "My favorite."

The wife motioned for the girl to come to her, half-hidden behind the doorway's curtain.

"You'll be safe," the *dragoman* said.

Chapter 5 - Chained by the Neck

By twenty and twenty, chained by the necks, they [Captain John Smith and the other prisoners] marched to this Great City [Constantinople or Stamboul]

John Smith

There is also a usual market in Constantinople, wherein they sell men and women of all ages as ordinarily as we do cattle in England, which are, for the most part, Christians, such as the Turks take captive in Hungary, or other places where they overcome….Their custom is to make slaves of all they can take alive, and, at their return, to sell them in the open market.

If Christians be moved in compassion to buy them, because they are Christians, the Turks will sell them exceeding dear to them, but cheap to a Musselman (as they call themselves) [Muslim] that is, true believers. But, if they cannot get their own price for them, they will for them to turn Turk, and so serve them in all servile labors, as the Israelites did the Egyptians.

"The Description of the Famous City of Constantinople"
by Guilielmus Biddulphus [William Biddle],
Collection of Voyages and Travels

Slave Camp, Edirne, *Rumelia*, Ottoman Empire, Nov. 1602

WITH NOTHING BUT his fine cloak to keep him warm, Captain John Smith spent another miserable night in the slave fields. Unable to use even a saddle for a pillow, the former captain of two hundred and fifty horsemen, spent inched up his collar. He could raise it no higher; the unbearable neck brace blocked its path. John writhed in cold agony.

Dampness greeted the break of day. Unlike the previous morn, the blacksmith was nowhere in sight. His tent had been torn down: the echoes of his pounding hammer silent, replaced by crackling campfires.

Camp cooks added kindling to their blazes and set large cauldrons on to boil. Guards, more numerous than before, spread out from the flaming fires and roused the Christian slaves to their feet. Other guards followed the directions of the head slave driver. Wearing a large turban and holding a long whip in his hand, he towered over his men. His guards dragged long chains and piled them onto round stacks. The slave driver stomped directly towards Smith. "Up!"

His bare fingers stiff, John pushed himself off the soggy ground. Light drizzle soaked the flattened grass. Nearby, the Italian officer sold in Axiopolis stirred, too.

The head driver cracked his whip. "Up!" A third snap pierced the air.

The driver whacked the back of a slumbering slave.

With an agonizing cry, the slave raised his arm to deflect the next expected blow. "No!" The slave staggered to his feet. Blood seeped through his torn shirt.

Unwilling to risk the same fate, scores of other prisoners—all with neck braces—jumped to their feet. More guards snapped their whips and the whole slave camp roused.

Guards pushed and shoved, lining them up and leading them by the fires.

Cooks took large spoons and slopped rice from the blackened cauldrons onto wooden plates. "*Pilaf.*"

Thankful for his first warm meal in days, John ate the rice with his fingers. Allowing barely enough time to down their morning meal, guards corralled John and the others. They lined them like sheep, ready for slaughter.

As quickly as they had been ordered to rise, guards ordered the captives down. Near piles of chains, they placed the prisoners into groups of twenty, parallel lines of ten.

John sat at the head of one line, while the Italian officer sat at the head of the next. The hurting slave, rice in his beard, grimaced behind them. No ointment would sooth his wound.

As soon as the prisoners finished their meal and the guards gathered the dishes, the head slave driver snapped his whip.

The slave drivers grabbed the chains and dragged the clinking metal across the ground. One driver pulled the end of one chain through the ring attached to John's neck, while another pulled the other end through the Italian's neck brace. Like seamstresses threading needles, the drivers pulled the ends through each neck ring of the twenty seated slaves. At the back of the gang, the two drivers secured the links together and locked the heavy chains tight.

The head slave driver mounted his horse and motioned to the first slave. "Up!"

The drivers, first one then another, cracked their whips. "March!"

Every muscle in John's body tensed. Latent pain returned to his side. His wounded ribs were not yet healed, lingering aches flared.

When the first group of twenty slaves slogged forward, John's pain could scarcely be assuaged. The heavy chain tightened, twisting the neck brace and rubbing against his collarbone.

In groups of twenty, hundreds of other Christian captives followed. Whenever a group bound by chains slowed, the slave drivers liberally exercised their whips.

John and the lead group crossed the stone bridge over the Tundzha River. After passing the Macedonian Tower, they entered Adrianople through an arched gateway. All along the narrow streets of the former Ottoman capital, older women stared. Some shook their heads, but most of the Greek, Armenian, and Turkish citizens of that old part of the city ignored their faces. Concentrating instead on their own daily business, some of them entered a long, covered market. Others unloaded goods and supplies from their mules.

Passing through to the other side of the walled town, the chained slaves crossed another bridge, not wide enough for two wagons to pass. On the long span, Smith nudged the elbow of the Italian officer walking beside him. "How long until we reach Constantinople?"

"At least several days, it's about one hundred and fifty miles."

The head slave driver turned his horse around, snapped his whip, and scowled.

John quit talking.

The nearly four hundred slaves in the human caravan plodded southeast through the mud and dampness. Like an armada of galleys sailing over the waves of the Mediterranean, the train of twenty slaves weaved up and down, over the rolling hills of what the Greeks called Thrace, but Ottoman Turks called *Rumelia*, the land of the Romans.

Now hundreds of miles away from Christian lands and frustrated at his lack of control, Smith did not know what to do, except to step forward and forward once more. The human merchandise trudged towards Constantinople.

By noon the next day the skies had cleared and the sun beat down. The slave right behind Smith stumbled, causing the chain to cut into John's neck.

The slave driver ran towards him. "Get up!"

Smith reached back and helped the hurt man to his feet. "You must make it."

Whip in his hand, the driver shoved the weakened slave back into line. "Move!" He stared at Smith, who acquiesced.

After another hour of marching without a break, the slave behind John panted. "Thirsty."

"Water." Smith pointed at the follower.

The slave driver on horseback answered with the crack of his whip. He met any resistance with instant brutality. "Keep moving." Demonstrating great efficiency in doling out punishment, the driver hit the wounded slave again.

Stymied and unable to intercede, Smith wanted to escape. But how? *Even if I could break the chains, who would help me? Any attempt will be futile and to escape through hundreds of miles of Ottoman territory? Impossible.*

The English slave trudged onward in pure misery. His feet, sorely blistered, ached with every step. Heavy chains weighed him down.

Dirty and fatigued from days of marching, Smith and the other slaves reached a small town. After passing a mosque with a single minaret, the slave caravan reached the top of a river embankment. Below, fresh water flowed.

Babaeski, Rumelia, Jamada II, AH 1011 (AD 1602)

THE *DRAGOMAN,* ALONG with the two Bulgarian boys and the young girl captured by the Grand Vizier, followed the *janissary* foot soldiers, returning to the heart of the vast Ottoman Empire, the great city of *Stamboul.* Wearing his tall hat instead of his turban, Ali *Agha,* the appointed leader of the *janissaries* and brother-in-law to the powerful Chief White Eunuch, the Sultan's most trusted advisor, rode at the head of four *ortas,* almost a thousand men. Another officer carried his standard, a pure white banner.

Since leaving Edirne, the *dragoman* had not heard any *janissary* complaints. The foot-soldiers of the Sultan had received their quarterly pay on time, unlike the summer when several *ortas* rebelled at Edirne. Those *janissaries* came to blows with *sipahi* horsemen, but Ali *Agha,* with the help of the treasurer, had quelled the discord. They had arrived with the necessary monies from the Imperial Treasury. Now, a half year later, Ali *Agha* was returning to the Ottoman capital.

The *dragoman* turned to the two Bulgarian boys and the girl riding on the horses behind him. Throughout the journey from Edirne, their horses had kept pace.

The older boy sat in front of his brother on the same horse. *"Dragoman*? What's the name of this town?"

"Mehmet *the Conqueror* asked that same question. He stopped here."

"He did?"

"Yes, when Mehmet *the Conqueror* led his Ottoman army from Edirne to Constantinople, he asked an old man what the name of this town was. The old man answered *'eski.'*"

"What does that mean?"

The *dragoman* translated from Turkish to Bulgarian. *"Eski* means old."

"That's a funny name," the girl said. "What did *the Conqueror* say?"

"Sultan Mehmet looked at the old man and laughed. He renamed the town *'Babaeski.'*"

"Babaeski?"

"It means 'Father of Old.'"

For the first time since leaving the Balkans, the girl smiled. *"Babaeski."*

On the far side of the small town, the *dragoman* stopped at the top of an embankment. Below, the *janissaries* had caught up with the slave train. One of Ali *Agha's janissaries* rode ahead. "Make way!"

Slave drivers cracked their whips and pushed the slave gangs of twenty to the side, but the head slave driver, mounted at the top of the far embankment, crossed his arms and refused to move the first gang of twenty. He clearly intended to let his slaves continue to drink on the far bank. They ate biscuits their biscuits and drank their fill.

Ali *Agha* led his horse to the middle of the creek. He directed his *janissaries* to rest upriver from the slaves.

The *dragoman* found Ali *Agha*. "I have not seen the *sipahi* leaders since we left Edirne."

"The leaders dismissed many to return to their *timar*s in *Rumelia*."

The *dragoman* heard neighs of horses and looked around. *"Sipahis?"*

"Not all are returning to their *timar*s," Ali *Agha* said.

"Move away!" The *sipahi* leaders remained mounted at the water's edge. "Our horses need water."

"My men are not finished," Ali *Agha* said.

His *janissaries* did not move.

Across the river, slave drivers snapped their whips. Chains tightened as the slaves rose and plodded uphill to the road leading to *Stamboul*.

As many of his horsemen crossed, the *sipahi* leader asked Ali *Agha*, "What about my men? They haven't been paid."

"Am I responsible for that?"

"You are on the Council."

"They were paid by the treasurer in Shumen. Do you not remember?"

"That was for the campaign," the *sipahi* leader from Anatolia said. "We must be compensated for the loss of our *timar*s."

"Losses?"

"There are even more."

"More?" Ali *Agha* asked.

"Haven't you heard about the rebellion in Anatolia?"

"Yes, we all know the rebels took Ankara last summer."

"More *timars* outside Ankara have been confiscated by the brother of the Black Scribe. The rebels are gaining power. My *sipahis* need compensation for the loss of their lands."

"The Grand Vizier must be told."

"We cannot wait for a response. We must meet his Lieutenant, Deputy Grand Vizier *Saatci* Hasan *Pasha* at the new palace in *Stamboul*." The *sipahi* leader turned away and encouraged his horse across the creek.

Minutes later after the companies of *sipahi* riders departed, Ali *Agha* pointed to the long-legged girl. "You never told me about her."

"I must present her to the Sultan's Mother at the New Palace," the *dragoman* said.

The next day, after crossing the stone bridge at Luleburgaz, the *dragoman* and his party spent most of the afternoon and that night at the *caravanserai*, the traveler's inn, more comfortable than open fields. *Stamboul* was still a hundred miles away.

Two days later, the *janissaries* marched ahead. The *dragoman* and the three children, along with their escorts, reached the northern shores of the Sea of Marmara, the main body of water connecting the Mediterranean and Black Seas. A merchant ship flew the flag of the Republic of Venice, while closer to shore two Ottoman galleys plied the waters. A pounding drum kept time and long oars, manned by unseen slaves, hit the water.

The steady drum beat faded as the *dragoman* continued. The road veered inland, the Ottoman Empire drew closer.

Theodosian Walls, Constantinople (*Stamboul*)

THE *DRAGOMAN* AND the two boys and the girl approached a double set of fortified walls.

"Those walls go on for miles," the girl said. "Where are we?"

Land Walls of Constantinople

"Constantinople." The *dragoman* led the children down the road that paralleled the wide ditch below the stone walls "More than one thousand years ago, the Roman Emperor Theodosius built those walls from the Castle of the Seven Towers on the Sea of Marmara to the Golden Horn, the protected harbor. Though the rest of the Roman Empire fell to the barbarians, those walls withstood their invasions, even the one led by Attila the Hun."

"Strong walls," the older boy said.

"Yes, but almost one hundred and fifty years ago, they could not withstand the Ottoman armies of Sultan Mehmet II." The *dragoman* pointed to a large gap in the double walls. "During a *Gaza*, or a Holy War, Mehmet *the Conqueror* brought his army, one hundred thousand strong but getting through was not easy."

"How did they break through?" the older boy asked.

The *dragoman* laughed. "Mehmet *the Conqueror* and his men brought the largest cannon ever built. The huge cannon took so long to load that it could be fired only seven times a day. Though the Greek defenders tried to repair the walls, the cannonballs breached them. *Janissaries* entered a smaller gate in the wall and overwhelmed the defenders of the breach. Afterwards, Mehmet the Conqueror placed three cannonballs by the gate the Turks call *Topkapi*, or cannon gate."

Edirnekapi, Constantinople

CAMELS LADENED WITH wicker baskets overflowing with thick sticks trekked toward the gate. The caravan, more than a dozen dromedaries, plodded slowly forward, through the stone archway protected by a pair of octagonal towers.

The *dragoman* and his small entourage caught up with the slave caravan. "Here we are," the *dragoman* said. "*Edirnekapi*, the Gate of Edirne." He approached the head slave driver at the gate. "The Grand Vizier asked me to personally deliver the 'Bohemian' he captured on the battlefield."

"You mean the one wearing the fancy clothes?" The slave driver gestured towards the brown-bearded slave sitting at the front of the first group of chained slaves.

"Yes. Can you spare a guard?"

"I can't do that, I only have one guard for every twenty slaves."

The *dragoman* pulled a coin from his purse and slipped it discretely into the Driver's hand. "Perhaps if you deliver him last."

"Meet me by the after mid-day prayers."

"By the Column." The *dragoman* remembered the burnt column was not far from the Palace of Ibrahim *Pasha*. "The Grand Vizier will appreciate your help."

Column of Constantine

"Don't forget to mention me." The driver squeezed the coin.

JOHN WATCHED THE *dragoman* take three children through the gate. As he and the rest of the slave caravan stayed seated outside the Gate of Edirne, several *janissaries* exited the gate and began to patrol.

One *janissary* held the leashes of two large dogs and as they approached, the dogs barked at John and the others. The slaves behind John and the Italian scooted away from the snarling canines. The largest dog jumped at the slaves, but the *janissary* tugged on the rope.

The head slave driver interposed his horse. The slave drivers forced Captain John Smith, his Italian friend, and the other chained captives up the sixth hill of Constantinople.

Chapter 6 - Aisha, Sister of the Sultan

Their robes and glorious luster of pearls and precious stones, which they carried, were worthy of the wife [Safiye Valide Sultana] and daughter [Aisha] of the most powerful and rich Monarch [Sultan Murad III] of the earth . . .

Built with incredible expenses, as we may see in the Hippodrome of Constantinople, by the Saray [Palace] of Ibrahim Pasha, where of the Turkish Emperors have been heirs, the which is capable to lodge a Great King. Their moveables and ornaments of their halls, are equal to their greatness, wherein they spare no cost . . .
History of the Imperial Estate of Grand Seigneurs by Michel Baudier
Translated from French by Edward Grimeston

That fair Palace, which is to be seen; now [AD 1594] the Lodging of this other Ibrahim Pasha, given him when [he] married the Emperor's daughter [Aisha].
"Discourse of the Most Notable Things of the Famous City Constantinople" by John Sanderson, Hakluytus Posthumus or Purchas his Pilgrim, Vol IX

Ibrahim *Pasha* Palace, *Stamboul*, *Jumada II*, AH 1011

BEAUTIFUL AISHA STEPPED out onto the balcony and peered through the latticed window of her palace facing the *Atmeidan*, the ancient Hippo-

Ancient Hippodrome and Hagia Sophia

drome of Constantinople. The Sister of the Sultan had heard about the *sipahis* returning from the European frontier. Her betrothed, Grand Vizier Hasan *the Fruiterer*, had sent most of the Ottoman army back at the end of the fighting season.

"So many *sipahis*," Aisha told her attendant.

"They set up their tents over there." Her veiled attendant gestured to an encampment set up beyond the tall monuments in the former stadium.

Though chariot races had ceased long ago, riders still exercised their horses in the largest open space within *Stamboul*. After Friday services ended at the mosques, teams of riders would compete, throwing long darts at each other.

"And there." Aisha pointed to a second encampment, larger than the first. The returning *sipahis* did not appear interested in contests or games.

One mounted *sipahi* leader rode to the largest tent of the encampment and dismounted. A turbaned leader, appearing as somber as the first, exited the open pavilion and greeted the visitor in the traditional Turkish manner. Each leader crossed his arm across his chest and nodded to the other.

"I wish my betrothed would return, too," Aisha said.

"It has been over a year since the Grand Vizier departed."

"Nearly two, but Ali *Agha* delivered the signed marriage contract last summer."

After her late husband *Damat* Ibrahim *Pasha* died outside Belgrade, Aisha's brother appointed Hasan *the Fruiterer* to be his new Grand Vizier. Sultan Mehmet III gave Hasan all of Ibrahim's tents, horses, camels and mules and even promised him that he could marry the widow Aisha when he returned.

Aisha added, "If only we could have peace, the suffering would end."

"And you could remarry."

"Yes, the time of mourning has passed."

Aisha gazed back at the encampment. When the two *sipahi* leaders looked up at her balcony, she did not avert her eyes. They did not stare long, for the loud neigh of an approaching horse garnered their attention. The taller one scowled at the sight of a white carriage passing below the Hagia Sophia, the former Byzantine church turned into a mosque. The round edifice dominated the skyline of the far end of the field.

"Your mother arrives from the New Palace," her attendant said.

Black eunuchs and palace guards, both on foot and on horseback, escorted the fancy carriage. Aisha had ridden in the white carriage, a wonderful present from Queen Elizabeth. After its delivery, the Sultan's Mother rode in it wherever she travelled around *Stamboul*.

The white carriage rolled down the wide field towards the main gate of the Palace of Ibrahim *Pasha*, named for the former Grand Vizier of Suleiman *the Magnificent*, who built the structure using stones once part of the Hippodrome. More than a hundred yards long, this grand palace had three courtyards facing the *Atmeidan*. The fourth one was in the back, part of the harem, the forbidden quarters. No man was allowed in it—only women, children, and eunuchs.

Memories flooded her mind, as her mother's carriage approached the palace. Twenty years earlier, when she was little more than a child, Aisha had stood with her mother on this very same balcony. Dressed in splendor, she and her mother and their court enjoyed days of colorful parades and plays. With his sword and cup bearers behind him and his Chief White Eunuch beside him, her father Sultan Murad III sat in a separate vestibule, a little bit higher to their right. They all watched the festivities surrounding the circumcision of her brother, Mehmet. Days later, her father sent him to govern Magnesia, the birthplace of both Aisha and her brother. The pretty city stood not far from Smyrna in western Anatolia, Asia Minor.

The white carriage slowed at the center gate leading to the First Courtyard. Aisha knew the reason for her mother's visit. Although the prescribed time of mourning for her late husband had passed, her mother insisted on showing proper respect. She often told her daughter, 'We must set an example'.

"We must go inside," Aisha said.

Great Hall, Ibrahim *Pasha* Palace

AISHA SAUNTERED ACROSS thick carpets inside the Great Hall, larger than the corresponding one at her brother's palace. Grand Viziers normally listened to petitioners at the Divan in the New Palace, but when the Council was not in session, Grand Viziers listened to petitioners in this room. Like those before him, Aisha's late husband *Damat* Ibrahim *Pasha* dispensed justice and issued commands from the large chair. Unlike the Grand Vizier of Suleiman *the Magnificent*, her late husband had died of natural causes. That first Ibrahim *Pasha* had abused his office, threatening the power of the Sultan, who had him strangled by palace mutes.

Aisha looked forward to the day—hopefully soon—when her betrothed, Hasan *the Fruiterer*, would return from Belgrade. The new Grand Vizier, like those before him, would run the daily affairs of the Ottoman Empire from here. Kept in perfect order, the Great Hall had high ceilings.

The widow Aisha normally ran the affairs of her palace from her well-lit salon, built in center of her harem garden, but occasionally, she used the darker Great Hall. Lamps and candles, however, illuminated the room. Long tapestries adorned the walls. The blue and white vases placed on two stands were empty.

Aisha told her Overseer, "Have them filled."

"But the season," the strong Overseer protested. Approved by her mother, the Black eunuch had been with her for years. "Tulips will not blossom until spring."

"I am certain we can find winter blooms."

"I will ask the gardeners."

"See what you can do."

"As you wish." The Overseer bowed and relayed the message to one of the fifty Black eunuch guards of the harem. He stood with his curved sword by one of the doors.

Aisha *Sultana* sat down on the cushioned bench attached to one wall. She straightened her perfectly tailored outfit and adjusted her jeweled headdress. Though her long black hair flowed to her shoulders, she did not feel particularly pretty because of the hooked nose she inherited from her father. But she had an attractive figure and also possessed an abundance of jewels, an inheritance from *Nur Banu*, her grandmother. A simple pearl necklace rested on her breast.

The line of women in the Great Hall had grown and Aisha needed to attend the pressing needs of her court. The first ones wanted her to choose the fabric for the harem from the samples draped over their arms.

"Yes, I like the feel of silk, but I like that pattern better." Aisha turned to the door and recognized her mother entering the Great Hall. "*Madre.*" Speaking in Italian, she asked, "What do you think?"

Her thin mother walked straight towards her. "The decision should wait," she answered in Italian, the *lingua franca* of the New Palace. She stopped and eyed Aisha from head to toe. "I see you are not ready."

Aisha's zest for life could not be dampened. "Mother, it takes me longer." In her hand she held a letter.

"Why does it take my daughter so long?"

"My hair needed combing."

"It does look pretty." Her mother straightened a loose strand. "A letter?"

"I received it last night."

"And what does your future husband say?"

"How did you know it was from—" Aisha caught herself in midbreath. She glanced at the Overseer chosen by her mother. Whether small matters or large, her mother had always found a way of knowing what was going on.

"Withhold no secrets from me."

"Keep secrets? From you, *Madre*?" Aisha invited her mother to sit down. "I thought we might have tea before we visit the graves."

"Not today." Her mother remained standing. "We must go, for I need to return to the New Palace early."

"I will decide about the pattern later." Aisha, speaking Turkish, dismissed her attendants.

Although she and her mother both wore white, the customary color for mourning, Aisha felt different this day. Her deep grief at the loss of her husband, who had died less than two years earlier, had dissipated. She did not feel like crying any longer. Aisha and her mother exited the Great Hall and descended the stone stairs into the Second Courtyard. They walked through the arched passageway leading to the First.

Attendants opened the door and helped the women into the white carriage waiting on marble stones. The fancy carriage looked as nice as the day it was delivered to Aisha's mother several years earlier.

The iron gate to the *Atmeidan* swung open and the horses surged ahead.

Atmeidan

AISHA PULLED BACK the carriage curtains and looked for the two *sipahi* leaders who had been meeting earlier. The leader with a scowl had disappeared and the other remained at the door of his tent. At the far end of the field, towards the arsenal and the water, the *sipahi* encampment had grown larger. As the carriage turned left, Aisha viewed the three ancient monuments marking the spina, the center spine of the ancient Hippodrome. In the center, three bronze serpents had their bodies wrapped around the center column, their heads pointed upward, their mouths open wide. Framing the Serpentine Column from Delphi

Egyptian Obelisk in Front of Palace of Ibrahim Pasha

in Greece were two, much taller columns. Faced with squared stones, the Column of Constantine Porphyrogenitus stood high on one side and the Egyptian Obelisk of Theodosius on the other. Emperor Constantine had it shipped from Luxor in southern Egypt, down the Nile, and across the Mediterranean Sea when he founded Constantinople as his capital.

Aisha pulled out the letter from the Grand Vizier. "I must reread it."

Her mother leaned forward. "And what does it say?"

Aisha held it to her heart. "The Grand Vizier was in a terrible fight."

"Was he injured?" Her mother's concern seemed real.

"Almost killed, but do you know what he promised?" Aisha asked.

"To send me a present."

"Speak up," her mother said. "What is it?"

Aisha shook her head. "He did not say."

"Well." Her mother straightened herself in her seat. "As soon as the Grand Vizier returns, you and he shall get married."

Although they normally attended prayer services at the Hagia Sophia at the end of the *Atmeiden* closest to the New Palace, today they would go to *Sehzade Camii*, the Prince's Mosque, where Aisha's late husband *Damat* Ibrahim *Pasha* was buried.

The carriage veered left, up a main road.

Eski Serai, Third Hill

THE CARRIAGE REACHED the Third Hill and the *Eski Serai* or Old Palace where the former concubines of her father and their unmarried daughters stayed. After Aisha's brother Mehmet ascended to the throne, he sent the concubines and virgin *odalisques* of their father here. Many of those concubines, including ones whose sons were of the nineteen killed upon the ascension of Mehmet to the throne, had been jealous of Aisha's mother whose other son had been spared, sent earlier to the farthest reaches of the empire. Their daughters, their attendants, their eunuchs, and most of the dwarfs who had amused Aisha's father, would keep them company. Unless an *odalisque* had a Jewish matron arrange a marriage to an important vizier, she, like all of the others, would live the rest of her days inside the high-walled palace.

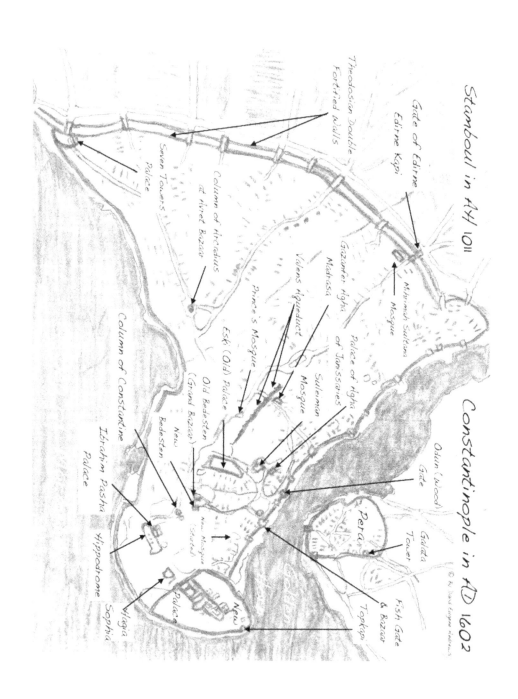

Aisha had stayed inside the *Eski Serai* for eight days of singing and dancing before her wedding to *Damat* or the Bridegroom. All the women of her father's Imperial Harem were allowed to join in the festivities. Four years after her brother was circumcised and sent to Magnesia, hundreds of sailors transported wedding presents to the teenage bride. Gifts included fifty life-size animals made of sugar and were received by black eunuchs at the Old Palace door. After sending one hundred female slaves and fifty noblewomen in raised coaches to take her bed and furniture and prepare her new quarters at the Palace of Ibrahim *Pasha*, the veiled Aisha rode on horseback under a *baldachin*, a moving canopy of gold cloth carried by four Eunuchs. Even after the marriage ceremony was concluded, the marriage was not immediately consummated. Her father, Sultan Murad III, waited fifteen or twenty days before granting permission for his vizier *Damat* Ibrahim *Pasha* to approach her.

The midday call for prayer broke her reflections and Aisha gazed out the window.

Standing high above, on the upper balcony of one of two minarets, a *muezzin* once more cried out the call to prayer at *Sehzade Camii*, the Prince's Mosque.

Prince's Mosque - Sehzade Camii

Turbe of *Damat* Ibrahim *Pasha*, *Sehzade Camii*, Third Hill

"AISHA, DO WHAT is proper," Safiye *Valide Sultana* told her daughter. "Ask Allah for the salvation of *Damat* Ibrahim *Pasha* and ourselves."

"*Sì, Madre.*" Aisha backed away from the sealed coffin of her late husband.

Inside the raised crypt, his corpse would have been turned on its right side, facing Mecca. Below a high dome, light streamed through both upper and lower windows of the octagonal *turbe*. Coral red Iznik tiles adorned the walls of the newly built mausoleum.

More than twenty years her senior, her late husband had gained Aisha's hand after he returned from Egypt. Her father Sultan Murad III had appointed Ibrahim to take the place of a eunuch governor of Egypt who had imprisoned in the Castle of Seven Towers for absconding with

Egypt's riches.

Ibrahim, who had been born in Herzegovina in Bosnia, searched for and found the treasures the eunuch had hoarded. After a thorough accounting, Ibrahim packed up the riches, including a huge emerald, later cut into six fine pieces. On his return by land via Syria, Ibrahim squashed a rebellion by the *Druze,* a minority sect, and forwarded four hundred of their heads back to *Stamboul.* Aisha refused to believe the charge that some of those four hundred heads belonged to Ibrahim's own men.

The Sultan rewarded him with the hand of his eldest daughter, Aisha. She often interceded with her father, who eventually gave in and promoted Ibrahim to be his Second Vizier. After her father's death, her brother Mehmet acceded to the Ottoman throne and *Damat* Ibrahim *Pasha* became his Grand Vizier.

The young widow stood at the foot of Ibrahim's crypt next to her mother. They turned towards the *Kaaba*, the House of Worship originally built by Abraham, in Mecca.

"We pray for Ibrahim's salvation and ours," Aisha concluded, following her mother's exact instructions. Wailing over the dead was not approved, but her eyes were moist and she shed a tear. Aisha could not escape the melancholy mood their frequent visits to the graves imbued. "Can we go now?"

The fully veiled mother and daughter exited Ibrahim's *turbe*. Instead of going to the garden area behind the mosque, where the large *turbe* for the Prince stood, they headed back to the carriage, parked by the main entrance.

Aisha handed alms to a poor man who said, "We will pray that the two black angels will not torment *Damat* Ibrahim *Pasha's* soul."

"Into the night." A second man held out his hand.

Aisha handed him a coin.

When they reached the main entrance to return to their coach, a religious man stopped them. "The imam wishes to see you inside."

"For what reason?" her mother asked.

"I do not know. The imam said it would not take long."

Aisha and her mother entered the enclosed courtyard of the Prince's Mosque and passed by the ablution fountain.

Before the devout prayed their midday prayers, all had washed their face, hands and feet, becoming ceremonially clean.

Nearly sixty years earlier, Suleiman *the Magnificent* and his wife Hurrem known as Roxlena or the Ukrainian had the *Sehzade* Mosque and Complex built in memory of their son. Contrary to tradition, Roxlena had persuaded Suleiman to formally marry her and their son was named heir to the throne, usurping the rights of his first born by Suleiman's first concubine. No sooner had the new heir been named than the prince became sick and died at the young age of twenty-one. Many in *Stamboul* claimed it to be a sign from heaven, but to honor the Prince, Sultan Suleiman commissioned the famous architect Mimar Sinan to build this, his first mosque in *Stamboul*. The Prince's body, was brought back from Anatolia, it was interred in the garden large octagonal *turbe*.

Mausoleum of the Prince
Turbe of the Şehzade

Aisha and her mother walked through the porticos, the covered walkways leading to the main prayer hall. Blue Iznik tiles adorned the ceiling of the central dome, as well as the four half domes on adjoining sides. Dozens of windows and lamps in the form of a circle suspended from above brightened the large room. Only one or two men remained kneeling and bowing on their prayer rugs, facing the mihrab, showing the direction of Mecca. Aisha glanced at the area reserved for members of the imperial family when they stopped below the minibar, where the imam would deliver his Friday sermon.

"What is it?" the Sultan's Mother asked.

"I thought you should know," the imam said. "The Chief White Eunuch and his brother-in-law, the *Agha* of the *Janissaries,* just returned from Belgrade. They are at the Chief White Eunuch's madrasa."

"We should meet him," her mother said. "Thank you, imam. When I return to the Imperial Harem, I will inform the Chief Black Eunuch of your attentiveness."

Gazanfer *Agha* Complex, Valens Aqueduct

THE WHITE CARRIAGE slowed beneath the double arches of the Valens Aqueduct. More than twenty feet thick, the arches, brick above stone, reached upwards more than fifty feet. Originally built twelve hundred years earlier by the Roman Emperor Valens, the aqueduct spanned the valley between the Fourth and Third Hills, bringing water from springs outside the city to deep cisterns built beneath the hills. Though once damaged by an earthquake, Suleiman *the Magnificent* had it repaired.

In the shadows of the aqueduct to their left, white smoke plumed upwards. Circular chimneys rose above the plain walls of the single story complex. The carriage rounded the corner and halted in front of the gate of Gazanfer *Agha* Complex. The largest dome stood over the mosque, but smaller domes marked the rooms of the first madrasa, or religious school, ever built in *Stamboul* by anyone other than an immediate member of the Sultan's family.

"Safiye *Valide Sultana*, you were visiting the graves?" The Chief White Eunuch and Ali *Agha* approached on horseback.

She pulled back the drapes and leaned forward. "Yes, with my daughter."

The beardless eunuch motioned to the *Agha* of the Janissaries. "This was the first time I was able to show Ali *Agha* the progress on the translation of the poems."

"I thought a collection would please the Sultan," Ali *Agha* said. "I know your son loves stories with moral lessons."

"And chivalry," Aisha interjected.

"The headmaster and the poet have worked diligently on translating the stories into Turkish." Ali *Agha* gestured to bearded students and their teachers standing in the gateway, before turning back to Aisha. "You received the letter from the Grand Vizier?"

"Yes, it was a surprise," Aisha said. "Did he say anything else?"

"Yes, he looks forward to returning," Ali *Agha* replied. "Sister of the Sultan, you must excuse me, but I must go."

"And we must go, too," the Sultan's Mother added.

"Shall I accompany you back to the New Palace?" the Chief White Eunuch asked.

"No, I must take my daughter back to her palace. Thank you." She closed the drapes.

"Mother?" Aisha asked, as the carriage turned around. "Perhaps, the Grand Vizier's present will soon arrive."

Chapter 7 - Italian Conversation

The streets of this City [Constantinople/Stamboul] are narrow, and shadowed with pentices [sloped roofs] of wood, and upon both sides the way is raised some foot high, but of little breadth, and paved for men and women to pass, the midst of the street being left low and unpaved, and no broader than for the passage of asses or beasts, loaded . . .

The buildings of the City, being partly of a matter like brick, but white, and (as it seems) unhardened by fire, partly of timber and clay . . . some few palaces, which are of free stone . . . built only two stories high, without any windows, after the manner of Italy.

Itinerary [AD 1597] by Fynes Moryson

To this Great City, where they were delivered to their several masters and he [Captain John Smith] to the young Charatza, Tragabigzanda [Aisha, Sister of the Sultan] . . . The Pasha [Hasan the Fruiterer] writ to her, a Bohemian Lord conquered by his hand, as he had many others, which ere long he would present her, whose ransoms should adorn her with the glory of his conquests. This noble gentlewoman took some time . . . to speak with him, because she could speak Italian.

John Smith

Edirnekapi, Constantinople, Ottoman Empire, Autumn 1602

STICKS OF ALL sizes overflowed wicker baskets strapped to the back of the last camel. Though smaller than any other in the long caravan, this camel carried a large load of firewood. Unlike the others with one hump, this one had two. Loosely tied to the one ahead, the double-humped Bactrian slogged. When the last herdsman smacked the beast on its rump, it kicked its hind leg and bellowed. The rope tightened and its loud howl subsided. The carrivan disappeared through the arched gate into the City, the herdsman trailed behind.

Citizens returned to their business, but hundreds of Christian slaves remained seated along the road below the Theodosian Walls. Among them, Captain John Smith waited to be delivered. When the English slave heard a click, he turned and saw the Head Slave Driver place a key into his purse. Pulling out his whip, the Head Slave Driver stomped towards

Smith. Behind him, the end of his chain tying the twenty slaves together jangled on the ground.

A pair of guards picked up the ends and unthreaded the chain from the neck braces, starting from the back. When they reached the front of the line, they circled the chain round and round. It rose higher and higher, coiled like a snake ready to strike.

The Head Driver stepped closer to John and held his hand out as though commanding a dog to stay still.

John remained frozen.

A guard, carrying a two-foot long cutter, rushed toward him. With jaws wide open, the cutter swept by John's face.

The Head Slave Driver tapped his whip.

Cold metal touched John's neck. The cutter snapped the metal link and the brace loosened. The guard pried opened the neck brace and tossed it next to the coiled chain.

John's neck itched badly. He stretched, but could not easily scratch it. His movement was restricted, his wrists still bound with leather. He reached up and rubbed his neck, but the rough leather only made it worse. When John brought his arms down, he found the Head Slave Driver towering over him. With a whip in his fist, he stared down at the English captain.

Unwilling to suffer more pain, John sat perfectly still. When the Driver turned his attention elsewhere, the Italian officer sitting next to John shook his head.

Behind them, guards took off more neck braces and tossed them into the pile. More groups of twenty waited to be unchained, to be delivered to new owners or resold in the slave markets of Constantinople.

In the distance, several horses meandered around the slave caravan, up the hill on the road to Edirne. John recognized the rider on the first horse. Days earlier, he had seen the Interpreter with The Grand Vizier in Bulgaria. Two young boys dressed in red shared the second horse, while a long-legged girl, wearing a brown hat, sat sidesaddle on a third. Two black men dressed in turbans held the reins of her steed.

As they passed each group of twenty, the *dragoman* eyed the Christian slaves. When he reached the first group, the Head Slave Driver intercepted him, and exchanged a few words. The *dragoman* pointed his finger at John, before slipping the Head Slave Driver a coin. He rode ahead with the two boys and the girl through the arched Gate of Edirne.

As soon as the Head Slave Driver returned, he ordered John's half of the group to stand. Smith had barely enough time to say *arrivederci* to his Italian officer friend. It seemed unlikely they would ever see each other again, at least in this lifetime.

John and the first wave of slaves traipsed through the Gate of Edirne. He counted his paces. *Nine, ten.* The Theodosian Walls were nearly thirty feet thick, strong enough to stop the Barbarian invasions, but not strong enough to stop the Ottoman Turks a century or so earlier.

Countless wooden houses, some with overhanging balconies, lined the narrow side streets.Beyond the mosque complex built inside the gate, the wide street grew crowded.

View of Constantinople/Stamboul from Galata/Pera in 1635

Constantinople, Ottoman Empire, Late Autumn 1602

THE HEAD SLAVE Driver led the slaves up a narrow street. Sloped roofs hung over wooden planks on both sides. Whenever a citizen approached, guards forced John and the others into the muddy ditch, an uneven chasm normally reserved for beasts and animals.

Looking at his list, a ledger written in Turkish script, the Driver stopped at the largest house on the block. After announcing his presence, he delivered a Hungarian slave to his new owner.

John and the few remaining slaves returned to the main thoroughfare. Just beyond where an ancient aqueduct spanned a valley between two hills, a white carriage, escorted by guards on horseback and on foot, exited a mosque.

A little further ahead, a small cadre of janissaries marched out of their barracks and patrolled the outer walls of an old palace. The plain walls, two stories tall and dotted with towers, extended for about a quarter mile on the left side of the main road.

At the eastern end, while the slave drivers took the remaining slaves to the palace gate, John motioned to the guard for a drink. At the fountain opposite the gate, John had barely moistened his lips, when a *sipahi* rider kicked the cup out of his hand. The rider yelled at the guard.

Clearly, slaves were not allowed to drink the clean water. As the argument between the guard and the rider grew louder, several *janissaries* rushed to the fountain.

Lucky for John, the Head Slave Driver quickly returned and the ruckus between the *sipahis* and *janissaries* quieted. As the Head Slave Driver departed, along with Smith and the guards, the spilt cup remained on the ground.

After passing a large mosque complex, men left a smaller mosque by the busiest of squares. They approached the burnt column in the midst of an intersection where the tall *dragoman* atop his horse, without the young girl or the two young boys.

Terrace above Second Courtyard, Ibrahim *Pasha* Palace

SMOKE DRIFTED AWAY from the chimneys behind Aisha, Sister of the Sultan. She walked along the terrace overlooking the Second Courtyard of the Palace of Ibrahim *Pasha* and watched her mother's white carriage disappear from sight. Her mother and sister had dropped her off at her palace, and were returning to the Imperial Harem at the palace of her brother, Sultan Mehmet III.

Inside the Great Hall of the Palace of Ibrahim *Pasha*, Aisha told the Overseer, "Before I continue with my court, have the servants bring me tea."

"At once." The Overseer bowed.

Though the Grand Vizier normally used the Great Hall for important state matters, Aisha made use of it while he was away. After being named Grand Vizier, her future husband Hasan *the Fruiterer* would not occupy the palace until their marriage was finalized. After putting things in quick order, he had been absent for more than a year, having gone directly to the European frontier.

Aisha took her seat on a bench attached to one wall. Her favorite attendants kept her company as she sat down on the cushion, placed higher than any other.

Minutes later, servants carried out a low table and set it in the midst of the seated women.

After letting the tea brew for several minutes, the head servant picked up the brass teapot and poured a cup. "I trust it is not too hot."

Aisha waved the steam towards her nose and breathed in the aroma. It was the kind of tea her father loved so much. Imported via the Silk Road from China through Trebizond on the Black Sea, some considered the tea too bitter, but not her. She nodded her approval.

The servant poured the tea into small cups for the other ladies and bowed. "I'll refresh the pot."

The Overseer and two guards appeared in the doorway and bowed. "Aisha *Sultana*."

"I am not ready to hear your report on the remodel."

"You have a guest."

"I do not recall inviting any friend."

The Overseer handed Aisha a letter. "The Grand Vizier sent his *dragoman* to deliver a message."

"From my betrothed?" Aisha straightened up.

"He sent you a present, too."

A guard set down a saber and a shield.

"What use do I have with these? What is the meaning?"

"I believe it may be in the letter."

"Invite the *dragoman* in," Aisha said.

The *dragoman* presently entered and bowed.

"Tea for our guest." Aisha motioned to the hand-woven rug that her servants had rolled out. "You must sit down."

"I respectfully decline your offer. I can only stay a short while. There is a banquet at the New Palace and I must attend."

"Yes, I heard." Aisha leaned back on the comfortable pillows.

"The Grand Vizier wanted me to deliver a slave."

"*Dragoman*, what shall I do with a slave?" Aisha asked.

"He is no ordinary slave. The Grand Vizier conquered the 'Bohemian' Lord by his own hand."

"How did he defeat him?" Aisha asked.

"He challenged him in single combat. On the battlefield, he charged him, but the Grant Vizier blocked his blow and struck him with his sword." The *dragoman* added, "See, he even took his shield and his saber. He sent me to deliver the nobleman to you, so you can ransom—"

"Ransom?" Aisha asked.

"Yes, a gift. The 'Bohemian' nobleman must be rich. His garments?

The best money can buy." The *dragoman* unsheathed the officer's sword. "This saber with its fancy handle? Crafted in silver."

"And the shield?"

The *dragoman* lifted it up for Aisha and her attendants to see. "The slave must be worth much."

"What do these three turbaned heads emblazoned on the shield mean?" Aisha pointed.

"The Grand Vizier did not tell me."

Aisha truly admired her betrothed. "You must tell me more."

"I would, but it is getting late. The Grand Vizier could only promise to send more conquests back to you."

"He will?" Aisha glanced once more at the saber with its ornate handle and the shield.

"Yes." The *dragoman* took one last sip of tea. "Thank you again for your hospitality, but I really must go." He placed the cup on the tray and bowed. "The Deputy Grand Vizier and the old and new Venetian ambassadors await me. I wish I could tell you more, I must say *arrivederci*."

Impressed with The Grand Vizier's feats of bravery and pleased with his thoughtfulness, Aisha decided she would use her merchant friends to contact the slave's family in the Kingdom of Bohemia. She determined to find out where the slave's family had their estate and calculated how much ransom she should demand.

As the *dragoman* departed, Aisha turned to the Overseer. "Bring me the Bohemian."

Arched Corridor, Ibrahim *Pasha* Palace, Late Autumn 1602

CAPTAIN JOHN SMITH barely had time to rest before the large Overseer brought him through a long, arched corridor.

When Smith arrived upstairs at the Grand Hall, he saw a single young noblewoman and her court, seated on a cushioned bench. She motioned to the well-dressed African Overseer to bring him closer. When he did, she issued a firm command in Turkish.

The Overseer hesitated before yielding to the woman's command. He grabbed Smith's bound wrists and stretched his arms forward. Smith stood still. After stepping back, the Overseer drew his scimitar sword and, with a swish, cut Smith's leather bands. Smith looked down, no nicks.

Sheathing his sword, the Overseer marched across the room and at the door turned around. He crossed his arms, stared at the English captive, and frowned.

For the first time since he had been captured by pillagers on the battlefields in Wallachia, Smith was unbound. His fine clothes, still soiled from wounds and the long journey from Axiopolis, needed cleaning. He peered straight into the Turkish noblewoman's eyes.

The young woman motioned for Smith to sit down, but there were no chairs. She spoke to him in Turkish, a language he did not understand. When he finally sat down across from her, she asked, *"Lei parla italiano?"*

"Sì." Smith was surprised to hear a familiar language. *"Parlo italiano."*

"Buono," she said, "what's your name?"

"Captain John Smith." When the noblewoman did not respond, he translated his name into Italian. *"Capitano Giovanni Fabbro."*

"Giovanni." She offered a small cup. "Tea?"

"Grazie," Smith said, "and who are you?"

"Il mio nome è Aisha, your new owner." She sipped her tea. "The way you walk? Are you a horseman?"

"Sì, a captain of two hundred fifty horsemen."

"And where in Bohemia are you from?"

"Bohemia?" The question perplexed the English captain.

"Yes, are you not an officer in the army of the Holy Roman Empire? Its capitol is Prague in the Kingdom of Bohemia."

"I'm not Bohemian."

"Well, you don't look Italian." Aisha pointed to his sleeve. "Your clothing, the stitching? You must be a rich Bohemian Lord whom I can ransom."

"I am not from Bohemia and I'm not rich." Captain John Smith shook his head. "I'm from England. I'm an Englishman."

"How can you be English?" Aisha asked. "The English and Turks are friends. The Grand Vizier told me you are from Bohemia."

"The *Pasha* said so?"

"The Grand Vizier captured you on the battlefield."

Smith straightened up and the Overseer touched his sword. "The Grand Vizier did not conquer me." Smith showed how money changed hands. "I never saw the man until he bought me at a slave auction at Axiopolis."

"The Grand Vizier did not buy you." Aisha pointed towards Smith's saber and shield near the door. "Look, your saber and shield. My betrothed defeated you by his own hand."

"He did not."

"Whom do you expect me to believe?"

"Believe the truth."

"Overseer!"

The Overseer stepped toward the English slave and Aisha waved her arm. "Take him away."

The Overseer wrapped Smith's wrists with leather and led him to the slave quarters.

Smith could not believe what Aisha had told him. No one had ever defeated him in single combat. As he crossed the courtyard, he wondered if his new owner would sell him. Would he end up on an Ottoman galley? Only Spanish galleys were worse.

Fourth Courtyard, Harem, Ibrahim *Pasha* Palace, *Stamboul*

UPSET AT THE claims of the capitano, Aisha paced her garden courtyard. *What can I do? My father never lied to me and neither did my late husband. It must not be true. Capitano Giovanni must be lying.* Her body tensed. *Or was he?* She stopped midstride.

If John told the truth, then my betrothed lied to me. How could he do that to me, the Sister of the Sultan? She gazed up at the sky. *Who is telling the truth? How can I find out?*

Aisha remembered her friend Emine spoke English, so she determined to test the man. *If Captain John Smith does not speak English, then he must be lying.* She told her head servant. "Bring me paper and pen."

Aisha scribbled a note and handed it back to her servant. "Deliver this to my friend Emine."

"I'll send for a messenger."

Aisha told herself, *I must know the truth. Nothing will stop me.*

Chapter 8 - New Palace Banquet

Yesterday, we had [an] audience of the Grand Signor [Sultan Mehmet III], with all the usual ceremonies. The banquet was extraordinarily splendid. The [Deputy] Grand Vizier frequently invited us to eat; and the conversation most cordial. When we went into the Sultan's presence, we found him of a cheerful countenance, smoking and turning his eyes with pleasure upon us, as though to show that he saw us gladly.

As the ship Martinella came into port she fired the usual salutes, and, being very close in shore, the shock broke some windows in the kiosk. The Acemi Oglan [Janissary Cadets] came out and made a row, demanding the Master of the ship. I sent Borisi to the Bostangi Pasha [The Chief Gardener] to make apologies, and he took Borisi to see the damage. Besides the broken glass, the plaster had fallen on the rich carpets.

Francesco Contarini and Agostino Nani
Old and New Venetian Ambassadors in Constantinople
Valley of Pera, Istanbul, 2nd December 1602

New Palace, *Stamboul, Jumada II*, AH 1011 (Dec. AD 1602)

"MAKE WAY!" THE crier exclaimed. "Safiye *Valide Sultana*! Make way!"

Her white carriage slowed and the Mother of the Sultan pulled back the curtains. She saw masses of people, Arab merchants donning baggy salvars and Anatolian refugees wearing tattered garb. Armenians scurried below the high walls of the New Palace.

"Make way!" The crier repeated. "Safiye *Valide Sultana*!"

A Greek woman grabbed her son's tiny hands and pulled her daughter aside.

As the carriage passed the Mausoleum of her beloved husband, Sultan Murad III, she remembered watching the funeral procession nearly eight years earlier. Her weeping could not then be contained, and even now, her sorrow remained.

Sultan Murad III

Next to that, the Hagia Sophia, the domed Byzantine church turned into a Sunni Mosque, *sipahi* horsemen remained mounted, moving slowly. Other riders reacted even less quickly, or not at all. Some did not show the respect the Mother of the Sultan deserved by moving out of the carriage's way.

"Make way!"

Affluent merchants and petitioners parted before the Imperial Gate.

The New Palace occupied the whole tip of the peninsula. Shaped in the form of a triangle, its outer fortified walls spanned nearly three miles. With two sides facing the water and one side facing the land, it housed thousands, always ready to serve the Sultan or his mother.

Guards waved the white carriage through the Imperial Gate and into the First Courtyard. Often referred to as the Courtyard of the *Janissaries*, the busy plaza was a quarter mile long and nearly as wide but was much quieter than the streets outside the palace walls.

On the right side of the courtyard, the *acemi-oglan* or *janissary* cadets tended the terraced gardens leading down to the Sea of Marmara. A company of soldiers, part of a *janissary orta* or battalion, exited their barracks. Dressed in white hats, loose-fitting coats, and baggy pants, the *janissary* guards carried curved scimitar swords at their side and arrows in their quivers.

The extra guards who had accompanied Sultan's Mother's visit to Aisha dismounted. While their horses were refreshed at the horse fountain near the *Janissary* Tree, their riders returned their weapons to the armory, a former Byzantine church. Christian symbols had been removed from the small domed church, once called Hagia Irene. Meanwhile, in front of the armory, a dozen *acemi-oglan* practiced sword fighting.

To their left, the massive stack of firewood grew larger. Basket after basket of wood was unloaded from a camel train. Workers dragged them higher up the massive stack, providing fuel to heat the palace and fire up the kitchens.

The carriage edged past another group of frowning *sipahi* riders. The Sultan's mother decided to talk to the Chief Black Eunuch about their insolence.

Gate of Greeting, New Palace, *Stamboul*, Ottoman Empire

CONICAL ROOFS TOPPED two stone structures, a pair of cylindrical towers framing the Gate of Greeting. At the entrance to the Second

Courtyard, archers peered down from narrow windows, vertical slits in the parapet tower. If any adversary of the Sultan ever ventured this far, those archers would have clear shots.

Today, the mood seemed festive. Gatekeepers, like the first ones, waved the white carriage through. Pathways criss-crossed the grassy turf of the Second Courtyard. Tall cypress trees lined the walkways and cast slender shadows. Raking up leaves and trimming broken branches, the *acemi-oglan* meticulously maintained the smaller fruit trees, a trade that the Grand Vizier, Hasan *the Fruiterer*, had previously mastered. On this late autumn day, none bore fruit.

Beyond the tall trees, countless servants trekked toward the kitchens. Some unloaded firewood from pushcarts. Others walked in single file and carried wicker baskets filled with produce, fish, and bread.

Distinctive domes covered more than a half dozen large rooms. Like calligraphy in the sky, smoke rose from the chimneys, drifting ever higher. A slight sea breeze kicked up, filling the yard with spiced aroma of the finest Turkish cuisine.

The Mother of the Sultan signaled for her carriage to stop. "I must check on the preparations." She alighted from her carriage.

The driver guided the carriage past the imperial stables, the ones housing nearly three dozen of the finest horses in the world. He stopped it outside the Carriage Gate, an entrance to the Imperial Harem manned by black eunuchs.

Although she would not partake of the fancy fare with the male guests at the Divan, the *Valide Sultana* wanted to make sure everything would run smoothly. She would enjoy the delicacies in her private quarters, the Imperial Harem, but the food must be prepared correctly.

When the Sultan's Mother entered the first kitchen, the one for her son, the cooks immediately stopped. The Sultan's Mother waved her arm. "Please, continue."

At the next kitchen, sometimes referred to as the Queen's Kitchen, a servant brought a platter of fish, yet uncooked. "Very fresh."

"Do not forget the garnish."

"Yes, for color."

By the time Safiye *Valide Sultana* reached the fourth of nine kitchens, she could tell the officers had everything in good order. The larders and cupboards were full, the food fresh and plentiful. The Mother of the Sultan nodded her approval and crossed the courtyard with her entourage.

On the left side of the courtyard, she entered the Divan, an open air building where the council of the Sultan often met to conduct imperial business. Numerous marble columns supported the overhanging roof. The Divan's square tower, more for ornamentation than protection, rose above.

After walking along the corridor on the far side of the Divan, black eunuchs snapped to attention. Those eunuchs, armed with tall pikes and curved swords, kept a vigilant guard at the Queen's Entrance to the Imperial Harem. No wandering eye could glimpse any of the nearly three hundred beautiful women in the harem, reserved solely for her son, the Sultan.

"Welcome back," the Chief Black Eunuch said. "The feast was more expensive than we planned."

"We'll discuss it later." The Sultan's Mother turned. "I see the first guests have arrived."

Those guests congregated by the Gate of Greeting.

BACK AT THE Imperial Gate, the *dragoman* and the three Bulgarian children waited for an unhappy troop of *sipahi* horsemen to exit. Because of a reduction in pay, the *sipahis* had already rebelled twice in the past three years. The *dragoman* wondered: *would they rebel again?*

After delivering the "Bohemian" slave to Aisha, the *dragoman* had returned to the *Sandal Bedesten,* housing the small silk market. Outside the market, slaves were often sold. Though the *dragoman* had left the long-legged girl in care of woman he thought he could trust, a slave buyer saw the girl and had made a large offer. She had almost been sold, but the *dragoman* had arrived just in time to stop the transaction and pay for the girl's new outfit. He scolded the two black eunuchs from Edirne for not intervening, but decided not to mention the incident to the Chief Black Eunuch. If the Sultan heard about it, he might hold him responsible. The *dragoman* did not want to take the risk. He also retrieved the two Bulgarian boys, the new *ghilman* Grand Vizier Hasan *the Fruiterer* had captured in the mountains of Bulgaria.

In the center of the gate, *Bostangi Pasha*, the Chief Gardener of the New Palace, stood. "*Dragoman.* We've been expecting you."

"Word travels faster than my horse." The *dragoman* patted his steed on the neck.

"A fine Arabian indeed. You must attend the banquet tonight. Both the new and old ambassadors from Venice will soon arrive and your services are needed."

The *dragoman* pointed out the *ghilman*, the two boys dressed in red. "The Grand Vizier collected the *Devshirme* in Bulgaria and wanted me to present these to the Sultan. And I must present the girl to the Safiye *Valide Sultana* for her approval." He turned to the girl. "This is the Chief Gardener."

Venetian Ambassador Arriving at Imperial Gate (early 1500s)

The girl eyed the man from head to toe. "You don't look like a gardener; your hands are not even soiled."

"The Chief Gardener is not only in charge of the grounds," the *dragoman* said, "but also responsible for the Sultan's personal security. *Bostangi* has more than a thousand guards at his command. The Sultan even awarded him the title of *Pasha.*"

"Like Hasan *the Fruiterer*?"

"Yes," the *dragoman* said, "like the Grand Vizier."

"The Sultan's mother will be most pleased." The powerful *Bostangi Pasha* turned to an aide. "Tell the Deputy Grand Vizier of the *dragoman*'s arrival."

"At once." The young messenger sprinted toward the Gate of Greeting.

The massive palace built by Mehmet *the Conqueror* was impressive.

Scanning the vast courtyard, the younger boy's eyes widened. "So many people."

Like flowers cloaking a meadow, the colorful decor of the Ottoman Empire covered the large First Courtyard. Some Arab merchants wore striped gowns, others long off-white robes. Their distinctive dress indicated whether they came from Alexandria, Baghdad, Mecca, Medina, or Sanaa in Yemen.

"The Ottoman Empire and its vassal kingdoms extend across all of North Africa, from Egypt to Morocco." The *dragoman* pushed past a group of dark-skinned Arabs from Upper Egypt, as well as Moors from

Tripoli and the furthest ends of the Sahara. "From Bosnia to Crimea, they all come here, to the home of the Sultan Mehmet III, the ruler of the world and caliph, the true successor to the Prophet Mohammed."

"Mehmet?" the boy asked.

"Mehmet means Mohammed in Turkish," the *dragoman* said.

The *dragoman,* the two boys, and the Bulgarian girl with long legs dismounted. As attendants led the horses away, one steed relieved itself. The boys pinched their noses. The long-legged girl jumped over fresh horse dung, bigger than bricks.

Steps behind, *Bostangi Pasha* ordered, "Clean up this mess."

Attendants, using brooms and shovels, quickly carted the stink away.

"*Dragoman.*" *Agha* Ali, the gray-bearded leader of the *janissaries,* approached. Behind him cadets continued to practice sword fighting by the armory.

"You made it back from the frontier before me." The *dragoman* gestured to the two boys in red robes. "I hope to present the two boys to the Sultan this afternoon."

Agha Ali looked down at them. "Once you are trained as cadets, you shall become *janissaries,* too." He turned back to the *dragoman*. "You must forgive me. I must go."

While *Agha* Ali crossed the courtyard, the *dragoman*'s party went deeper into the palace grounds. The sound of clashing swords faded.

In front of the Second Gate, the *dragoman* recognized the Emissary of the Crimean-Khan, *Ghazi* Giray II. The representative of the Emperor's most trusted ally wore a large turban as fine as any Turk. His Crimean-Tartar escorts maintained their traditional black sheepskin dress, but their fierce expression seemed to frighten the young girl.

"Your Emissary?" The *dragoman* spoke the Crimean dialect of the Tartarian language. "I didn't realize you were in *Stamboul*."

"Nor I you."

"What brings you to the New Palace?"

"The Crimean Khan has not been fully compensated for sending his warriors into Wallachia." The stout Emissary added, "And, of course, the banquet."

The *Bostangi Pasha* told the guards. "You may let these guests through."

Normally, like the first gate, no one could enter without first stating his business. Identities had to be confirmed.

Second Courtyard, New Palace, *Stamboul*

THE *DRAGOMAN* LED the boys along one of the diagonal walkways of the Second Courtyard, toward the Divan, the open building on the left side.

"The smell?" The younger boy looked across the courtyard, toward the kitchens.

The older one smiled. "I can almost taste it."

"If you behave," the *dragoman* said, "I'll make sure you get all of the food you want."

At the Divan the runner sent earlier waved for the *dragoman*. "Deputy Grand Vizier *Saatci* Hasan *Pasha* will see you now."

"Good." The *dragoman* turned to the three young Bulgarians. "Come with me." The *dragoman*'s party walked toward the Divan, where dozens of servants finalized preparations for the planned banquet. Some guests had already arrived. The *dragoman* walked past the pillars and around a hanging divider.

"The messenger informed me you were nearby." Deputy Grand Vizier *Saatci* Hasan *Pasha* waved the *dragoman* forward. "I need to hear your report."

"Other business detained me," the *dragoman* answered.

"You mean the slave you delivered to Aisha?"

"Is nothing secret?"

"Not to me." The Deputy Grand Vizier laughed. "The *devshirme*?"

"The tribute to the Sultan has been collected. Most have been delivered to the *Janissary* School in Edirne."

"Excellent. Sultan Mehmet III will be pleased."

"But these two boys show great promise." The *dragoman* motioned to his guard to bring the Bulgarian boys forward. "The Grand Vizier wanted them delivered personally to you."

"It will not do."

His response surprised the *dragoman*. "What do you mean?"

"It won't do for me to take delivery of these boys," the Deputy Grand Vizier said.

"But the boys show great promise."

"I would not want to take credit for your efforts. You must deliver them to the Sultan yourself."

The *dragoman* relaxed. "As you wish. I also wanted to give this girl to the Sultan."

Saatci Hasan *Pasha* waved for the girl to come to him. "Pretty, but the Sultan's Mother will want to examine any candidate." He motioned to a messenger. "Bring *Kislar Agha*."

The messenger scurried toward the main entrance to the Imperial Harem, behind the open-air Divan. The *dragoman* knew that the Chief Black Eunuch ran the large harem. Osman *Kislar Agha* was responsible for protecting all of the Sultan's wives and hundreds of concubines.

Within minutes, *Kislar Agha* appeared. Dressed in a long robe and in a turban more impressive than the one worn by the Crimean emissary, Osman *Kislar Agha* stepped up to the Divan. "I can stay only a minute. The *Valide Sultana* just returned from her carriage ride."

The *dragoman* removed the Bulgarian girl's cap. Her long hair flowed down to the small of her back. "A gift for the Sultan."

The *Kislar Agha* eyed the girl from head to toe. "Long legs." He turned to the *dragoman*. "*Valide Sultana* will be pleased, but an *odalisque* must be trained before she is presented to the Sultan."

"What a pretty carriage," the girl said.

Attendants unhitched the horses from the white carriage parked at the Carriage Gate.

"Queen Elizabeth of England gave it to *Valide Sultana*," *Kislar Agha* said. "I'll take you to see her now."

The girl turned to the *dragoman*, who told her, "You'll be an *odalisque* until you are trained both in the arts and how to act."

"Follow me." *Kislar Agha* reached for the girl.

"*Dragoman*!" The girl appeared frightened and upset.

The *dragoman* motioned. "Now go." He smiled to reassure her. "You will not be harmed, as long as you obey."

Still looking uneasy, the girl followed the *Kislar Agha* up to the Sultan's Mother, where the Eunuch presented the Bulgarian girl. *Valide Sultana* lifted the girl's chin and acknowledged the *dragoman*.

The *Agha* of the *Janissaries*, who had arrived from the First Courtyard, leaned toward the *dragoman*. "*Valide Sultana* appears pleased with the gift. She will present the girl to her son after she is trained to fulfill her duties."

As soon as the Sultan's Mother took the girl through the Queen's Gate and into the Imperial Harem, the older of the two Bulgarian boys asked, "Will we see her again?"

"Unlikely." The *dragoman* knew that no man except the Sultan could enter.

"*Janissaries* aren't allowed into the harem," the *Agha* of the *Janissaries* said. "White eunuchs guard this court, but only women and black eunuchs are allowed inside."

The *dragoman* turned back to the Deputy Grand Vizier. "And the two boys?"

"You can present them to the Sultan after the banquet."

The *dragoman* rejoined the Emissary of the Crimean Tartars in the Divan. The two Bulgarian boys sat down in a separate area, but within sight. Their attention immediately turned back toward the center of the courtyard, where senior officers of the *janissaries* had joined their *Agha*.

The loud sound of marching soldiers arose as an *orta* of *janissaries* stomped into the courtyard. Within minutes, more than a thousand *janissary* soldiers had paraded through the Gate of Greeting. They marched in place and lined up in formation in the center of the yard. As quickly as the marching had started, it stopped. The *janissaries* stood at attention in absolute silence.

Gate of Greeting

The Deputy Grand Vizier leaned toward the *dragoman*. "The new and old Venetian ambassadors have arrived."

Bostangi Pasha escorted the two ambassadors in front of the silent *janissaries* and to the Divan. Several servants followed, carrying more than the requisite gifts from the Venetians to the Sultan.

After introducing the ambassadors to the *dragoman* and the Crimean emissary, the Deputy Grand Vizier signaled the beginning of the banquet.

While the guests conversed and started the first course, guards collected the gifts the new ambassador had brought and carried them through the Gate of Felicity. The gifts of fine linen, soft silk, and polished silver would be deposited into the Imperial Treasury.

On the far side of the courtyard, in full view of the banquet, the *janissaries* sat down, cross-legged on the ground. While many servants streamed across the courtyard, bringing dish after dish to the esteemed guests, other servants brought food to the *janissaries*, the Sultan's chosen.

As soon as the guests in the Divan had finished the first course, the

Deputy Grand Vizier motioned to the servants. "Bring the second." More tasty dishes arrived. "Ambassadors, I must conduct some business, but you must eat." He quickly disappeared behind a curtain.

The banquet, meanwhile, progressed. Palace chefs had prepared dishes of rice, lamb, fish, and pastries. After more than a dozen courses, the *dragoman* lost count of how many had been served. The Deputy Grand Vizier returned and insisted the guests eat more.

"It's all delicious," the new Venetian ambassador said.

The former ambassador finished chewing. "Most splendid."

The *dragoman* agreed. He bit into a sweet grape, harvested from the palace gardens.

The Deputy Grand Vizier told the Emissary from *Ghazi* Giray II. "You may see the Sultan now."

After two more courses, the emissary of the Crimean-Tartars returned to the feast.

The *dragoman* asked him, "How's the Sultan's mood?"

"Good." The happy Tartar emissary handed two large moneybags to his guard. "The Sultan rewarded us for sending our army to Wallachia."

"Don't all of the Sultan's tributaries pay into the treasury?" the new Venetian ambassador asked.

"All do," the Deputy Grand Vizier said, "except Crimean Tartars . . ."

The *dragoman* remembered the reason. "Because they fight."

As soon as the Crimean-Tartar Emissary sat back down, the Deputy Grand Vizier leaned toward the *dragoman*. "The Sultan will see you now."

The *dragoman* waved to the guards and escorted the two boys the short distance to the entrance to the Third Courtyard, the Sultan's private quarters.

Gate of Felicity, New Palace, *Stamboul*

AFTER THE *DRAGOMAN* announced his business at the Gate of Felicity, the Chief White Eunuch, Gazanfer *Agha*, appeared. Also known as the *Kapi Agasi* or the *Agha* of the Gate, he escorted the *dragoman* and the boys past a group of the *acemi-oglan*.

"I just met with the emissary from the Crimean Tartars," Gazanfer *Agha* said. "This past year has been very costly. The *janissaries* and the Crimean-Tartars won a great victory in Wallachia, but *Ghazi* Giray II lost thousands of men. What news do you bring me?"

The Chief White Eunuch's interest in the affairs of the frontier did not seem unusual, for Gazanfer was close not only to the Sultan, but also his mother.

"Perhaps our fortune has changed," the *dragoman* said. "I learned that the Grand Vizier has successfully defended Buda."

"When I take you into the Sultan's presence, do not talk about the fighting. All news must be handled carefully."

Throne Room, New Palace, *Stamboul*

INSIDE THE THRONE Room palace guards stood at attention, as Sultan Mehmet III plopped down onto his rich throne. He wore a large white turban topped with a small plume and a dark tassel. With a square diamond ring on his thumb, the warrior Sultan kept his scimitar at his side. Stuffed from the banquet, the black-bearded Sultan finally settled himself into his chair, covered with rich silk and adorned with jewels, mother-of-pearl.

The Sultan recognized Gazanfer *Agha*, his most trusted advisor, at the door. The Chief White Eunuch had not only loyally served the Sultan, but also his father and grandfather before him. Gazanfer *Agha* had received the title of Chief White Eunuch more twenty years earlier and had been allowed to build his own *medrese*, the first Islamic school in *Stamboul* not built by a member of the royal family. The Sultan also recognized the *dragoman*, who often translated when foreigners or Tartars gave their respects.

Behind the Sultan, four hundred men stood in three ranks. In one section, two hundred pages, some holding small axes, kept watch. Beneath their gold caps, all of the young men had shaved heads, save for a single lock of hair behind their ears. Their faces likewise were clean shaven except for their mustaches. Silk belts secured their gowns of gold above leggings of red leather.

Next to them, one hundred dwarfs were also dressed in gold. Though short, each carried a scimitar at his side, ready to use at a moment's notice. Sultan Mehmet III had less need for the dwarfs than his father who sometimes used them for his amusement.

In a third section, the last one hundred men, who could neither speak nor hear, watched with interest. All wore velvet caps. Even though no one else dared to whisper in the Sultan's presence, the mutes signed and understood each other perfectly. On his orders, some of the older mutes were the ones who killed his own brothers. On his ascension to the throne a decade earlier, he had nineteen of his brothers killed around this same Throne building. Only the brother birthed by his own mother remained alive in Tartaria, at the furthest reaches of the empire, near the border with Muscovy. His mother assured him that her youngest son posed no threat to his reign.

When he, the third sultan of the House of Osman named for the Prophet, stretched out his arms, one of the pages brought a jug and poured the water for the Sultan to wash his hands. As soon as the Sultan finished the ceremonial cleaning, the page handed him a towel. When he finished drying, another page handed the Sultan the end of a long flexible tube.

The Sultan inhaled and the water pipe percolated with the tobacco smoke. He exhaled and smiled at the Chief White Eunuch.

"Your Excellency," Gazanfer *Agha* said. "*Dragoman.*"

The *dragoman* bowed low and slowly approached the ornate throne over the thick silk carpets. He did not advance too far and kissed the hem of the Sultan's robe. When Mehmet III acknowledged his presence, the *dragoman* stepped back, always facing the ruler of the Ottoman Empire. If he had done otherwise, it would mean certain death. Like King Nebuchadnezzar in ancient Babylon, all peoples feared him. The Sultan chose who would live and who would die, who would be set up and who would be put down.

Out of the corner of his eye, the Sultan glimpsed his mother standing behind the throne. The floor length curtain hid her presence, but a windowpane reflected her image.

When the *dragoman* reached the wall, the Sultan inhaled more tobacco smoke from his *nargile*, the Turkish water pipe. He raised his eyes and glanced out the window. Outside, guards carried more Venetian gifts to the Treasury at the far corner of the Third Courtyard.

"The Grand Vizier was successful in collecting the first of this year's *devshirme.*"

"Yes, the tribute."

"The ranks of the *janissaries* will soon be replenished." The *dragoman* pointed to *janissary* cadets out the window. "Even as we speak, more *acemi-oglan* like those outside are being trained in Edirne." He added, "And the Grand Vizier personally captured these two boys in the Balkan Mountains. In several years they will become your newest *janissaries*."

"Bring them here." Sultan Mehmet III coughed. He took another long drag of pungent tobacco, exhaling the smoke mostly out of his nostrils.

Two pairs of guards grabbed the forearms of the two young boys. With each holding one arm, the four guards brought the tribute forward and forced the boys to kneel. At the foot of throne, they pressed a corner of the Sultan's robe to the boys' lips. "Kiss the gown."

As soon as the boys complied, the guards helped them back up. They retraced their steps, continually facing the Emperor.

They did not bow again until *dragoman* forced their heads down.

"They have much to learn, don't they?" the Sultan asked.

"They do, sire, but I am sure the *Janissary* School *Agha* will persuade them of the path that they should travel. He will teach them in the ways of Allah and his prophet.

"The school will teach them to be loyal to me."

"Yes, sire." The *dragoman* kept his eyes gazed at the ground. "If they please you, I can take them to the school."

"If the younger one excels in talent and loyalty, perhaps the *Janissary* School *Agha* will make him a White Eunuch."

"I'll mention that to him."

The Sultan was pleased. The *dragoman* and the boys bowed once more.

As soon as the *dragoman* departed, the old and new Venetian Ambassadors, whose turn to see the Sultan had arrived. They, too, approached the Sultan on bended knee.

Garden, New Palace, *Stamboul*

OUTSIDE THE THRONE Room, the *dragoman* met the *Bostangi Pasha* who took the boys to watch tropical fished housed in a pond near a kiosk in the garden.

Bostangi Pasha asked the boys, "Would you like to see the organ, a gift from Queen Elizabeth of England?"

The two boys nodded.

"Perhaps you can show us," the *dragoman* said.

Bostangi Pasha took them inside to the organ room.

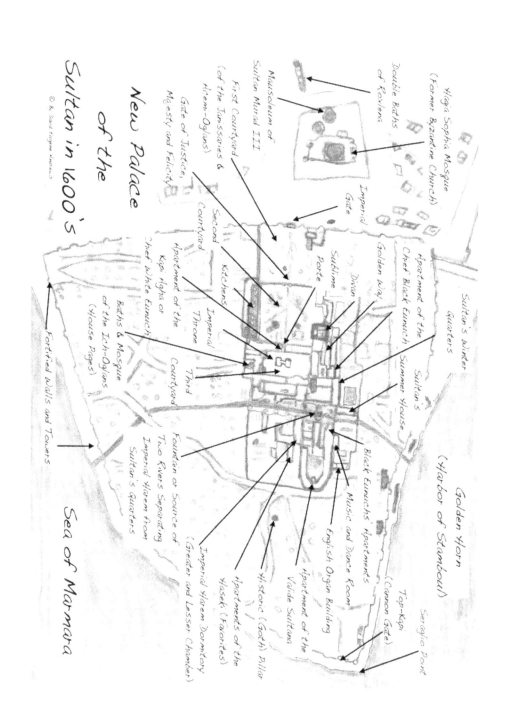

New Palace
of the
Sultan in 1600's

© B. David Eugene Havens

Hgia Sophia Mosque
(Former Byzantine Church)

Double Baths
of Roxiena

Mausoleum of
Sultan Murad III

First Courtyard
(of the Janissaries &
Hicem-Oglans)

Gate of Justice,
Majesty and Felicity

Imperial
Gate

Apartment of the
Chief Black Eunuch

Golden Way

Divan

Sublime
Porte

Second
Courtyard

Kitchens

Imperial
Throne

Kep Agha or
Chief White Eunuch

Apartment of the
Baths & Mosque
of the Ich-Oglans
(House Pages)

Third
Courtyard

Sultan's Winter
Quarters

Sultan's
Summer House

Black Eunuchs' Apartments

Music and Dance Room

English Organ Building

Apartment of the
Valide Sultana

Historic (Goth) Pillar

Apartments of the
Haseki (Favorites)

Imperial Harem Dormitory
(Greater and Lesser Chamber)

Fountain at Source of
Two Rivers Separating
Imperial Harem from
Sultan's Quarters

Fortified Walls and Towers

Golden Horn
(Harbor of Stamboul)

Top-Kap
(Cannon Gate)

Seraglio Point

Sea of Marmara

The younger boy looked up at the sixteen-foot-high organ with a built-in clock. "So large."

As the clock moved to the hour position, *Bostangi Pasha* lifted a small pin on the side. Immediately, the keys began to move. The organ played a tune. When the organ hit the low notes, the sound reverberated throughout the room. After a refrain, figurines on the second tier raised their silver trumpets and played short notes. When the whole song finished, bird figurines on the very top of the organ flapped their wings. The blackbirds and smaller birds returned to their resting place.

"Because the Sultan liked Queen Elizabeth's gift so much," *Bostangi Pasha* said, "Mehmet III persuaded his tributary in Algiers to release two Scotsmen who had been captured."

The *dragoman* stared at the large clock. "It's getting late."

The whole building shook, but the organ was not playing.

Plaster fell from the ceiling and the walls. The *dragoman* recognized the unmistakable sound of cannon fire. Several windows shattered. Cannons boomed again. The *dragoman, Bostangi Pasha,* and the frightened boys rushed outside.

The buildings shook again. Shattered glass from the kiosk windows splintered and rained on the ground. *Janissary* cadets, the *acemi-oglan,* swarmed the building and the courtyard. "Who's firing?"

The *dragoman* and the *Bostangi Pasha* reached a gazebo and viewed the harbor. On the blue and gray waters, not far from shore, a large ship flew a flag from its highest mast. It displayed a lion, the symbol of Venice.

"The Venetian ship *Martinella* fires her cannons," *Bostangi Pasha* said.

Venetian cannons fired a fourth round. The boom caused the building to shake again.

"A salute?" the *dragoman* asked.

"How many times?" one *acemi-oglan* asked. "The Shipmaster must be punished."

While several cadets ran down to the water's edge, other *janissary* cadets headed back into the palace.

"They will confront the two Venetian ambassadors," *Bostangi Pasha* said.

Minutes later, a Venetian representative arrived. *Bostangi Pasha* picked up a large piece of plaster. While *janissary* cadets brought other damage, he pointed out the broken panes of glass. "What do you have to say?"

"We must apologize profusely," the Venetian representative said.

"What kind of salute was that?"

"No harm was intended."

"This breach of the peace cannot stand," *Bostangi Pasha* said. "Amends must be made."

"What did you have in mind?" the Venetian asked.

"Silk carpets must be cleaned. And the windows? All must be replaced." *Bostangi Pasha* turned. "Have I missed anything, *Dragoman*?"

The *dragoman* glanced at the Venetian and smiled at the Chief Gardener. "You like to go hunting?"

"That's right. What an excellent idea." *Bostangi Pasha* spun to the Venetian diplomat. "How about some sporting dogs?"

"Sporting dogs?" The diplomat paused. "I will pass your request to the new ambassador."

After the Venetian interpreter left, the *dragoman* and the two boys returned to the palace. The Deputy Grand Vizier intercepted him not far from the Divan. "The Sultan was pleased with your gifts."

The *dragoman* nodded.

"Take the two boys to the *Janissary* school tomorrow. The *agha* will be expecting you."

"I'll take them to noon prayers first." The *dragoman* escorted the two boys to the Court of the *Janissaries* where he left them. "I'll return tomorrow and you can begin your training."

Chapter 9 - English Translator Emine

Seraglio [Ibrahim Pasha Palace] as it then stood was built upon vaulted arches springing from three rows of columns, which had belonged to some building of the late empire.
Studies in the History of Venice, Vol. II by Horatio F. Brown

This noble gentlewoman [Aisha, Sister of the Sultan] took some time . . . to know how Bogall [Beylerbey or Lord of Lords] took him [Captain John Smith] prisoner; and if he were . . . a Bohemian lord conquered by his hand. To try the truth, she found means to find out many [who] could speak English . . .
John Smith

Ibrahim *Pasha* Palace, *Jumada II*, AH 1011 (Dec. AD 1602)

ON THE TERRACE overlooking the Second Courtyard of the Palace of Ibrahim *Pasha*, Aisha paced back and forth. Still upset that her betrothed might have lied to her, she glimpsed a carriage on the *Atmeidan*, the former Hippodrome. At the top of the stairs, Aisha warmly greeted her friend. "Emine. Thank you for coming so soon."

"You look as lovely as ever." Emine squeezed Aisha's hand and stepped back. "What's wrong?"

"You can tell?"

"How long have we been friends?"

"Years." Aisha ushered Emine through the Great Hall to a wing with windows stretching from the carpeted floor to the high ceiling. She motioned to her friend. "Please."

Emine sat down on the divan, the cushioned bench attached to the wall. A dwarf fluffed her pillow.

Aisha dismissed the old dwarf, who had once served her father. "You may return later." Her brother had no use for the little people, so most went to the *Eski Seray*, the Old Palace, after he acceded to the throne. The old dwarf did not seem too happy, but slid off the divan and bowed before exiting.

"How can I help?" Emine asked.

"The Grand Vizier sent me a rich slave to ransom."

"A slave? To ransom?" Emine smiled. "How unselfish."

Aisha brought out the letter. "He wrote me how he captured the officer on the battlefield and promised I would receive a ransom. All I need to do is contact the slave's rich family in Bohemia."

"His family is rich?"

"That's what The Grand Vizier wrote me, but the slave says 'no'. I do not know whom to believe." Aisha leaned closer to her friend. "I need you to translate."

"I speak neither German nor Bohemian."

"But you do speak English."

"Yes, you know I was born in England, before being captured as a young girl by corsairs off the Barbary Coast. But I thought you said the slave's family lived in Bohemia?"

"The slave told me he's not from Prague in Bohemia. He claims he's from England."

"How did you find out? You don't speak English."

"The slave speaks Italian."

"Ah. Like you and your grandmother."

"I need to find the truth." Aisha peered directly at Emine. "Can you help me? How good is your English?"

"Excellent. I translate for my husband all the time. In fact, your messenger caught up with me just as I arrived from Izmir."

Aisha heard movement from behind the wall. Her mother appeared from behind the lattice divider.

"When did you arrive?" Aisha asked.

"Minutes ago. If you were more observant . . ." She glanced at the Overseer. "Overseer, bring the new slave here." She turned back to Aisha. "We need to contact his rich family, so we can ransom him and receive the reward."

"The Grand Vizier gave the slave to me."

"Yes, but you're still my daughter."

Aisha wondered how long her mother would dominate her every action. "Will you be staying?"

"No. Your sister and I are going to the bazaar." Her mother stepped back. "Fatima!"

Aisha's sister presently appeared, fully covered and ready to go out.

As soon as Aisha's mother and sister exited, the large Overseer arrived and pushed the bound slave forward. The slave wore rich but soiled attire.

"No doubt," Emine whispered, "a Lord of immense worth. His family would certainly pay much to get him back."

"*Ciao, Capitano Giovanni Fabbro.*" Aisha called Captain John Smith by his Italian name.

"Ciao, Signorina Ch'Aratza Tragabig-Zanda."

Aisha was not impressed with the mispronunciation of her name or title. She gestured and the Overseer loosened the slave's hands, before moving to the door and crossing his arms, just like the day before.

The *capitano* remained standing, not moving an inch.

"You didn't tell me your slave was so handsome," Emine whispered in Turkish.

"Handsome?" Aisha took a second look at John. "You think so?" She addressed her brown-bearded captive in Italian. "This is my friend Emine, an English translator."

"I haven't spoken English in weeks." John replied in Italian and did not smile.

"A pleasure to meet you." Emine asked, "What is your name?"

He straightened. "Captain John Smith."

Aisha gestured. "*Capitano*, have a seat."

When her slave sat down, Aisha clapped her hands twice.

A servant appeared. "You called?"

"Bring food for our guests."

"The slave, too?"

"Everyone."

The servant hurried out.

"Where in Bohemia are you from?" Aisha asked.

"I told you yesterday, I'm not from Bohemia," the Captain said. "I'm from England."

"But Emperor Rudolph II rules from Prague."

"I told you, I am not from Bohemia."

"What do you mean?" Aisha asked. "The Grand Vizier captured you on the battlefield."

"The Grand Vizier bought me at a slave auction at Axiopolis on the lower Danube." The Captain tensed. "I never saw him before. How many times must I tell you?"

The Overseer stepped forward.

Aisha turned to Emine. "His story does not waver."

"He doesn't act like any slave I know."

"What do you think?"

"I have no idea."

Aisha lowered her voice and leaned closer to Emine. "If he speaks the truth, this means that the man my mother insists I marry has lied to me. Find out where's my slave's home."

"Where in England are you from?" Emine asked.

"Lincolnshire," John replied.

Emine commented, "Well, he speaks English even better than I. He speaks with a distinctive accent—that I know."

"Then he's not a Bohemian nobleman?" Aisha said.

The servants returned with two trays. Aisha handed Emine and John figs and honeyed pastries. "Go ahead, eat."

"*Grazie.*" The slave bit into a piece of baklava.

"How do you like it?" Aisha asked.

"It's delicious," Emine said. "Made with *bal*?" She referred to the flavorful Anatolian honey.

"Yes," Aisha turned back to John and peered directly into his blue eyes. "Who are you?"

"An English Captain of two hundred and fifty horsemen. I fought for the Army of the Holy Roman Empire."

Aisha considered the value of the captain's attire again, the fabric and his style proved its worth. But how did an English soldier end up fighting against the Turks? "Start at the beginning."

Emine translated the question.

"When my father died, he left me competent means," Captain John Smith said, "but I was young and could not handle money."

Aisha listened to the translation from English into Turkish.

Emine translated more. "John says he's not a nobleman."

Aisha reflected. How could he be an orphan? How could her slave have such fine clothes if he were not a nobleman? She motioned for her slave to continue.

"Almost ten years ago, after my father died, I set my heart on adventure."

Chapter 10 - Fatherless in Lincolnshire

[Captain John Smith] so honestly reported to her [Ch'aratza Tragabig-zanda/Aisha, Sister of the Sultan] . . . His parents, dying when he [Smith] was about thirteen years of age, left him a competent means, which he not being capable to manage, little regarded; His mind being even then set upon brave adventures, sold his satchel, books, and all he had, intending secretly to get to sea.

John Smith

Outside Louth, Lincolnshire, England, Autumn 1593

YOUNG JOHN SMITH swung his tan satchel onto his shoulder, hurdled over a fence, and darted across a wet field. Weaving past haystacks, the English lad ran through a cold mist into a small grove. Huge water drops falling from drizzle-soaked trees did not bother the blue-eyed boy of thirteen.

The lad reached the rutted road leading to Louth, but a slow-moving cart blocked his path. He scurried around it and through tall grass. Jogging alongside the ox-driven cart, John looked up and recognized the driver, a friend of his father's. "Going to the market?"

"John Smith, is that you?" the yeoman farmer asked. "We miss your father."

"So do I." The English lad skipped ahead, but he was not as fast as the hare crossing his path. The brown creature hopped away, disappearing through a hedge of green.

In his satchel John carried valuable items—books his father had bought for him. Some came from time spent at the grammar school at Alford where he had studied under Reverend Francis Marbury whose classroom overlooked the church porch. Other books came from the grammar school of Louth, a very old school formerly supported by Catholic guilds, but later endowed by King Edward VI during his short reign before passing away only months shy of age sixteen.

Interspersing fast sprints with short walks, John slowed his pace at the outskirts of Louth. In the months since his father's death, he had spent his whole allowance. The lawyer in charge of his father's estate told him to spend it wisely, but the monies did not last as long as intended.

John approached his grammar school on School House Lane, a school he no longer attended. His father's death had brought an end to his formal education.

"John!" His schoolmaster, who had taught him Latin, stood at the schoolhouse door. "Where are you going in such a hurry?"

"I must meet someone at St. James Church."

John failed to reveal that he planned to sell all of his books. He certainly did not want to tell the schoolmaster what he intended to do with the monies he would receive. He did not want to become a yeoman farmer like his father, even though he had inherited seven acres of land near Carleton Main, many miles away.

John could resist the call no longer, having set his heart on brave adventures. He planned on leaving England one day soon, to sail the waters beyond the isle shores.

Church of St. James, Louth, Lincolnshire

NOT FAR FROM where his father had owned a couple of tenements willed to his younger brother, John rounded the corner into Westgate. At the eastern end of the street, the spire of the Church of St. James rose nearly three hundred feet. On this foggy morning, heavy mist hid the tip of one of the tallest spires in all of Lincolnshire.

A woman wearing a long overcoat strolled towards him. A younger boy appeared from behind her. "That's John!"

The woman took several steps and stopped. "John Smith?"

John caught his breath. "Yes?"

"My son said you have books to sell."

"I won't need them any longer." John slipped the satchel from his shoulder.

"New books cost so much. Can you show me what you have?"

"Every book your son needs." John started to open his leather satchel, but the heavy mist turned to rain. "Let's go under that tree."

The young mother pulled her son along. Water ran down the boy's cheek. Beneath the overhanging tree, he gathered several drops together on his tongue. While he licked more liquid off his lips, his mother pushed several strands of dripping hair up under his cap.

She turned to John. "You don't want to go to school any longer?"

"I'm done with school for now." John raised the flap of his satchel and reached inside. "Here's my Latin book."

The mother flipped through the pages.

"It's used," the boy said. "I wanted something new."

"I've read them all." John pulled out two more books. "My father bought all of these for me."

"I heard he passed away." Sad tones tinged her words, sorrow marked her face.

"Yes, he died."

"You're an orphan?" the young boy asked.

"Fatherless." John paused. "But I have plans."

"What about your mother?" the lady asked.

"She married another man. They'll take care of my seven-year-old sister Alice and my younger brother Francis, but not me. I'm thirteen. I can take care of myself."

"You're alone?" Her eyes moistened. "I'm so sorry."

"It's all right," John said, "I have plans."

"Do you have other relatives who can take you in?"

"My father was of the ancient Smith's of Cuerdley in Lancashire and my mother was of the Rickands near the Great Heck of Yorkshire, but I have little contact with them."

"What about your guardians? You must have a guardian." The mother raised her eyebrows. "Will he take care of you?"

"They gave me some money and even talked about making me an indentured servant for seven or eight years." John pulled out a wooden paddle with parchment pasted on it. On the top part of it the ABC's had been written and on the bottom half, the Lord's Prayer. "I also have this hornbook from the free school at Alford." Alford was not far from Willoughby, named for the local Willoughby family. John's father had worked for Lord Willoughby.

"I already know my ABC's," the boy said.

"If you take them all, I'll even give you the satchel to carry them, too." John asked, "What will you offer?"

"The satchel looks good, but these books look worn."

"They can be used for years longer."

The woman pulled out several coins. "Is this enough?"

"Plenty," John said.

"Very well." The mother placed the coins into John's hand. "What are you going to do?"

"Don't tell anyone." John looked down the street for any signs of his schoolmaster. "I want to sail and see faraway lands, lands of beauty and intrigue."

"Won't that be dangerous?" she asked.

"I'm not afraid."

"You're going to sea?" the young boy asked. "Truly?"

"Others may be satisfied with living out their whole life in their hometown, but I'll seek adventure." John smiled. "The world is so large; I want to see it all."

The young son, fully enthralled, showed more interest in John's words than his new schoolbooks. "That sounds like more fun than going to school."

"You're just a boy," John said. "Not everyone gets to go to school. Don't be idle, listen to your mother."

"Godspeed to you, young man." The mother placed the books back into the satchel and grabbed her son's hand.

"Thank you." John pulled the strings to his coin purse tight. "I'd better get going. I hope to catch a ship at Boston."

As the mother and her son walked in front of St. James Church, the boy squirmed away. He jumped up and landed with both feet in the middle of a large puddle. Water splashed everywhere. It soaked the bottom of the boy's pants, as well as his mother's overcoat.

She frowned, scolded him with her finger, and grabbed his elbow.

Turning away, John soon reached the thrice-weekly market several blocks away. Though it was still early, farmers and merchants had already set up their booths. He recognized and smiled at the farmer he had passed on the road. Some early shoppers browsed through the merchandise and produce.

John picked up a piece of fruit and flipped a coin from his purse to the vendor. "Keep the change."

Biting into an apple, John exited Louth and headed south. It would take him two days to reach Boston, the closest and most important Lincolnshire port, about thirty miles away.

All day and into the evening, John walked through the familiar countryside of Lincolnshire, bypassing Alford and also Willoughby, where he had been baptized as an infant by his parents, George and Alice Smith.

Although his feet were sore after walking so far, he didn't care. John needed to find a ship.

The yellow light in the distance signaled his arrival at Boston, the Lincolnshire Port Town. Miles away, lanterns placed high in the tower of the parish of St. Botolph beckoned him.

Boston Harbor, Lincolnshire, England

EARLY THE FOLLOWING morning, John walked along the tidal waterway of Boston. At the first ship, dockworkers lugged cargo up a ramp. Other workers rolled wooden barrels leaking fresh water up another.

"Ahoy!" John yelled. "I want to go to sea."

A shipmate put his hands on his hips. "You'll have to see the captain."

"Where's he?"

"Captain! Someone to see you."

The captain drew near to the rail and peered at John. "Where?"

"Here." John waved his arms.

"You're just a boy, and not too large at that."

"I'm strong. I helped my father with the cows and hogs."

"No cows or hogs here." The captain laughed. "I've got no need for a farmer boy like you. And I already have a cabin boy."

All morning long John searched the docks for a ship that would take him. He walked to each ship tied to the docks and yelled to others anchored in the waterway. Despite his best efforts, John's persistence did not pay off.

"You'll need a license from the Queen Elizabeth to leave England," one sailor said.

"I don't want to leave. I just want to sail."

St. Botolph's Church, Boston, Lincolnshire

WITH EVENING APPROACHING and feeling dejected, John Smith sauntered towards the parish church of St. Botolph. When he reached it, he almost bumped into a man swinging a lantern.

"Where are you going?" John asked.

"Every night I light the lanterns in the stump," the parish worker said.

"The stump?"

"That's what we call the tower of St. Botolph." The worker pointed up. The square bell tower rose almost as high as the church in Louth, yet it had no spire.

"Oh, the stump with no spire. I saw the lanterns last night from miles away," John said, "but who was St. Botolph?"

"Saint Botolph founded a monastery when this area was merely an island. It was known as Icanhoe or Ox Island, but later this place became known as Botolph's Town."

"Boston."

"Exactly. The name was shortened to Boston." The church worker entered the stump tower to light the lanterns.

When John turned, a pair of carriages rolled towards him. Its wheels screeched to a stop. The door opened.

"John Smith?

The voice was very familiar. John recognized the youth leaning out the carriage door. "Peregrine!"

"We've been looking for you." Peregrine Bertie, the youngest son of Peregrine Bertie, Lord Willoughby jumped out. "My brother is here, too."

"Robert!"

Peregrine's older brother Robert stepped out. "John!"

"How did you find me?"

Robert laughed. "Boston's not that big."

"But how did you know I was here?"

"The woman you sold your books to told us you went to Boston," Peregrine said.

"I told her to keep it a secret."

"Secret or not, Louth's a small town." Robert Bertie laughed. "Are you ready?"

"For what?" John turned his attention to a man stepping out of the second carriage. He recognized his guardian.

The lawyer stepped forward. "We found a place for you."

"What do you mean?" John asked.

"An agreement has already been signed." The lawyer handed John a rolled parchment. "The merchant Thomas Sendall wants you to begin working tomorrow."

"But I wanted to go to sea."

"You're a little young for that."

The lawyer's stern expression made John hesitate.

"I couldn't find a ship." John lifted his purse and realized the money from the sale of his books and satchel was already half gone. The remainder would not last long.

"The merchant will give you a place to stay," Robert said. "My father would have wanted it for you."

"Where is Lord Willoughby?" John asked.

"Our father has journeyed back to the continent," Robert Bertie said.

"Where he was born?"

"No, not to the Duchy of Cleve in Germany. The last time we heard from him he was in Venice, but he may have gone to Vienna."

The lawyer motioned to the open door. "John, you must climb in."

John paused, looking over his shoulder toward the ships before hopping into the carriage.

"We'll take you clear to Great Lynn." Peregrine followed John into the carriage.

After Robert sat down, John asked the lawyer, "Are you coming too?"

"No. I have to go to London. Queen Elizabeth's council of advisors is expecting me." He shut the carriage door. "You'll learn much from that famous merchant."

With Robert and Peregrine seated opposite John, the driver snapped the whip.

After leaving Boston, the carriage bumped along the road in the fens. The squeaky wheels scattered the birds. Dotting the skies like black specks in the sand, the birds soared above the verdant marsh.

The carriage rounded a bend and a large bay came into full view on their left.

They traveled further away from Boston in Lincolnshire. The road reached the salt-water marshlands. The water buttressed against the tidal lands, the Wash.

"The Wash seems so large," John said.

"It extends many miles," Robert said. "We won't reach Lynn in Norfolk for many hours."

Later, the carriage crossed over a small bridge spanning the River Witnam.

"Is it true King John lost his treasure along this road?" John asked.

"Just a legend, I heard," Peregrine said.

"But his crown jewels?"

"I believe King John did lose them," Robert said. "His crown jewels have never been found, though many have searched for more than four centuries."

"Maybe they're lost forever," John said.

"Maybe," Peregrine said. "Perhaps someday we'll receive a treasure."

The carriage hit another bump, jostling the three friends.

"As soon as we drop you off, we're going to return to our home at Grimsthorpe Castle," Peregrine said

Happy to have friends like Peregrine and Robert Bertie, John Smith remembered his father's advice: honor and love the good Lord Willoughby.

"I heard about that famous song your father's soldiers sang after a battle in Flanders." John asked, "Do you remember all of the words to The Brave Lord Willoughby?"

Peregrine glanced at Robert and smiled. "We remember."

"Let's sing it." The two brothers chimed in with John:

"The fifteenth day of July, with glist'ning spear and shield,
A famous fight in Flanders was fought'en on the field:
The most courageous officers were the English captains three,
But the bravest in the battle was brave Lord Willoughby."

The carriage swayed. The three sang the end of the tune:
"Then courage noble English men, and never be dismayed,
If that we be but one to ten we will not be afraid
To fight with foreign enemies, and set our country free,
And thus I end the bloody bout of brave Lord Willoughby."

Southgate, King's Lynn, Norfolk County, England

LATER, THE CARRIAGE reached the fortified walls of the port of Lynn Regis, where the Ouse River flows into the Wash. When they stopped in front of the stone Southgate, John pulled out and perused the indentured servitude agreement: he would be bound for years; perhaps until he turned twenty-one, after the start of the next century, he would be stuck there.

He looked back at a ship unfurling its sails.

John longed for the sea.

Chapter 11 – Indentured Servant in Lynn

Lynn Regis, vulgarly called King's Lynn.
Royal Charter, King Henry VIII

*About the age of fifteen years he [John Smith] was bound an apprentice to Master
Thomas Sendall of [King's] Lynn, the greatest merchant of all those parts;*

"What is, the anchor away?
Yea, Yea.
Let fall your foresail."

John Smith

King's Lynn, Norfolk County, England, Summer 1595

ON BOARD A small shallop docked behind a warehouse, John Smith
wrestled with a heavy trunk. The strong youth from Lincolnshire pushed
it to the edge of the flat-bottomed boat, gained a firm grip, and raised one
end of the wooden container. He leveraged the trunk onto the quay fronting the fleet, the small tidal stream that emptied in the Great Ouse River.
When he scooted it forward, the knot holding the boat to the dock suddenly slipped. The vessel rocked, so did the trunk.

John straddled precariously between the dock and the boat. With all
his might, he squeezed his legs together. The shallot did not draw closer.
He stretched to reach the dangling rope, but could not reach it. The trunk
teetered over the water.

"Need a hand?" The merchant Thomas Sendall grabbed the line.

"The knot slipped."

Sendall pulled the small boat closer to the quay. "What a wooden
monstrosity."

"It's heavier than it looks." The youth from Lincolnshire kept his hand
on the trunk. He regained his balance. With Master Sendall's help, the
young apprentice maneuvered the trunk onto the dock.

Together, they carried it into the adjacent warehouse and returned to the shallop, now fully secured. When John retrieved several burlap sacks, he noticed that one emanated a pleasant odor. "Do you know what's inside?"

"Must be the spices." Master Sendall pointed to an overflowing basket. "And those must be the currants."

"Currants?" John retrieved the heavy wicker basket.

"Used in scones and cakes."

John bit into a juicy morsel, half of the size of a grape raisin.

"We previously called them the raisins of Corinth." Sendall picked out a few bad pieces and tossed the dried fruit into the water. Several gulls swooped down and pecked at the discards drifting toward the Great Ouse. "I purchased this from the Levant Company, who shipped it all the way from Izmir."

"Izmir?"

"In the Levant, the eastern end of the Mediterranean, beyond Spain and Rome, the Ottoman Empire controls much of the trade with Cathay, China, Persia, and the Indies. But sailing can be dangerous, because of pirates."

Sendall's last words piqued John's curiosity. "Pirates?"

"Yes, when the Barbary Pirates capture a ship, they often hold both the ship and her crew for ransom."

Several sailors swabbed the deck of a triple-masted ship anchored in the waterway. As other sailors prepared the ship for departure, John followed the merchant.

Inside the warehouse, Master Sendall pried open the trunk. "Let's see what's in it." He pulled out a bolt of purple cloth. "Excellent. I've been waiting for this silk. The mayor's wife wanted a new dress and may be on her way over this morning." He handed the heavy roll of smooth cloth to John. "Put it next to the other fabric."

"Isn't purple the color of royalty?" John asked.

"Yes, and Lynn was chartered as Lynn Regis," Sendall said. "Lynn means pool because the waters gathered here before emptying in the sea. And Regis means—"

"I know, Royal."

"There's no town in the entire Kingdom more loyal to the throne."

John returned to the storeroom to put away the rest of the shipment. "I'll line up all of these goods in perfect order, just like you want." He put away the last of the spices and positioned the basket of currants by the front door of the store.

Master Sendall meanwhile helped customers. The Mayor and his wife entered the establishment. Using a yard stick, Sendall measured the purple silk for the Mayor's wife.

When the brass bell on the door jingled again, two Flemish weavers entered. "We heard you received a shipment from the Levant."

"Word travels fast." Sendall smiled.

Having labored for the merchant for two years, John knew Sendall often sold fabric to the immigrant weavers from Flanders. They worked on the other side of Purfleet, one of the tidal waterways dividing Lynn.

Finally, all of the customers left. The store was empty and quiet.

"Master Sendall?"

"What is it, John?"

"Will you let me go to sea?"

"Absolutely not," Sendall said. "We've talked about this before. A contract is a contract. You're an indentured servant for the term of years."

"But that's so long."

"Now don't think of running away. You know what the law says."

"If an indentured servant leaves early, he'll be a servant for all of his life." John went back to the warehouse and stared toward the Great Ouse and the triple-masted ship. When the breeze picked up, sailors raised the anchor and John could hear the commands bouncing over the water.

"Is the anchor away?" the sea captain asked.

"Aye! Aye!" sailors shouted.

"Let fall your foresail."

Sailors at the top of the foresail obeyed and John sighed with regret. Another ship sailed away without the youth from Lincolnshire on board.

That night John climbed the wooden stairs to the living quarters above the store. The window well extended over the entryway. As John peered out, he wondered if he would ever be able to sail the high seas. He yearned for adventure. Perhaps he would even be able to fight pirates.

Dining Area, Sendall's Store, King's Lynn, Autumn 1595

ON A SUNNY autumn day, John Smith finished eating a late breakfast prepared by Master Thomas Sendall's cook. When Sendall arrived in the dining area behind the store, the cook showed him an empty container. "We're running low on corn."

John swallowed his last bite and wiped his mouth. "Do you want me to get more at the Corn Exchange?"

"Several pounds," Sendall said. "But it might be crowded in that part of town."

"Yes." John jumped up and grabbed his cloak. "There's a fair at Tuesday Market."

"Don't take too long."

The young John Smith quickly exited the store, holding the door for the first two customers of the day. He walked down a narrow street and crossed the bridge over Purfleet, the small stream and tidal waterway. When he reached Damsgate, the cross street that bisected the newer part of Lynn, he looked towards East Gate. Royal Arms adorned that gate leading to Norwich, the main city of Norfolk County.

A smartly dressed boy ran ahead of a man, most likely his father. He intercepted John. "Do you know where the fair is?"

John stopped and pointed. "At Tuesday Market."

"But it's not Tuesday."

"Tuesday's the name of the square."

The boy turned. "Father!"

The father, also clad in fine wool attire, caught up with his son. He placed his hand on the boy's shoulder. "We've just arrived from Heacham."

John had heard of the small town. "North of here?"

"Yes, what's your name?"

"John. John Smith."

The man extended his hand. "John Rolfe."

"Good name."

"And this is my son. He's also named John."

John Smith looked down. "Hello."

"I'm ten," the young boy said.

"I'll show you the way to the market."

Tuesday Market Square, King's Lynn, Autumn 1595

VENDORS SET UP booths at Tuesday Market Square. A nobleman approached a woman selling green apples. Her elderly father sat on a nearby stool and kept a wary eye.

A jester jumped in front of John Smith, Mister Rolfe, and his son.

"You're early." He blocked their path.

Smith stood his ground. "Be gone, fool!"

"Call me a fool?"

"You are a fool."

"I prefer jester." The green-clothed man wore a triangular hat. "And this is my friend."

A young man holding two colorful balls in his hand bumped into the jester. He shoved him out of the way. "Watch!"

The juggler kept the two balls in the air. While tossing one ball up and down, the juggler let the other ball roll up his arm. When it hit his bicep, the juggler snapped his arm. The ball sprung five feet into the air.

Smith watched with amazement at such dexterity. "How do you do that?"

"Yes," the younger John Rolfe said. "How?"

The juggler added another ball. The three balls formed a circle. "Concentration."

As soon as the juggler spoke, one of the three balls escaped, rolling to Smith.

"Something in short supply today." John tossed the leather ball behind his back to the juggler and turned to Mister Rolfe. "I almost forgot. Master Sendall needs several pounds of corn."

"You've got to go?"

"I should." Smith stepped toward the Corn Exchange on the opposite side of square. The double masts of a ship garnered his attention. He turned toward the two Rolfes. "What I'd really like to do is go to sea." The vessel slowly approached Common Staith, the quay nearest Tuesday Market. "I wonder where that ship is from."

"Can we see?" the younger Rolfe asked his father.

"If you want."

By the time the boy and his father caught up with him, John had reached some fish stands. Vendors displayed their assorted morning catch. A fish vendor leaned over, picked up a handful of salt, and tossed it onto the fish.

"How much are the herring?" A woman shopper holding a small basket stepped in front of Smith. "How fresh?"

"Just arrived this morning," the vendor said.

While the lady and the vendor conversed, Mister Rolfe, his son and John watched the rickety Dutch ship drift alongside the dock. Sailors secured the lines and straightened two planks.

"Where are you from?" John yelled up to the Captain.

"Enkhuizen on Holland's inland sea." The old Dutch Captain walked down the plank. "I've got to find a mate to replace my last one."

"I'd like to go," Smith said, "But I have to get permission from Master Sendall."

"We cannot wait." The old Captain peered at several men sitting near the Corn Exchange, the large warehouse near the quay.

"Can I go?" the ten year-old asked his father.

"You're too young." His father turned to the Captain. "What happened to the last mate?"

"Died at sea," the craggy Captain said. "Buried him in the deep, we did."

"God rest his soul," a woman shopper said. "I'll remember to pray for him along with my husband at St. Nichols Church."

"Your husband dead, too?" The Captain, who had several teeth missing, smiled.

"Oh me, the gods! Nay!" the lady said. "He's at sea. Two months now, I believe."

"He just likes to take a drink now and then." The fish vendor pointed. "You might find a mate at that inn over there."

"I need someone who speaks Dutch and obeys orders."

"I can learn Dutch," Smith said.

The Sea Captain pivoted. "Don't bother asking your Master. I don't need novices."

Dockhands raised full sacks of salt over their shoulders and walked up a plank. Other dockhands carried even larger sacks of grain from the Corn Exchange.

"Hurry, lads!" the Captain yelled. "Winds are favorable."

At the stern of the ship a small dog began yapping. It stuck its nose through the rails and paced back and forth.

Smith walked closer. "What are you barking at?"

The young John Rolfe pointed. "Look!"

Two small rats scampered down the taut line holding the ship. Near a boulder at the corner of the Corn Exchange, the two vermin stopped to feast on grain that the spilled into a pile.

The dog yapped again.

One rat continued to nibble on the spilt mush, but the other rat scampered through a puddle. It perched itself on the boulder, raised its nose, and sniffed the air. When a fly buzzed too close, the rat snapped, but its sharp teeth missed the target. Filled with dark emptiness, its hollow eyes could put a chill up many a spine, but not Smith; he had seen fatter rats.

"Begone!" A worker with a broom rushed out of the exchange. The rats disappeared behind the boulder and around the corner.

"We best get back to the fair," the older Rolfe said. "We don't come to Lynn that often." The father and son from Heacham waved goodbye.

"I still need to buy grain." John entered the Corn Exchange and walked past piles of corn that butted against the wall. At the far end of the large warehouse, he reached the scales.

"John Smith! What can we do for you today?" the Weigh Master asked.

"I need to buy ten pounds for Master Thomas Sendall."

"How's that great merchant doing?" The man removed two large metal weights from one side of the balance scale.

John handed over a small sack to fill. "Very well. We just received another shipment from the Levant."

"A dangerous place," the Weigh Master said. "If the Spanish don't get you, then the Barbary pirates might. Those Barbary folks have even hired some Englishmen, I hear." The iron scale balanced. "Ten pounds."

John took back the now filled sack. "Put it to Master Sendall's account."

"His credit is good."

Minutes later, John Smith arrived back at the store. He handed Master Sendall the sack of corn. "A Dutch ship's arrived at Common Staith."

"Let me guess. You wanted to go?"

"Yes, but he wanted a sailor with experience."

"There's plenty of work to do here," Master Sendall said. "I'll even teach you some accounts. Remember, we always want to make a profit."

Frustrated he could not leave and go to sea, John did not sleep well that night. He peered out his window towards the water. The full moon illuminated the masts of yet one more ship.

Someday, he promised himself, someday.

Chapter 12 - Master Thomas Sendall

The hazard of the merchant . . .

But . . . he [Master Thomas Sendall] would not presently send him [John Smith] to sea.
John Smith

King's Lynn, Norfolk County, England, Spring 1596

MONTHS PASSED SLOWLY and, as winter lingered into spring, John Smith felt even more trapped inside the store. Like he did every day, the indentured servant for Master Sendall swept the floor. Unlike so many farm boys, content never to leave the boundaries of their own hometowns, his longing to sail had not abated. John, having heard too many tales from sailors, wanted brave adventure, now more than ever.

On this stormy morning, John picked up a towel and swiped it across the foggy window. Sheets of rain pounded hard against the windowpane. He could hardly see across the cobblestone street. Every few seconds, another wave swept against the glass.

Feet away, a pair of horses broke the stormy spell; a carriage pulled up in front of the store. Two men climbed out, but John did not recognize them: their collars were upturned and pulled-down hats covered their faces. They darted to the store. The door creaked when it opened.

The storm accompanied their entrance. The cold wind whipped across the room. Loose fabric samples blew from shelves. When the two scrambled inside, the door slammed with a bang. It latched shut. The pair stomped their feet and shook water from their sleeves. Water flew from their cloaks, like a pair of English sheepdogs after a bath.

When the taller of the two newcomers took off his hat, John recognized his friend, the younger Bertie brother. "Peregrine!"

"I'd recognize that voice anywhere," Peregrine said, "a little bit lower than the last time I heard it." He reached out and grabbed both of John's arms. "It's good to see you again."

"What a cheery sight on a gloomy day." John smiled.

The remembrance of several childhood experiences flashed across his mind. He and Peregrine, a couple years older, had often played together.

Footsteps approached John from behind. "Master Sendall, you remember Peregrine Bertie? We grew up together in Willoughby in Lincolnshire."

"Of course I do." The merchant extended his hand. "How's the son of Lord Willoughby?"

"Good, Master Sendall," Peregrine said. "How's your apprentice?"

"John's a good worker."

"Just like his father," Peregrine said. "At least that's what my father always told me."

"And how is Lord Willoughby?" Sendall asked. "I heard he's still recuperating."

"'Tis true. The Queen recently wrote to him, saying she misses his advice—"

"And counsel." The older man, who had accompanied Peregrine into the store, stepped forward.

"My father wrote and said he might be home soon from his long stays at Venice and Vienna . . ."

"Peregrine, have you forgotten your manners?" the older man asked.

"Master Sendall, this is my French tutor."

The tutor extended his hand. "A pleasure."

"What brings you to Lynn?" John asked.

"My brother is at Orleans," Peregrine said.

"In France?" John asked. "What's Robert doing there?"

"Helping King Henry IV."

"The King?" Sendall asked.

"Yes," Peregrine said, "like our father."

"What do you mean?" John asked.

"Acting at Queen Elizabeth's request, my father once helped King Henry IV," the tutor said. "That was before King Henry purportedly said, *'Paris vaut bien unne messe'.*"

"My French needs some work. What does that mean?" John asked.

"Paris is worth a mass. Even though King Henry had the advantage a few years ago, he didn't attack Paris during the Wars of Religion. At the time King Henry espoused the Reformed Religion of Jean Calvin instead of Roman Catholics."

"What did King Henry do?"

"The French King became Catholic," the tutor said. "Henry forsook the Reformed Religion and partook of the Catholic Mass."

"Paris opened her gates," Peregrine said, "but the fighting between Henry and the Catholic League continues."

"How so?" John asked.

"The Catholic League did not believe Henry's conversion, even though the Pope himself accepted it. King Henry IV fights against Philippe Emmanuel *de* Lorraine, the Duke of Mercoeur."

"How does your brother help?" John asked.

"English soldiers aid the French in their fight against the Duke," Peregrine answered. "The Duke of Mercoeur, supported by King Philip II of Spain, rules all of Brittany, but King Henry considers Brittany to be part of France." Peregrine glanced at the store shelves. "As soon as we get the supplies we need, my tutor and I will take them."

"You're going to France?" John stared intently at his friend.

"What kind of supplies?" Mr. Sendall asked.

"Everything. Cured meat, of course. But iron tools, tin, and lead, if you have it."

"Oh, we can get all of those things for you." John glanced out the window. The intense rain had abated.

"I'll gather the tools," Sendall said. "John, you go on ahead to the butcher shop."

The butcher shop was located next to Trinity Guild Hall on Saturday Market Place. "Certainly, Master Sendall. I can do that."

"I'll meet you in front of Trinity Guild shortly," Sendall said.

Peregrine Bertie and his tutor put their hats back on. John threw on his cloak and the three walked through the doorway in much lighter rain.

Trinity Guild Hall, Saturday Market Place, King's Lynn

BY THE TIME John Smith, Peregrine Bertie and his tutor had reached Saturday Market Place, the morning rain had tapered off completely. Vendors straightened their booths. Farmers unveiled their produce and merchants their wares.

A forlorn-looking boy leaned against the checkerboard façade of nearby Guild Hall. He watched the Market Place happenings. The square slowly began to fill with people.

"That's the Guild of the Holy Trinity." John pointed to the old building with two doors and two small windows. "The important merchants of the town set up the guild to provide for the poor."

Decades ago King's Lynn was known as Bishop's Lynn.

John pointed to a church with large, square, twin towers. "And that's St. Margaret's Church. "

The Bishop of Norwich founded St. Margaret's Church and many monasteries. When the Pope in Rome refused to grant King Henry VIII a divorce, Henry declared himself head of the Church in England and King Henry confiscated the properties of all the monasteries throughout England, including those at Lynn. That's when Bishop's Lynn became known as Lynn Regis, or King's Lynn.

Peregrine stared at the small statue stood atop the peaked roof the Guild building. "So the merchants meet at Trinity Guild Hall to help the poor?"

"Well, that was during the Catholic times. That's when the merchants even hired their own priests, paying for their room and board at Thoresby College. The priests prayed for the souls of departed members in this hall, but now this hall houses many prisoners."

John, Peregrine, and his tutor stopped in front of the butcher shop, located in the building adjacent to Guild Hall. Three small sheep carcasses hung in one of the two front windows.

A larger carcass hung in the arched doorway. A couple of flies alighted near the feet of the slaughtered cow. Two hooves almost reached the ground. Drops of blood mingled with lingering pools of water.

"Peregrine, I was thinking." John paused. "Could take me with you?"

"To France?"

"You'll need Master Sendall's permission," the tutor said. "As an indentured servant, you have no liberty to leave and do as you please."

"I know, but if the son of Lord Willoughby asks, I'm sure Sendall would let me go."

"We could use a strong body to carry the supplies," the tutor said.

"It won't hurt to ask," Peregrine said.

"I'll let you do the talking." John smiled. *If I could go to France?* As he pushed the cow's carcass aside, he swatted at an annoying fly, an unusual sight after a cold rain.

Inside the shop, the butcher sharpened his knife. He spat on a smooth rock and pulled the blade across the wet stone in a circular motion. He repeated this several times. Seconds later, he rubbed his thumb across the grain of the blade.

"Looks sharp," John said.

The butcher waved the blade. "Got this knife at the Hanse Steelyard, the warehouse for the German Hanseatic League."

"The Hanseatic League?" Peregrine asked.

"A group of merchants throughout the Baltic Sea. They control most of the trade," his tutor said. "Merchants who join pay a membership fee, but then get to export and import without large tariffs and taxes, but Queen Elizabeth might expel the Hanseatic League. The League doesn't allow the English the same rights in the German cities of the Holy Roman Empire."

"What do they bring here?" Peregrine asked.

John remembered what Master Sendall had taught him. "Fur from Moscow, cloth from the Rhine, as well as timber and iron from Sweden."

"Swedish knives are the best," the butcher said. "How about some meat? I have mutton and beef from this morning, the freshest meat in Lynn."

"How much is your beef?" John asked.

"How much do you want?" The butcher, ready to cut the fresh meat with his sharpened knife, moved toward the carcass.

"We don't need fresh meat," the Tutor said. "We're going to France."

"Have you any dried or salted beef?" John asked.

"Can't say I have much cured." The butcher reached for a chunk. "Only this, a couple pounds of dried beef."

"Let me taste it." John tore a small strip.

"How is it?" Peregrine asked.

John chewed. "A little tough."

"We'll take it all." Peregrine handed the butcher several coins and handed the cured beef to John to carry.

As soon as they left the butcher shop, they walked by Guild Hall.

The forlorn looking youth, who had been leaning against the wall, had sat down. "Can you spare something?"

"You're new to Lynn?" John asked.

"I was on my way to London to look for work."

"You'll have to go through Cambridge." John turned to Peregrine. "What do you think?"

"Give him a strip."

John tore a slice of dried beef and gave it to the boy.

"Peregrine!" Master Sendall carried a large bag across Saturday Market Place. "I've gathered all of the necessary supplies."

"Thank you." Peregrine took the bag. "We've bought some dried meat."

"Master Sendall," John said. "The son of Lord Willoughby has a request."

"And what's that?"

"It's more a proposition than an outright request," Peregrine said.

"Go on."

"I know that John is under contract with you for five or six more years."

"John's help is invaluable," Master Sendall said, "a most trustworthy servant."

"You must know that John wants to go to sea."

"He talks about it every day."

"With so many supplies, we could use another hand." Peregrine glanced at John. "I would like John to be my attendant in France."

Master Sendall did not immediately respond.

John felt as anxious as he had ever been. He wanted to go. He waited seconds, but it seemed like minutes.

The tutor broke the silence. "You might want to consider the Queen."

"What do you mean?" Sendall asked. "I know that Queen Elizabeth helps King Henry, but I need someone to help me."

"You can get another servant." John pointed to the boy he had given the beef to minutes earlier. "That boy needs work."

"How do I know he's trustworthy, like you?"

"You might have to give us both a chance." John waved for the boy to approach.

Master Sendall asked the boy. "You want to work?"

"I was going to go to London, but I work hard."

"You have two days to prove your worth." Master Sendall turned to John. His countenance had changed. "How can I stop you from helping a friend of England?"

"Lynn's reputation of loyalty to the crown is well deserved," the tutor said.

"Ever since the time of King John," Master Sendall said.

"Then you'll let me go?" John asked.

"Yes." Sendall smiled. "And I will send you with a parting gift."

"What's that?" John asked.

"A knife from the Hanse Warehouse."

John turned to Peregrine and his tutor. "I'll meet you at the docks," he said. "I only have a few things to bring."

Back at the shop, John gathered his belongings and Sendall handed him a knife.

John rubbed his thumb across the eight-inch blade. He took the sheath and tied it to his belt. He put the knife inside. "Thank you again, Master Sendall."

"Be of good service to Peregrine and his brother," Master Sendall said.

"I will." John waved goodbye to the greatest merchant of Lynn.

Outside, Sendall pointed to clearing skies. "With fair weather approaching, your ship to France will leave soon."

Quay, Great Ouse River, King's Lynn

WITHIN AN HOUR, John reached the quay on the Great Ouse River.

"Hurry up!" the Captain yelled. "We want to reach the open sea before nightfall."

Peregrine, his tutor, and John carried the supplies up the plank to take to Peregrine's older brother Robert in France.

Dockhands cast off the lines. Carried by the river's current and the outgoing tide, the ship drifted away from the dock.

Peregrine leaned against the rail. "I can't wait to see my brother in France."

As the North Sea beckoned and the ship neared open water, John smiled broadly. "On to Orleans."

West winds filled the mainsail, the vessel surged forward.

Chapter 13 - Safiye *Valide Sultana*

Lest her [Aisha's] mother [Safiye Valide Sultana] . . .

John Smith

Sultan Murad lately dead, in January, began his reign about 1574. Gra [Safiye Valide]
Sultana his wife liveth being of 45 years, a very wise woman being wife of the Turk 32
years.

The State of Turkey in 1594
Reported by Salomone Uschehebrea, Jew in Constantinople
to English Ambassador Barton

Ibrahim *Pasha* Palace, *Jumada II*, AH 1011 (Dec. 1602)

EMINE FINISHED TRANSLATING the words of the slave from English
into Turkish. "On to Orleans."

"In France?" Aisha asked.

"Yes," *Capitano* John Smith said, "Orleans in France."

The Sister of the Sultan peered at her slave. "So you were born in England?"

"I told you." He took the last fig from the tray. "I would not lie."

The stoic Overseer uncrossed his arms and turned.

Aisha's mother, Safiye *Valide Sultana*, appeared at the door. "What's
going on here?"

"Nothing, Mother." Aisha rose to her feet. Her friend Emine and her
slave followed her lead. "I was learning where the slave's family lived."

"And did you find out where his castle is?" Her mother pulled back
her hijab. Her sister mimicked her mother and let her hijab rest on her
shoulders.

"Not yet," Aisha said. "Emine translated everything."

"I did not know you spoke Bohemian," her mother said.

"No," Emine said. "English."

"That's right. Your father trades with the English Levant Company in
Izmir. But how does that help? The slave is Bohemian."

111

"I can explain," Aisha said.

"Explain? Explain what? You can explain what our slave is still doing here, eating figs." The mother of the Sultan pivoted. "Overseer, take the Bohemian back to the slave quarters, at once!"

"Mother! He's my slave."

"You'll do as I say."

"I am not a child." Aisha longed for day she would be wholly in charge of her own life. She told her slave in Italian, "You need to go back to your quarters."

"*Grazie,*" the captured captain said.

Aisha wondered if her slave understood everything she had said.

The Overseer grabbed the slave's elbow and led the Englishman back to his quarters.

Emine reached for her scarf. "I'd better be going."

"Thank you for translating, I'll send for you soon."

"Yes, we aren't finished," Emine said, "I can bring our friend Filiz back next week."

"Good, she speaks French, doesn't she?"

"Yes." Emine exited the Great Hall.

As soon as Emine left, Aisha's mother restarted the conversation. "I must insist that you do as I say."

"Yes, Mother." Aisha headed through the fourth courtyard.

Vaulted Apartment, Ibrahim *Pasha* Palace, *Stamboul*

INSIDE HER VAULTED apartment Aisha removed her headdress. After an attendant helped her take off her embroidered jacket, she loosened her belt and sat on her bed. Settling on her pillow, Aisha thought about her slave and how he sold his books and satchel to the English mother. She laughed when she remembered the story of the lady's son jumping into a puddle.

The Sister of the Sultan closed her eyes, but could not fall asleep. The image of her captive, especially his smile, did not leave her mind. She wondered what kind of man he was? He loved adventure. If he didn't, how could he ever have entered into her life? She could not wait until her friend Emine brought back the French translator Filiz.

She asked herself, was it a sin to think about John? After all, both her mother and her brother insisted Aisha marry the Grand Vizier.

Chapter 14 - Pillars of Hagia Sophia

Solomon! I have surpassed you!
Byzantine Emperor Justinian, AD 537

Sultan Murad II subsequently built two minarets on the north and west side, each with only one gallery. The ensigns (alems, i.e. the crescents) on the top of these four minarets are each of 20 cubits, and richly gilt; but that on the great dome is 50 cubits long, and the gilding of it required 50,000 pieces of gold coin. It is visible at the distance of two farasangs by land, and 100 miles off by sea . . .

They are the imams (reciters of the form of prayer); . . . muezzins (criers, who call to prayers from the minarets); . . . in all, full 2,000 servants, for the revenues of the mosque settled upon it by pious bequests (evkaf) are very large. The Hagia Sofia is, in itself, peculiarly the House of God.
Narrative of Travels in the 17th Century
by Evliya *Effendi*, Translated from Turkish

Hagia Sophia, *Stamboul*, 17 *Jumada II*, AH 1011 (Dec. 2, 1602)

THE MORNING FOLLOWING the banquet the turbaned *dragoman* escorted the two Bulgarian brothers out the Imperial Gate of the New Palace and stopped in front of the Hagia Sophia. The imperial mosque with its four minarets dominated the first of the seven hills of *Stamboul*. Its large dome rose above the dark-pink walls of the main structure.

High up, from minaret balconies, muezzins called the faithful to prayer. A crescent, a symbol of the Ottoman dynasty topped each minaret. Osman, the founder, dreamed his empire would dominate the earth under the moon. Sunlight hit the larger gilt crescent atop the main dome.

"Before I take you to the *janissary* school, you must learn the Five Pillars of Islam," the *dragoman* said.

"What do you mean?" the older boy asked.

"Just like the four pillars that hold up the great dome of the Hagia Sophia, you must do these five things to get to heaven."

"I don't care about your heaven," the younger brother said. "I want to see my mother."

"I've told you, forget your mother." The *dragoman* waved his finger. "You belong to Sultan Mehmet III now."

"But—"

"It's a great honor to be *ghilman*. Just like the *ghilmun* who serve True Believers in heaven, you will serve the Sultan. First, you must be trained in the ways of Allah and of Mohammed the Prophet." The *dragoman* asked the older boy, "Do you remember the first pillar of Islam, the *Shahadah?*"

"No."

"Both of you must learn it before we go into the Hagia Sophia."

"I thought you were taking us to the *Janissary* School," the older boy said.

"I am, but first you must learn the *Shahadah*. If you want to go to paradise, you must submit to Allah. Now, both of you repeat after me: There is no god but Allah, and Mohammed is his Prophet." The *dragoman* waited.

The boys stood in silence.

Criers above again called out for prayer. Other muezzins across *Stamboul* echoed the refrain.

"There is no god but Allah, and Mohammed is his Prophet," the *dragoman* repeated.

The boys acquiesced. "There is no god but Allah, and Mohammed is his Prophet."

"Excellent." The *dragoman* stepped toward the Hagia Sophia and pointed south. "You can see this Mosque from across the Sea of Marmara, even from Asia."

"The church looks ancient," the oldest boy said.

"More than a thousand years old. When Emperor Justinian first saw it, he proclaimed, 'Solomon! I've surpassed you!' Solomon built the Temple in Jerusalem to hold the Ark of the Covenant, which held the Ten Commandments, Aaron's rod that budded, and manna from heaven. For more than a millennium, a statue of Emperor Justinian stood in front of this church named Hagia Sophia, meaning Holy Wisdom. The statue held an apple in its hand, but do you know what happened?"

"What?" the older boy asked.

"The apple fell to the ground," the *dragoman* said. "Later, Mehmet the Conqueror waged jihad against Constantinople and the Byzantine Empire fell. Mehmet the Conqueror, like previous Sultans who had conquered Bursa and Edirne, converted the largest church in the city into a mosque."

"The Hagia Sophia?"

"Yes, this mosque."

Above them, the call for prayer rang out.

"Why do they always do that?" the younger boy asked.

"The Salat is the second pillar of Islam. You must pray five times every day," the *dragoman* said.

The call rang out again and a company of *sipahi* riders approached the mosque. The two boys followed the *dragoman* past two large mausoleums—one built for the father and the other for the grandfather of Sultan Mehmet III.

A beggar sat by one of the tombs. He held out a cup, but the *dragoman* ignored him and walked around a corner. The boys followed through the outer narthex. Inside the Hagia Sophia, the *dragoman* took off his shoes. He ordered the boys, "Take them off, show respect."

The boys reluctantly obeyed and slipped their shoes off. The older boy straightened the two pairs.

At the inner narthex, the *dragoman* washed his hands and face at one of the two marble urns. "Now wash."

The younger boy shook his head. "I'm not dirty."

"You must wash." The *dragoman* handed the towel to the older boy. They waited for the younger one to sprinkle water on his hands and arms. When both boys completed the religious cleansing, the *sipahis* then took their turn.

Inside the main room, the older boy peered up at the dome, nearly one hundred feet across. "This room is huge."

Four triangular pendentives came to a point in each of four corners. These triangular arches supported the massive dome, resting on four huge pillars in the corners. High above, light streamed through the glass and illuminated the large sanctuary.

"So this is a church?" The younger boy pointed. "There is a picture of Jesus." The mosaic depicted Jesus pointing his finger and holding the New Testament. "That's Jesus, the Creator."

"Allah, the God of Abraham, is the Creator," the *dragoman* said. "That mosaic should be plastered over."

"It will still be there." The younger boy added, "Even if there are no crosses in this church, Jesus will still be there."

"At least Sultan Mehmet the Conqueror did not plunder the Hagia Sophia like the Doge of Venice did during the Christians' Fourth Crusade." The *dragoman* waved to a religious leader. "I want you to meet the imam."

"The imam?" the older boy asked.

"The leader of the mosque."

The imam greeted them. "*Dragoman*, I see you have brought the *ghilmun*."

"Yes," the *dragoman* said. "These *ghilmun* need to learn the Salat."

"I would teach them, but prayer time must begin soon." The imam adjusted his head covering. "But if you have any questions, the ulema here can answer them." The imam headed to the preacher's platform to recite a prayer.

"What's an ulema?" the older boy asked.

"A scholar. Everyone respects them."

After the *dragoman* introduced the boys to the ulema, the younger boy looked around. "There are no women."

"They pray in a separate place." The ulema pointed to a screened-off area.

More men, including another group of *sipahis*, came into the mosque. They took off their shoes and lined up in rows on mats laid upon the

Hagia Sophia Interior

marble floors.

"We face toward the Ka'bah in Mecca in Arabia," the *dragoman* said. "The mihrab niche is in the middle of the qibla wall. The mihrab points the direction toward the Ka'bah."

"Why do you bow in the direction of Mecca?" the older boy asked, softly.

"Because that is where Abraham, who fathered Ishmael by Hagar the Egyptian, built an altar, the Ka'bah."

"Wasn't Abraham the husband of Sarah and the father of Isaac?" the older boy asked.

"Yes, that is why we consider Jews and Christians to be people of the Book," the ulema said. "We even allowed Jews to settle here when the Inquisition kicked them out of Spain. And the Christians can worship, too."

"But I haven't heard any bells since we arrived."

"Church bells are never allowed to ring."

"Why?" the younger boy asked.

"It's the law."

The prayer ritual began. Facing Mecca, the men touched their ears with their thumbs and cupped their hands beside their ears. They recited the key and the appropriate verses from the Qur'an in the proper sequence. All of the men stood, bowed, and prostrated themselves in unison.

As required, the men repeated the sequence four times. At the end of the prayer, each man said saalam to the man on his left and on his right.

After the sermon about the importance of giving to the poor, the younger boy pointed to the second floor and to the Sultan's loge. "Is that the Sultan?"

"Yes," the *dragoman* said. "Mehmet III is the caliph."

"What's a caliph?" the older boy asked.

"The caliph is the Successor to Mohammed. Years ago when he conquered Cairo and Mamluk *Sultana*te of Egypt, Sultan Selim I brought the caliph back here. When the last caliph died, the Ottoman Sultan inherited the title of Guardian of the Faithful. The caliphate was reestablished here in *Stamboul*."

"So Mehmet III is the Successor to Mohammed?"

"Yes."

Exiting the mosque, the *dragoman* and the boys stopped and peered up at a mosaic of the Virgin Mary holding the baby Jesus. On one side of the picture, Emperor Constantine held a model of the city of Constantinople. On the other side of the mosaic, Emperor Justinian held a model of the Hagia Sophia in his hands.

The younger boy pointed. "Look! The emperors are presenting Constantinople and the Hagia Sophia to baby Jesus, just like the shepherds and the three wise men did."

"Jesus was just a prophet," the ulema said.

"It looks like both this church and this city belong to Jesus," the younger boy said. "When Jesus comes a second time you will know."

"When He comes again, we will all know," the ulema said. "*Dragoman,* you will excuse me. I must talk to Sun'Ullah *Effendi*."

"The former Grand Mufti?" The *dragoman* knew that Sun'Ullah *Effendi* was the most important religious leader in the Ottoman Empire; however, he had been deposed after a *sipahi* rebellion, more than a year earlier.

"The *sipahis* remain unhappy about events in Hungary, but especially in Anatolia. You will excuse me." The ulema rushed to the former Grand Mufti.

The *dragoman* and the two boys, meanwhile, put their shoes back on and exited the Mosque. When they reached the large mausoleum of Selim II, the grandfather of Mehmet III, the *dragoman* again saw the man begging. This time, however, he stopped and reached for his purse. "Followers of Mohammed must pay the Zakat, the third pillar of Islam." The *dragoman* gave the man a coin. "Muslims must pay one-fortieth of their income to the poor."

"So much work to get to paradise."

"To get to paradise is not easy. When you are older, you must also observe the Sawn. You must fast during the month of Ramadan."

"You mean we can't eat for a whole month?" the older boy asked.

"You can eat, but only at night. From dawn to dusk, you must fast. It is called the Sawn, the fourth pillar of Islam." The *dragoman* added, "And the fifth pillar is called the Hajj. Someday you may go on a Hajj, a pilgrimage to Mecca."

"What if we can't afford to go?" the older boy asked.

"Allah can forgive you. But if you're able, the Qur'an requires you go."

The younger boy pouted. "The only place I want to go is home."

"I told you. Forget your mother," the *dragoman* said. "As a *ghilman*, you belong to the Sultan."

"And if I don't?"

"You might end up like Sultan Mehmet III's brothers."

"What do you mean?" the younger boy asked.

The *dragoman* pointed. "Sarcophagi hold the bodies of nineteen boys inside Murad III's mausoleum."

As soon as the *dragoman* finished his translation, a stunned expression swept over the older boy's face. "You mean?"

"Yes," the *dragoman* said. "When Mehmet III acceded to the throne, he had nineteen of his younger brothers strangled."

"We'll go to the *Janissary* School."

Chapter 15 - Janissary School *Agha*

The discipline and obedience taught in the Janissary schools was the most strict, austere, and perfect of any military education instituted, and had in it all the abstinence, privation, and total submission peculiar to the monkish orders of La Trappe [Trappists] and Ignatius Loyola [Jesuits].

This splendid body of infantry, which was never known to retreat from a field of battle . . .
Imperial Reference Library, London, 1808 edition

One of the grandest of these [palaces of Stamboul] is that of Ibrahim Pasha, the Vizier of Sultan Suleiman, on the Atmeidan, in which 2,000 pages of the Saray were formerly educated.
Narrative of Travels by Elviya *Effendi*

Stamboul, 17 *Jumada II*, AH 1011 (Dec. 2, AD 1602)

DECIDING IF THE two Bulgarian boys should see part of the city, the *dragoman* led them towards an intersection. Several *janissaries* stood at the corner and acted as policemen. Like all of the *janissaries* within *Stamboul*, these *janissaries* were armed with curved swords, not muskets. Two of them also held maces. One swung a wooden club to and fro.

The *dragoman* knew that local citizens preferred *janissaries* to *acemi oglanlar*, since the cadets were prone to excesses. The punishment meted out to shopkeepers and other citizens by the cadets was not always deserved. Their fervor against the Christians and Jews was also well-known.

"Everything is much bigger than in our village," the older Bulgarian boy said.

The younger boy stepped out of the way of two *janissaries* carrying a cauldron. "And crowded, too." Behind them, a third *janissary* balanced a long ladle over his shoulder.

"*Dragoman*, what are they doing?" the older boy asked.

"Bringing food to members of their *oda*." The *dragoman* stopped and watched.

119

The two *janissaries* set down the black cauldron by the acting police-men. A third one scooped out a steaming mixture of rice and mutton onto plates. Each of the *janissary* guards removed the wooden spoon lodged in his cap and began to eat.

"Nothing is more important than the cauldron to an *orta*." The *drago-man* referred to the *janissary* regiment.

"What do you mean?" the older boy asked.

"Many armies will fight to the death to protect their company flags, but *janissary orta*s must never lose their cauldron in battle. The whole *jan-issary* corps is called an *ocak*, which like the smaller *orta* means hearth."

"Like the hearth by a fireplace?"

"Yes, the *orta* always brings its large cauldron when it marches." The two *janissaries* picked up the small cauldron to continue their rounds. The *janissary* with the ladle followed them towards the next police post as-signed to members of their *oda*, or barracks.

The *dragoman* led the boys around a corner and down a narrow street. *Janissary* cadets swept up litter and trash.

"Do cadets have to work, too?" the younger boy asked.

"It's all part of the discipline and training."

Rounding a corner and returning to the *Atmeidan*, the *dragoman* stopped at the main gate of the magnificent Palace of Ibrahim *Pasha*."

"We're finally here, the *Janissary* School."

"This looks like a palace."

"The Sister of the Sultan lives here, but part of the palace is a school for two thousand, some of whom will become pages."

At the gate to the third Courtyard, two young *janissaries* blocked the *dragoman*'s entrance. "State your business."

"Do you know who I am?" The *dragoman* did not wait for the guards to answer. "I represent the Grand Vizier Hasan *the Fruiterer*. Bring the *Agha* of the *Janissary* School to me, at once."

"Wait here." The taller of the two guards left his post.

A minute later the *Agha* appeared. "*Dragoman*, come in. You must for-give the new guards."

"I can see I've been gone too long. Sultan Mehmet III wants you to train these boys."

"You saw the Sultan?"

"Yes, after the two boys were circumcised as Muslims, I presented them to the Sultan." The *dragoman* lowered his voice. "But I must tell you something."

"Please come inside."

The two boys, dressed in the dark red robes that they had received when they were taken from their mother, entered the Third Courtyard of the Palace.

The *dragoman* pushed the youngest boy ahead. "Move!"

When the group reached the schoolmaster's office, the *Agha* peered down at the two boys. "You are now *acemi oglanlar*, novice boys.

"After you are trained, you will become *janissary* soldiers," the *dragoman* said.

"Let me take a good look at you." The *Agha* lifted the chin of the oldest boy and turned to the *dragoman*. "Where did you find them?"

"The Grand Vizier issued a firman in the name of the Sultan and collected them in the Balkan Mountains of Bulgaria." The *dragoman* recalled the mother of the boys calling it 'Blood Tribute', but failed to relay the anger she had shown the Grand Vizier. "I just brought them from the Hagia Sophia Mosque."

"Do they know the first pillar of Islam?"

"I know the *Shahadah*," the older boy said.

"Tell me."

"There is no god but Allah and Mohammed is his Prophet."

"I see he learns quickly." The *Agha* turned to the *dragoman*. "With an aptitude like that he might become a provincial governor or even a vizier for the Sultan."

"But the younger one will probably take more time."

"We have time. We normally would first assign them to good families in Anatolia to learn Turkish, but not this year."

"The rebellion?"

"It grows."

"I thought the rebel leader *Scrivano* died." The *dragoman* knew *Kara Yazici* had been called *Scrivano* because he was a scribe.

"He did, but his brother took over," the *Agha* said. "We can teach the boys Turkish here. According to the rules, they will be here for seven years."

"Seven years?" the older boy asked. "Will we ever go home?"

The *Agha* ignored the protest. "We will teach you the Sharia, the law of the Qur'an and the hadith, the traditions. Your teachers will instruct you in calligraphy and arithmetic. And if you show an aptitude, you will learn languages, including Arabic and Persian."

"Do I have to?" the younger one asked.

"If you don't change your attitude, you will be known as a reject," the *dragoman* said. "Don't disappoint me."

"On the other hand, I could send you to the Topkapi Palace School," the *Agha* said. "You could become a white eunuch."

As soon as the *dragoman* translated, the older boy shook his head. "Eunuchs lose body parts. I don't want my brother to lose any body parts. It isn't right."

"It won't hurt," the *dragoman* said.

"Liar!" the young boy said. "I'm still in pain from the circumcision."

"Do you want the cane?" the *Agha* asked. "Remember, *Yeniceri* or *janissary* means 'New Troop'. Sultan Murad I originally created the corps to be loyal to him. It is a great honor to serve the Sultan. "

"The *dragoman* told us that."

The *Agha* waved for a white eunuch, who had arrived in the doorway. "Boys, you are assigned to the leader of your barracks." He told the eunuch. "Take the boys through the courtyard."

When the boys and their new leader exited, the *Agha* turned. "What were you going to tell me at the gate?"

"When I saw the Sultan, he coughed and turned pale."

"You mean?"

"It's just what I saw."

"The older *janissaries* like Sultan Mehmet III, because he once led them into battle."

"The Grand Vizier, too, likes the Sultan," the *dragoman* said. "At the Battle of Keresztes in Hungary, the Sultan picked up the banner of Mohammed that had been brought from Damascus and turned the tide."

"If the Sultan dies, his able son, Prince Mahmud would reign."

"Will there be a change?" the *dragoman* asked. "I saw Sun'Ullah *Effendi* talking with the *sipahis* after prayers."

"Rumors are that the *sipahis* are upset because of the rebellion in Anatolia," the *Agha* said. "The Chief White Eunuch Gazanfer *Agha* persuaded the Sultan to appoint one of his own eunuchs as commander."

"But that campaign failed."

"Yes, and now the *sipahis* may want Sun'Ullah Effendi to be reinstated as Grand Mufti."

"They want a new religious leader?"

"Be careful, *dragoman*. These are tumultuous times."

The *Agha* and the *dragoman* rejoined the two boys and their eunuch leader in the courtyard. Along one wall some of the *acemi oglanlar* worked out with weights. Using a pulley system, one of the students reached with the right arm, and braced himself against the wall with his left.

"The weights start as low as twenty pounds, something even the young ones can carry," the *Agha* said. "But it can increase to over one hundred pounds."

Across the yard, older *janissary* students carried heavy timbers, also to build strength.

"Will we also learn to fight?" the older boy asked.

"Yes, we will teach you to wage Ghaza, the Jihad." The *Agha* gestured to another part of the courtyard, where students shot arrows at targets. In a corner, other recruits practiced sword fighting. "But you must remember the Greater Jihad is the quest for a perfect spiritual life. It is the struggle against sin within oneself."

"What's the Lesser Jihad?"

"The Lesser Jihad is the struggle against the environment. It includes armed conflict. A person who fights is called a *mujahideen* or *ghazi*."

"So that is why we will be training?" the older boy asked.

"Yes, you will be *janissaries* for the Sultan," the *dragoman* said. "And the Sultan himself is a *Ghazi* because after he led our army to victory at the Battle of Keresztes, he gained the title of *Ghazi* warrior."

"And the Khan of our allies, the Crimean Tartars, is known by his name, *Ghazi* Giray II," the *Agha* said.

The eunuch quickly moved towards the two boys. They jumped back. The eunuch smiled. "Only testing your reactions."

"Within the Lesser Jihad," the *Agha* said, "there is a defensive jihad and an offensive jihad. The defensive jihad is in *dar al-Islam* or the 'land of Islam,' while the offensive war is in the *dar al-Harb* or 'land of war.'"

"This feels like school," the older boy said.

"This is school."

"Before Sultan Mehmet II, who was later known as Mehmet the Conqueror, captured Constantinople, the city was in the *dar al-Harb*, or the Land of War," the *dragoman* said. "Now, the city is in the *dar al-Islam*, the Land of Allah."

"The Lesser Jihad continues," the *Agha* said. "Sultan Mehmet III wants to expand the empire into the heart of Europe, even to Vienna."

"We call Vienna the apple of the Danube," the *dragoman* said. "If the Persians don't attack from the East, the Grand Vizier might lead the army up the Danube."

"According to the Sultan's wishes," the *Agha* said, "I will teach these two boys."

"Very well." The *dragoman* turned to the boys. "You two must obey. The *Agha* will tell me if you do not."

"But from now on, only your leader can punish you," the *Agha* said. "According to the code of the corps, you must obey and submit to your superiors, but within the compound you are protected from outsiders."

"You will be staying in the barracks with about twenty-five other cadets." The Eunuch led the two boys past their cauldron. The youngest boy looked at the *dragoman* one last time, before disappearing into the barracks.

Pleased with delivering the *devshirme*, the *dragoman* left the *Janissary* School.

"Where to now, *dragoman*?" the guard asked.

"To the baths."

Chapter 16 - French Translator Filiz

*To try the truth, she [Aisha, Sister of the Sultan] found means to find out many [who]
could speak English, [and] French . . .*

John Smith

*In the middle of the seraglio were the women's apartments, with gardens, courtyards,
loggias, baths, and fountains. In the center of one of the gardens, and quite surrounded by
fountains, was a chamber entirely inlaid with precious marble.*

*But, beautiful as these apartments were in their decoration, they were too dark for the
modern taste, and somewhat melancholy. The captain of the sea accordingly constructed
an apartment especially for the use of the bride [Aisha, Daughter of Sultan Murad III].*

*It consisted of a salon adorned with mosaics like majolica. Next to this was a vaulted
chamber in mosaics and gold, and frescoed in part; in this chamber was a fountain.*

"The Marriage of Ibrahim *Pasha*: An Episode at the Court of Sultan Murad III,
1586"--per accounts by the Venetian Ambassador
Studies in the History of Venice, Vol. II by Horatio F. Brown

Salon, Ibrahim *Pasha* Palace, *Jumada II*, AH 1011 (AD 1602)

"MADAM AISHA." THE Overseer bowed at the entrance of the salon,
where the Sister of the Sultan read her Qur'an.

"What is it?" Aisha raised her eyes from her desk.

"You have guests waiting."

"Ah, my friends?"

"Yes, the English translator Emine and another by the name of Filiz."

"Don't stand there. Bring them to me, at once." Aisha closed her gold-
bound Qur'an.

Low sunbeams streamed through the tall windows of the salon and
caught the facets of jewels inlaid in her golden desk. Outside, on the other
side of the harem garden, her two friends crossed on a broad path, walking past a kiosk, a perfect place for private conversations.

At the door of the salon, beneath the loggia, the arched walkway that enclosed her apartments in the midst of the garden, Aisha embraced her trustworthy friend. "Emine, so good to see you and so soon."

"I promised I would bring Filiz."

"It's been so long." Filiz stepped back. "I like your jacket."

"Thank you." Aisha appreciated the compliment. As servants helped her friends with their coats, she led them past the mosaic walls and to a couch. "To be honest, I am a little confused."

"What do you mean?" Filiz sat near the powerful Sister of the Sultan.

"I do not know whether the slave Hasan *the Fruiterer* gave me is Bohemian or English." Aisha rehearsed how the Grand Vizier had written to her about how he had defeated the Bohemian on the battlefield. "Emine, like me, questions whether John is indeed English."

"Yes," Emine interjected. "He speaks English fluently, but what does that prove?"

"When we stopped," Aisha said, "John told us he planned to go to France."

"Well, I know French." Filiz pulled back her hijab. Her wavy hair reached her shoulders. Like Aisha and Emine, Filiz wore a short jacket over her silk blouse.

"And so does John, at least that's what he told Emine and me." Aisha rose and, leaving the servants, led Filiz and Emine to the kiosk in the garden. Sitting inside on the benches, the morning sun warmed them.

Filiz looked around. "And where is this John?"

"My mother insists that he work all the time," Aisha said. "She says a house slave needs to earn his keep."

"But Emine told me he was injured."

"John's feeling better." Aisha glanced toward the Overseer, who had followed them within earshot. "I sneak food to him in the slave quarters every day."

"Your shish kebab is so tasty," Filiz said. "I remember the last time I visited."

"And your soups are delicious," Emine added.

"That's so kind of both of you," Aisha said. "We'd better get started. My mother went to the grave of my father and will not return for hours. I want to learn as much as I can."

"Your mother didn't insist you come along?" Filiz asked.

"She wants the ransom more than I." Aisha waved to the Overseer.

"Bring John to us, and have the servants bring coffee."

The tall, black eunuch frowned. "As you wish." He bowed.

Minutes later, her new slave walked past a leafless apple tree and appeared at the door.

Aisha extended her arm and with her palm facing down, curled her hand and motioned. "Come here, capitano." As the brown-bearded captain slowly walked through the center of the kiosk, Aisha gestured, adding in Italian, "Have a seat."

Captain John Smith sat down opposite the three women. After the servant girl served him coffee in a small cup, he sipped the brew. "It's bitter." He squinted and coughed, then picked loose grounds from his teeth.

Aisha almost laughed. "Add some sugar." As John regained his composure, she motioned. "My friend speaks French."

"A pleasure to meet you." John extended his hand, but took it back when he saw the coffee grounds on his fingers.

"Comment allez-vous, Jean?" Filiz asked.

"Bien, merci, mademoseille," John said. "Comment vous appelez-vous?"

"Je m'appelle, Filiz."

Filiz told Aisha in Turkish that she had translated her name and turned back to John. "Emine told me that you went to Orleans. Can you tell us about that?"

"Naturellement." John paused. "Filiz? Where did you learn French?"

"My father, who was French, along with other merchants from Nice and Marseilles, sailed in the Mediterranean. When a terrible storm disabled our ship, pirates plundered the vessel and took the passengers to Algiers. I was presented to the Ottoman governor."

"I see," John said, in French.

"As you may know, until about ten years ago all Christian vessels, other than the Venetians, flew under the French flag, so it was not uncommon for those taken or captured to end up in women's market in Constantinople. But you? Tell us about your journey to France."

"When I left King's Lynn in England," John began, "I sailed with Peregrine Bertie and his French tutor to Orleans. The English Queen Elizabeth aided King Henry IV in the French King's fight against the Duke of Mercoeur. With the support of the aging King of Spain, that ardent Duke of the Catholic League controlled the whole of Brittany. King Philip II lived outside Madrid, at his palace monastery at *San Lorenzo d'el Escorial."*

"We heard about him sending an armada and attacking England," Emine said.

"Even though Queen Elizabeth had defeated the Spanish Armada in 1588, King Philip II still caused much mischief in France and the Lowlands."

"John, tell us about your adventures in France." Aisha sipped her coffee.

"After sailing past Dunkirk we saw the Flag of Spain flying over the captured fortress at Calais."

Chapter 17 - Bertie Brothers at Orleans

At last, he [John Smith] found means to attend Master Peregrine Bertie into France, second son to the Right Honorable Peregrine, that generous Lord Willoughby and famous soldier; where coming to his [older] brother Robert, then at Orleans . . .

John Smith

They [German students] are not only attracted by the lessons given there [the University of Orleans], but the purity of the language. The French now spoken in Orleans is as pure as [the Greek] once spoken in Attica [ancient Athens].

Paul Hentzner, German Lawyer
Voyages in Parts of Europe, 1596 to 1600
Translated from French

English Channel, Late Spring 1596

THE MOON HAD not quite faded from sight when a breeze stirred the low fog below the cliffs of Dover. Like whiffs of smoke from a candle, the light fog dissipated. With each passing moment the sun edged higher; its morning rays brightened the cliffs pure white. As the swells rolled across the English Channel, fishing vessels dipped and rose again.

The captain brought the wheel around. "Mates! Keep a sharp eye!" Wind filled the foresail of the small vessel from King's Lynn. It tacked closer to the shores of France.

"Aye! Captain!" The sailor in the crow's nest shaded his eyes. "No sign of pirates this morning."

At the bow of the ship, sixteen year-old John Smith stood next to Peregrine Bertie and his French tutor. John could not believe he was actually sailing. Several English merchant vessels and Dutch Men-of War plied the channel waters.

Only a day earlier, John had departed Lynn, where Master Thomas Sendall had employed him as an indentured servant. Now John attended the needs of Peregrine Bertie on the sea going to France, for what he hoped would be the first of many travels.

"We used to only worry about pirates from Dunkirk, but they were further away," the French tutor said. "Now, we worry about Calais in Picardy."

"What do you mean?" John asked. "That's part of France."

"In late April, Calais fell to Cardinal Albert of Austria. He captured Fort Risban and now Calais belongs to Spain." The tutor gestured to the far shoreline.

A flag—a simple red cross on a plain background—waved above a fort. The tower of Fort Risban controlled the entrance to the town's harbor.

"An Austrian?" John asked.

"The House of Austria rules Spain, but make no mistake," the French tutor said, "Spain is the enemy of both France and England."

"And the Free Dutch Republic," Peregrine Bertie added.

John remembered hearing how years earlier, Peregrine's father had fought against the Spanish in Holland. "Calais is so close to Dover."

"Spain's capture of Calais is very serious," the tutor said. "Queen Elizabeth had offered to help King Henry IV by sending the Earl of Essex."

"What happened?"

"The Earl of Essex was at Plymouth and prepared for a major expedition. When the Queen received Ambassador *de* Sancy from France, she said she would defend Calais, but on one condition."

"What condition?"

"The Queen wanted to occupy the town for herself," the tutor said.

"She did?"

"Yes," the tutor said, "the French Ambassador told Queen Elizabeth that King Henry IV could still prevent Calais from being taken, or recapture it, if lost. The Ambassador added that King Henry IV would much rather see the place in possession of the Spaniard than in the hands of her Majesty."

"And the Queen's response?" Peregrine asked.

"She told him that she thought the Ambassador had overstepped his authority, but *de* Sancy replied, 'the King, my master, could not imagine that such a demand could possibly have been made, so dearly he cherishes the honor of your friendship.'"

"And after the ambassador left?" John asked.

"Queen Elizabeth sent Sir Robert Sidney to Boulogne to ask King

Henry for Calais for herself. The King responded that he was ready to conquer Calais in person, but would never give it up to the Queen."

"He did?"

"*Oui*," the tutor said. "The French King added, 'If I am to be bitten, I should like as well to submit to the lion as the lioness.'"

"King Henry sounds very upset." John asked, "But happened to the Earl of Essex?"

"Along with Francis Vere, the Earl of Essex and Lord High Admiral Charles Howard have gathered their fleet. The English expedition is sailing south and may raid the Portuguese coastline or the Azores. They want to intercept this year's Spanish Silver Fleet from the West Indies."

"Is Sir Francis Drake going, too?" John asked.

"Haven't you heard?" Peregrine asked.

"What?"

"After almost capturing a silver ship in Puerto Rico last autumn, Sir Drake went to Panama and attempted to capture the Spanish gold." Peregrine frowned. "That's when it happened."

"Did Drake die in an attack?"

"No, but after he returned to his ship, Drake passed away from illness. He died in January. The bad news reached London in April."

"The Spanish consider the hero Drake to be the worst pirate in the world," the tutor said, "but another knight will soon be going."

"Who?" John asked.

"Sir Walter Raleigh, who once planted a colony in Virginia, a colony lost and never found." The tutor added, "The fall of Calais may change everything."

"What do you mean?" Peregrine asked.

"King Henry IV is determined to get Calais back and the Queen cannot allow a Spanish port to be in sight of Dover. Even as we speak, France and England have negotiated a treaty."

"And the Dutch?" John asked.

"The Stadtholder Maurice of Nassau and his cousin, Lewis Gunther, along with hundreds of Dutch sailors and soldiers have joined the Earl of Essex and Francis Vere in the expedition south," the tutor said. "Queen Elizabeth appreciates their help, but still considers the Dutch Republic to be under her protection."

French Countryside, Spring 1596

AFTER THE SHIP landed and the three travelers disembarked, they hired a carriage. Riding on the rough road across the French countryside, John peered out the window. Many fields were unattended, overgrown with weeds. Pockmarked buildings needed repair. They passed scores of families fleeing the war.

"Probably heading to Paris for food," the tutor said.

After several days of travel, John, Peregrine, and the tutor reached Orleans, passing over a moat and through a strong gate. In a sparsely occupied square, they alighted from the carriage as a few French noblemen exited the cathedral.

John looked up at the large church. "Damaged in the wars?"

"*Oui*. King Henry IV would like to rebuild Sainte Croix Cathedral," the tutor answered in French.

The shortest French nobleman shook his head. "Our King won't be able to restore it to its former splendor until Cardinal Albert leaves Calais."

"We're looking for an Englishman named Robert Bertie, the son of Lord Willoughby," Peregrine said.

"The army encampment is across the river. You might try there." The French nobleman pointed the way.

Stone Bridge, Orleans, France, Early Summer 1596

THE LATE AFTERNOON sun cast long shadows onto the Loire River. A small vessel sailed beneath one of the dozen arches of the long stone bridge connecting Orleans to the South embankment. The river flowed steadily southwest. Towers on both ends, as well as on the island in the middle of the river, protected the bridge and Orleans from attack.

"Do you see the North Tower?" the tutor asked.

"*Oui*," John said.

"And you certainly must have heard of Joan of Arc?"

"Who hasn't?"

"In French she is known as Jeanne *la Pucelle*."

"The maid."

"Yes, around 1429, towards the end of the Hundred Year's War, Joan of Arc was only a teenager," the tutor said. "She received visions from God, who told her to help the Dauphin Charles."

"Dauphin?"

"Dauphin means the dolphin, but it also means 'King to be.'"

"What does that have to do with this bridge?" John asked.

"The English, who were still Catholic, had laid siege to Orleans," the tutor said. "They bombarded the North Tower and Orleans was ready to fall, but *La Pucelle* arrived in time."

"A French maid attacked the English?"

"The Maid of Orleans not only attacked, but also rallied the French to victory. She went overland, but waited for favorable winds to bring supplies down the Loire. With her white standard flying high, she wore a metal breastplate. Against all odds, she led the French to victory with a frontal attack on the two-towered gatehouse, *Les Tourelles*." The tutor pointed. "Over there."

"You mean she dressed up like a man?" John asked.

"That's what the English claimed, but to the French, she was dressed as a soldier."

When they reached the far side, a noblewoman in a hooped skirt watched several groups of women washing clothes. They beat the clothes with sticks and rinsed the garments along the river banks.

Peregrine pointed to a small encampment. "I see Robert!"

John, too, recognized the eldest son of Lord Willoughby. The carriage came to a stop.

A narrow saber at his side, Robert Bertie ran across the field. "Peregrine! You made it."

The two brothers embraced and Robert turned to John. "And John Smith! What a surprise to see you."

"How do you like my new attendant?" Peregrine asked.

Robert smiled. "You couldn't have found a better one."

"We brought you victuals." John showed him the salted meat they had purchased from the butcher in Lynn.

"And the supplies you wanted," the tutor added.

"The wars over religion have devastated France," Robert said. "It is difficult to find everything we need."

"We noticed much destruction on the way here," John said.

"Last year's poor harvest did not help," Robert added, "and Cardinal Albert's attacks in Calais and La Fere cost France much."

"We saw refugees from Picardy fleeing the frontier. Will we be staying here?" John asked.

"No," Robert said, "at the Hotel Groslot, at least for a while." He tied his horse to the back of the carriage.

All climbed inside. When they crossed the bridge back into Orleans, a woman of the evening approached the carriage. "Perhaps you fellows would like to have some company?"

"Not tonight," the tutor said, firmly.

Hotel Groslot, Orleans, France, June 1596

THE CARRIAGE THAT held the English travelers soon stopped in front of a red brick building. Peregrine Bertie and his French tutor exited first. The hotel owner stood at the hotel entrance and greeted Robert.

"This is my younger brother, Peregrine."

While the hotel owner escorted the Bertie brothers inside, an older woman came out and greeted the tutor. John, meanwhile, went to retrieve the luggage. He noticed that the prostitute had followed them.

She approached him once more. When John set down a bag, she said, "Surely you can use some company."

John shook his head and picked up the luggage.

As he carried the supplies they had brought from King's Lynn in England into the Hotel, John breathed in the aroma of freshly baked bread.

"You must be famished." Robert watched John step towards the source. "The fare here may be simple, but it's good."

At the door of the dining area, the wife of the hotel owner asked, "Both of you are sons of Lord Willoughby?"

"We are." Robert gestured to his brother. The familial features were unmistakable.

"Come. Have the best seat. Your Queen Elizabeth once sent Lord Willoughby to help our beloved King Henry."

"As soon as the treaty with France is signed, the Queen will once more help your King," Robert said.

"Though the English were once our enemies, today you are our friends." The owner motioned to the slender girl beside him. "My daughter will take care of you."

While the tutor conversed with the owner, the owner's daughter came over and smiled. *"Bon Jour."*

John stood up and tipped his hat. *"Bon Jour, Mademoiselle."*

"Parlez vous francais?" she asked.

"Oui, un peu. Our tutor teaches us more each day." John's stomach growled.

The daughter looked at him and laughed. "What language is that?"

"I guess I'm hungry."

"Tonight, we serve my mother's favorite onion soup with cheese." She led them to a table. "Have a seat."

"I've had it before." Robert sat. "Onion soup is particularly good."

Minutes later, the French maid returned with the soup. John caught a whiff. "It smells delicious."

"Go ahead, eat," she said.

He picked up the spoon. *"Merci, beaucoup."* It tasted unexpectedly different.

Merchants, soldiers, and students sat at the long tables in the crowded dining room.

Interior of a French Hotel in 1500s

"We couldn't help but overhear your conversation." A German student turned his chair. "We're also learning French."

"The French spoken in Orleans is as pure as anything in all of France," a second student added. "We study French at the University of Orleans."

"Perhaps, you can introduce Peregrine and John to your instructor," the tutor suggested. "I must tutor them in French every day."

"Perhaps we can," the German said. "And you?"

"I want to help King Henry like my father," Robert said.

"Against the Cardinal?"

Robert agreed. *"Oui."*

"You must not underestimate him," the German student said.

"What do you mean?" John asked.

"My father is a banker for the Spanish King," the German student said. "I accompanied him to the admired palace, talked at length with the King's servants, and learned how strong the Spanish truly are."

"Do you mind if we listen in?" a French officer asked.

Robert made room for two French officers. Both pulled their chairs closer.

"About a year ago, in the spring of 1595, King Philip II had his daughter *Infanta* Isabella at his side at their Palace Monastery outside Madrid, *San Lorenzo d'el Escorial.*"

Chapter 18 - *Infanta* Isabella of Spain

"Simplicity in construction, severity in the whole, nobility without arrogance, majesty without ostentation."

King Philip II of Spain
Instructions to the Architects of *San Lorenzo d'el Escorial*

The King's [Philip II's] health is still causing alarm. The doctors say that his body is so withered and feeble that it is almost impossible that a human being in such a state should live for long.

Francesco Vendramin, Venetian Ambassador to Spain
Madrid, 13 May 1595

Royal Library, *San Lorenzo d'el Escorial*, Spain, Spring 1595

INFANTA ISABELLA CLARA Eugenia, the daughter of the King of Spain, shut a large book in the Royal Library. Her father, King Philip II, had asked her to find and retrieve it the previous afternoon. Meticulously dressed in a blue-green gown with a silk bodice and gold embroidering, *Infanta* Isabella rose from the marble and jasper table. A barrette held her long, dark hair in place. She walked past a large globe of the earth, and approached the elderly librarian. "Thank you again for helping me to locate this. My father will be pleased."

The barrel-vaulted library of *San Lorenzo d'el Escorial*, second only to the Vatican in size and quality, contained thousands of volumes. Tall bookcases lined the walls of the long room, built over the main entrance

Infanta Isabella Clara Eugenia

of the massive Palace Monastery. The forests outside Havana provided some of the wood.

"Sometimes books are difficult to find," the male librarian said. Unlike other libraries, the edges of the pages in the Royal Library faced outward, in order to preserve the books. "As are relics of saints."

"You refer to my father's search to find and bring back relics."

"King Philip II has been more successful than most. Not only with relics, but also with books and manuscripts."

Infanta Isabella's father had accumulated more than forty thousand volumes, including a Bible written on gold leaf. Several thousand manuscripts could also be found—some more than one thousand years old. In addition to Arabic manuscripts from Granada and assorted Persian manuscripts, the library contained a copy of the Qur'an, richly decorated. In a secure part of the library, those with special permission could even gain access to books banned and confiscated during the ongoing Inquisition.

"As soon as I finish reading the passages to my father, I promise to return it." *Infanta* Isabella handed the book to her Lady-in-Waiting to carry.

"I hope so." The librarian smirked. "You do know the penalty for stealing from this library, don't you?"

"Certainly," *Infanta* Isabella said, curtly. "But that does not apply to the royal family. It is the Royal library. Has theft been a problem lately?"

"Not since Pope Gregory XIII issued the decree. The threat of excommunication from the church more often than not suffices to keep potential perpetrators in line."

"If any book is stolen, that thief would face God Himself on Judgment Day," *Infanta* Isabella said. "Only the Catholic Church could save him."

"No good Catholic would risk excommunication and the fires of hell." The librarian asked, "Will there be anything else?"

"No," *Infanta* Isabella replied. She glanced up at the rounded ceiling. The fresco of King Solomon entertaining the Queen of Sheba looked as fresh as the day it had been painted. Her father believed that rulers should be wise like Solomon. And her father had a great need to be wise as he had vast dominions under his crown encompassing not only the Kingdom of Spain, but also of New Spain, including Mexico and Peru. He also ruled Naples and Sicily, as well the Lowlands, including Brabant and Flanders. Holland and Zeeland were in rebellion.

The more than twenty-five hundred windows of the granite palace showed the morning sun rising higher. The rays illuminated the *Sierra de Guadarrama*, the mountains northwest of Madrid. A little more than three decades earlier, *Infanta* Isabella's father had moved the capital of Spain from his birthplace in Valladolid to the geographic center of the Iberian Peninsula.

"I must go to prayer before I see my good father," she said.

"Is King Philip II well?" the librarian asked.

"Better, the gout has subsided." *Infanta* Isabella grabbed her white-laced handkerchief. "But as you know, my father likes to start work promptly at 8:00. I must be going."

Puerta Principal del Monasterio, San Lorenzo d'el Escorial

WHEN *INFANTA* ISABELLA and her Lady-in-Waiting reached the ground floor, a guard by the *Puerta Principal de Monasterio* greeted her "*Infanta* Isabella?"

"Sí?"

"Albert of Austria, the Cardinal Archbishop of Toledo, arrives."

Infanta Isabella touched her kerchief to her lips. "Albert comes early." Cardinal Archbishop Albert was the younger brother to the Holy Roman Emperor, Rudolph II, to whom she was promised in marriage at the age of two. Though the contract had been signed, Rudolph waited twenty years then broke the agreement. She had grown up with the expectation of her marriage to Rudolph. That had never happened.

Infanta Isabella headed through the main door. A man led a monk riding on a donkey away from the Palace Monastery. Tall towers anchored the four corners of the yellow granite palace-monastery that overlooked the small town. The whole structure of the palace with its plain, straight lines and smooth facades resembled the gridiron on which the ancient Romans had crucified Lorenzo.

Infanta Isabella waited for the carriage of the Archbishop, still in the distance. The territo-

ry of Toledo provided her cousin Cardinal Albert the richest income of any Archbishopric in the Roman Catholic Church.

Meanwhile, an attendant exercising *Infanta* Isabella's white horse approached the daughter of the King of Spain and bowed. "My Lady, will you be riding your horse this afternoon?"

Infanta Isabella stroked the young horse on the forehead. "I won't have time today. We have guests."

"I see. Yes, My Lady." The attendant led the white horse away.

She turned to her Lady-in-Waiting. "You may go."

The Lady-in-Waiting took the book back to the Royal Apartments.

When the carriage pulled up, *Infanta* Isabella greeted her cousin. "Archbishop Albert, you arrived quickly."

Cardinal Archbishop Albert, dressed in ecclesiastical regalia, alighted from the carriage. "Your father urgently asked for my presence, so I rode all night from Toledo."

"He'll be expecting us after prayers."

Cardinal Albert nodded and stared back at the Western wall through which he had just passed. Like the other three walls surrounding the palace, it was more than four stories tall and seven hundred feet long. Framed by huge granite blocks which had taken forty-eight pair of oxen to transport, the white door with copper knockers stood twenty feet high and twelve feet wide. "I had forgotten how large this magnificent palace was."

"My father oversaw many of the details," *Infanta* Isabella said.

"Truly a reflection of him," Cardinal Albert said.

"He told his architect that he wanted, 'Simplicity in construction, severity in the whole, nobility without arrogance, and majesty without ostentation.' Most of all, my father wanted to build a final, resting place for his father."

"Holy Roman Emperor Charles V."

"And to honor Saint Lorenzo," *Infanta* Isabella said as they walked towards the doors of the main entrance.

"Yes, your father named this palace in honor of the Saint he credited for his victory against the French at the battle of San Quentin." Cardinal Albert pointed to a huge figure of Saint Lorenzo carved above Philip's Coat of Arms and the door.

"But the honor he gave to the Saint was more than just in naming this monastery *San Lorenzo d'el Escorial*."

The two cousins entered through the main door of the large palace. The palace not only housed the Royal Apartments and the Basilica, but also a college for priests and a monastery for monks. The mausoleum, though planned, had not yet been built underneath the church. Panels in relief on each side of the main doorway depicted gridirons.

Basilica, San Lorenzo d'el Escorial, Spain

INFANTA ISABELLA AND Cardinal Albert strolled together across the *Patio de los Reyes.* Like each of the sixteen palace courtyards, walls nearly four stories high fronted the enclosed Courtyard of the Kings, named for the Old Testament Kings of Judah. Six large statues on a ledge above the arched doors of the Basilica depicted six of those kings. A pair of bell towers framed the front of the Basilica, the central building of the whole complex. A simple, round dome rose high above the far end of the nave.

Cardinal Albert, whose first assignment after he entered the priesthood was to serve the Pilgrim Church in Rome, a church founded by the mother of Emperor Constantine, would have recognized the similarity between this dome and the open one in the Basilica of St. Peter's in Rome.

Bells rang out from the two towers.

Students from the college and monks from the monastery entered through the side doors. *Infanta* Isabella, accompanied by her cousin, climbed the steps and entered the Basilica through the center door, the one reserved for members of the Royal Family.

At the far end of the nave, beyond the light streaming from the dome, *Infanta* Isabella saw the high altar.

A priest walked toward Cardinal Albert. "Archbishop, will you help with the mass this morning?"

"It will be my honor." Cardinal Albert moved to the front of the high altar, while *Infanta* Isabella took her position of honor in her family's section.

Beyond the altar, three reredos or screens reached more than fifty feet high. In the center of the red granite and jasper screen, an artist had drawn the final minutes of Saint Lorenzo's life.

The nearly naked Saint sat on an iron grill. Bright flames rose from below. She could almost feel the heat. A Roman guard with a small pitchfork poked at the beleaguered saint who seemed to accept his fate. Lorenzo was a martyr for the faith in the century before Constantine became the first Christian Emperor of the ancient Roman Empire. *Infanta* Isabella's father would be willing to make sacrifices, too.

Below the Basilica, the remains of her Grandfather Charles V would be kept. Charles was a true King of Spain, the grandson of Ferdinand of Castile and Isabella of Aragon. They had united their kingdoms in marriage before Granada fell and Columbus discovered the New World.

Below the high altar, the yet-to-be completed Mausoleum would be the final resting place for other members of the Royal Family as well, including Don Juan of Austria. Don Juan, the half-brother of King Philip II, had led the Christian victory over the Turks at the Battle of Lepanto in 1571, ending Ottoman domination of the Mediterranean Sea.

The pious *Infanta* Isabella did not want to think of her father's impending death. When the gout severely afflicted him, he finalized his will. Her younger brother, Philip, would inherit the Spanish crown.

King Ferdinand and Queen Isabella in 1486

Infanta Isabella glanced at the opposite chair. Her brother Philip was not there. Nearby, however, she recognized Philip William of Nassau, the Prince of Orange.

Other women might not consider the weighty matters of state, but the daughter of the King of Spain had been groomed to rule. Her father had once attempted to install her on the throne of France. *Infanta* Isabella had a claim, since her mother was the daughter of the French King Henry II. But the Valois dynasty had passed. Henry of Navarre and the Bourbons claimed the French throne.

At the end of the Latin Mass, *Infanta* Isabella knelt before the altar. Her cousin gave her the elements—the bread and the wine. When she raised her eyes, *Infanta* Isabella saw her father looking down from his bedroom window up above, to the side of the altar.

The Royal Apartments of the House of Austria had been built behind the high altar. Behind the shuttered window on the left, *Infanta* Isabella had her bedroom. The other window, however, was open. Her father acknowledged her.

After the service, *Infanta* Isabella approached her cousin Cardinal Albert. "I believe my father is ready to see us."

"I'd like to go through the Hall of Battles."

"You seem to know my father's plans," *Infanta* Isabella said.

Prince Philip William of Orange approached. "Sorry to intrude, but I just wanted to greet you." The forty-year-old Catholic Prince of Orange asked, "Archbishop Albert, are you here to discuss the Lowlands?"

"The King might want some spiritual insight," Cardinal Albert replied.

"The infidels have grown too strong," *Infanta* Isabella said.

The Archbishop looked at the praying monks. "Perhaps it would be best if we continue this discussion upstairs in the Hall."

Salas *de* Batallas, San Lorenzo d'el Escorial, Spain

PRINCE PHILIP WILLIAM of Orange accompanied Cardinal Archbishop Albert of Austria and *Infanta* Isabella of Spain to the *Salas de Batallas*.

Inside the Hall of Battles, *Infanta* Isabella asked Prince Philip William, "How long have you been in Spain?"

"I was only thirteen years old and studying at the University in Brabant, when the former Governor of the Netherlands, the Duke of Alba sent me to Spain." Philip William's father, the former Prince William of Orange, had rebelled against the King of Spain nearly thirty years earlier. After a Catholic zealot had assassinated the teenage boy's Calvinist father, agents of the Duke of Alba, the Spanish Governor of the Netherlands, kidnapped Philip William. The teenager was taken to Spain and raised in the Roman Catholic faith under the watchful eye of the Jesuits and King Philip II.

"Do you have any doubts about your faith?" Cardinal Albert asked.

"No, Archbishop," Philip William said. "I am thankful that I've been brought up in the true faith; the Roman Catholic faith is all I know."

Large frescos lined both sides of the Hall of Battles. The paintings depicted the Battle of Higuera in 1431, when King John II of Castile defeated the Moors of Granada in the borderlands outside their capital. "This is my father's favorite painting," *Infanta* Isabella said.

Cardinal Albert pointed to the flags. "The Cross triumphed over the Crescent, but the *Reconquista* of Spain was not completed until sixty years later."

"When Granada fell in 1492," *Infanta* Isabella said.

On the opposite wall, one painting portrayed the Spanish *flotilla's* expedition to Teicera in the Azores against the Portuguese. "And this one?" Philip William asked.

"My father's first wife was *Infanta* Mary of Portugal but she died in childbirth. After that my father moved to England and married the Catholic Queen Mary of England." The *Infanta* did not voice that the English called her Bloody Mary, because she had persecuted so many Protestant heretics. "During this time the English joined with the Spanish to fight against the French at San Quentin."

The three stopped. Several paintings detailed her father's victory over the French.

"And these?" Philip William asked.

"Spanish Infantry defeated the French," *Infanta* Isabella said.

"The Feast Day of Saint Lorenzo," Cardinal Albert said, "on August 10, 1577."

"In honor of that Saint," *Infanta* Isabella added, "my father vowed to build this palace, *San Lorenzo d'el Escorial.*"

Infanta Isabella remembered the story how the year following her father's victory, Mary of England became ill and died. Her father then proposed to Mary's half-sister, Queen Elizabeth, but the English Parliament opposed the marriage, so Elizabeth declined her father's advances. It was not that bad for *Infanta* Isabella, however, since the following year her father married *Infanta* Isabella's mother, Elizabeth of Valois, the daughter of the French King Henry II. She had just turned fourteen.

Infanta Isabella never knew her grandfather. During the jousting match to celebrate her parent's marriage, her grandfather King Henry II was mortally wounded by the captain of his Scottish guard. Because of *Infanta* Isabella's lineage to the French throne, her father King Philip II felt *Infanta* Isabella had a claim not only to the throne of France, but also to the throne of England because of his previous marriage to Queen Mary.

Cardinal Albert, *Infanta* Isabella, and Prince Philip William entered the Royal Apartments, the Palace of the Austrians. When they reached her father's study, *Infanta* Isabella turned to her cousin. "I wonder if my father's gout has flared up today."

Nearing thirty years in age, *Infanta* Isabella also remained single, but things might change. She knew her father had plans for her.

Chapter 19 - Spanish Silver Fleet

After long labor and great danger of going to the bottom, the West Indies' fleet has safely come to port. It is very rich.

13th May 1595

This fleet has brought in the revenues of the years 1593 and 1594, and this autumn the revenue of this year is expected. If this reaches home safely, they reckon that in the course of five or six months thirty millions of gold [silver] will have been brought into the country. This is amazing and surpasses any record in the memory of man.

Francesco Vendramin, Venetian Ambassador to Spain

Madrid, 19th May 1595

Palacio de los Austrias, San Lorenzo d'el Escorial, May 1595

UNLIKE THE LAVISH High Altar of the Basilica, the King of Spain's apartment inside the *Palacio de los Austrias* was simply furnished. It was referred to as the Palace of the Austrians because the royal Habsburg family originally came from Austria. The study of King Philip II had white-washed walls and terra cotta tile floors, just like he wanted: majesty without ostentation.

Infanta Isabella turned to the Prince Philip William of Orange, "Wait here."

Infanta Isabella and Cardinal Archbishop Albert of Toledo approached the open bedroom door. The bedridden King raised his eyes. His stern expression lifted when he saw his daughter.

"How is the Most Catholic Majesty feeling today?" Cardinal Albert said.

"Thank you for asking." The King grimaced and clenched his teeth. "The gout is painful."

Cardinal Albert placed a relic, a tooth of a saint, on the side table. "I hope this will help."

"You know how much relics provide comfort to me."

"Let me shut the windows." *Infanta* Isabella walked to the window

144

that connected her father's bedroom to the Basilica. The strong smell of incense lingered. The contrast between the rich High Altar of the Basilica and her father's plain apartment was unmistakable.

At the High Altar where she had been praying minutes earlier, a monk prayed and interceded by the statues of Charles V. The statues of her widowed father and three of his wives stood, unmovable on the opposite side. She closed the shutters. The pure sound of the hand organ faded.

The view on the other side of her father's bedroom overlooked the forested foothills her father treasured. The King of Spain loved nature. It provided solace.

Of all the palaces surrounding Madrid, *San Lorenzo d'el Escorial* was her father's favorite. When her father was healthy, he could accomplish more in one day in the Royal Apartments than he could in four days at the Palace at Alcazar, the former Moor fortress inside Madrid.

King Philip trusted no one more than his loyal daughter *Infanta* Isabella, who read and translated all of the King's correspondence.

Beneath the canopy and atop the covers, the fully dressed King propped himself up from his pillows. "Where's my son?"

"Philip's gone hunting." *Infanta* Isabella leaned over and gave her father a kiss.

When *Infanta* Isabella's mother Elizabeth of Valois died, the King of Spain married for a fourth time. Ever since Anna of Austria, the mother of Philip, died more than a decade earlier, King Philip II had remained a widower. "Good daughter, help me up."

Assisted by *Infanta* Isabella and a waiting attendant, the King sat up, swung his legs over the edge, and requested, "Hand me my cane."

Infanta Isabella escorted her father into the study. "We took the Prince of Orange through the Hall of Battles."

"I see." The King sat down into a chair and lifted his foot onto a stool.

Philip William bowed and kissed the King's extended hand. "Your Majesty."

"You may stay."

"Does it concern the Lowlands?" Philip William stepped back.

"Yes, the Netherlands are of utmost concern to me." The King turned to Cardinal Albert. "Thank you for coming so quickly."

"I came as soon as I received your request," Cardinal Albert said.

"Your work overseeing the Inquisition when you were Viceroy of Portugal served me well," the King said. "I am pleased with your work as Archbishop of Toledo, but let me get to the point. The death of Archduke Ernest in the Lowlands last February has caused a vacancy for far too long."

"And you need someone to govern?" Cardinal Albert glanced at *Infanta* Isabella.

"I need someone I can trust." The King's voice grew stronger. "And no one is more trustworthy than you."

"Me?" Cardinal Albert stepped back. "I appreciate the honor, but what about my flock? I've not been Archbishop of Toledo that long."

"I know that being Archbishop meets your style. Your adherence to the Catholic doctrine is most admirable," the King said, "unlike your older brother, the Holy Roman Emperor Rudolph II."

"He's too interested in alchemy and collecting art," *Infanta* Isabella said.

"To accept such a position, I will have to be defrocked," Cardinal Albert said. "Even if I agree, will Pope Clement VIII agree? The Pope and you have not always seen eye to eye."

"Another Archbishop will be found," the King said. "But we can make sure part of the three hundred thousand *livres* a year stipend remains with you."

"How much?"

"Fifty thousand *livres*, but you may receive more. We expect the silver fleet from the West Indies to arrive soon."

"Is it not early in the year for the fleet?" *Infanta* Isabella asked.

"If winds are favorable, they should have already passed Havana," the King said. "I will need to communicate with the Pope."

"About stepping aside?" Cardinal Albert asked.

"About marrying Isabella." The King reached for his daughter's hand.

Infanta Isabella squeezed the King's hand to indicate her approval.

"Me?" Cardinal Albert eyes widened. "Marry my cousin?"

"We need to keep the obedient provinces of the Netherlands in the family," the King said. "And bring the rebellious provinces back into submission, by the Inquisition if necessary."

Cardinal Albert, not normally at a loss for words, stared at *Infanta* Isabella.

"Albert, I propose that you marry my daughter. As soon as the Pope gives his blessing to the union and you are married, the two of you will rule the Lowlands as co-sovereigns."

Infanta Isabella smiled.

"In the meantime?" Cardinal Albert asked.

"You must go to Brussels," the King said. "One last thing."

"What's that?"

The King gestured to the Prince of Orange. "Philip William of Orange will accompany you," the King ordered. "He will help you rule his father's lands for the Catholic faith."

"That would please me much," Philip William said.

"I see we are all in agreement," the King said.

"As you wish." *Infanta* Isabella knew the importance of the Lowlands to her father. The Counterreformation would proceed.

"I will start organizing my belongings," Cardinal Albert said. "But about the funds?"

"If the fleet does not arrive, we'll have to borrow from the bankers of Genoa or the Fugger family of Germany," the King said. "We can't let the King of France succeed."

Cardinal Archbishop Albert of Austria bowed and left the presence of his future bride and the King. The Prince of Orange followed the Archbishop out of the King's quarters.

When the King stood up, he swayed. *Infanta* Isabella rushed to steady her father and placed her hand on his forehead. "You have a fever."

King Phillip II of Spain

Her father stumbled forward toward the bed. "Help me."

"Doctor!"

SEVERAL DAYS AFTER he had agreed to be Spanish Governor in the Netherlands, Cardinal Albert rejoined his future bride *Infanta* Isabella in the King's study. *Infanta* Isabella arranged the stacks of letters on the desk and placed the petitions in order of importance. Cardinal Albert knew the King trusted his daughter, especially now: the King's recent flare-ups of gout had been serious.

With the aid of his doctors and the help of his crutch, King Philip II entered his study and crossed the room. When he sat down on a simple wooden chair beneath the crucifix, he slowly lifted his leg onto a resting stool. The white-bearded King did not look well.

When a doctor attempted to wipe the King's forehead with a towel, the King waved him away. "Leave us alone."

The doctor complied with the King's wishes. "We'll be outside."

A servant closed the door.

"Where's my son?" the King asked.

"Prince Philip has gone hunting," *Infanta* Isabella said.

"Again?" The King turned to his nephew. "Thank you for joining us, Albert."

"A delegation from the Council at Brussels has arrived," Cardinal Albert said. "They request more aid in the war against France."

"Let them wait. Send for my Foreign Minister."

Infanta Isabella went to the door.

"And my Chief Domestic Minister, too."

She told the messenger. "Bring Juan *de* Idiaquez and Cristobal *de* Moura to us."

As soon as the messenger left, *Infanta* Isabella asked, "Shall we begin?"

Her frail father sighed. "*Sí.*"

Like she did every day, *Infanta* Isabella began reading the letters. She lifted the first one. "We have correspondence about our aid in the fight against King Henry IV of France."

"How dare the French King declare war against us." the King said. "The Kingdom of Navarre should be ours, too. It should not belong to the House of Bourbon."

Shortly, the Foreign Minister Juan *de* Idiaquez appeared at the door. "I was down the hallway." He bowed. "One Jesuit attacked King Henry IV after Christmas with a knife. The French also found letters to the Spanish ambassador, so King Henry IV has expelled all of the Jesuits from France."

"We also have a message from Rome." *Infanta* Isabella picked up a letter. "Pope Clement VIII is still considering Henry's petition to officially rejoin the Catholic Church."

"That must be stopped." Philip leaned forward and coughed. "How can Henry ever claim to be a true Catholic?"

"I agree," Foreign Minister Idiaquez said. "After a supporter of the

Catholic League assassinated King Henry III, many Parisian Catholics wanted your daughter *Infanta* Isabella to be Queen of France. They refused to accept Henry III's distant cousin, the Huguenot King Henry of Navarre's claim to the French throne. But then the Parisians heard that Henry had partaken of the Catholic Mass, so they opened the gates of Paris to Henry of Navarre before *Infanta* Isabella could assume the throne."

"Not all members of the Catholic League agree with the Parisians." The King looked at his daughter. "By birthright of her mother Elizabeth of Valois and Elizabeth's father King Henry II, *Infanta* Isabella is entitled to the throne of France."

"The French believe in Salic Law," the foreign minister said.

"I know, only males can inherit the French throne." The King paused. "But there is still one member of the Catholic League who takes up arms against Henry of Navarre who calls himself King Henry IV of France."

"*Sí*, Sire. Philip Emanuel *de* Lorraine, the Duke of Mercoeur."

The King turned to Cardinal Albert. "When you go to Brussels, you must do everything you can to support the Duke of Mercoeur in Brittany."

"Already an army is being raised." Cardinal Albert glanced at the Chief Domestic Minister Cristobal *de* Moura entering the room. "But the funds are limited."

"How can we give more?" the King asked. "Our creditors from Germany want more security. The Silver Fleet from the West Indies has not arrived for two whole years." King Philip II turned to his daughter. "Any word from Lisbon?"

"I see letters." *Infanta* Isabella scanned the correspondence from Portugal. "The Portuguese nobility has been mustered because the English may attack."

The chief domestic minister stepped forward. "Provisions have been sent, but no sign of the English fleet."

The King's son entered the room. The young Philip still wore his riding boots. He scowled at the chief domestic minister, before turning. "Father, you're feeling better?"

The King shook his head. "Work must be done." He coughed again. "My rebellious northern provinces of the Netherlands must be brought back into submission."

"Yes, those are your lands," said the chief foreign minister.

"We will talk to the Genoese and the Fuggers about additional monies," the chief domestic minister said.

When the two ministers left, *Infanta* Isabella helped her father up and into his bedroom.

"I wonder how long it will take the Pope to give permission for you and your brother Philip to marry your cousins," the King said.

Like *Infanta* Isabella's marriage to her cousin Albert of Austria, King Philip II had arranged for Prince Philip to marry Philip's cousin, Margaret from Austria, but Pope Clement VIII had not signed that waiver.

When the King sat down on his bed, his doctors who attended to him both night and day returned to his side.

Cardinal Albert peered out the window and saw a man led a mule carrying a monk. As it headed back toward the Monastery-Palace on the rocky road, a messenger on a fast horse appeared. It kicked up dust as it passed the monk.

A minute later, the messenger, accompanied by the Foreign Minister Idiaquez and the Domestic Minister *de* Moura, came to the suite. "A message for the King!" He waved a letter in his hand. "From the commander of the fleet."

"The silver fleet?"

"Yes, it has landed at Seville," the messenger said.

Infanta Isabella took the letter and brought it to the resting King.

"What's the news?" The King raised his head.

Infanta Isabella unsealed the letter.

"What does it say?" Cardinal Albert leaned closer.

Infanta Isabella scanned the letter. "The English failed in their attacks." She proclaimed to her father, "Your fleet has arrived in Seville with twenty-two million in silver and gold."

The King sat up. "We've never had that much."

"Our share is six and one-half million," *Infanta* Isabella said. "Enough to pay all of our debts."

The King's countenance lifted. "Build a fleet." His voice grew stronger. "Raise an army."

Chapter 20 - Cardinal Albert of Austria

The French, who are very anxious for peace, have sent to Flanders to inquire whether Cardinal Archduke [Albert of Austria] has authority to treat. The answer was that he had the authority to treat with England, with the States [The Republic of the Seven United Netherlands], and with France, but separately. This rouses suspicion.

Piero Duodo, Venetian Ambassador to France
Paris, 10th February 1596

Cardinal Albert's Encampment, Brabant, Winter 1596

IN THE DEAD of the following winter, Cardinal Albert of Austria exited his large tent in the flat Brabant countryside outside of Brussels. The crisp air of Brabant reminded him of his native homeland in Austria where he had spent his much of his youth. Spain, where he spent all of his adult life, was not nearly as cold.

His journey from Madrid had taken months to prepare, but even longer to complete. Leaving his future bride *Infanta* Isabella at San Lorenzo d'el Escorial, the newly appointed General Governor of the Spanish Netherlands had sailed from Spain to Genoa during the warmth of the previous August after Pope Clement VIII had allowed him to relinquish his position as Archbishop of Toledo.

Cardinal Albert had not arrived in the Lowlands alone. He had also brought Prince Philip William of Orange, who, before being taken hostage at the age of thirteen and sent to Spain, had studied at the University of Brabant in nearby Louvain. After the assassination of his Calvinist father, Philip William had inherited William the Silent's title, Prince of Orange.

Cardinal Albert and his Head of Household, *Mayordomo Mayor Don* Francisco *de* Mendoza, met Prince Philip William by the fire. Prior to his appointment as Cardinal Albert's Head of Household, Mendoza had obtained the title of Admiral of Aragon.

"We're almost there." Cardinal Albert, with his blonde hair and beard, appeared Austrian on the outside, but his stark Spanish garb reflected his Spanish heart.

"Everything is in order," the Admiral of Aragon said.

The journey from Spain via Genoa had been made less arduous because of the able work of the Admiral of Aragon. The Admiral had managed Cardinal Albert's large retinue exceptionally well throughout the difficult journey over the Alps along the Spanish Road. The overland journey had to be made, because English and free Dutch ships controlled the seas, especially the English Channel between Calais and Dover.

After crossing over those tall mountains and traversing through Burgundy, they had arrived in Luxembourg in late January. Nearly three hundred and fifty mules carried Cardinal Albert's personal belongings.

Waiting in the Brabant countryside for their formal entry into Brussels, Cardinal Albert waved for a light-bearded Frenchman to join them. When he did, the Cardinal Albert told Jean Richardot, "I will announce your appointment as President of my Privy Council after this morning's inspection."

"I will not disappoint your trust." Jean Richardot smiled.

Cardinal Albert rubbed his hands together. "We must begin our task at once."

Cardinal Albert's experience as Viceroy and Grand Inquisitor of Portugal would serve him well. Including Holland and Zeeland, seven of his seventeen provinces had abjured the Spanish Crown. In the ensuing war, the previous governors had failed to bring the rebellious provinces back into the fold; their efforts had been stymied. Cardinal Albert did not doubt his own ability to bring them back under the rule of Spain.

Richardot stretched his hands out over the fire. "Count Fuentes, the acting governor of the Netherlands, should be arriving shortly."

The Admiral of Aragon gestured. "That must be him now."

Acting Governor Fuentes, along with other officers and guards, rode towards them. One of Cardinal Albert's older brothers, Archduke Ernest of Austria, had died the previous February. King Philip II of Spain had appointed *Don* Pedro Enriquez *de* Acevedo, Count of Fuentes, to be his acting governor until Cardinal Albert could assume control. That meant the Netherlands had been without a permanent governor for almost a year.

After Count Fuentes and two important officers dismounted, Count Fuentes began introductions. "This is my most trusted officer, Marshall Savigne *de* Rosne."

Marshall *de* Rosne, a heavyset Frenchman, saluted.

"And Giorgio Basta," Count Fuentes said.

Cardinal Albert had heard of the reputation of the Albanian Catholic Giorgio Basta. After the fall of Albania to the Ottoman Turks, the Basta family had relocated to an Italian town outside Naples. Two members of that family had risen to positions of importance, including Giorgio.

"At your service." Giorgio saluted.

The determined look in Basta's eye pleased Cardinal Albert. He was happy to have him on his side.

After the greetings were exchanged, Count Fuentes told Cardinal Albert, "Preparations for your arrival in Brussels are finalized."

"Excellent." Cardinal Albert preferred everything in perfect order. The official transfer of power would take place later, after his formal entrance into the capital of the Lowlands.

"Brussels anxiously awaits your arrival," Count Fuentes said.

The Admiral of Aragon gestured to one of the servants. "We will need to pack the mules by morning."

"We'll start before daybreak." His Spanish servant headed toward the mules corralled at the edge of the encampment. Other servants fed the beasts hay. Heavily armed guards were posted by the luggage.

"Shall we review the troops?" Cardinal Albert asked.

In addition to Prince Philip William, Cardinal Albert had brought a *tercio*, a formidable regiment of three thousand men. The troops began to assemble in a vast field.

"Flanders and Brabant can use all the help the King of Spain can lend." Count Fuentes referred to two of the largest of the ten obedient provinces. The seven other provinces, who called themselves The Seven United Provinces of the Netherlands, had been fighting for independence for nearly thirty years.

The Admiral of Aragon gestured to a waiting servant. "Bring the Cardinal's horse."

"At once." The Spanish servant quickly complied and brought the black stallion to Cardinal Albert.

"We will wait in your tent." The Admiral of Aragon led Jean Richardot and Prince Philip William away from the fire to the tent, where other members of the council of advisors waited.

Cardinal Albert mounted his horse. With his arrival in Brussels, Cardinal Albert would be not only the new Governor of the Lowlands, but also Lieutenant General of the army. Count Fuentes and the two Catholic officers, Marshall *de* Rosne and Giorgio Basta, remounted their horses and accompanied the Cardinal. They rode to the front of the regiment standing in formation. The three greeted the commander of the regiment, Ferrante Loffredo III, the *Marquis de* Trevico, who saluted.

"An impressive addition to the Spanish Army in Flanders," Marshall *de* Rosne said.

The *tercio* of nearly three thousand pikemen, musketeers, and swordsmen formed a single fighting square. Pikemen in the middle of the *tercio* pointed their sharpened pikes skyward. The pike blades glistened in the morning sun. Outside the pikemen, musketeers stood at attention. Hundreds of cavalry in company formation flanked the *tercio*.

"They are well-trained for battles against Queen Elizabeth of England, the Dutch rebels, or King Henry IV of France," the *Marquis de* Trevico said.

"You might have to fight them all," Giorgio Basta said.

"We have the will and the funds." Cardinal Albert knew that the silver and gold brought by the Spanish fleet from Peru to Spain in the past year was the largest influx to the Spanish treasury since Columbus discovered America. He glanced towards the guards standing by the mules that had carried more than a million *florins*. "Where is King Henry now?"

"At La Fere, south of Cambrai and Saint Quentin," Count Fuentes said.

Cardinal Albert remembered seeing King Philip II's victory over the French at Saint Quentin depicted in the Hall of Battles in *San Lorenzo d'el Escorial*. He wanted no less a victory, but knew that King Henry IV was a great general. "Go on."

"After I took Cambrai last October," Count Fuentes continued, "Henry countered and surrounded the town of La Fere."

"How long can La Fere hold out?"

"Unless we relieve the siege, only a few months."

Cardinal Albert completed his inspection and led the other officers back to the fire, where they dismounted and entered his large tent.

Inside, members of his council of advisors waited.

Cardinal Albert motioned Jean Richardot to stand. "I've decided to appoint Jean Richardot as President of my Privy Council."

As soon as he announced his decision, a messenger arrived by horseback. The man dismounted and immediately appeared at the tent's entrance. "Cardinal Albert."

"What is it?"

"A message from King Henry IV of France." He held a letter high and handed it to him.

Cardinal Albert broke the seal and scanned its contents.

"What does it say?" Philip William asked.

"The French monarch wants to know whether King Philip II of Spain has authorized me to treat."

"It sounds as though King Henry seeks peace."

"Perhaps he has heard the strength of my army," Cardinal Albert replied in all seriousness. He never joked or laughed in front of his officers or his advisors.

"What is your response?" Philip William asked.

Cardinal Albert turned to his secretary and began to dictate. "Tell the King of France that King Philip II of Spain has given me authority to make peace with England, with the rebellious States, and with France." He paused. "Only separately."

As soon as the messenger left, Cardinal Albert turned to Philip William. "We'll enter Brussels together." He leaned toward him. "The King and I need your help to rule."

The soon-to-be Governor of the Lowlands, Cardinal Albert of Austria, wanted to impress the citizens of Brussels, the capital of the Lowlands, but he would do it without the *tercio* of Spanish and Italian soldiers of the *Marquis de* Trevico. Along with the Albanian Giorgio Basta, the *tercio* would be sent to the vicinity of La Fere.

Porte Louvaine, Brussels, The Lowlands, February 11, 1596

CITY CANNONS SALUTED the arrival of Prince Philip William of Orange and Cardinal Albert of Austria. At the front of the long procession, Philip William rode between two dukes. Right behind the trio, Cardinal Albert, dressed in splendid Spanish attire—a golden embroidered cape draped over a black uniform with golden embroidered sleeves and belt, and an elaborate ruffled white collar—sat atop his black stallion and rode next to Count Fuentes.

The two companies of Cardinal Albert's personal guard remained close. One company carried lances, the other arquebuses, a firearm longer

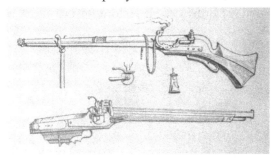

than a pistol but shorter than a musket. Other companies of cavalry, totaling more than one thousand horsemen followed. At the end of the procession were the three hundred and fifty mules carrying the Cardinal's possessions and some of his two hundred

Arquebus Mechanism

and fifty servants. Scattered crowds had gathered to watch the spectacle, even before they reached the city walls.

The gates of Port Leuven opened before them. Bells tolled long and loud above the fortified walls of Brussels. After entering through the covered gateway with its two parapet towers, Cardinal Albert waved and acknowledged the growing crowds. Nobles, burghers, and citizens lined the cobblestone streets.

Cardinal Albert leaned toward Count Fuentes, "The people seem to love me."

"As well they should."

After passing St. Gudula Cathedral, the crowds grew larger. Women and children leaned out second story windows and waved.

The entourage rode under a wooden Arc Triomphant spanning the roadway. A huge square opened in front of them. Trumpets blasted high notes.

The procession stopped in front of the Hotel *de* Ville. Its three hundred-foot high spire dominated one side of the the Grand Place. On the other side, next to the Guild-Houses stood the *Maison du Roi*, Cardinal Albert's new residence. The first of Cardinal Albert's mules reached the building.

When Cardinal Albert dismounted, the bells in the belfry of the Town Hall's spire stopped ringing. The crowds quieted. As their new Governor General, Cardinal Albert acknowledged the crowd, thanking the citizens for their warm welcome in a short speech.

The trumpets sounded again and once more, the bells tolled. The festivities began anew and lasted well into the evening. Torches lit up the Grand Place and facades of the magnificent buildings in the square.

Cardinal Albert knew this was his new home. He could not wait until his cousin and future wife *Infanta* Isabella could join him.

Council Chambers, *Hotel de Ville*, Brussels, The Lowlands

THE FOLLOWING WEEK, Cardinal Albert called a meeting of his advisors to order in an amply furnished chamber in the Hotel *de* Ville. President Jean Richardot of the Privy Council sat in a chair on one side of the room, while Prince Philip William of Orange sat behind a table on the opposite side.

"You have the floor, President Richardot," Cardinal Albert said.

President Richardot rose. "I'm happy to inform the Prince of Orange that King Philip II wants to return your father's estates in Brabant to you. It will be worth tens of thousands of *florins*." He hesitated.

"But?" Philip William asked.

"But 18,000 *florins* will continue to be paid to the heir of Balthazar Gerard."

The former Governor of the Netherlands, the Duke of Alba, had rewarded Gerard more than a decade earlier for killing William the Silent, Philip William's father, the former Prince of Orange, before Alba kidnapped and sent Philip William to Spain.

Philip William jumped up. "My father's assassin?" He pulled a dagger from his waist. "How dare you pay him!" Knife raised, he charged the Privy Council President Jean Richardot.

President Richardot stepped back. Two other council members stepped in front of him. Other nobles grabbed the Prince by the arms before he could hurt Richardot, or worse.

"If you cannot accept these generous terms," President Richardot said, "then the estates will not be returned!"

Prince Philip William peered at Cardinal Albert.

Cardinal Albert remembered how Philip William, while playing chess with a Spanish officer in prison, threw the officer out the window. He had killed the officer for bringing up his father's death.

"You will continue to receive your allowance," Cardinal Albert said.

Philip William stormed out of the room.

Cardinal Albert still needed the Philip William's help to bring the seven rebel provinces back into obedience.

Chapter 21 - Count Varax Bombards Calais

"There, (Señor) [Cardinal Albert of Austria], is Calais, who calls us, guarded by inexperienced young men, and defended solely by an aging reputation: the soldiers of Monsieur de Gordon have been neutral in all of the wars, and, because of this, have no experience in any manner."

Marshall *de* Rosne to Cardinal Albert
Las Guerras *de* los Estados Baxos by Carlos Colomo
Translated from Spanish

News has this minute arrived that the Castle of Calais has fallen. That event took place on Thursday the 25th [of April]. The Spanish bombarded it and then carried it by assault, cutting to bits all who were in it. This is a loss of immense importance to all Christendom and the consequences will be most grave.

Piero Duodo, Venetian Ambassador to France
Deciphered and translated from Italian
Paris, 1st May 1596

Outside Valenciennes, Hainaut Province, March 30, 1596

IN THE HAINAUT countryside outside Valenciennes, Cardinal Albert, the former Archbishop of Toledo, no longer wore ecclesiastical garb, but military armor. He stood next to Prince Philip William of Orange, who no longer displayed the anger he had shown against President Richardot in Brussels weeks earlier. On their journey to the Lowlands, the Philip William had made an excursion to Rome on behalf of Cardinal Albert and successfully petitioned Pope Clement VIII to allow him to wear a sword while still a cardinal.

Philip William, however, had been less successful in more recent matters. He was unable to persuade his younger brother, Count Maurice of Nassau, to once again submit to the Spanish Crown. The seven rebellious provinces of the north would not listen to gentle persuasion and end their decades-long struggle against their rightful ruler, King Philip II of Spain.

Only fiery irons can cure such a long illness, Cardinal Albert mused. Despite that, aid from England appeared unlikely because Queen Elizabeth

158

had withdrawn companies from Holland and reassigned them to her fleet. The time was not yet ripe to apply the cure to those rebel states. Bringing Holland and Zeeland and the other states of the north back into the fold would have to wait.

Cardinal Albert had traveled southwest from Brussels at the end of March. He looked out at his assembled troops, nearly eighteen thousand strong, including more than fifteen thousand infantrymen and nearly three thousand horsemen. They had assembled near the woods outside Valenciennes, toward Douai in Flanders. The footmen included the *tercio* of Neapolitans and Milanese under Ferrante Loffredo III, the *Marquis de* Trevico. Keeping close to the borders of Germany along the Spanish Road, those Italians had marched over the Alps through the rain, snow, and ice of early winter.

Though Cardinal Albert was in his first military campaign, his army consisted of experienced warriors. They included six thousand Walloons, divided into several regiments, including one led by Colonel la Barlotte. The *Maestro de Campo* General was Marshall *de* Rosne, whose Spanish foot were five thousand strong. Marc *de* Rye, the *Marquis de* Varambon, who had better connections than almost anyone else throughout Christendom, led nearly one thousand men from Burgundy.

The horsemen included both Lancers and riders armed with arquebuses. Besides the Spanish and Italian riders, the obedient Lowlands also contributed companies of horsemen, including the experienced Lancers of the Baron of Achicourt.

Cardinal Albert wanted to build upon the success of Count Fuentes. The former Governor of the Lowlands had left to be the Spanish Governor of Milan. Now Cardinal Albert needed to thwart King Henry IV of France in order to save the besieged town of La Fere from falling into French hands. He turned to an important Albanian officer. "*Seigneur* Giorgio Basta. Give us your report."

"After Count Fuentes and Marshall *de* Rosne took Cambrai last October, King Henry IV surrounded the town of La Fere. In the middle of the month, I took nearly eight hundred horses loaded with wheat and supplies and rendezvoused with the men from La Fere after dark. Those men took all of the horses back to La Fere and replenished the besieged town. La Fere has enough food to hold out for many more weeks."

"And the losses?"

"Gratefully, we did not lose a man," Basta said.

"La Fere defends itself admirably, but cannot last forever."

"Over the last two weeks, we have also gathered great quantities of goods and supplies." Basta pointed to a long caravan of wagons stopped alongside the road. "But King Henry has learned of our intentions and strengthened his earthworks. We broke their levee and lowered the water, but the French repaired it the next day."

 "King Henry expects us to attack and relieve the siege of La Fere." Cardinal Albert knew the prowess of the King of France and Navarre. "*Seigneur* Giorgio Basta. Take two thousand infantry and two thousand horsemen to Cambrai."

"Yes, your Highness." Giorgio Basta mounted his horse and led the riders and footman away to reinforce the strongest town north of La Fere under Cardinal Albert's rule. His brother, Nicolo Basta, a commander of horse, did not go with him. He remained near three companies of horse.

Valenciennes, Hainaut, the Lowlands, Wed., April 3, 1596

SEVERAL DAYS LATER, Cardinal Albert called his trusted officers together. "We must discuss the options."

"My brother will either attack Saint Quentin or skirt that town and probe La Fere directly," Nicolo Basta said.

"And the movements of enemy?"

"King Henry has sent forth scouts and knows you are in the field," Nicolo Basta said. "He has urgently sought assistance from all of his nobles, who make haste and come to his aid. The French King fears you will attack him any day."

"I would not underestimate him." Cardinal Albert knew of the fearless reputation of the French King. Henry IV had personally led his cavalry against the Constable of Castile at the Battle of Fontaine-Francaise the previous year. Riding without his helmet, Henry had turned the tide. "What else is our foe doing?" Cardinal Albert asked.

"He prepares for our counterattack and digs trenches night and day in the earthworks surrounding La Fere. We need to relieve that besieged town." Nicolo Basta asked, "Will we march south and attack the French King directly?"

"It risks the whole army," Marshall *de* Rosne said.

"We should attack Paris, instead," a Spanish officer said, more loudly.

"No." Cardinal Albert knew the Pope wanted peace between France and Spain. A direct attack would upset the Pope. "I have other plans."

"A diversion?" Nicolo Basta asked.

"Yes," Cardinal Albert said, "Marshal *de* Rosne will explain."

Marshal *de* Rosne stepped forward. He was joined by his second officer, Gaspard Zapena, as well as the General of the Artillery, Count *de* Varax Philibert *de* Rye who served previously as Governor of Burgundy. The Count *de* Varax had a receding hairline making it difficult to distinguish that he was the younger brother of the *Marquis de* Varambon.

"No one can doubt my loyalty to the Catholic cause, but we risk much if we attack King Henry directly," Marshall *de* Rosne said. "We may, however, be able to draw the French King away from La Fere."

"What do you mean?" the Spanish officer asked.

"Calais beckons us. Its young men are inexperienced and the soldiers of Monsieur *de* Gordon have remained neutral in all the wars. They are untested in all matters."

"But how will that help?" Nicolo Basta asked.

"King Henry will either be forced to immediately lift the siege of La Fere or see Calais fall," Marshall *de* Rosne said.

"We would have a very important port," the Count *de* Varax said, "and we would be able to control the English Channel."

"I like that plan." Cardinal Albert knew that the French port of Calais in Picardy was situated on the English Channel south of Nieuwpoort, Dunkirk, and Gravelines, ports already controlled by the obedient states. "We should not wait. Marshall *de* Rosne, take the *tercios* of *Don* Alonso *de* Mendoza and *Don* Luis *de* Velasco, and the Walloon regiment of La Barlotte. Go directly to Calais."

"And the artillery?" Marshall *de* Rosne asked.

"The Count of Varax will join you and take some of the cannons from Gravelines, the port just north of Calais."

"Adding Calais to Dunkirk will hurt not only King Henry, but also Queen Elizabeth," Marshall *de* Rosne said.

"Yes." Cardinal Albert nodded. "I will follow with the bulk of our army tomorrow."

Cardinal Albert had decided to send a separate regiment to conduct raids along the French border. He wanted to to create havoc and divert French attentions, so his true aims in Calais would remain hidden.

Marshall *de* Rosne issued the command, "Mount up!"

Colonel La Barlotte with his Walloon regiment and Count *de* Varax with his cannons joined the two Spanish *tercios*. The Vanguard of three hundred horsemen and thousands of foot soldiers moved with great speed on the road to Saint Omer to the northwest.

Nieulay Bridge, Calais, Monday, April 8, 1596

THE COUNT OF Varax stood next to Marshall *de* Rosne. "Will you need my artillery?"

"We'll see," Marshall *de* Rosne said, "but Nieulay Bridge is only guarded by forty Frenchmen."

Minutes later, the Count pointed. "They've surrendered!"

The Count of Varax accompanied Marshall *de* Rosne and inspected the bridge and the fort guarding the sluiceway.

"For the French to relieve Calais from Boulogne, they need to pass this point." The Marshall turned to *Don* Alonso *de* Mendoza. "Guard this."

"And us?" the Count of Varax asked.

"To Fort Risban."

Marshall *de* Rosne led the rest of the Vanguard further west. Across the rising tide to their right stood the town of Calais with its citadel fronting the water. After passing some wetlands, the *tercio* of *Don* Luis *de* Velasco marched at the front.

They reached a spur of land that hooked north. The water widened into a deeper harbor. Several ships remained docked outside the town's wall. At the very end of the narrowing peninsula stood the Tower of Lancaster and Fort Risban, occupied by one hundred French defenders.

Fort Risban, Calais, Picardy, Late Afternoon, April 8, 1596

THE REST OF the Vanguard, along with the Count of Varax, arrived at the tip of a narrow strip of land that separated the harbor from the English Channel, but only two hours of daylight remained. He urged his men to bring up four cannons taken from Gravelines in the north. When he looked across the harbor and saw French soldiers gathering, he turned to Marshall *de* Rosne. "Won't those soldiers help?"

"They can't," Marshall said. "The tide is too high." He signaled *Don* Luis *de* Velasco. "Attack!"

Velasco relayed the order. His *tercio* stormed the fort. The one hundred French defenders fought back, but when the Walloon regiment of

Colonel la Barlotte seconded the charge, they surrendered.

Presently, the Count of Varax entered Fort Risban, the key to the harbor of Calais. He ordered, "Man the cannons!"

"Musketeers!" Marshall *de* Rosne yelled. "Along the shore!"

Several companies of musketeers took up positions along the harbor side of the peninsula. That night, those three hundred musketeers fired at boats leaving the harbor.

When the Count of Varax spied twenty Dutch warships the next morning, his men fired warning shots. The Count of Varax controlled the harbor entrance.

Bridge at Nieulay, Calais, Maundy Thursday, April 11, 1596

BY THE TIME Cardinal Albert arrived at Calais with the bulk of his army, the outlying posts had been secured. Meeting the Count of Varax on a knoll east of town, Cardinal Albert viewed the well-fortified town. Directly before him, beyond the mainland gate, the main part of the seaside town had a large square. On its southwestern side, a large citadel occupied nearly a quarter of the town. He ordered two of the *tercios* who had just arrived to take up positions east of town and turned to the Count of Varax. "We need to plant batteries."

"I've already scouted locations," the Count of Varax said. "Sixteen cannons can be planted on the dunes. I'll take six more guns and plant them by Fort Risban and the sea."

"We cannot let Calais be resupplied." The Cardinal turned to the *Marquis de* Trevico. "Plant your *tercio* along the peninsula between the bridge of Nieulay and Fort Risban.

The *Marquis de* Trevico saluted. "Your Highness."

"Make certain no relief comes from France."

"You have my word."

Fort Risban, Calais, Tuesday, April 16, 1596

ON THE TUESDAY after Easter, Cardinal Albert joined Prince Philip William, Marshall *de* Rosne, and the Count of Varax by the dunes east of the town. "Much progress had been made."

"We have protected the approaches to Calais," Marshall *de* Rosne said. "Both by the bridge of Nieulay and the peninsula."

"We sank several Dutch ships trying to enter the harbor." The Count of Varax pointed to the English Channel. "But now there are nearly one hundred Dutch, French and English ships offshore. More English ships can be expected if the Queen of England ends her delay. Robert Devereaux, the Earl of Essex, still amasses his large fleet."

"And the Dutch?"

"*Stadtholder* Maurice of the so-called Free Dutch Republic has arrived. He brings thousands of Hollanders and Zeelanders."

Prince Philip William appeared astonished.

"Reports say that your brother Maurice sails on the flagship of the Dutch fleet," Marshall *de* Rosne said.

"The States-General were quick to respond." Cardinal Albert counted seventeen Dutch warships belonging to the seven rebellious provinces offshore.

"And my brother?" Prince William Philip asked.

"As long as we hold Fort Risban, *Stadtholder* Maurice cannot stop us."

"We must not wait. We need to establish a beachhead across the harbor," Cardinal Albert said.

"The walls are weakest by the gate." Marshall *de* Rosne pointed.

"Count of Varax, commence firing," Cardinal Albert ordered.

Both battery positions began firing. A tower fell. By two o'clock in the afternoon a wide breach had been made in the walls.

The pleasure of the attack did not last, though, when a cannon shot exploded near Cardinal Albert. Several officers fell in the explosion, including the *Mayordomo,* head of household, of Prince Philip William.

Blood splattered on Philip William, but he refused to leave. "I come from too good a house to be afraid."

Spanish cannons again pounded the town walls.

Towards dusk, at low tide, small boats ferried men and cannons across the harbor. By nightfall, the Spanish army of the Lowlands had established a beachhead at the docks. The *tercio* of *Don* Alonso *de* Mendoza prepared to assault the town.

The next morning, a messenger saluted Cardinal Albert at Fort Risban. "King Henry IV of France has entrusted the siege of La Fere to the Duke of Montpensier. He has arrived at Boulogne with more than one thousand horsemen."

Cardinal Albert glanced south, but he saw neither the King nor enemy scouts.

"And to the north, *Stadtholder* Maurice has sent eight companies of horse to Breda."

"He wants to draw us away from here," Cardinal Albert said.

"Should we send men?" Marshall *de* Rosne asked.

"And abandon our cause? When we are so close to victory?" Cardinal Albert turned to Nicolo Basta. "Stop the Dutch Cavalry."

"All I need is three hundred horsemen." The Albanian officer mounted his horse and headed back to the Bridge of Nieulay to meet his companies of horse.

Sporadic cannon fire hit the outer walls of the town, probing for weakness. Muskets fired back, but the response from Calais was ineffective.

A flag of truce flew at the harbor gate.

"Stop the shelling," Cardinal Albert ordered.

A French messenger crossed the harbor. When he arrived at Fort Risban, he said, "Governor Visodan of Calais would like a truce for six days."

"And allow King Henry to come to your aid?" Cardinal Albert said, emphatically, "No."

"How about a day?"

"No." Cardinal Albert shook his head. "If you do not surrender immediately, you will suffer the same fate as those as Dourlens." The former Spanish Governor of the Lowlands, the Count of Fuentes, had killed many who had refused to surrender Dourlens the previous autumn.

"I'll tell the governor." The French messenger returned to town. Spanish batteries once more pounded its walls.

"Prepare for the assault," Cardinal Albert ordered.

When the pikemen lined up in position and waited for the tide to ebb further, the French messenger reappeared at the Harbor Gate. After crossing the waterway, he said, "We will surrender the city, but not the citadel."

"Very well," Cardinal Albert said, "But you cannot take any of the city artillery with you."

"If, at the end of six days, King Henry IV of France does not come to our aid," the Frenchman said, "the Governor will surrender the citadel."

"If you do as you say, we will spare your lives."

The messenger returned to the town to relay the message. Within four hours the town was abandoned and the Spanish of *Don* Alonso *de* Mendoza, seconded by the Walloons of Colonel la Barlotte entered the town. By the time the Count of Varax arrived with his cannons, the Governor and all of the French soldiers had retreated into the citadel.

When the artillerymen of the Count of Varax started to plant a battery, the French fired. From the far side of the Plaza, the citadel's cannons pounded the forward Spanish positions. Houses burned and the fires could not be put out.

The Count of Varax relocated his cannons. He planted twelve pieces in a protected arc alongside the right side of the plaza, nearest the sea.

The French, meanwhile, reinforced the walls of the citadel.

For the next five days, the Spanish Army in Flanders prepared for the final assault.

Fort Risban, Calais, Tuesday, April 23, 1596

ON THE MORNING of the sixth day, the officers gathered at Fort Risban. Among others, the Count of Varax and the *Marquis de* Trevico were in attendance. Marshall *de* Rosne reported to Cardinal Albert, "French soldiers from Boulogne entered the citadel last night."

The news irritated Cardinal Albert. "How?"

"They waded through the water."

"They got through our defenses?"

"Through the section of the *Marquis de* Trevico."

Cardinal Albert spun to the Italian. "You promised."

"I don't know how," the *Marquis de* Trevico said.

"This cannot happen again," Cardinal Albert said. "How many got through?"

"We do not know."

"Will the citadel surrender tonight?" Cardinal Albert asked.

"I'll send a messenger," Marshall *de* Rosne said.

Hours later, when the messenger came back, he reported, "They answered, 'No.'"

Cardinal Albert turned to the Count of Varax. "Your cannons ready?"

"At your command."

"At dawn."

Main Square, Calais, Wednesday, April 24, 1596

THE NEXT MORNING at the Main Square opposite the Citadel, the Count of Varax commanded. "Fire!"

All twelve cannons commenced firing. The citadel walls exploded. Rocks flew. The cannons reloaded.

"Fire!"

Again, the twelve cannons blasted away at the walls.

"Fire at will!" the Count of Varax ordered.

With precision, powder and cannonballs were loaded. The cannoneers lit the fuses and turned. The cannons blasted away with fury for nearly six hours, until noon.

The blasts had brought down the wall in two large sections. The cannons silenced.

"Prepare for the assault!" Marshall *de* Rosne ordered.

The pikemen of the *tercio* of *Don* Alonso *de* Mendoza stood side by side.

"Do we take prisoners?" a Spanish officer asked.

"Cardinal Albert gave them a chance to surrender," Marshall *de* Rosne said. "Show no mercy." He signaled.

"Storm the castle!" *Don* Alonso motioned with his sword.

His pikemen marched through the breach, but the French defenders repulsed them.

Minutes later, Marshall *de* Rosne turned to *Don* Luis Velasco. "Attack!"

The second assault began. Muskets fired. Swords clashed. More French officers died, but the second wave was repulsed.

"Charge!" Marshall *de* Rosne ordered a third wave.

Colonel la Barlotte led the third assault. His regiment of Walloons stormed the breach and assaulted the leaderless French defenders.

The Count of Varax heard the clashes and screams echoing across the square. Less than an hour from the time of the first assault, the battle was over.

Frenchmen who had scaled the walls and run through the water were pursued by the cavalry. None escaped. All were slaughtered.

Towards evening, Cardinal Albert left Fort Risbon and entered the town of Calais. He allowed the one thousand women holed up in the cathedral to leave and go to Boulogne.

Marshall *de* Rosne then gave his report. "All of the French defenders have been killed. Only the lives of Hollanders and Zeelanders have been spared."

Cardinal Albert viewed the bodies lining the citadel walls. "How many dead?"

"They lost over a two thousand six hundred men, including Governor Visodan and the Governor of Boulogne, who arrived yesterday with several hundred men."

"And us?"

"Less than a hundred dead."

Cardinal Albert turned to his officers, including the Count of Varax. "Excellent work."

~ ~ ~

THE FOLLOWING MORNING Cardinal Albert peered over the Channel. In the distance, about nine leagues away, the Cliffs of Dover brightened above calm seas. "No sign of the English Fleet of the Earl of Essex." He turned his attention to the south.

French flags approached, but already defenses were ready.

"King Henry is too late," Marshall *de* Rosne said.

Later, when the French King turned back to Boulogne, Cardinal Albert told his officers, "Calais is ours."

Immensely satisfied with his quick and complete victory, Cardinal Albert peered at the flag of Spain. It waved over Fort Risban. "Even if we lose La Fere, we will not give back Calais."

Chapter 22 - King Henry IV at Chartres

"I am," says this amiable and worthy Prince [King Henry IV], in a letter to me, "very near my enemies, and hardly a horse to carry me into the battle, nor a complete suit of armor to put on; my shirts are all ragged, my doublets out at elbow, my kettle is seldom on the fire, and these two last days I have been obliged to dine where I could, for my purveyors have informed me, that they have not the wherewithal to furnish my table."

King Henry IV letter to Maximilian *de* Bethune,
Baron *de* Rosny [Later, Duke of Sully]

Being then but little youths under tutorage: his [John Smith's] service being needless, within a month or six weeks, they sent him back again to his friends.

John Smith

Hotel Groslot, Orleans, France, June 1596

ABOUT A MONTH after John Smith arrived at Orleans, he again ate a meal with Peregrine and Robert Bertie at the Hotel Groslet. The German students who studied French at the University had told them about Cardinal Albert and the *Infanta* Isabella. They all sat at the table closest to the fireplace still smoldering on this warm July day.

The French officers, who had accompanied the oldest son of Lord Willoughby into the Hotel that afternoon, finished their story, "And so that is what the Walloon prisoner told us about the fall of Calais."

"The women from the Cathedral confirmed the account to King Henry IV at Boulogne?" Robert Bertie asked.

"*Oui*," the French officer said, "after Calais fell, Cardinal Albert captured several other towns and immediately invested Ardres, also in Picardy. Several weeks later, in mid-May, the Spanish inside La Fere capitulated to King Henry IV, who left a residual force and swiftly set out to defend Ardres with forteen thousand of his men."

"So the King relieved the siege at Ardres?" John asked, in French.

"King Henry IV did not arrive in time. The acting Governor of Ardres had surrendered before a shot was even fired. He retired with his men, but as soon as the King heard about the disaster, he had that governor arrested. The King planned to execute him as an example to any other governor who would do the same."

"But a relative of his from Orleans heard about it," Robert said. "I saw him leave Orleans with his men at the beginning of June."

"That relative of the governor told the King that if the Governor of Ardres were not released, he would turn the fortress of Ham over to Cardinal Albert," the French officer said.

"Did King Henry execute the governor?" John asked.

"No," the French officer explained, "Instead the King relented, since it would have been too costly. Following the death of King's minister of Finance, the Treasury has not been replenished; the French are short of funds to pay for the costly wars."

"Short of money?"

"Many of the Swiss infantry and German horsemen the King has hired have not yet been paid. When I saw the King in the field, his leggings were torn. And the garment by his sword was worn through to his thigh."

John finished his soup and set down his spoon.

The friendly daughter of the owners approached. "More?"

"*Non, merci,* too warm a day," John said.

"Your French improves day by day," the daughter said.

John smiled. "Thanks to our tutor." Both John and Peregrine had finished their French lessons for the day.

The French officer turned to Robert. "Shall we be going?"

"You're leaving?" Peregrine asked.

"To the coast to join the English fleet." Robert rose. "The rest of my company has been reassigned and needs to move to the front with French regiments. King Henry IV of France confers at Amiens."

"Are more English soldiers arriving in France?" John asked.

"Not beyond the two thousand soldiers Queen Elizabeth has already sent." Robert paused. "John, I appreciate the victuals that you brought, but I can't use your help anymore."

"You mean?"

Robert secured his saber at his waist. "Yes, you need to return to England."

"But we traveled all this way." John touched the pocket holding the papers that had allowed him to travel out of England. "We've only been here a month."

"Six weeks, but you'll have more chances later, I'm sure. I've arranged for a carriage to take you through Chartres."

"When?" John followed Robert to the door.

"In the morning."

That night John did not sleep well. He did not want to return to Lincolnshire.

Cathedral of Our Lady of Chartres, Chartres, Summer 1596

PEREGRINE BERTIE AND the French tutor accompanied John north from Orleans, to the city of Chartres. As soon as they exited the carriage, Peregrine told John, "You'll be able to catch another carriage to the coast from here."

"You're not going back?"

"Not yet," Peregrine said. "The plague has subsided in Paris, so we wanted to go there."

John remembered hearing about the plague that accompanied the influx of French refugees earlier in the year. The streets were so crowded that workers hadn't even cleaned up the garbage. It had afflicted the poorer sections of Paris. Some nobles had fled the city.

"The streets of Paris are being cleaned for the arrival from the Vatican of the Papal Legate, Cardinal Alessandro *de* Medici," the Tutor told John. "Your carriage to the coast won't leave for an hour. We have enough time to see the Notre Dame *de* Chartres."

When they reached the gothic Cathedral, John peered up at its two towers. Inside the Cathedral of Chartres, John viewed some of the more than one hundred and fifty beautiful windows adorning the walls. "So much stained glass."

"Unlike much of the Lowlands." The tutor shook his head.

"What do you mean?"

"Many Anabaptists and Calvinists considered stained glass pictures of saints to be idolatry, so during the time of William the Silent in a *Beeldenstorm*, they destroyed many windows in the churches from Dunkirk to Antwerp and Ghent."

A man in a robe led scores of children through the narthex and into the sanctuary. "You'll excuse us, but rehearsal must begin." The choir director had the children line up in rows.

"Rehearsal? Today?"

"Haven't you heard? King Henry IV will be arriving this afternoon to meet the Papal Legate, Cardinal Alessandro *de* Medici."

"The Legate from Pope Clement VIII is here?"

"*Oui.*" The director glanced to a side entrance. He tapped his baton twice. The children silenced and just as quickly began to sing.

At the side entrance, meanwhile, a priest stood next to a white-haired man. They watched the children and smiled. John gestured at a man with a cap. "Who is that?"

"It must be the Legate *a latere.*" The Tutor leaned closer. "A legate is much more important than a *nuncio*, or papal ambassador. Pope Clement VIII has sent the Cardinal of Florence to secure the promises he had issued in his Bull of Absolution."

"What promises?"

"Last September, the Pope finally granted King Henry absolution. With the forgiveness of sins, the King will be fully admitted to the Catholic Church, but only upon the fulfillment of certain conditions."

"Conditions?"

"Such as setting up monasteries. When the Legate Alessandro *de* Medici approves these conditions, then absolution will be ratified. Even the Jesuits and Spaniards will no longer be able to question whether King Henry IV is the lawful Sovereign of France."

When John, Peregrine, and the Tutor exited the Cathedral, trumpets sounded. "The King arrives."

Royal guards secured the square in front of the Cathedral. Several carriages pulled to a stop and the jubilant King Henry IV of France stepped out of the first one.

John elbowed Peregrine.

"What is it, John?"

"His leggings are not ripped like we heard."

"You're right." Peregrine laughed. "Perhaps his finances have improved."

"The King has brought Maximilian *de* Bethune, the Baron *de* Rosny into his Council of Finance," the Tutor said, "but the problems may be larger than one man can solve. The King may call an Assembly of Notables in Rouen this autumn."

"I've always wanted to see the King, ever since I heard how my father helped him," Peregrine said.

John remembered the story of how Queen Elizabeth had once written to King Henry and told him that Lord Willoughby was one of her most trusted advisors. After the defeat of the Spanish Armada, Peregrine's father had assisted the French sovereign.

King Henry warmly greeted the Papal Legate at the top step of the Cathedral, where inside Henry had been crowned King of France two years earlier. The smiles both wore seemed sincere.

French Franc with King Henry IV, King of France and Navarre

"The Pope is very happy that the French King has returned to the Catholic Church," the French Tutor told them.

John knew that King Henry *de* Bourbon had been raised as a Calvinist by his mother. After Henry abjured that faith and the French bishops accepted his conversion, he entered Orleans and then Paris over objections of many in the strict Catholic League.

"The Catholic Church in France will not become independent of Rome like the Church of England." The Tutor paused. "But the Papal Legate has two other tasks besides restoring the Catholic Church inside France."

"What do you mean?" John asked.

"First, King Henry IV wants to annul his marriage to the Queen, Marguerite *de* Valois, whose mother was Catherine *de* Medici from Florence."

"Related to the same family as Papal Legate Alessandro *de* Medici?"

"Yes, the same family, and the second task—peace between France and Spain—must also be addressed. After the loss of Calais and Andres to Cardinal Albert, King Henry IV cannot afford to stop the war that France formally declared against Spain last year."

"And us?" John asked.

"We must get you back to England. Peregrine and I will go to Paris." The Tutor pointed across the square. "John, your carriage is ready."

While the Legate and King Henry IV entered the Cathedral to celebrate Mass and listen to the choir, John climbed into the carriage. The carriage hurried out of the city on a bumpy road straight to the French coast.

SEVERAL DAYS LATER, John peered over the port side of the ship to England. When it tacked and its foresail billowed, he reflected. Disappointed and frustrated at not being needed in France, he did not want to return home. John certainly did not want to become an indentured servant for Thomas Sendall in King's Lynne again. The travels to Orleans had whetted his appetite. He wanted more adventure.

At least for now, John had the monies from the inheritance his father had left him. Perhaps he could use them to get back to sea.

The coast of England drew closer.

Chapter 23 - Feigning Herself Sick

This noble Gentlewoman [Aisha, Sister of the Sultan] took sometime occasion to show
him [Captain John Smith] to some friends . . . Would feign herself sick . . .

John Smith

On the return journey to the Seraglio [Palace] of Ibrahim [Pasha] 100 female slaves
riding astride, and all of them richly dressed in brocade, followed the 50 coaches, and
scattered money among the crowd. Each horse was led by a slave, and the whole band was
escorted by 50 handsome black eunuchs on horseback.

After the slave women, [there] came a gold-bound Qur'an carried on a golden desk
studded with jewels; then six silver candelabra with lighted torches, a crystal box full of
gems, and many other caskets of jewels; then the bride's [Aisha's] bed, made of silver-gilt,
and carried in several pieces, to be put together, and bedquilts and coverlids of gold
brocade embroidered with pearls . . .

The Marriage of [*Damat*] Ibrahim *Pasha* [to Aisha, Sister of the Sultan], 1586
Venetian Ambassador, May 1586

Kiosk, Ibrahim *Pasha* Palace, *Jumada II*, AH 1011 (Dec. 1602)

INSIDE THE GARDEN kiosk, Aisha, Sister of the Sultan, listened to her friends. Filiz and Emine finished translating John's words from French and English. Sadness tinged Aisha's heart as she peered into John's eyes. "So many Frenchmen died at Calais."

"Not even one of the French soldiers escaped." John waved his index finger. "After the Count *de* Varax pounded the walls of the garrison, the Spanish Army in Flanders gained a great victory. Although Cardinal Albert later lost La Fere, he showed his mettle, winning Calais in his first campaign."

"But he let the women go?"

"He must have realized that the tides of war ebb as well as flow, so, yes, Cardinal Albert let the one thousand French women, holed up in the Cathedral, go to King Henry IV at Boulogne."

Aisha sipped the last of her drink and set down her cup. She retrieved a laced kerchief from her sleeve and patted her lips. "So you learned French in Orleans?"

"Oui," John replied, "juste un peu francais."

"I like your accent." Filiz, the French translator, smiled.

"I must give credit to my tutor. He insisted that I repeat each word, until my accent matched those native to Orleans."

"The French spoken there must be pure," Aisha said, "but I didn't realize that France was so poor."

"It was," John said. "The years of war had devastated the countryside. The Spanish had used their millions to fight the French."

"And you? At least you had your inheritance." Aisha wondered if the remainder could be used for John's ransom.

Filiz reached for her scarf. "I didn't realize how late it is."

Aisha's eyes widened. "You are right." She glanced out the window; the sun had shifted. "My mother will be back soon."

"The time has gone by so quickly," Emine said.

Filiz pivoted. "We must bid you *adieu, Jean* Smith."

John bowed. "*Adieu.*"

Aisha clapped her hands twice and the Overseer stepped forward. "Take the English slave back to his quarters."

"As you wish." The Overseer grabbed John's elbow.

While he led John back to his quarters, Aisha escorted her two friends to the door. "Can you come back next week?"

"Let me know the time," Filiz replied.

"Let me know the time as well." The English translator Emine tied the belt of her coat.

"Thank you again." Aisha embraced her two friends and watched them disappear beneath the loggia on the other side of the garden.

Vaulted Chamber, Harem, Ibrahim *Pasha* Palace, *Stamboul*

AISHA RETURNED TO the vaulted chamber of her apartment, built by the captain of the sea before she married her late husband *Damat* Ibrahim *Pasha*. While a servant lit one of the candelabras, another servant helped her take off her favorite pair of shoes.

The head chambermaid pulled back the bedquilt, embroidered with golden thread and pearls. "Are you feeling better?"

"I'm a little tired." Aisha's head flopped onto her pillow.

"Perhaps a bath." The servant pointed in the direction of the toilet closet, furbished in gold, and the baths beyond.

"That might be refreshing, but not now." Aisha turned her head. "You may leave me alone."

They closed her door.

Aisha heard the soft sound of the fountain and reflected on all the stories John had told her during the day: the stories of him going to Orleans and finding Robert Bertie, as well as the stories of *Infanta* Isabella of Spain and her ailing father, King Philip II. *Infanta* Isabella was going to marry her first cousin, Cardinal Albert, who had arrived at Brussels and become a general. Though she didn't like wars, Aisha had to find out the truth. John had journeyed to France, but was forced to return to England. If all this was true, how did he ever meet the Grand Vizier, her fiancé?

Like John, Aisha wanted to see Paris, but she had to stay in *Stamboul*. But John had an inheritance. If it were large enough, maybe his friends could send it and pay his ransom. After all, John was her slave and she deserved to collect it. The Grand Vizier had promised as much.

Aisha's thoughts were interrupted by a knock. Her mother reappeared in her doorway. "Aren't you going to eat?"

Aisha raised her head. "I'm not hungry."

"Not hungry?" Her mother stared. "Aisha, I'm worried about you. The Grand Vizier won't appreciate someone who is too skinny."

"The Grand Vizier has more important things to worry about."

Chapter 24 - Turkish Bathhouse in Belgrade

The castle is next worth notice (if not chief): it standeth with the City [Belgrade] on the very point, which the two rivers make, showing without to be a very great, fair and strong thing, being very much beautified with turrets, bulwarks, battlements, and watchtowers round about, wherein is, as it were, another city, having churches [mosques], baths, etc., all the dwellers, Turks.
Travels of Peter Mundy in Europe and Asia, 2nd June 1620

Sekul Murish, one of the independent princes of Transylvania . . . came to the Serdar and solicited his aid [in 1602], promising he would, if thus supplied with sufficient means, subdue the whole of the region of Transylvania under the Mohammedan yoke. The Serdar [Commander-in-Chief] placed confidence in his promises, and therefore determined to aid him in person . . . but he had scarcely time to hold a council of his great men, when, behold! Messengers with evil intelligence from Buda waited upon him . . .

The Grand Vizier had reached Belgrade...he ordered the troops to be paid their wages.
Annals of the Turkish Empire, Vol. I by Mustafa Naima
Translated from the Turkish by Charles Fraser

Lower Belgrade, Ottoman Empire, AH 1011 (AD 1602)

AT THE FOOT of the steep incline, just inside the Eastern Gate of the Lower Fortress of Belgrade, the Grand Vizier pulled the reins of his brown Arabian. Dusty from his long trek, he abruptly stopped in the front of the *hamam*, the Turkish bath.

A stablehand grabbed the bridle. "The Grand Vizier, welcome back. It's been a long time."

"Weeks." The turbaned Ottoman leader, the Grand Vizier of the whole Ottoman Empire, dismounted and calmed his steed. He noticed a white stallion. "Sekul Murish is here?" The Grand Vizier knew his friend, the former independent Prince of Turtzfeld, the Turkish Field in Transylvania, had lost his valley kingdom to the Holy Roman Empire at the very end of the previous winter.

"He crossed the Danube from Timisoara earlier today." The groomer removed the hair from the brush.

"Excellent." The Grand Vizier remained confident they would regain Transylvania and once more make it a vassal state of the Ottoman Empire. Earlier in the summer, the armies of the Holy Roman Empire besieged Buda, interrupting the Grand Vizier's planned invasion, but in the autumn the Ottoman's strongest allies had taken to the field. *Ghazi* Giray II and his army of Crimean-Tartar warriors were nearby.

"Poiraz Osman is also inside." The stablehand held out his hand."

"I promoted Poiraz Osman to the *Bey* of the *sipahis*."

"I heard," the stablehand said. "One of his officers mentioned how difficult recapturing Buda had been been. He lost many men."

"Feed and water my horse." The Grand Vizier retrieved a coin from his money pouch, but put it back. "You will get your reward later."

The Grand Vizier turned his attention to the far end the *hamam*, the entrance for women. Three Turkish women, arriving from their Turkish neighborhood of the lower town, congregated at the far entrance. Though each wore a *hijab*, the last one had her face only partially covered. When she caught the Grand Vizier's eye and winked, the important *Pasha* acknowledged her with a grin. The women disappeared into the women's side of the double bath.

The Grand Vizier walked through the arched doorway and entered the first room. Steam, rising from the floor, smothered his face. High above, light streamed through the windows and the thickening mist. Reaching the head attendant, he removed his turban and exchanged it for a towel. "Take good care of this."

"As always." The head attendant set the white turban on a dry bench. While another young attendant folded his clothes, the Grand Vizier wrapped the towel around his waist.

In the second room, the Grand Vizier placed his hands into a basin filled with soapy water. After he finished washing, another attendant brought a second basin for rinsing, but when he dipped his hands, it was too hot. "How many times do I have to tell you?" He pulled out his hands. "This water is scalding!"

The attendant drew a deep breath. "Yes, Grand Vizier."

Another attendant quickly brought another basin. "Here's some cold water."

"I don't want cold water, you fool." The Grand Vizier knocked the basin onto the floor.

"Yes, *Pasha*." The attendant scrambled and picked up the broken pieces.

Yet another attendant sheepishly offered a cotton towel. The Grand Vizier snapped it out of his hand and wiped the soap away, without ever bothering to rinse. "Clean up this mess." He tossed the hand towel back to the attendant and entered a third, cooler room.

"Grand Vizier, what was that noise?" Sekul Murish joined his friend at the edge of the large pool.

"I thought I recognized your white stallion." The Grand Vizier paused. "The noise? Attendants made mistakes."

"Did the Sister of the Sultan appreciate your gift?" Poiraz Osman *Bey* asked.

"You heard?" The Grand Vizier had rewarded the *sipahi* officer Poiraz Osman with both position and riches. The Grand Vizier sat down at the pool's edge. "I do not know, but both she and her mother should be impressed with my heroism. I told them how I had captured that Christian officer on the battlefield."

"But we did not even have a chance to fight."

The Grand Vizier chuckled and lowered his voice to a whisper, "Well, if you must know, I actually bought him at a slave auction in Axiopolis."

"You're so clever," Sekul Murish said.

"You are so right."

On a bluish-green marble bench, a man with full cheeks and a triple chin leaned forward. "Grand Vizier, did you say you captured an enemy officer?"

"I forgot to tell Aisha that I had bought him at the slave auction."

Though Poiraz Osman *Bey* eked out a smile, other *sipahi* officers did not chuckle.

After a second, the fat man on the marble bench belted out a hardy laugh. He rose and rushed across the white and gray marble floor. "Let me—"

Before he could finish his sentence, his towel loosened. He reached for it, but started to slide. His body twisted and he reached out to catch himself, but it was too late.

The Grand Vizier cringed. The fat man's thick feet slipped out from beneath him. His momentum carried him forward. He belly-flopped into the pool and water splashed everywhere. The Grand Vizier raised his hand and protected his face, as a large wave spilled over the pool's side. Sekul Murish wiped his eyes.

When the fat man popped his head out of the water, the Grand Vizier frowned in disgust.

"Are you all right?" one man asked.

The fat man shook his head and spouted water out his mouth, like a kettle pouring tea. "So sorry."

The Grand Vizier was not pleased. "Despite our religious admonition to be clean, perhaps some should not be allowed inside the *hamam*."

The fat man wiped his eyes. "It won't happen again." He caught his breath.

"Aren't you afraid that Aisha will find out you bought the officer at the slave auction?" Sekul Murish asked.

"How can she find out?" The Grand Vizier asked. "The slave doesn't know Turkish and she doesn't know Bohemian."

"Do not underestimate your betrothed," Poiraz Osman *Bey* said. "I hear she is smart."

"She is not as clever as I."

"But, "Poiraz Osman *Bey* said, "she does know Italian, like her grandmother."

"Fair enough, but whom will she believe?" The Grand Vizier asked. "Me? Or that foreign devil?"

"You, of course." Sekul Murish chuckled.

"Besides, when she receives the ransom money, she will forget the details and I will be her hero."

"You're so smart," the fat man said.

"I know." The Grand Vizier stroked his beard. "Aisha and I will make a perfect couple. She is so young and pretty and I so wise."

"I do not know about you," Sekul Murish said, "but no one disputes that the Sister of the Sultan is the richest woman in all *Stamboul*."

"In the whole world. Soon she will be even richer. As soon as Aisha finds out where the nobleman's family lives in Bohemia, they will gladly pay a huge ransom. And the money I have spent? I can make plenty more selling slaves; I am good at it."

"That you are," Poiraz Osman *Bey* said. "How long will you stay here in Belgrade?"

"Through the winter or until the Sultan calls me back. I have promised Aisha I would conquer more enemy officers," The Grand Vizier replied. "The steady supply of slaves means more opportunities." He knew any good buyer determines the field slave's value by his strength. With winter approaching, the weak field slaves would have to be fed until the new crops ripened. It all came down to how much a slave costs and how much food it takes to feed him, at least until he worked the fields or entered the mines of Anatolia. He added, "The selection at the Marketplace in *Stamboul* is limited."

"Limited?" Sekul Murish asked.

"Yes, prices usually are higher there." The Grand Vizier remembered seeing the slave auction at the New *Bedesten*, not far from his palace. Like the slaves sold at Axiopolis and other towns bordering the Ottoman frontier, the slaves in *Stamboul* were tested for fitness and strength. Many, including women, were taken into rooms to be stripped naked and examined for defects.

"I heard the prices for female slaves are still high," Sekul Murish said.

"Yes, ever since *Nur Banu*, the Venetian mother of the previous Sultan Murad III, increased the size of the Imperial Harem. About fifteen years ago, *Nur Banu* realized she was losing influence to Safiye, the Albanian favorite of her son Sultan Murad III. *Nur Banu* sent her servants to the slave marketplaces and chose the most beautiful ones. She paid the highest price and presented them to her son, one by one. Through the Chief White and Black Eunuchs, *Nur Banu* regained influence over the empire, but only until she died. Safiye then regained power over the affairs of her husband Sultan Murad III and later continued her influence over her son. Safiye learned from *Nur Banu* and she provided her son Sultan Mehmet III with *odalisques* and concubines."

"Are you afraid of getting married to Sultan Mehmet's sister?" Sekul Murish asked.

"In what way?" the Grand Vizier asked.

"When *Damat* Ibrahim *Pasha* married Aisha, he was only allowed one wife. He even had to refer to himself as 'her slave,'" Sekul Murish said.

"He did not know how to handle power."

The mist, even thicker than before, obscured the marble walls and wooden beams high above.

"And Aisha?" Poiraz Osman *Bey* asked. "The Sultan will only allow you one wife."

"I will be satisfied with just one." He turned to his friend, Sekul Murish. "How many wives do you have?"

"Two, but they were captured when my kingdom fell. When I get it back, I would like three, maybe four." Sekul Murish paused. "I do not know what happened to all of my concubines."

"The teachings of Mohammed and the Qur'an allow four," the Grand Vizier said. "How about you, Poiraz Osman? How many wives do you want?"

"I only want my one wife. She's more than enough for me."

"I'll never have one hundred concubines, like the Sultan." Though he was the second most powerful man in the empire, the Grand Vizier had only seen the outside of the Imperial Harem. No man was allowed to go inside, only the Black Eunuchs. The Grand Vizier knew that almost all of those eunuchs had been selected from young Africans from the Upper Nile. They had been made eunuchs when they were children. "That young girl I sent to the Sultan's Mother won't be allowed to leave the Imperial Harem at the New Palace."

"Except when the Sultan visits his other palaces."

"Yes, but on short travels, usually only one of the Sultan's favorites accompanies him."

"Grand Vizier?" Poiraz Osman *Bey* asked. "Are you planning to return to *Stamboul*?"

"Not anytime soon," the Grand Vizier said. "As soon as the Great Khan arrives in Belgrade, I intend to honor him with a feast."

The other *sipahi* officers grew more attentive.

"After his losses in Wallachia last month?" Poiraz Osman *Bey* asked. "I heard thousands of warriors died at the Battle of Targoviste."

Sekul Murish shook his head. "The Crimean Tartars were not as successful as we had hoped."

"The Crimean Tartars suffered greatly in their victory against men sent by the Holy Roman Emperor Rudolph II," the Grand Vizier said. "*Ghazi* Giray II, the Khan of the Crimean Tartars, had not appeared on the battlefield in years."

"The Khan's half-brothers have been helping the rebel *Deli* Hasan in Anatolia," Poiraz Osman *Bey* said. "The Khan worried that if he did not join Ottoman efforts, the Sultan, in attempt to forge peace, would appoint one of the Khan's half-brothers as Khan in his stead." The *sipahi* officer leaned closer. "But since that did not happen, the Ottoman Empire must deal with its bigger problem."

"What do you mean?" the Grand Vizier asked.

"In Anatolia, because the rebel *Deli* Hasan grows stronger, turmoil is now everywhere."

"I have written *Stamboul*. The Chief White Eunuch, Gazanfer *Agha* has appointed another to command our forces in Anatolia." The Grand Vizier scoured the attentive audience. "*Ghazi* Giray II will go neither to Anatolia nor fight along the frontiers of Persia. The Khan and his Tartar fighters will winter here, with me."

"Belgrade is not big enough for all his men," Poiraz Osman *Bey* said.

"Accommodations will be found."

Poiraz Osman *Bey* rose. "With your permission, I will return to *Stamboul*."

"Yes," the Grand Vizier said, "after the banquet."

"As you wish." Poiraz Osman *Bey* bowed.

Minutes later, the Grand Vizier and Sekul Murish returned to the first room and retrieved their clothes. After the Grand Vizier wrapped his turban around his head, he exited the *hamam*. At the far end, the woman who had winked at him earlier stood with her friends. Her face was not hidden and her wet black hair flowed over her shoulders. She ran her finger along the bottom of her chin.

The Grand Vizier raised his eyebrows and smiled.

"Grand Vizier!" The stablehand held the reins of his brown Arabian.

The Grand Vizier handed him a small coin, took the reins, and turned to his friend. "Will you join the feast I am hosting for the Khan tonight?"

Sekul Murish paid his groomer and mounted his white stallion. "My pleasure."

The Grand Vizier brought his horse around. Fully relaxed from the baths and with his guard and entourage in tow, he stopped at the top of the incline of Belgrade, a Serbian word meaning 'white castle'. Below, on the Danube, the wooden waterwheels of a dozen floating mills clapped rhythmically, more slowly than the spring. The noise continued both day and night.

To the east, waves of warriors, all on horseback and most clothed in black sheepskin, approached. Recent autumn rains kept the normal dust clouds from rising on the road paralleling the Danube. *Ghazi* Giray II and his personal guard of Crimean-Tartars, ten thousand strong, would arrive within the hour.

Inside the gates of the Upper Citadel, the Grand Vizier proclaimed to hundreds waiting in the square, "Preparations for the banquet must be completed!"

Chapter 25 - Letter to Pasha Tymor

A crystal box full of gems, and many other caskets of jewels; . . . then 125 mules laden with boxes of precious stones, silver, gold, cushions, carpets, curtains. . .

By the time this long procession of household furniture reached the Seraglio [Sarai/Palace] of Ibrahim [Pasha], the 50 waiting-women, under the direction of the Governess of the Harem, were ready to receive it, and in a short time the rooms of the bride [Aisha], the kitchen, and the rest of the house were in order.
"The Marriage of [*Damat*] Ibrahim *Pasha* [to Aisha]
An Episode at the Court of Sultan Murad III, 1586"

To her . . . brother [Tymor, Pasha of Nalbrits], this kind Lady writ so much . . .
John Smith

Vaulted Chamber, Ibrahim *Pasha* Palace, AH 1011 (AD 1602)

LIGHT RAIN PITTER-PATTERED against Aish's window and melded into her dreams. The rhythm slowed and Aisha awakened in her Vaulted Chamber. She fluffed up her pillow and leaned back, watching the water wash down her high window. She decided to rest a little longer and mused about how she would discover the truth about her slave. Soon her mother would arrive to take her to the baths. Aisha dreamed up other plans.

Her betrothed, the Grand Vizier, had written her that John was Bohemian, but John insisted he was English. She was still unsure which man was telling the truth. Only a week earlier, her friend Filiz had translated John's story from French. His journey to Orleans ended abruptly when his services were no longer needed by the Bertie brothers, Robert and Peregrine.

Aisha decided to send for Emine. The English translator could relay *Capitano* John Smith's story of his return to England.

I must find out about John's life there.

The pitter-patter against her windows quieted, signaling the end of the morning shower. She swung her legs over the side of her bed and pulled back the thick drapes. Streaks of water slowed, the dreary sky brightened, the garden very damp. She donned a robe and glided across the marble floor.

Aisha's head servant, always ready at Aisha's door, arose from the marble bench. "What is it?"

Aisha opened one of her cedar chests. "I need help picking out what I will wear today." She retrieved an attractive outfit.

The servant pulled out two more. "This one will impress the women at the baths." She placed the outfit next to the other ones on the bed.

Aisha touched the fabric of each outfit. "I do not plan to accompany my mother today."

"You are going to the baths alone?"

"No, I am staying home."

"I don't understand."

Aisha lifted the first outfit to her chin. "When my mother arrives, tell her I do not feel well."

"You don't mean?"

"Just tell her."

"Oh, I see, you are dressing for—"

Aisha raised her finger and quieted her servant's thoughts.

The servant picked up the silk one with repeating emerald patterns. "This one looks prettiest on you."

"I like it, too." Aisha rushed and opened the crystal jewelry box. She picked out a choker adorned with a single large pearl. "This once belonged to my Venetian grandmother."

"Yes, *Nur Banu.*"

Because *Nur Banu,* whose name meant woman of splendor, and Aisha's mother did not get along, Aisha's father, Sultan Murad III, had bestowed the whole of his mother's jewelry to Aisha. She received the inheritance shortly before her marriage to *Damat* Ibrahim *Pasha.* No one doubted she was her father's favorite daughter.

While the head servant placed the other two outfits neatly into the chest, Aisha folded the emerald dress. After setting the costly necklace on top of all, the young widow closed the chest and climbed back into her bed. "Tell me when my mother and sister arrive."

"As you wish."

Minutes later, she glimpsed her door opening. The voice of her mother rang out. "I must see my daughter."

The Overseer appeared first, then her mother.

"I told my servant I was tired," Aisha said.

Her mother brushed the tall, black eunuch aside. "Do you mean you will not be joining us?"

"I am unable to." Aisha moaned and put her hand on her waist. "My stomach aches."

Her younger sister poked her head around her mother. "The baths will do you good."

"We will not force her to go," her mother said.

"I am sure I will feel better by next week." Aisha sank her head deep into the pillow.

"I think I will send for the doc—"

Aisha bolted up. "No need."

Her mother peered at her, intently.

"I am sure I will feel better, later." Aisha sank back.

"We will see you later." Her mother turned and looked back.

"I hope to be rested." Aisha pulled up the rich covers. Out the corner of her eye, she saw her mother and sister exit. As the door closed, the sound of their footsteps faded; their chatter subsided.

Her servant presently reappeared. "Your mother's departed."

Aisha stepped out of her bed, her toes touched thick Persian carpet, and she looked toward the door. "Where is my Overseer?"

"Making sure the slaves build the new addition."

"I must see him."

"The slave?"

"The Overseer." Aisha retrieved the emerald green outfit and the jewelry. "But first, bring me pen and paper."

"Aren't you going to eat breakfast?"

"Not now. I must write my brother in Nalbrits."

"Ah, *Pasha* Tymor?"

Aisha admired her youngest brother, who lived at his Castle of Nalbrits in the Province of Cam-bria in Tartaria. Tymor had been granted a large *timar*, or estate, across the Black Sea in the lands of the Tartars east of Azov, at the edge of the Ottoman Empire. "I must tell him about the slave the Grand Vizier gave me."

The head servant returned with the writing instruments and shortly afterwards, the Overseer arrived. "You called me?"

"I need for you to bring my friend Emine."

"Emine? What about your mother?" her Overseer asked.

"The *Valide Sultana* does not need to know. You shall not tell her."

"As you wish, Sister of the Sultan." He bowed. "I will send a messenger."

"Good."

Her Overseer exited the Vaulted Chamber and Aisha sat down at her desk. With the perfect posture her tutors had always insisted on, the petite noblewoman picked up the feathered pen. Making sure she did not spill the jar of ink, she hurriedly penned a short letter to her brother. After waiting for it to dry, she rolled it the traditional way, from top to bottom.

Meanwhile, other servants had entered the Vaulted Chamber. One held a towel by the fountain, and, after Aisha washed her face and hands, handed it over.

"Excellent." Aisha's eyes sparkled. "Now, what shall I wear?"

With younger servants watching, her head servant smiled. "You'll want to reveal your beauty today." She opened the cedar chest, placed the pearl choker aside, and picked up the low-cut, emerald outfit they had previously chosen. "How about this one?"

Aisha smiled at the friendly banter. "Perfect." She picked up the silk outfit, and brought it to her chin, just like she had done before.

The servant smiled and helped Aisha dress, combing her long, black hair. With the final stroke, the servant set down the brush. "You are as gorgeous as ever."

Aisha glanced into the mirror. "Thank you."

"Not a strand out of place."

Carrying her letter to her brother in her hand, Aisha intercepted the Overseer. "The messenger?"

"He should be back soon."

"Excellent." She sauntered outside, through the garden to the kitchen. "Any pastries this morning for my friend Emine?"

"Something sweet?" her favorite chef asked.

"That would be nice."

"I'll get started right away." The chef reached for the tongs to break off a piece of the sugar loaf, a one-foot high cone.

Aisha walked across a garden path back to the salon, the meeting place built in the midst of the courtyard garden.

Salon, Ibrahim *Pasha* Palace, *Stamboul*

SURROUND BY THE beautiful mosaics inside her salon, Aisha paced back and forth. *What was taking the messenger and Emine so long?* She straightened the pillows on the bench attached to the wall. The young woman wanted to know more about the slave her fiancé had given her to ransom. *Capitano* John Smith had worn fancy clothes. Certainly, someone must be willing to pay a huge ransom for him. If not, John had his inheritance. His freedom must be worth thousands.

Minutes later, her guests arrived.

She rushed to the opening door and embraced her friend. "Thank you for coming, Emine."

"I came as soon as I could."

"I know." Aisha's servant helped Emine with her coat.

When the messenger started to take off his coat, too, Aisha turned. "Messenger?"

"Something else?"

"Yes." She waved the letter she had written. "I need you take this letter to the docks."

"A letter?" Emine asked.

"To my brother. I told him about the slave the Grand Vizier gave me."

The messenger buttoned his coat and took the letter. "I know a sea captain sailing across the Black Sea. With the rain lifting, the winds should be favorable very soon."

As soon as the messenger departed, the Overseer appeared. Before Aisha could say a word, the Overseer interrupted her thoughts. "I know, I'll bring the slave."

"Good." Aisha took Emine's hand and sat down. "My mother wanted me to go the baths."

"You didn't want to go?" Emine asked.

"How could I? I wouldn't enjoy it."

"Aren't you afraid that your mother will find out?"

"About what? I'm only trying to find out where John lives."

"But he's so handsome."

"Can I help that?"

By the time the Overseer and *Capitano* John Smith arrived from his slave quarters, a servant stuck her head into the room. "The water's hot for tea."

Aisha gestured for the servant to bring it and turned to her slave.

"John?" Aisha motioned to the adjacent cushioned bench. "Sit, please."

"*Gracie*." John nodded to her friend. "Emine, it is good to see you again. I haven't spoken English all week."

"I like to practice it, too." Emine took a cup from the silver tray. "Aisha just sent a letter to her brother, *Pasha* Tymor of Nalbrits in Tartaria."

John turned to the young noblewoman. "I didn't know you had another brother. He's probably as noble as you." John lifted the small cup. "I must say that you've been kind to me, considering my position."

Emine translated.

"You mean as my slave?" Aisha sipped her tea and peered at her servant, who had lingered too long. "That will be all."

"England does not have many slaves, just indentured servants," John said. "Most slaves in Europe come from Africa in trade controlled by the Portuguese. Many of the Africans are sent to the plantations of the Caribbean, Mexico City in New Spain, or the silver mines in Peru."

"Muslims cannot enslave other Muslims," Aisha said.

"And Arabs are no longer allowed to own white slaves," Emine said. "But your brother must own slaves at his castle in Nalbrits."

"Many," Aisha said.

The servant returned with a tray of freshly baked pastries.

"And Christians are not allowed to enslave other Christians." John set down his cup. "Well, at least Catholics do not enslave other Catholics."

"So did you return to Lynn and work for Master Thomas Sendall as an indentured servant again?" Aisha asked.

"No, I prefer adventure. After I reached the coast of England, the vessel I boarded in France sailed towards Gravesend on the Thames. The river was crowded with ships—some freshly damaged, needing repair."

Chapter 26 - Tussle on the Thames

The whole country [England] is diversified by charming hills, and from the summits of those, which are nearer to the sea, they sweep the whole horizon. On these summits are poles with braziers filled with flammable material, which is fired by the sentinel if armed ships of the enemy are sighted.

The Queen [Elizabeth] has every opportunity to muster fleets, for not only are the ports full of ships, but especially the Thames, which, from London to the sea, measures some forty or fifty Italian miles, where one sees nothing else but ships and seamen.

Francesco Gradenigo, Young Venetian Nobleman
Letter to Piero Duodo, Venetian Ambassador in France, Summer 1596

Gravesend, Thames River, England, Summer 1596

HIS SHORT JAUNT inside France having abruptly ended, John Smith found himself back in England. After sailing past the white cliffs of Dover and the Downs of Kent, the triple-masted vessel he was on tacked west. It soon reached the wide mouth of the River Thames. The rolling hills of the Kent countryside reminded John of peaceful days in Lincolnshire, but those thoughts did not last.

Above the riverbanks of Kent to the south and Essex to the north, round braziers, metal pans mounted on tall sturdy poles and filled with oil and tar, dotted nearly every hilltop. Ready to be lit, the large braziers could quickly signal an alarm if enemy ships ever threatened to attack. Ever since the Spanish Armada of 1588, when John was only eight years old, he had heard rumors that the Spanish might again attempt to invade England. For nearly a decade, those rumors had never come to fruition, but the recent capture of Calais by Cardinal Albert had raised the angst of many: though aging, King Philip II of Spain might yet attack his nemesis Elizabeth, the virgin Queen of England.

The river grew crowded with ships. One large Man-of-War was pockmarked, a sign of a recent skirmish or battle.

"First Mate!" the Captain yelled.

"Aye, Captain?"

"We'll drop anchor at Gravesend, beyond Rouge Hill." The Captain gestured beyond the bow.

With its wide arms turning in the steady breeze, a windmill stood next to its adjoining mill atop the hill just east of a small town. Downwind, a shorter brazier remained unlit—no enemy ships were in sight this day.

"Mates! Make Ready!" The first mate relayed the command.

Several sailors shimmied up the mainmast.

"I thought we were sailing to London," John said.

"Too crowded." The Captain gestured. "We're anchoring at Gravesend."

A company of armed horsemen trotted away from Rouge Hill and down the road leading into Gravesend. The road ended at a long pier extending out into the Thames. At that pier, soldiers had already embarked on a flat-bottomed boat ferrying them to a fort on the opposite shore. Star-shaped bastions protected land approaches to Fort Tilbury in the County of Essex.

A second boat docked to carry the band of approaching riders from the pier to the river's northern shore.

The Captain brought his ship into the wind. "Drop the mainsail!"

"Aye, aye, Captain."

Sailors loosened the lines holding the mainsail. They let the lines slip through their hands. Others secured the mainsail to the boom.

"Drop anchor!"

The anchor splashed. When the ship was secured, sailors lowered the small skiff attached to the ship's side. John noticed an English officer disembarking from the pockmarked Man-of War and wondered what had happened. He stepped into the skiff. When the skiff drew close to a fishing vessel, he recognized its markings: it was owned by Lord Willoughby. He waved to two of his friends, who worked for the same Lord that his father had before his untimely death.

"John Smith." One friend waved back. "I thought you were in France."

"I was. What are you doing here?"

"We had such a good catch, we decided to take it to London."

John cupped his mouth. "I'll meet you on the quay."

Docks, Gravesend, County of Kent, England

AT THE DOCKS of Gravesend, ferrymen led the first horse John had seen onto the second flat-bottomed boat. The first boat had already reached Fort Tilbury on the opposite shore. Ferrymen calmed that steed and led a second horse aboard.

When John's two friends transferred a small flat of fish to the dock, one pointed. "We just have to make a quick delivery to the pub over there."

The eatery fronted an open square. Beyond the square, the wooden houses stood side by side on curved streets. A steeple rose above the two-story structures.

"And after that?" John asked.

"We go to London."

"That's where I wanted to go."

"We have plenty of room on board," John's friend said. "Lord Willoughby wouldn't mind."

"He's back from Venice?"

"No, not yet, but he's already in Lower Saxony."

"In Stade on the lower Elbe River," the second friend added.

"Is he well?"

"He still suffers from the gout, but despite the royal proclamation that no one lame can serve, he's petitioned the Queen to be Governor of Berwick on our border with Scotland."

John helped his two friends deliver the fish to the pub near a small market square. After eating a quick meal by St. George's Church—its steeple he had seen earlier—John and his two friends returned to the dock and located their fishing vessel.

The English officer, whom John had seen earlier on the water, limped towards them. "Did you say you're going to London?"

"Yes," John's friend said. "We're going now." John stepped into the skiff, followed by his friend.

The officer looked down. "I need to go London, too."

"Come on in."

A local man rushed forward. "You can't take him to London."

"He wants to go," John said.

"And who are you?"

"John Smith from Lincolnshire."

"Only the local ferry from Gravesend can transport passengers up the

Thames." The local pointed to a ferry boat. "We claim that right."

"John's not a passenger. He's our friend."

"And him?" the local man asked.

"I'm an officer in the service of the Queen."

"Still, you must pay."

John remembered seeing the officer before. "You're from Lincolnshire, too, aren't you?"

"Yes, I led some soldiers to Cadiz." The officer turned to the local. "You wouldn't want to delay my report to the Privy Council, would you?"

"The rules."

"I have to report to the Queen's secretary about Cadiz," the officer said.

"You were at Cadiz?" the local asked.

"Wounded and knighted," the officer said. "The Privy council wants an accounting of the booty captured at Cadiz."

"What booty?" John asked.

"Haven't you heard?" the officer asked. "The English sacked Cadiz in Spain. The Earl of Essex knighted me in the marketplace."

"You're a knight?" John stared at him in awe.

"Yes." The knight turned to the local man. "The Queen will be displeased if you delay me any further."

The ferryman huffed and walked away.

The skiff carrying John, his two friends, and the knighted officer soon reached Lord Willoughby's fishing vessel. After his friends helped the officer onto the deck, the vessel weighed anchor. It sailed west, slowly, up the Thames.

Before the first bend, the knighted officer sat down. John and his two friends gathered round.

"What happened at Cadiz?" John asked.

When the officer raised his pant leg, he showed off a wound, not fully healed. Around its edges, the skin was red. "It's not that bad." Pus oozed from it. "It occurred after the Earl of Essex scaled the walls. We captured many Spaniards and held the nobles for ransom, but let me start at the beginning."

"Do."

"By early June, the English fleet had mustered at Plymouth. Francis Vere and many Dutch allies had arrived from Holland and Zeeland, but few of us knew what our destination was. Some thought we would attack the Azores, others the coast of Portugal."

That must have been about the time Robert Bertie had joined the expedition, John thought.

"Later, after we had captured Cadiz, we learned from the Spanish prisoners that King Philip II of Spain thought we would attack Lisbon," the officer explained. "At the beginning of this year, the Spanish King, who also claims the title of King of Portugal, received two Ambassadors from the Kingdom of the Congo. They had arrived at San Lorenzo d'el Escorial outside Madrid to complain to His Most Catholic Majesty about his Portuguese slave traders."

Chapter 27 - Ambassadors from Africa

Two ambassadors, uncle and nephew, have arrived here from a King of the Congo provinces to renew their obligations toward his Majesty [King Philip II of Spain]…to beg him to prohibit the Portuguese in the region of Cape Verde and along that whole coast from buying the Blacks, who are Christians.

Some of the Portuguese . . . have been making large purchases; and this has led the neighboring princes to capture these [Christian] Blacks in order to sell them again.

Agustino Nani, Venetian Ambassador to Spain

Madrid, January 1596

Ambassadors' Hall, *San Lorenzo d'el Escorial*, Spain, 1596

THE DOUBLE DOORS of the Hall of the Ambassadors swung open. The room had an air of freshness, for the palace of San Lorenzo d'el Escorial had been built less than twenty years earlier, while *Infanta* Isabella Clara Eugenia was still blossoming into the woman she had become. Less austere than other parts of the palace, this room had several large paintings and tapestries adorning the walls. The ceiling was somewhat low, but, like the rest of the palace, everything was in perfect proportion.

The Foreign and Domestic Ministers, as well as other members of the Court of her father, were in attendance. The Spanish King sat on his throne.

A Spanish crier stepped forward, stopping just inside the double doors. He pronounced, loudly, "Ambassadors from the Kingdom of Congo."

Dressed in colorful African attire, the brother and son of the King of the Congo ambled forward to the center of the room. The two ambassadors bowed to His Most Catholic Majesty, King Philip II.

When the two Africans Ambassadors rose, the Spanish King waved them forward. "Welcome."

They approached the King and kissed his hand. When they stepped back, *Infanta* Isabella noticed that both Africans wore crucifixes around their necks.

"What may we do for you?" the King asked.

"We have always paid homage to the King of Portugal," the brother of the King of the Congo said.

Infanta Isabella knew that her father had claimed the title of King of Portugal after the previous king died without a legitimate heir in 1580.

"Yes, and to me, personally, for nearly twenty years."

"Recently," the younger ambassador said, "the problem of the Portuguese slave traders has grown."

"Those Portuguese traders have purchased many blacks for Mexico City, the Potosi mine in Peru, and the plantations in the Caribbean," his uncle added.

"Yes, but what's the problem?" the King asked.

"Lately, the traders have made even larger purchases, buying Christian Blacks, taking them to Cape Verde Island off the African coast, and transporting them to New Spain."

"Certainly, the Portuguese slave merchants know it is illegal to enslave any Christian," the King said, "whether *negro*, *blanco*, or *mulatto*."

"Neighboring princes have been raiding our fields and villages, capturing our strong men," the older ambassador added. "Once captured, they keep them all together. The traders claim they cannot tell the difference."

"Enslaving Christian Negroes is prohibited." King Philip II of Spain rose to his feet. "If slave traders buy Christians from your kingdom, they must be released and returned." The King glanced at his ministers.

The Domestic Minister stepped forward. "I will tell the governor of Portugal to enforce the order at the Island of Santiago off Cape Verde, St. George's Castle at El Mina on the Gold Coast, and Island of Sao Tome—"

"Close to Congo. *Gracias*." The older ambassador turned to his nephew. "We have a second request."

The King sat back down. "Go on."

"We would also like our own Cathedral at Sao Salvador."

"An excellent idea," King Philip II of Spain said. "I will support your petition to the Pope."

"*Gracias*." The ambassador glanced at a young African standing by the door. "One last favor, if it would please your Highness."

"Yes?"

"One of the young officers from my court would love to sail with your fleet to New Spain."

"We can arrange that. Perhaps on our most powerful ship, the *Saint Philippe.*"

"I will talk to the Admiral," Domestic Minister Cristobal *de* Moura said.

After the two ambassadors bowed and departed, a servant helped the King lift his leg onto a stool. *Infanta* Isabella could read her father's face: his gout was still painful. The Foreign Minister Juan *de* Idiaquez and the Domestic Minister drew closer.

"The work on the fleet goes well," Minister *de* Moura said. "Nearly one hundred ships are being built in Biscay, Lisbon, and Seville."

"Later this year we'll be able to send a new Armada to Flanders or Ireland," the King said.

"The Earl of Tyrone, Hugh O'Neill," Foreign Minister *de* Idiaquez said, "has made some progress against the English General Sir John Norris and his brother. At the Battle of Mullabrack in Ireland, O'Neill did wound one of the two brothers last autumn. When Norris offered gold in exchange for the release of four of his officers, O'Neill refused."

The King Phillip II of Spain declared, "As well he should."

"O'Neill told Norris that he would never exchange a heretic for gold, but that he would gladly spare their lives if they would abjure and live by the Catholic faith."

"So the English prisoners converted?"

"Unfortunately for them, no," the Foreign Minister responded. "The four heretics refused to renounce the Church of England. They declared that they would gladly die in the religion of their Queen."

"And O'Neill?"

"He burned the four English officers at the stake."

Infanta Isabella, like her father, voiced no objection or surprise. She knew fire was the punishment for heretics, both in this life and the next.

"We must see how we can aid the Irish Catholics," the King said.

"What about sending the fleet to England?" Minister Idiaquez suggested.

"With Cardinal Archduke Albert now in the Lowlands, we must consider an invasion of England." The King glanced at his daughter. "Should Elizabeth die, perhaps I can place my daughter on that throne. Our claims are better than King James VI of Scotland."

"I agree," Foreign Minister d'Idiaquez said. "That is why I've asked

Father Robert Persons to come from the nearby English College in Valladolid, Castile to meet with us."

The English Jesuit entered the hall. After an exchange of greetings, he spread his papers on a table. "I have begun the work of detailing the *Infanta's* claim to the English throne."

Infanta Isabella knew that her father once was married to Queen Mary of England. *Infanta* Isabella also had an independent claim to the English throne through the lineage of her maternal grandfather, the late French King Henry II.

"The lineage must be clear," the King said.

"It will be," Father Persons said. "After I finish the work I will translate it into Latin and deliver it to the Pope."

"What does the *Infanta* say?" Minister d'Idiaquez asked.

Infanta Isabella smiled. "May God's will be done."

Alcatraz Palace, Toledo, Castile, Spain, Late June 1596

SEVERAL MONTHS LATER, the Spanish Court relocated from the Palace at San Lorenzo d'el Escorial to the fortress Palace of Alcatraz in Toledo, south of Madrid.

For the past thirty-five years, King Philip II of Spain had divided his reign among his palaces, both inside Madrid and at the ones nearby, including Alcatraz in Toledo.

Two servants helped King Philip II of Spain out of his bed. When the servants escorted her father to his study, *Infanta* Isabella heard bells ringing. She stopped and peered out a palace window.

The steeple bells of the Cathedral of Toledo swung back and forth. She thought of her cousin Albert, who had once been Cardinal of Toledo. She wondered when her future husband would return, since he was in the Lowlands. His capture of the port of Calais in Picardy had raised everyone's spirits, but the capitulation of La Fere to King Henry IV had lowered them almost as far. Her cousin had not been given a fair chance to keep the French King from capturing it.

"Any further word from the Lowlands?" her father asked.

"Very little since the fall of La Fere," *Infanta* Isabella said.

"Isabella?" The King motioned for his daughter's help.

"What is it?"

"Gout."

Infanta Isabella read the pain on his face and lifted his leg up on a three-legged stool.

Her father asked, "Did the order to the Portuguese ship captains get delivered?"

"Yes, we received a note from your Viceroy." *Infanta* Isabella picked up the top letter from the stack. "The Viceroy in Portugal has sent word to all Sea Captains that no Christian slaves can be purchased and those on board must be released, but he also requests aid."

"Aid?" the King asked.

"The Portuguese nobles want your help." *Infanta* Isabella knew that Antonio Perez, the pretender to the Portuguese throne had visited England and caused mischief in London. Rumors that Queen Elizabeth would support him had surfaced several times. Despite Cardinal Albert's able rule when he was Viceroy of Portugal, not all Portuguese wanted Spanish rule.

"With the death of that pirate Drake in Panama last January and the dispersion of his fleet, the virgin Queen certainly won't attack this year."

"Especially after the conquest of Calais in April," *Infanta* Isabella added.

"You and I think the same. The Portuguese worry too much; their concerns are exaggerated. Things are going so well; we prosper on all sides. What is the worry? Who can stop us?"

Infanta Isabella agreed with her father.

An hour later, the guard at the door let a messenger into the study. He waved a letter. "From Cardinal Archduke."

The King motioned for his daughter to retrieve it. She broke the seal and scanned the writing.

"What is it?" her father asked.

"Albert remains in the field until he knows where the English fleet has sailed."

"The Queen sends her fleet?"

"He reports the flower of the English nobility is on board." She turned the page. "The Dutch, too, have added both soldiers and sailors."

"Does he say how large?"

"He reports an enemy fleet of fourteen thousand soldiers and four thousand sailors has sailed south from Plymouth."

"So large?" The King leaned back. "Are they headed to Lisbon or the Azores?"

Minutes later, a second messenger arrived at the door.

"What is it?" the worried King asked.

The messenger bowed. "On the Feast Day of the Nativity of St. John, a scout ship sighted fifty English ships off the coast of Portugal, north of Lisbon."

Infanta Isabella knew the feast day was June 24th, only a few days earlier. Part of the Spanish fleet was still being built at Lisbon, though several ships had relocated to Cadiz, south of Seville.

"Panic has struck Lisbon," the messenger added. "Nobles move their goods out of town."

"Send Adelanto of Castile." King Philip II of Spain and Portugal dictated an order. "Lisbon must prepare to receive an attack."

Chapter 28 - Queen Elizabeth in London

I am convinced that we shall never have a fair and trustworthy peace with the King of Spain as long as he is on the flood of success, and does not realize that his career may be checked, his power overthrown, his greatness humiliated.

Queen Elizabeth to the Duke of Bouillon
Deciphered from Italian and reported by Piero Duodo,
Venetian Ambassador to France from Paris, 17th August 1596

When he [John Smith] came from London . . .

John Smith

London, Thames River, England, Summer 1596

"MAKE WAY! MAKE way!"

The sound echoed over the water.

"Make way for her majesty, the Queen!"

The fishing vessel swerved. Leaving the knighted English officer in the middle of his story, John Smith rushed to see the Queen. His two fisherman friends joined him at the rail of the small ship.

Ten oars simultaneously hit the water and the lead boat surged. The lines tightened and pulled the trailing Royal barge a few feet forward. "Make way!"

The fishing captain tacked his vessel harder. Lord Willoughby's ship yawed violently to port. John widened his stance and steadied himself. The boat straightened.

Twenty oarsmen once more slapped their oars against the water. The Royal Barge swooshed forward.

Fitted with draped curtains, the plush barge pulled alongside Willoughby's fishing vessel. Beneath an overhanging awning, the aging Queen Elizabeth, short and ruddy in complexion, sat on her throne.

In the thirty-seventh year of her reign, members of her court swarmed around her. Her Ladies-in-Waiting, all dressed in long gowns and high-starched collars, attended the Queen's every need. Well-dressed guards provided protection.

Oars again slapped in perfect timing. The lead boat cut through the placid water. The barge edged further away from the Tower of London, Queen Elizabeth's point of departure.

Round towers anchored the corners of that ancient castle. Its gray outer walls rose above the Thames. Behind the outer walls, the White Tower with its four spires reached higher. Built at the time of William the Conqueror, over five hundred years earlier, the White Tower was the oldest part of the castle. Weather vanes swiveled atop each spire, before steadying beneath the blue London sky.

The Tower of London was an ancient castle, but oftentimes it also held prisoners. When Elizabeth was young and just a Princess, the ardent Catholic Queen Mary once imprisoned her inside that same tower.

The knighted officer with the wounded leg joined John at the rail and pointed to a gate facing the river. "When guards ordered Princess Elizabeth to go through Traitors Gate, she refused."

"Elizabeth knew she was no traitor," John said.

"But when it started to rain, she relented."

"Times change," John said. "England is no longer Catholic."

"Yes, and now Queen Elizabeth heads the Church of England. She holds the title 'Defender of the Faith'. That's part of the reason she sent us

Queen Elizabeth of England

to Cadiz," the wounded officer said. "Queen Elizabeth also said that peace cannot come until King Philip II realizes he cannot win."

"What do you mean?"

"The Queen told the Duke of Bouillon that there can be no peace until King Philip II realizes that his work may be checked, his power overthrown, and his greatness humiliated."

Further up the Thames, along the shoreline, a small crowd grew noisy. An array of citizens waved. Several younger ones jostled to the fore to glimpse their Queen and her court.

John moved to the bow to get better look. A bridge appeared straight ahead. Nineteen sarlings or piers supported the bridge and shops spanning the length of it. "That must be London Bridge. I knew the bridge had buildings on it, but those are tall." Many of the buildings stood three stories high.

London Bridge, the Thames River, and the Tower

From a few windows and irregular gaps between buildings, spectators peered down at the Queen. Her barge disappeared beneath the bridge.

"Trim the sails!" the fishing boat captain shouted. "Make ready, men!"

John's friends brought in the remaining sails. They cinched knots. The vessel drifted towards the busy dock at Billingsgate.

Billingsgate, London, England

AFTER THE WOUNDED, knighted officer departed, John grabbed one end of a flat filled with fish. "London's much busier than Lynn."

John and his Lincolnshire friends pushed their way through the busy dock and reached the fish market. After they delivered the catch, one of his fisherman friends asked, "You're staying?"

"I have to see the lawyer," John said.

"Be careful here," his friend advised. "London has many migrants and vagrants."

"Those bloody vagrants." A woman yelled from behind a fish stand. "Always trying to grab a fish or two."

"That's mighty foul language coming out of the mouth of one of the fairer sex," his friend whispered to John.

"What did you say?" the woman asked. "You'd better mind your own mouth, if you don't want me to flail this fish over your pretty little head!"

"Feisty are we?" his friend asked.

"Reckon you'd be, too, if you had to smell sailors all day."

"I bathed last week," the other friend said.

"We'd best be going." John nudged his friends. "Let the woman be."

Walking a little further, his friend gestured to several men, gathered together. "These migrants just move from one town to another, looking for work."

John noticed that when a nobleman or merchant walked by, several of the migrants offered to haul goods. Others pressed sea captains, their vessels docked, to go sea.

A man sitting at a corner held out his hand. "Can you spare a penny?" He repeated. "Mister, a penny?"

John took a coin out of his purse. "Here, now get up and go on your way."

John's friend interjected, "They're usually looking for workers down by the warehouses. Go see them."

When the man walked away, John's friend told him, "I don't like giving money to vagrants."

"He looked hungry."

"When vagrants can't find work, they sometimes steal. A couple of years ago, vagrants surrounded Queen Elizabeth's coach, so she decreed that all must leave London. Since then, any found are returned to their home shires and counties."

~ ~ ~

A COUPLE OF weeks later, John returned to Billingsgate. "What's the commotion?"

"Cadiz in southern Spain has been sacked and the whole English army has arrived back at Plymouth. I'm looking for my son." A nobleman pointed to sailors disembarking a ship. "And Rear Admiral Sir Walter Raleigh is here."

The dashing adventurer limped down the ramp. A few years earlier Sir Walter Raleigh had secretly married Elizabeth Throckmorton, a Lady-in-Waiting to the Queen. When she found out what had happened, Queen Elizabeth imprisoned both Raleigh and his wife Bess in the Tower of London for marrying without her permission. Later, they were both released and Raleigh again received the Queen's favor.

"Why is he limping?" John asked.

"Splintering wood injured him," a voice from behind answered.

John turned to the familiar sound of his friend. "Robert Bertie."

"Sir Robert, now."

"You're a knight?"

"Yes," Robert Bertie said. "The Earl of Essex knighted me at Cadiz."

"How so?"

While Sir Walter Raleigh entered a waiting carriage, Robert led John through the fish market. "About two months ago, Rear Admiral Sir Walter Raleigh was on the *Warspite*, the flagship of the fourth and final squadron. I arrived on board with my uncle, Sir John Wingfield, and his Lieutenant, Colonel Horace Vere, not far from Portugal's coast."

"You must tell me all."

Chapter 29 - English Fleet Sails

Our Navy in this port beautiful to behold, about one hundred fifty sail, whereof eighteen of Her Majesty's own, since her reign never so many before.
Anthony Standen to Francis Bacon aboard "The Repulse"
Plymouth Harbor, England, 30th May 1596

Lastly, as the end of war is peace, so she [Queen Elizabeth] might have had peace when and with what conditions she would, and have left out whom she would; for she only should force him [King Philip II] to wish for peace;
--Robert Devereaux, the Earl of Essex to the Council, 13th June 1596

Cadiz, among the seaports, may truly be called the Heart of Spain . . .
Agustino Nani, Venetian Ambassador in Spain
Madrid, Spain July 1596

Off the Northeast Coast of Portugal, Mid-June 1596

THE SMALL PINNACE, or boat, shuttling Sir John Wingfield, Lieutenant Colonel Horace Vere, and Wingfield's nephew Robert Bertie from the large ship, the *Vanguard*, drew alongside the *Warspite*, a great ship under the command of Rear Admiral Sir Walter Raleigh. The sailors of the small craft retrieved the oars and secured the lines.

The three Englishmen grabbed the meshed ropes overhanging the *Warspite's* side and climbed up past tiers of cannons. Some cannons protruded out open portholes, but most stayed hidden behind covered ones.

Sword at his side, Robert slipped over the rail after his uncle and Colonel Vere.

A deckhand yelled, "Welcome aboard, Sir Wingfield."

Robert steadied himself on the deck of the flagship of Sir Walter Raleigh, the leader of the fifth and final squadron of the English and Dutch fleet of two hundred fighting ships and support vessels. With a crew of three hundred, the *Warspite* was larger than any other vessel in the final squadron of fifty. It was also fast.

Most importantly, though, was its commander: Sir Walter Raleigh, the most famous seaman in all of England. Like most English lads, Robert had heard of Raleigh's encounters with the Spanish Main in the New World, his organized—though failed—expeditions to Virginia, and his more recent exploits in Guiana in the Americas.

Sir Walter Raleigh, standing near the helm, shouted to the sailor in the crow's nest above, "Keep a sharp eye!"

One arm around the mast, the sailor leaned southeast. "Land ho!"

Robert rushed to the rail. He viewed the northwestern coast of the Iberian Peninsula. "Is that Portugal?"

"Yes," his uncle said.

Sir Walter Raleigh pivoted to his helmsman. "Prepare to tack."

"Whereto?" the helmsman asked.

"West, away from land."

"Mates!" the helmsman shouted. "Make ready!"

Sailors ran past Robert, Sir Wingfield, and Captain Vere to their stations. Two sailors shimmied up the foremast, others grabbed lines attached to the boom.

"Ship ahoy!" The lookout pointed to the south.

Robert spied a Spanish frigate over the port bow. Many leagues away, the Spaniard hoisted its mainsail and veered due south, toward Lisbon.

"Shall we give chase?" the helmsman asked.

"Nay!" Sir Walter Raleigh replied. "We're on a mission."

Robert wondered what the true mission was. His uncle, like all of the other captains, had orders, but they would remain sealed until they reached their destination. If separated by tempest or attacked by the Spanish, the orders were to be destroyed, tossed into the sea.

"Bear west!" Sir Walter Raleigh ordered the helmsman, "Away from the coast!"

"Aye, aye, Rear Admiral."

The helmsman turned the wheel. The *Warspite* tacked west.

Robert glanced back at his uncle's vessel. Sails unfurled, the *Vanguard* matched the *Warspite*'s movements. The rest of the squadron of nearly fifty vessels did the same.

With a steady breeze and on calm seas, the open ocean lay ahead. While the squadron raced towards the sun lowering over the Atlantic, Robert reflected on how he had arrived here so quickly.

When summoned at Orleans, Robert had thanked his younger brother

Peregrine and attendant John Smith for bringing him supplies and victuals. He told John he had no further use for him, for he was going to sea.

Robert hurried to the French coast, where he had boarded a waiting
English vessel, quickly crossing the Bay of Biscay. He met up with the
English Fleet at Plymouth in Devonshire on the southern coast of England
at the beginning of June. About one hundred fifty fighting vessels had
gathered there, including eighteen of the Queen's own.

Lord Admiral Charles Howard and the Earl of Essex, the two Generals of the fleet, received final orders from the Queen's Council. Grand
Admiral Howard, the Baron of Effingen, had command of the fleet at sea,
while Robert Devereaux, the Earl of Essex, would command her Majesty's
forces on land. Though some officers had speculated that the fleet might
sail east and confront Cardinal Archduke Albert at Calais, most knew that
the fleet would sail south, toward Spain. The die had already been cast:
King Philip II must be confronted on his own land.

Aboard the ships were six thousand three hundred English soldiers
under pay, as well as nearly one thousand young noblemen, volunteers
from almost every noble house in the land. Nearly seven thousand sailors
manned the one hundred fifty fighting ships in the fleet.

Although delayed a day by contrary winds, the massive English fleet
sailed south during the first part of June. Slightly more than a week later,
Sir Walter Raleigh had summoned his officers by raising his Flag of
Council at the stern of the *Warspite*.

Robert's uncle Sir John Wingfield, the commander of the *Vanguard*,
had heeded Raleigh's summons. He brought his Lieutenant Colonel, Captain Horace Vere, as well as his nephew Robert Bertie along.

Now here he was on the *Warspite*.

"What day is it?" Robert asked.

"The Catholics call this the Feast Day of the Nativity of St. John," his
uncle said.

"So many saints," Robert said. "Can't keep track of them all."

"Guess you're no priest." His uncle led him across the deck. "When
we reach our destination, you'll fight alongside me."

"Do we know where?" Robert was anxious for battle.

"Until we pass Cape St. Vincent at the southwest corner of Portugal,
my orders are sealed."

"Sir Wingfield." An important officer intercepted the three Englishmen.

"Sir Francis Vere." Sir Wingfield saluted. "Your younger brother here is my Lieutenant Colonel."

Horace Vere saluted his brother, too. "You remember Lord Willoughby's son?"

"Robert, isn't it? You were very young that last time I saw you." Sir Francis Vere chuckled. "But even then, you wanted to examine my saber and my dagger."

Sir Francis Vere was Lord Marshall of the expedition. He commanded the *Rainbow*, another ship in Sir Walter Raleigh's squadron. The able general of the English land forces in the Lowlands, Sir Francis Vere, had followed in the footsteps of Robert's father, Lord Willoughby. After a battle, Robert's father had knighted Francis Vere.

"An honor to be in your command, Sir Vere." Robert saluted.

Dutch Man-of-War in 16th Century

"I've brought my best men, all experienced in warfare." Sir Vere gestured to his ship, the *Rainbow*.

Sir Vere's veterans were scattered amongst various ships of the rear squadron, but Sir Vere had not arrived with only the English—he had also brought the Dutch. Like Sir Vere's veterans, the Dutch and Zeeland soldiers had fought against the Spanish in the Lowlands for many years. Dutch and Zeeland flags flew above some of the ships in Raleigh's squadron.

Sir Vere waved for a Dutch officer to approach. "I persuaded Lewis Gunther of Nassau to take command."

"We heeded the call of our English allies and your Queen. I've chosen two thousand two hundred of our best soldiers." Lewis Gunther of Nassau, the cousin of the *stadtholder* Count Maurice, had joined Sir Vere in late April and brought twenty-four Men-of-War and three thousand sailors. His Dutch musketeers and pikemen from Vlissingen in Zeeland had drilled with the already growing English force at Plymouth.

"Do we know our destination?" Sir Wingfield asked.

"Wherever it is," Lewis Gunther said, "we draw our swords for the good of Christendom." He looked askance at Sir Wingfield.

Robert wondered why, but then remembered that his uncle had once commanded the garrison at Geertruidenberg in the Lowlands. When Sir Wingfield's English soldiers did not receive their pay, they mutinied and turned the fort over to the Spanish. The Dutch considered Sir Wingfield's soldiers as not much better than traitors. Many Dutchmen considered Sir Wingfield a traitor, too.

"I will lead the fight myself," Sir Wingfield said.

"As one of my countrymen said, 'we have not surer way of putting an end to our war for independence than to transport that war nearer to the heart of Spain'," Lewis Gunther said.

"I agree."

"Though Sir Walter Raleigh wants the honor," Sir Vere said, "I can tell you our purpose is to intercept Spanish trade with the Indies and the rest of Europe. The capture of Calais by Cardinal Albert has been awful. We can no longer protect the trade with northern Europe."

The group walked past the helm and climbed the ladder up to the poop, the high deck above the captain's cabin, finding Sir Walter Raleigh.

"Do we know our destination?" Sir Wingfield repeated his earlier question.

"Nothing will be revealed until we pass Cape Saint Vincent," Sir Walter Raleigh said.

"What is the purpose of this meeting?" Sir Vere asked.

"I called this meeting to reiterate what was said before." Sir Walter Raleigh peered at Sir Vere. "At sea, I am in command of this squadron. Should we encounter the Indies fleet, I'm in charge."

Sir Walter Raleigh had crossed paths more than once with Sir Vere, a man ten years younger than the Rear Admiral.

"On shore, the army reports to the Earl of Essex and me," Sir Vere replied. "The Earl of Essex has written the Articles of War."

"With your help," Sir Walter Raleigh said.

Sir Vere, who had been chief advisor to the Earl of Essex, was appointed Lieutenant General, the Lord Marshall of the land expedition. Sir Vere would second Essex, the general of the invasion on shore.

"Queen Elizabeth insists the lives of all women and children must be spared." Sir Walter Raleigh turned to Lewis Gunther. "We will only kill those who resist."

The officers returned to their respective ships and Sir Walter Raleigh's squadron sailed southwest. The fifty escorts, including Sir Wingfield's *Vanguard* and Vere's *Rainbow*, surrounded Sir Walter Raleigh's *Warspite*.

Sails billowed full in the setting sun.

Cape Saint Vincent, Southeastern Portugal, End of June 1596

SEVERAL DAYS LATER, Sir Walter Raleigh's squadron rounded the southwestern tip of the Iberian Peninsula. In the long journey from England, no vessels had been lost. Below the rocky cliffs of Cape St. Vincent, the fifty ships drifted to a stop.

Sir Walter Raleigh's rear squadron, with the *Warspite* at its head, was formidable, but it was only a portion of the total.

Months in the making, the English and Dutch fleet was impressive by any measure. Besides the one hundred fifty fighting vessels, smaller ships held ammunition, supplies, and horses. Flyboats, built to hold companies of soldiers for boarding or landing men in shallow water, also accompanied the fleet, bringing the total number sailing to Spain to roughly two hundred.

Larger than the infamous Spanish Armada of 1588, this fleet included twenty Great Ships, each fitted with three tiers of cannon. Ever since that Armada had visited England, the Queen had never truly returned that favor: never, until this day. The favor would be returned with a fleet larger than any other during Queen Elizabeth's entire reign.

The fleet was divided into five squadrons of equal size. Sixty years old, Grand Admiral Charles Howard, the general at sea, had overall command and sailed aboard his flagship, the *Ark Royal*. Nine year's earlier Sir Walter Raleigh had built that massive vessel himself, calling it the *Ark Raleigh*. When Queen Elizabeth purchased it, she renamed it the *Ark Royal*. Grand Admiral Charles Howard used the *Ark Royal* as his flagship when he led the English to victory over the Spanish Armada the following year.

Less than half the Grand Admiral's age, the Earl of Essex, Robert Devereux, sailed on the *Repulse*, at the lead of the second squadron. The ambitious Earl of Essex had overall command of the land forces and held the title of Lord General.

A third squadron consisted of Dutch vessels.

A fourth squadron sailed closer to Sir Walter Raleigh's forces. Lord Thomas Howard, a little older than the Earl of Essex, but still much younger than his kinsman Grand Admiral Charles Howard, commanded that squadron.

Sailing aboard the Great Ship *Mere-Honour*, Lord Thomas Howard had seen the Spanish before, in the Azores. While gathering supplies there, a huge Spanish fleet drew near. Though Lord Thomas Howard escaped with his half-dozen ships, one of his vessels, the *Revenge*, stayed behind. Its Captain wanted to pick up stragglers, sailors still on shore.

Sailing alone, the *Revenge* boldly faced a Spanish fleet of fifty three ships. With his ship badly damaged, the Captain of the *Revenge* refused to surrender, preferring to die instead. He had even ordered his Master Gunner to destroy his ship by shooting cannonballs down through his hull. When the Spanish offered safe passage for his crew, however, the sailors convinced their leader to finally surrender.

On the way back to Spain, a storm sank the captured *Revenge*, commanded by the Spaniards and a skeleton crew. Most survivors from the previous encounter, including the brave captain, died at sea. The *Revenge* remained on the minds of Lord Thomas Howard and his friend Sir Walter Raleigh, the Rear Admiral of the fleet.

The officers of the *Vanguard* gathered on the ship's poop deck. Some were from Lincolnshire, friends of Robert Bertie's father.

"Where will we go?" Robert asked.

"There are only two places we can intercept Spain's trade with Europe and the Indies," Sir Wingfield said. "Most trade flows from Lisbon and Cadiz."

"We're going to Lisbon?"

Sir Wingfield unsealed the letter. "We are going to Cadiz." He finished reading. "The Queen says first Cadiz, then backtrack to Lisbon."

When an Irish vessel approached the fleet from the east, Grand Admiral Charles Howard sent three flyboats to intercept it.

Hours later, after the Irish merchant had been captured, a messenger from the *Ark Royal* boarded the *Warspite*. Another messenger from the *Warspite* came to the *Vanguard*. "The Irish captain says that no one at Cadiz knows we're here."

"Excellent," Sir Wingfield said. "A complete surprise."

"And that's not all," the messenger reported. "The fleet to the Indies still lies in port, fully loaded with supplies worth millions."

"Its escorts?"

"The four Apostles, including *Saint Philip* and *Saint Andrew*."

"They fought against the *Revenge*." Sir Wingfield pointed to the *Warspite*. "Sir Walter Raleigh will want to avenge the *Revenge*."

Bay of San Sebastian, Cadiz, Spain, June 30, 1596

AT THE BAY of San Sebastian, a southerly wind grew stronger, the breaking waves grew higher. Whitecaps dotted the choppy waves all the way to the end of the bay, where a guard tower stood.

Aboard the *Vanguard*, Robert Bertie, having arrived several hours earlier with the rest of the English fleet, saw Spanish riders riding back and forth along the rocky shore.

At the tip of a narrow sliver of land, five or six miles in length, the Spanish port of Cadiz stood strong. On the far side of the walled city, Spanish flags waved over Fort St. Philip, commanding the harbor entrance. Inside the harbor, the Bay of Cadiz was crowded.

The last of forty Indies merchant ships, fully laden and riding low in the water, sailed up the Puntales channel to Puerto Real. Like threatened cubs cowering in the darkest part of a cave, these weaker vessels retreated to the innermost part of the harbor. Galleys and larger ships, including the four Apostles, protected them.

About to step onto one of the landing boats, Robert Bertie turned back when his uncle grabbed his arm. "Not yet."

"What's wrong?"

Sir Wingfield pointed. "Sir Walter Raleigh arrives."

Grand Admiral Charles Howard had ordered the Rear Admiral to watch for Spanish Men-of-War that might attack from behind, but he must not have encountered any ship from St. Lucar, for here he was.

The *Warspite* dropped anchor near the *Repulse*, the vessel of the Lord General, the Earl of Essex.

Robert could tell the invasion was not going well. The landing might be a disaster. The waves grew rougher, the wind did not subside. Saltwater splashed over several vessels.

~ ~ ~

SIR WALTER RALEIGH reached the deck of the *Repulse*. "General Essex! What are you doing?" Sir Walter Raleigh pointed to the boats in the bay.

"You risk everything!"

At the stern of the *Repulse*, more soldiers boarded landing crafts.

Another gale hit, like a slap across the face. One of the landing craft below the ship capsized. Soldiers flailed in the water. Some reached for their muskets, other for pikes. Heads bobbed, some towards jagged rocks.

"We were going to land on the west side and take the town," the Earl of Essex said.

"But the Spanish fleet?"

"Fort St. Philip protects the harbor entrance and—"

"If we continue this path, our ruin is guaranteed!" Sir Walter Raleigh said. "The whole army will be overthrown! Call the boats back!"

"Grand Admiral Charles Howard would not allow us to enter the harbor," the Earl of Essex said, "unless we first captured the town."

"I agree with Sir Walter Raleigh," one commander interjected. "We cannot win. Even if we land, we will be overcome by those defenders." He pointed to Spanish musketeers lining up by the Guard Tower at the end of the bay.

"Go and persuade the Grand Admiral," the Earl of Essex told Sir Walter Raleigh. "You have my support."

Sir Walter Raleigh reentered his skiff and his sailors rowed him to the *Royal Ark*, the greatest of the English ships.

Minutes later, Sir Walter Raleigh's boat once again approached the *Repulse*. Not waiting to board, Raleigh cupped his hands around his mouth and yelled up to the Earl of Essex, "*Intramus*!"

Upon hearing the Latin phrase for we enter and with much joy on his face, the Earl of Essex threw his hat into the air. A gust carried it onto the water, but he did not seem to care.

"Bring them back!" the Earl of Essex commanded.

One by one, each of the landing craft in the water turned around. Other vessels, farther away, took longer to return. Several vessels capsized, some soldiers drowned. By the time the rest of the boats returned, it was already dusk. For Sir Walter Raleigh, a nighttime attack on the Spanish seemed too risky. They must wait until morning.

That night, the *Warspite* and the rest of the English fleet edged closer to Las Puercas, the rocks at the harbor entrance. In the bay, on the other side of those rocks, the four Apostles remained anchored, prepared to defend the Indies supply fleet at any cost.

Chapter 30 - Sir Walter Raleigh

You shall receive many Relations, but none more true than this.

The spectacle was very lamentable on their side: for many drowned themselves; many, half-burnt, leapt into the water; very many hanging by the ropes' ends by the ships' sides, under the water even to the lips; many swimming with grievous wounds, strucken under the water, and put out of their pain;

And withal so huge a fire, and such tearing of the ordnance in the Great Philip, and the rest, when the fire came to them, as if any man had a desire to see hell itself, it was there most lively figured.

Sir Walter Raleigh
A Relation of Cadiz Action in the Year 1596

Bridge, the *Warspite*, Cadiz, Spain, Sunday, July 1, 1596

DAY BROKE OVER the port of Cadiz, the oldest city in Europe, the ancient Phoenicians' Cradle of the Sun. The morning's first rays illuminated the tall masts of the Spanish fleet, anchored in the bay.

At fifty-five vessels strong, the Spanish fleet was not only large, but also well-protected. Two forts commanded the peninsula side of the bay. Fort St. Philip jutted out at the tip of the peninsula, while Fort St. Puntales stood further south, at the narrowing of a channel. Beyond that second fort, the rich merchant ships of the fleet had already sought refuge.

Most importantly, the more than forty merchant ships were protected by the four Apostles, the largest ships in the Spanish navy.

For Sir Walter Raleigh, the *St. Philip*, anchored dead ahead, was the most tempting of targets. With the Admiral of the Spanish fleet on board, the largest of the four Apostles weighed more than fifteen hundred tons. The *St. Philip* with its one thousand two hundred men would be a worthy match to Sir Walter Raleigh's *Warspite* and his three hundred-man crew.

The previous night, after the landing was abandoned, Grand Admiral Charles Howard had called a War Council aboard his flagship, the *Ark*

Royal. The Council had chosen Sir Walter Raleigh to lead six English ships into battle, but those ships would not include the *Ark Royal*. It would not participate in the attack. The Flagship of the English fleet had a draft too large to maneuver in the shallower parts of the Cadiz harbor.

On the *Warspite*, Sir Walter Raleigh stood next to his Master Trumpeter. Atop the poop, the high deck behind the wheel, Rear Admiral Raleigh signaled his trumpeter.

The Master Trumpeter took a huge breath and brought his trumpet to his lips. He blasted a refrain: "All hands on deck!" He repeated the tune. "All hands on deck."

Ship bells clanged.

"All hands on deck!" Quartermasters in the midship echoed the refrain. "All hands on deck!"

Sailors rushed from below to their appointed stations: some near tackle and rigging; others up masts and across booms. Soldiers likewise appeared in force. Musketeers readied their shot and lined up at the rails: their powder dry; matches lit.

"Gunners! Beat open the ports!" Sir Walter Raleigh ordered. "Out with your lower tier!"

Visible through open grates in the deck below, cannoneers rolled their ordnance into position. At the prow, next to the foremost cannons, gunners stacked bags of powder and more cannonballs. The Lieutenant at the forecastle signaled. 'All ready'.

"Weigh anchor!" Sir Walter Raleigh commanded his Boatswain.

The Boatswain and his men cranked a wheel, bit by bit. The cable creaked in the hawse pipe as the anchor was slowly raised.

The ship shifted, but Sir Walter Raleigh wanted to be sure it was more than buffering winds. "Is the anchor aweigh?"

"Yea!" The Boatswain shouted. "Yea! Admiral! Anchor aweigh!"

Raleigh shouted to the bow. "Let the foresail fall!"

"Aye, aye!" The sailors obeyed.

The sail flapped in the southerly breeze. Two sailors pulled the lines taut and the foresail billowed out. The *Warspite* surged forward and sailed past Las Puercas, the outer rocks.

Less than a mile ahead, the *St. Philip* weighed anchor and sailed up the middle of the harbor. It retreated to the narrow channel between Fort Puntales and the Spanish mainland.

The *St. Philip* slowed and turned. It retreated no further and stopped.

Its broadside faced the hard-charging *Warspite*, a ship Sir Walter Raleigh had outfitted with his personal fortune, now expended. The *St. Philip* opened all of its portholes. Its bronze cannons, primed and ready, poked through every opening.

The other three Apostles—the *St. Matthew*, the *St. Thomas*, and the *St. Andrew*—set sail. With fifty cannons and four hundred-man crews, each Apostle exceeded the *Warspite*, both in tonnage and firepower. Like the *St. Philip*, they stopped at the narrowest part of the channel and turned their broadsides toward the harbor entrance. Augmented by three frigates on their right side, the four Apostles formed an impenetrable curtain.

Pushed by the wind, the *Warspite* eased past the front of Fort St. Philip at the harbor entrance. The fort fired rounds at the *Warspite*, but her cannons remained silent. She did not engage.

Sir Walter Raleigh respected neither the fort nor its cannons; he would not fire back. He turned to his Master Trumpeter, who blew a single blast of his horn. That flat sound was Raleigh's only answer to cannonballs that whizzed by the *Warspite*, already at the town walls of Cadiz.

Like the fort, cannons aligned atop the notched walls of Cadiz fired rounds at Sir Walter Raleigh and his well-built ship. Again, Sir Walter Raleigh refused to engage; he fired neither cannon nor musket.

The town's cannonballs wholly missed. Sir Walter Raleigh's Master Trumpeter wailed a single blast of his instrument. The note was loud, the tone flat.

Immediately ahead, seventeen galleys with their oars out of the water lined the shore from the walls of Cadiz to Fort Puntales, two miles distance. Their prows faced the center of the harbor. The *Warspite* sailed in front of each of them and they fired, one by one. Again, Sir Walter Raleigh answered, but only with seventeen blasts of the trumpet. He did not want to waste ammunition on slave-powered galleys.

With a good wind filling his foresail, Sir Walter Raleigh kept his eyes fixed on the prize: the *St. Philip*, anchored below the fort in the middle of the channel, directly ahead. Through his spyglass, Sir Walter Raleigh spotted two individuals conferring on the deck of the *St. Philip*: the Admiral of the Spanish fleet and an African officer, most likely a loyal Catholic from the Congo.

"Drop anchor!" Sir Walter Raleigh ordered.

His sailors furled their sails. The Boatswain dropped the anchor. The Rear Admiral yelled to the Master Gunner. "Fire!"

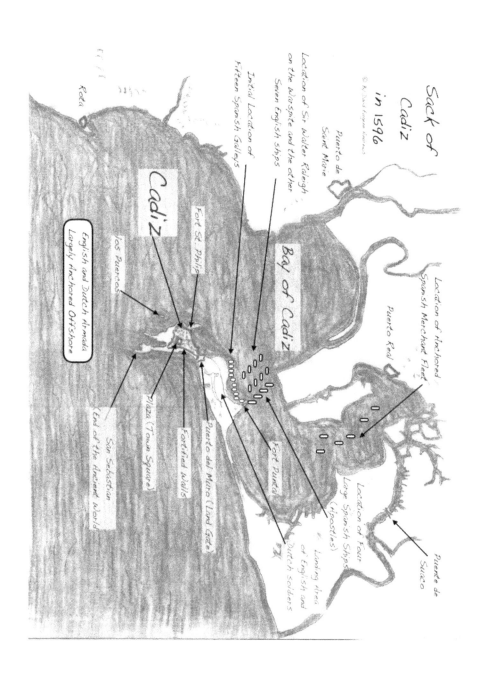

Sack of Cadiz in 1596

© By David Lawson Lawson

Rota

Puerto de Sant Marie

Location of Sir Walter Ralegh on the Vanguard and the other Seven English Ships

Initial Location of Fifteen Spanish Galleys

Cadiz

Fort St. Philip

los Puercas

English and Dutch Armada Largely Anchored Offshore

Bay of Cadiz

Location of Anchored Spanish Merchant Fleet

Puerto Real

San Sebastian End of the Ancient World

Plaza (Town Square)

Fortified Walls

Puerto del Mino (Land Gate)

Fort Punta

Location of Four Large Spanish Ships

Landing Area of English and Dutch Soldiers

Location of Four Large Spanish Ships (Hipostles)

Puente de Suazo

The Master Gunner relayed the command. The *Warspite*'s prow cannons fired at the *St. Philip's* side, well-within range.

In reply, the *St. Philip* unleashed a terrible barrage. Cannon blasts from its powerful broadside hit the *Warspite*'s bow and its unsecured foresail.

The Battle of Cadiz had begun.

Five English ships seconded the *Warspite* into battle. The *Rainbow* under the command of the Lord Marshall, Sir Francis Vere, fired a broadside at Fort St. Philip and a second one at the walls of Cadiz, before engaging the galleys lining the shore. Sailing close to the peninsula, the *Rainbow* fired at the first galley. It responded by firing its prow guns.

The other sixteen galleys fired at the four English ships advancing up the channel. Two sailed on the far side near the Spanish Mainland and two closer along the shores of the peninsula.

On the far side, the *Nonpareil* had Vice Admiral Thomas Howard at its helm. He had transferred his flag from the *Mere-Honour*, because that ship, like the *Ark Royal*, was too large to maneuver in the harbor. Vice Admiral Thomas Howard anchored the *Nonpareil* off the *Warspite*'s port side. He fired his cannons at a second Apostle fronting him. Like the *St. Philip*, that Apostle and yet another answered English cannons with broadsides of their own.

In front of the rocks of the peninsula, the Spanish galleys fired their prow guns incessantly at the *Rainbow*, but to little effect. They were no match for that well-built ship.

The two other English ships sailing nearest to the *Rainbow* joined her and fired well-aimed broadsides. They dislodged several galleys, whose oars soon smacked the water.

Those two last English ships soon anchored slightly astern of the *Warspite*'s starboard side. All four Spanish Apostles faced their broadsides against the English attack vessels. They blocked their path to the inner harbor with power.

The rest of the seventeen galleys sailed in single file, perhaps hoping the cannons of Fort Puntales would protect them. They were mistaken, and garnered little support. When the galleys passed the *Warspite*, Sir Walter Raleigh decided to offer more than sour notes.

This time, instead of a blast from his trumpeter, Sir Walter Raleigh unleashed his cannons. His powerful broadsides blasted several galleys and damaged them severely.

The galleys, however, survived and edged along the shore. Under the Apostles' protection, they turned. Three by three, they slid into the openings between the bows and sterns of four Apostles. Those remaining galleys joined two large galleons, reportedly transferred from Lisbon, as well as two argosies, formidable vessels built at Ragusa. The Admiral, Vice Admiral and Rear Admiral of New Spain, within firing range of the *Warspite*, provided even more support to the four Apostles, still lined stern to bow below Fort Puntales at the narrowest part of the channel.

Galley - 16th Century

Behind all of those fighting ships, the rest of the Spanish fleet and the rich merchantmen destined to the Indies, were anchored at Puerto Real in the inner harbor. In open seas, the four Apostles would have provided ample protection against English corsairs, who were authorized by Queen Elizabeth to harry Spanish trade.

The six English ships vied for position, but Sir Walter Raleigh remained at the head of all. The previous night, the Council of War had stipulated this, as well as gave orders not to board the enemy directly. Sir WalterRaleigh and the others were ordered to wait for Fly-boats that Grand Admiral Charles Howard would send forward.

The *St. Philip*, the *St. Matthew*, the *St. Andrew*, and the *St. Thomas* fired more broadsides at the six English ships. The battle intensified. The *St. Philip* fired at the *Warspite*, more rigging and tackle fell. Booms became unhinged, the foremast fractured.

Sir Walter Raleigh fired back. "More powder to the prow!"

"Gunners! Another round!" The Master Gunner and his men reloaded.

Gunners lit fuses and fired. The *St. Philip* was hit. Wood shattered, splinters flew.

Sir Walter Raleigh realigned his ship. Broadside faced broadside, cannons fired ceaselessly. Over three hours, the *Warspite* scored countless hits, receiving just as many if not more.

After another hour of ever-increasing cannon fire, at about ten o'clock in the morning, the Earl of Essex joined the fray. Lifted by a rising tide, the *Repulse* and an eighth English ship joined the fight. The remainder of the English and Dutch ships remained anchored at the harbor entrance.

The Earl of Essex anchored the *Repulse* on the port side of the *Warspite*. More cannonballs hit the *Warspite*.

"We're taking on water!" the head carpenter said.

"Fix it!" Raleigh ordered.

"Sailers! Bail!"

Another enemy shot shook the vessel.

"Where are those Flyboats?" Sir Walter Raleigh wanted to board the *St. Philip*. He peered astern, toward Cadiz and the harbor entrance. No flyboats were in sight.

"The *Warspite* might sink," the boatswain yelled.

"I must avenge the *Revenge*!" Sir Walter Raleigh was determined to win or die in the fight.

Sir Walter Raleigh exited the stern of the *Warspite* and took his skiff to the *Repulse*. He wanted to confer with the Earl of Essex, one of the two generals of the whole operation.

"There are no flyboats!" Sir Walter Raleigh said. "If we don't attack, the *Warspite* will sink."

They peered over the stern and confirmed Raleigh's assertion. Grand Admiral Charles Howard was approaching in a small boat, but he was joining Vice Admiral Thomas Howard on the *Nonpareil*. With even more cannonballs hitting the *Warspite*, it might be too late.

"I'll support you," the Earl of Essex said.

Having decided to board the *St. Philip* with his crew and soldiers, Sir Walter Raleigh stepped over the rail and entered his skiff. He noticed something different: Sir Francis Vere had slipped anchor. Contrary to orders, his *Rainbow* had edged ahead of the *Warspite* on the starboard side.

Sir Walter Raleigh told his oarsmen, "Hurry!"

Only fifteen minutes after he had first departed, Raleigh exited the skiff and again boarded the *Warspite*. He peered to port and saw something just as disturbing as Vere's maneuver. Vice Admiral Thomas Howard had slipped anchor, too; the *Nonpareil* was now the closest English ship to the Four Apostles.

Instead of being first in battle, Sir Walter Raleigh found himself third. *This cannot stand*, he told himself. "Boatswain! Weigh anchor!"

"Aye! Admiral!"

The *Warspite* slipped its anchor. It surged ahead of the *Rainbow* and *Nonpareil*, before anchoring again.

"Fire!" Sir Walter Raleigh ordered.

Much closer now, the *Warspite* fired its cannons again. The *St. Philip* responded in kind, its barrage even more intense.

"Admiral!"

"What is it?"

"We're taking on more water below, and—"

"Speak up!"

"Sir Francis Vere, the Land Marshall, has tied lines to our stern."

Sir Walter Raleigh peered over starboard. Sailors on the *Rainbow* drew that vessel closer to the *Warspite* and closer to the action.

"Cut Sir Vere away!"

The sailors obeyed and cut the tie lines. The *Rainbow* drifted away, protected by the *Warspite*, ever more crippled.

The cannonade continued. Shots blasted through the aftcastle, splintering wood and injuring Sir Walter Raleigh's leg.

Sir Walter Raleigh leaned on his good leg and glanced over the portside. The *Repulse* edged closer to an enemy Apostle. It fired at the *St. Thomas* at point blank range.

Straight ahead, the *Warspite*'s bow almost touched the *St. Philip*, now less than twenty feet away.

Soldiers readied themselves for boarding.

"Lay out a warp!" Raleigh ordered.

Sailors tossed grappling hooks across the water.

Vice Admiral Thomas Howard and the *Repulse* matched Sir Walter Raleigh's initiative. They tossed grappling hooks at the *St. Thomas.*

Another English ship drew closer.

The *St. Philip* slipped its anchor and surged away. The other three Apostles did likewise, heading for rocks and mud opposite Fort St. Puntales. *St. Philip* and *St. Thomas* immediately ran aground.

The *St. Philip* tipped. Scores of its sailors hit the water and the mud. Others dangled from lines; some were pulled below the surface. Bodies and timbers floated side by side. The *St. Philip* began to burn. Many sailors, clothes aflame, jumped ship.

A black officer dove like a swan. As he hit the water, the powder in the greatest Apostle, the *St. Philip,* exploded. The Admiral of the Spanish fleet must have ordered his African officer to light a fuse and ignite the magazine to keep the ship from falling into Sir Walter Raleigh's hands.

Flames swirled up the shooting mainmast. The massive ball of fire spread across the water, consuming timber. From the sea below to the masts and sails above, the hellish inferno engulfed Spanish sailors flailing in the water.

Some sailors screamed, "*Misercordia*!" requesting to be put out of their misery and the English musketeers obliged. Firing from the rails, they shot the gasping sailors dead, ending their lives before they could drown.

The *St. Thomas* burned, too, but English soldiers and sailors captured the *St. Matthew* and and *St. Andrew* before the Spanish set them aflame.

Dutch and Zeeland ships engaged and attacked the two argosies that had supported the Apostles. After finding them full of ordnance, they boarded and killed many sailors. When the Dutch brought more Spaniards to the deck and started executing them, Grand Admiral Charles Howard rushed to one argosy to intervene.

Rear Admiral Sir Walter Raleigh, as fast as his injured leg allowed him, rushed to the other. "Stop!" he told the Dutch. "Stop the slaughter! We've won!"

The veterans from the Lowlands halted their killing.

Most of the Spanish galleys, meanwhile, retreated deeper into the harbor. While dozens of rich merchantmen remained anchored near Port Real on the eastern side of the inner harbor, the galleys stayed closer to the peninsula.

~ ~ ~

NEAR THE SOUTHERN end of the five-mile-long peninsula, where it connected with the Spanish mainland, Robert Bertie stood next to his uncle aboard the *Vanguard*.

Sir Wingfield had already captured two galleys, so he turned the wheel. The *Vanguard* tacked and aimed at a third, fleeing towards the narrowest part of the peninsula. With only a slight chance of escape on a narrow waterway leading to the open ocean, the enemy oars hit the water to the faint beat of a drum.

Robert peered ahead. On shore, near a bridge on the peninsula, an ingenious machine raised another galley out of the harbor. Beyond it, a second galley slid into a small canal, further away from the bay. Both vessels followed about ten other galleys that had already escaped to the Atlantic.

Those dozen galleys sailed southeast and hugged the coast leading to the Strait of Gibraltar.

"That one shall not escape." Sir Wingfield ordered, "Fire!"

The *Vanguard's* prow cannons fired across the galley's bow. The pounding of the enemy drum ended. Their oars were raised out of the water. The galley drifted to a stop. The Spaniards on the deck of the galley dropped their weapons and surrendered.

Robert Bertie jumped on board and helped secure the prisoners. He looked below and found countless white slaves, ragged and worn. He called up to the English sergeant, "Get these men out!"

The English sergeant appeared below deck, found a key and unlocked the chains of the galley slaves.

"Thank you," one English slave said. "I've been here for months, ever since I was captured in the Caribbean last winter."

After having released the slaves and transferred them to other vessels, Robert headed back onto the deck of the *Vanguard,* now reunited with the rest of the English fleet. Robert looked to the harbor.

The larger of the forty or so merchant ships anchored in the inner harbor had no hope of escape. The *St. Philip* and the *St. Thomas* still smoldered from consuming fire. Though badly damaged, the *St. Matthew* and *St. Andrew* were in English hands. Sir Walter Raleigh was wounded on the *Warspite*, but the sea battle had been won.

At Earl of Essex's command, bows pointed toward shore. Landing craft lined the harbor.

The Earl of Essex prepared to lead the Army.

The time had come to take Cadiz.

Chapter 31 - Farther No Man Dares to Go

He [Robert Bertie] was knighted in the Marketplace [of Cadiz] where he said, "An old woman with a stone knocked down the Esquire [Bertie], and the General [Robert Devereaux, the Earl of Essex] commanded him to rise a Knight."
Attributed to Robert Bertie by David Lloyd in Memoirs of the Lives, Actions, Sufferings, and Deaths of Those Noble, Reverend, and Excellent Personages, That Suffered by Death, Sequestration, Decimation, or Otherwise for the Protestant Religion

Beyond th' old pillars many have traveled
Towards the sun's cradle, and his throne, and bed.

A fitter pillar our Earl did bestow
In that base Island, for he well did know
Farther than Wingfield no man dares to go.
"Il Cavaliere Gio: Wingfield" by Sir John Donne

Cadiz, Spain, Mid-Afternoon, July 1, 1596

FIVE REGIMENTS OF English and Dutch soldiers crowded into scores of vessels. To the beat of the drum, the landing craft approached the whole length of the harbor shores, from Cadiz to Fort Puntales. The bodies of Spanish sailors drowned or burned in the fiery destruction floated in the strait below the fort. Though two Apostles had been captured, the St. Philip and the St. Thomas still smoldered in the mid-afternoon sun. The Dutch were recovering many bronze cannons; the sea battle had just ended.

Select soldiers, including Robert Bertie, prepared for a second battle, this time on land. Robert ate strips of dried meat, the final victuals that John Smith had brought to him when he was in Orleans. Ahead of Robert, the walled city of Cadiz remained in Spanish hands.

Riding in two separate boats at the head of their respective regiments, the Earl of Essex Robert Devereaux and Lord Marshall Sir Francis Vere neared the rocks below Cadiz. One of Sir Francis Vere's most important officers, Sir John Wingfield, sat at the bow of a large landing craft, directly in front of Robert.

On either side of Robert, oarsmen pulled in perfect rhythm. Like all of the other oarsmen in the regiment, they pulled to the beat of a loud drum. It resounded across the bay.

The skiffs of the other three regiments moved closer to the shore, but further south, toward Fort Puntales. In the wake of the vessels carrying the five regiments, other boats and skiffs transported hundreds of young English noblemen, including two named Thomas Gale and John Donne. Those volunteers would soon experience their first land action.

Squeezed between the oarsmen, Robert peered over the shoulder of his uncle. Sir Francis Vere touched the shores and disembarked. His regiment readied, but the landing would not be easy.

On shore, eight hundred enemy horsemen had already exited the gates of Cadiz. Galloping hard, they approached the landing party with lances upright, arquebuses across their chests, and swords at their sides.

Sir John Wingfield stood up and motioned. Wearing no helmet, Robert's uncle urged his rowers. "Catch up!"

Robert grabbed the end of the nearest oar and pulled harder. Within seconds, his skiff landed.

The English musketeers in Sir Francis Vere's regiment jumped into the shallow water and climbed onshore. Dozens of them fired at the horsemen charging them. In front of the standing gunmen, English pikeman moved into position, steadying their pikes. When the charging horsemen stopped, they used the pikes' curved hooks and pulled the riders off.

Further south, all the way to Fort Puntales, the Dutch and English soldiers disembarked along the shore. The two thousand fighting men confronted the outnumbered Spanish horsemen and drove them off. Pursued by the other three regiments, most of the Spanish caballeros and cavalrymen galloped toward the Spanish mainland.

While the Earl of Essex and Sir Francis Vere organized their men along the shore, the other three English regiments captured Fort Puntales, destroyed the engine that had raised the galleys from the bay to the Atlantic, and secured the Puento Souse where peninsula met the mainland. They formed defenses that would confront the relief army that King Philip II would certainly send.

Most of the remaining Spanish cavalrymen who had escaped the encounter returned to the walls of Cadiz, either directly or through rolling hills leading to the western side of the peninsula. Enemy soldiers and horses under the cover of those hills reentered Cadiz or patrolled its walls. They were prepared to resist any siege that may begin the next day: the Earl of Essex wanted to bring cannons on shore.

Sir Thomas Wingfield accompanied by his nephew joined Sir Francis Vere and the Earl of Essex. Lewis Gunther, the commander of the Dutch forces, also attended the ad hoc meeting.

Sir Francis Vere told Earl of Essex, "We don't have to wait for the artillery."

"What do you mean?"

"Do you see the Spanish troops before the town?" Sir Francis Vere pointed toward Cadiz, less than a mile away. "If we draw them out, they will lead us inside."

The Earl of Essex did not hesitate. "Let it be done."

Vere turned. "Sir Wingfield?"

Robert Bertie's uncle stepped forward. Robert knew that his uncle wanted to atone for his English soldiers who had surrendered the Dutch fortress at Geertruidenberg to the Spanish. The Dutch had never forgiven Wingfield, forbidding him to fight with them in the Lowlands. Wingfield's chance at redemption was at hand.

"Our two regiments will cross through the hills and hide as close as we can to the city." Sir Francis Vere pointed. "Take your two hundred men and advance to those Spanish troops. If they counterattack, skirmish with them and retreat until—"

"Until what?" Sir Wingfield asked.

"Until you meet your support." The Earl of Essex had assigned his Lieutenant Colonel and three hundred men to second Sir Wingfield.

"Then we'll turn and together drive the Spanish back." Sir Wingfield acknowledged.

"We'll follow with the main force." Sir Francis Vere glanced at the Earl of Essex and Count Lewis Gunther.

The Earl of Essex gestured his approval.

When Sir Wingfield returned to his select company, Robert Bertie joined him. With most of the English soldiers hidden behind the hills, the plan proceeded.

Sir Wingfield, along with Robert Bertie and the rest his men, attacked the light horse outside the walls of Cadiz. When the skirmish intensified, they turned and ran, until they reached the support.

Those soldiers and Sir Wingfield turned back on the pursuers. Together, five hundred pikemen, swordsmen, and musketeers attacked the Spanish horsemen.

Some Spaniards escaped to the city through the fortified gate. When that gate shut, the last of the Spanish riders abandoned their horses and surmounted the walls that extended shore to shore.

The Earl of Essex and Sir Francis Vere followed with five hundred more men. Lewis Gunther of Nassau and the Dutch soldiers attacked the guard towers d*Effend*ing the Bay of San Sebastian, where the previous night's landing had been abandoned.

From the very start, the Dutch had been the most aggressive. Before the English fleet surprised Cadiz the previous afternoon, Dutch ships, disguised as merchantmen, had entered the harbor. When Admiral Charles Howard and the English fleet first appeared, those merchantmen raised the flags of William the Silent and opened fire. No longer merely defending their ancient liberties from overreaching governors, the Seven United Provinces of the Netherlands had brought their War of Independence to Cadiz and sent shockwaves throughout Spain. Lewis Gunther and his attackers overwhelmed the Spanish defenders and planted their flag atop the tower bunker.

Robert Bertie and the other English soldiers crossed a broad ditch and the outer ramparts of Cadiz. In front of them, the old city walls were more than six feet high. The English musketeers fired a volley. Pikemen climbed up the walls. Musketeers pushed the thin line of defenders back with more shot.

The Earl of Essex reached the top of the walls. Two of his captains led their men down the streets, as the enemy retreated to the center of town.

About a block from the wall, a Spanish officer held firm with his men. Sir Wingfield grabbed an abandoned pike and ran directly at him, piercing him all the way through. Another defender wounded Sir Wingfield in the thigh. Bertie drew his sword and delivered a mortal blow to that Spaniard, but Sir Wingfield's leg bled.

"Bring me a horse." Wingfield told his nephew.

The only horses were far ahead, ridden by *caballeros* mounting a stubborn defense against the few English footmen.

Down another street, the main gate remained strongly defended. If it were not opened quickly, the scores of English attackers within the town would be annihilated. Order was gone.

Sir Francis Vere with a small company of men attacked the gate. The

Spaniards fired muskets. The brave English fought back. For nearly a half hour, the firefight intensified.

In the midst of that fighting, Robert found an abandoned horse near Sir Francis Vere, who continued to direct the assault. Robert brought it to his uncle, who held his bandaged leg.

"Help me up!"

Robert lifted his uncle up onto the captured horse.

"Put your helmet on!" Sir Francis Vere yelled.

Sir Wingfield drew his sword. "I must fight!" He rode forward without his helmet. A few of his men, including his Lieutenant Colonel Horace Vere and Robert Bertie, followed him toward the main square. Spanish musketeers fired from the second floor and the bell tower of the town hall.

Meanwhile, Sir Francis Vere overcame the last of the Spanish defenders. The iron gate slowly rose and the Earl of Essex led his men down the main street to the square, where Sir Wingfield directed his men.

Swords drawn, Robert and five other soldiers edged along the side of the square, past an eight-foot high white cross, and toward the corner of that hall. More Spanish defenders retreated through the center door of the town hall, while Robert advanced past shuttered windows, below a balcony.

Suddenly, Robert heard a noise. Above him, citizens began throwing down large rocks from the overhang. Robert raised his arms, but it was too late: a Spanish lady had released a rock with both hands. Robert ducked, but it hit him in the shoulder and knocked him down. While he pushed himself against the wall, he turned his attention to the middle of the square, where his uncle slew one of the last defenders.

Suddenly, a shot rang out. It hit Sir Wingfield in the head. The knight slid off the horse and slammed the ground hard.

Robert Bertie wanted to run to his uncle but the volleys pushed him back to the wall.

Seconds later, the helmeted English general, the Earl of Essex, led the main force into the square. Two companies of musketeers lined up. They aimed and fired a round at the musketeers who had shot Robert's uncle dead.

After several more volleys, Spanish weapons became silent, the defenders atop the walls stayed hidden. The civilians, who had thrown rocks, likewise disappeared, drawing back inside the town hall.

An hour later, Grand Admiral Charles Howard and others entered the town. Sir Walter Raleigh entered, too, but upon the shoulders of his men. The splintering wood had so badly wounded his leg that he could not stand.

Sitting next to his fallen uncle at the base of the white cross, Robert massaged his sore shoulder. Soon, the hundreds of citizens locked inside the town hall surrendered and were taken prisoner.

Robert learned that the *caballeros* who had not escaped to the mainland had entered the convent of San Francisco. By nightfall, they, too, surrendered. Sir Francis Vere's prisoners included one of the wealthiest men in Cadiz, the President of the *Casa de Contratacion*, the House of Trade.

Most of the remaining Spanish forces and citizens had retreated to Fort St. Philip on the bay side side of Cadiz. Surrounded, the five thousand inside that fort had no means of escape.

At nightfall, the looting began. Officers chose houses for their own; their men began to pillage. In every section and down every street, the chaos spread.

The Rear Admiral Sir Walter Raleigh, pressed on all sides by the looters, grimaced. He told the two generals. "I'm returning to the *Warspite* to order the fleet."

Sir Walter Raleigh ordered his men to lift him onto a captured horse. He rode out of Cadiz.

With torches lit in the main square, the Earl of Essex visited his wounded officers. He drew out his sword. He knighted those several men who had jumped over the walls and led the initial attack. He now stood in front of Robert Bertie whose shoulder throbbed from the thrown rock.

The Earl of Essex told the son of Lord Willoughby, "Kneel."

Robert Bertie knelt before the General, who tapped the Esquire lightly on both shoulders with his sword. "Rise a knight."

Sir Robert Bertie rose.

Fort St. Philip, Cadiz, Spain, July 2, 1596

THE NEXT MORNING, Sir Robert Bertie stood next to Sir Francis Vere and the Earl of Essex in front of Fort St. Philip.

"Will you surrender?" the Earl of Essex asked the priest in charge of negotiating the terms for the Spanish. "No one will be harmed. Spanish prisoners will be exchanged for English galley-slaves. Everyone else in the fort can depart with the clothes on their back. Only forty prominent citizens will be held for ransom."

"How much?" the priest asked.

"One-half million *ducats*."

An hour later, the priest returned with the terms agreed to by the Spaniards inside. Fort St. Philip surrendered without a further shot. Five thousands Spaniards, including all of the women, children, and priests, exited and headed to the shore. They departed with only their clothes and jewelry and were ferried to Puerto Santa Maria on the far side of the bay.

When one Spanish lady walked towards the dock, however, an English soldier grabbed her. He ripped the lady's garment and stole some jewels.

"Arrest him!" the Earl of Essex ordered. "Harm no women."

"What do you want done?" The guard kept a firm grip.

"Hang him," the Earl of Essex commanded.

When another guard brought a rope, the priest who had negotiated for the Spanish intervened. "So harsh?"

"Orders must be obeyed," the Earl of Essex said. "Spanish ladies must be respected."

The priest of Cadiz pleaded, "Spare him."

The Earl of Essex finally relented. The soldier's life was spared, the jeweled necklace returned.

When all of the others had departed, one Spanish lady, however, refused to go. She pleaded to stay with an English Captain, her captor. When that Captain told her he was promised in marriage to another in England, the Spanish lady told him, "I will become a nun." She offered a chain from her neck as a present.

The sack of the city, meanwhile, continued. All resistance had evaporated; its citizens and soldiers had departed. The Earl of Essex secured one house with a large library.

That afternoon, a messenger from the merchants of Seville arrived. "We offer two million for our merchantmen ships at Port Real."

Out of earshot of the messenger, Sir Walter Raleigh spoke, "We must consider it."

"We were commanded to capture the fleet or destroy it," Grand Admiral Charles Howard said. "Those West Indies Merchantmen cannot escape."

Chapter 32 - Candelabrum of Toledo

The courier who brought his Majesty [King Philip II of Spain] news of the English landing [at Cadiz] and what followed, arrived at Toledo while the King was reposing . . .

And although overcome by the news, yet it seemed to lend him vigor, for he rose from his chair and walked a few paces, a thing which the weakness of his legs and the remains of the gout had not hitherto allowed him to do.... Straightway, without any signs of a perplexed mind, he began to issue numerous orders and various provisions. The King then seized a candelabrum and with energy declared that he would pawn even that, in order to be avenged on the Queen [Elizabeth of England].
Agustino Nani, Venetian Ambassador in Spain to the Doge and Senate
Madrid, 14th July 1596

Alcazar Palace, Toledo, Castile, Spain, July 2, 1596

SQUAWKING CROWS AWAKENED *Infanta* Isabella from her afternoon nap. When she pulled back the curtains of her room in Alcazar Palace, she spied the noisy culprits. Under blue skies, the black birds flew away from the mountaintop palace and over Toledo, the ancient capital of Castile.

While her Lady-in-Waiting smoothed the ruffles in the bed, *Infanta* Isabella straightened her dress in front of a long mirror. "I must check on my father."

The King's gout had worsened over the past few months.

Earlier in the day, the *Nuncio* sent by His Holiness Pope Clement VIII had presented his case. He told *Infanta* Isabella's father that he had no further reason to fight against King Henry IV of France. His Holiness had absolved the French King and accepted him back into the Roman Catholic Church. His Most Catholic Majesty King Philip II of Spain should do the same. The King listened but did not agree.

After the *Nuncio* departed, *Infanta* Isabella's father confided that he could wear out the French. He did not want to negotiate with a King he did not consider to be a true Catholic. He expected more gold and silver from the mines of Peru to continue his campaign against France.

In the hallway leading to her father's suite, the Venetian ambassador and other dignitaries waited patiently. At the door of the suite, her father's most trusted advisor, the Chief Domestic Minister *Don* Cristobal *de* Moura, paced back and forth.

Great consternation afflicted the countenance of *Don* Cristobal *de* Moura. *Infanta* Isabella asked him, "What is wrong?"

"I did not want to awaken the King."

Infanta Isabella entered the suite and found her father already awake. With the help of his crutch, the Spanish King reached his desk and *Infanta* Isabella rushed to help him sit down. "*Don* Cristobal *de* Moura is here."

The King waved the Chief Domestic Minister forward. "What is it?"

"The English Fleet has attacked Cadiz."

"Cadiz? When?"

"The courier arrived three hours ago."

"You didn't wake me?" King Philip immediately rose, stepped forward, and hit the Chief Domestic Minister with his cane.

Don Cristobal *de* Moura suffered the blows. "Yesterday, at dawn they attacked."

The King put down his cane. "The Four Apostles?"

"Gone."

"The Saint Philip?"

"Our Admiral fired broadside after broadside for hours. When Sir Walter Raleigh prepared to board, the *St. Philip* cut anchor. Her captain ran it aground. It's destroyed, burned."

"And its cannons?"

"Eighty-two bronze cannons are at the bottom of the bay."

"And the other Apostles?"

"*St. Thomas* suffered the same fate; her captain fired the vessel."

Infanta Isabella shared her father's astonishment.

"The other two Apostles were captured," *Don* Cristobal *de* Moura added.

"And Cadiz?" the King asked.

"Late yesterday, three hundred cavalry met the enemy, but they could not withstand the English pike and shot. When they retreated to the city, the English and Dutch attacked. Cadiz has been sacked."

Not using his crutch, the King stepped forward towards his minister. "Send a message to Seville. Double the watch. Set chains across that harbor. Seville cannot be lost."

"The English may demand ransom."

"I'll pay no ransom."

Don Cristobal *de* Moura leaned back. "None?"

"Lest other towns capitulate so easily," the King declared, "we must make an example."

Prince Philip, the younger brother of *Infanta* Isabella entered the room. "I should go and relieve the city and defend our kingdom."

"It would not be wise," the King said.

"But I've never been to battle," the Prince said.

"I do not wish for you to go," the King declared. "The Duke of Medina has lost two fleets, the Armada to storm and now this fleet to fire. Bring *Don* Pedro *de* Velasco to me. He will retake Cadiz."

"We'll need more money," *Don* Cristobal *de* Moura said.

King Philip II grabbed a candelabrum and raised it above his head. "I will even pawn this candelabrum to take my vengeance against the Queen!"

Infanta Isabella had never seen her father so upset. She knew he would not be satisfied until a second armada sailed and attacked England.

English Encampment, Ramparts of Cadiz, Spain, July 3, 1596

THE ENGLISH LOOTED Cadiz for a second night and on the third morning after the initial attack, Sir Robert Bertie peered over the ramparts of Cadiz. "The Spanish burn their Merchantmen fleet."

Forty separate plumes of smoke rose over the inner harbor, where the merchant ships had taken refuge after the Four Apostles had been destroyed or captured. Richly laden with supplies bound for Havana, Mexico City, and Lima, the ships were worth millions.

Later that day, when the summer sun beat down, Robert learned that the Duke of Medina did not like the offer by Cadiz and Seville merchants. Without King Philip II's permission, the Spanish duke had ordered the fleet burned. The West Indies merchant ships, worth at least eight million *ducats*, were destroyed. None fell into English hands.

Over the next several days, the General Earl of Essex Robert Devereaux negotiated for the release of all English galley slaves. The negotiator from Spain had relayed the King's initial reaction to the Sack of Cadiz, but the English remained firmly entrenched. They would not be easily dislodged despite the heat, humidity, and stench.

On the sixth day after arriving, Sir Robert Bertie, along with many officers, gathered at the main cathedral of Cadiz. A minister of the Church of England led prayers for his uncle. The coffin with Sir John Wingfield's body was slowly lowered into the grave.

"A right valiant knight," Sir Francis Vere summed.

The poet soldier John Donne added, "Farther than Wingfield no man dares go."

After long moments of silence, the generals of both the land and the sea, the Earl of Essex and Grand Admiral Charles Howard, one after the other, tossed their moistened handkerchiefs onto the coffin.

The next day, the Earl of Essex and the Grand Admiral brought many of their key officers and other gentlemen soldiers into the square to knight them. Among those knighted were the younger brother of Sir Francis Vere, Lieutenant Colonel Horace Vere, and a nobleman named Thomas Gale, as well as an officer from Lincolnshire with a wounded leg. The Earl of Essex had already knighted Lewis Gunther of Nassau and the Grand Admiral had knighted his kinsman Vice Admiral Thomas Howard. Together, the generals knighted more than sixty men.

With the summer heat rising and with many soldiers falling ill, Grand Admiral Charles Howard ordered all to leave Cadiz and sail back to England. The large library that the Earl of Essex had captured was loaded onto his ship. The two captured Apostles had been repaired and readied to be taken out of the harbor.

Cadiz, Spain, July 14, 1596

TWO WEEKS AFTER arriving, the English set fire to a Jesuit church and burned more than two hundred homes along all four corners of Cadiz.

Most of the English fleet departed to the west and a dozen Spanish galleys attempted to follow from the east. Waiting until the rest of the fleet sailed, Rear Admiral Sir Walter Raleigh feigned a counterattack. Those Spanish galleys turned back toward Gibraltar.

The next day, with the whole fleet in the distance, Sir Walter Raleigh prepared to weigh anchor outside the entrance of the Bay of Cadiz. A lone galley approached and English gunners fired. A cannon shot hit the galley, before an English officer commanded, "Stop firing!"

Sir Robert Bertie saw the galley flew a flag of truce. When it drew closer, he knew the reason the galley was not attacking. "It must be the promised release."

The Spanish captain of the galley came aboard and after Rear Admiral Sir Walter Raleigh served dinner to the enemy officer, thirty-nine English slaves were freed. Many, over dinner, told stories of how they had been

captured at sea and held in bondage for years. Some had been resold in the Mediterranean slave markets. Others had been seized in the Caribbean. Most had once been English sailors, soldiers or merchants. All were eager to go home in freedom to England.

The Duke of Medina had promised the release from the previous day, but the English slaves' freedom had been delayed.

The last English ship sailed west.

Soldier & Chained Galley Slave - 1500s

At Cape St. Vincent, a strong north wind carried the five squadrons and the two captured Apostles far out to sea.

Queen Elizabeth would be pleased.

Chapter 33 - Bowls of Tripe Soup

But at last there came commandment
For to set the ladies free,
With their jewels still adorned,
None to do them injury,
Then said this lady mild, "Full woe is me;
O let me still sustain this kind captivity!"
"The Spanish Lady's Love" by Anonymous

"Osman Bey, I showed you respect and attention in the late war on the [European]
frontiers; I conferred on you offices of trust and profit, and have heaped favors upon you."
Grand Vizier Hasan *the Fruiterer* to Poiraz Osman Bey
Annals of the Turkish Empire, Vol. I, by Mustafa Naima
Translated from Turkish by Charles Fraser

Salon, Ibrahim *Pasha* Palace, *Stamboul*, Early December 1602

THE HEAD SERVANT, appearing in the doorway of her reception room, bowed. "Aisha *Sultana*?"

"You are back?"

"The tripe soup is hot." Servants lifted two small kettles. "Would you like for us to serve you here?"

"Yes, yes," Aisha, Sister of the Sultan, said. "That would be nice."

While her friend Emine, the English translator, and her slave, *Capitano* John Smith, adjusted their seats, the servant set the soup down. Two more servants arrived from the kitchen with bowls and spoons.

"Smells delicious." John accepted the bowl. "Pork?"

"No, John," Aisha said. "Muslims cannot eat pork."

"Like the Jews?" John asked and Emine translated.

"I suppose, but these cuts of meat came from calves." Aisha had sent the servant to the butcher after her mother and sisters had gone to the *bagnos*, the baths.

"And the spices?" Emine asked.

"We always insist on a touch of paprika." Aisha acknowledged her servant, who lifted the cover. The paprika had been sprinkled on top of the white soup. The hints of butter, lemon, and garlic rose within the steam. Aisha swallowed the bite-sized morsel of tripe and turned back to John. "What happened to your good friend, Robert Bertie, after he went to fight in Cadiz?"

"As the son of Lord Willoughby told the story about himself, 'The squire was knocked down by a rock, but the Earl of Essex raised him up a knight.'" John's countenance saddened and he paused. "The fate of his uncle was not quite as happy."

"Robert's uncle died in the square?" Aisha asked.

"Yes," John said. "Sir John Wingfield inspired his men. As Sir John Donne said, 'Farther than Wingfield no man dares to go.'"

"But the generals won the battle?"

"Yes, with victories at Cadiz on both sea and land, an Englishman summed it up best, repeating Latin words coined by Julius Caesar."

"What was that?" Aisha asked.

"*Veni, Vidi, Vici.*" John paused. "It means 'I came, I saw, I conquered.'"

Emine translated John's English words into Turkish.

"The Spanish were certainly surprised."

"Not only by the success of the attacks, but also by how the English treated their prisoners. The soldiers did not touch any woman or child."

"More courteous than expected?"

"Yes, the Spaniards had always been told that the English were pirates. After the sack of Cadiz, they still considered the English to be heretics, but in other things the Spanish referred to us as 'warriors, provident, and truly noble.'"

"How so?"

"Queen Elizabeth had commanded women and children should not be harmed. The English generals enforced her Majesty's command and threatened pain of death to any soldier who disobeyed."

"But that Spanish lady?"

"The rich one held captive?"

"*Sì, dal capitano inglese.*" Aisha said, in Italian.

"The Spanish lady fell in love with her captor and even asked the captain to take her back with him to England."

"He did not oblige?"

"No, the English captain told her that he had been promised to another. The Spanish woman gave him an expensive necklace to present to his future wife, promising him she would become a nun instead."

The answer surprised Aisha. "A nun?" When John nodded, she gazed into John's blue eyes. "Are you promised to someone back in England?"

"Why do you ask?"

"*Curiosità.*" Aisha finished her tripe soup. She lifted a refreshed teapot. "More tea?"

"How can an Englishman refuse?" John handed her his cup.

"What about the slaves?"

"During the initial attack by Sir Walter Raleigh, thirty-eight Turkish slaves escaped from the Spanish galleys. The generals provided the freed Turks with clothes, provisions, and a pilot to take them across the Mediterranean to Ottoman Barbary."

"The English freed the slaves? What about the English ones?"

"As part of the bargain with the Duke of Medina, Spanish prisoners were exchanged for the thirty-nine English slaves, some of whom had been captured with Sir Francis Drake earlier in the year, but others had been chained beneath the decks of the Spanish galleys for more than twenty years."

Aisha sipped the strong tea from her small cup. "But you have not answered my earlier question. What became of your friend, Robert Bertie?"

"He returned to London, England which is where we were reunited."

"So when your friends sent you from France back to England, you then traveled to London?"

"Yes, I looked forward to claiming my inheritance."

"Then indeed you are rich."

Emine touched her friend's hand with a smile and said in Turkish, "Aisha, I think we are finally going to learn about his wealth."

"After such delay." Aisha couldn't wait to discover how much ransom she would receive from the first of the rich conquests her betrothed, the Grand Vizier, had promised to send her from Belgrade—so long as everything John was about to tell her was in fact the truth.

Kale-Megdan, **Belgrade**, *Jumada II*, **AH 1011 (Dec. AD 1602)**

INSIDE THE LARGE banquet hall of the Upper Castle in Belgrade overlooking the Danube in Ottoman Europe, Grand Vizier Hasan *the Fruiterer* motioned to his servants. "More tripe soup for my guest of honor."

"Your hospitality overwhelms us." With both hands, *Ghazi* Giray II, the fierce Khan of the Crimean Tartars, accepted the steaming bowl. More than one hundred Tartar leaders, including two of the Khan's sons, partook of the feast. Many sat in circles, as if eating around campfires. Others, like their Turkish hosts, ate at low tables. All sat cross-legged on the floor.

"Tripe soup is made differently here in Belgrade than *Stamboul*." The Grand Vizier breathed in the aroma of garlic and onion. "We boil lamb instead of cow's stomach."

Ghazi Giray II sipped his soup. "It does taste delicious, but you should sample our fare. My own chefs will return your hospitality and prepare a banquet in your honor, Hasan *the Fruiterer*."

The Grand Vizier raised his hands. "There is no need to do so."

"I insist, tomorrow."

"Very well." As soon as the Grand Vizier relented, he turned. "Let me introduce a few of my officers. You remember my treasurer?"

"Yes, of course."

"And this is Poiraz Osman *Bey*, a leader of the *sipahis*."

"No need to stand," *Ghazi* Giray II said. "Tell me about the siege of Buda."

"We repelled the besiegers less than a week after the beginning of autumn," Poiraz Osman *Bey* said. "My *sipahi* horsemen, followed by the *janissary* footmen and volunteers stormed out of the Gate of Vienna. We helped our commander *Lala* Mohammed *Pasha* save Buda."

"I have conferred many honors on Poiraz Osman *Bey*," the Grand Vizier said. "I also sent word to *Lala* Mohammed *Pasha* and hoped he would attend this banquet."

Poiraz Osman *Bey* pointed to the hall's entrance. "He has made it."

The Grand Vizier stood up to welcome his commander. "*Lala* Mohammed *Pasha*, you must have known we were anxious for your arrival."

The *Pasha* had kept his former title of *Lala*, a tutor. "Only an unexpected attack would have kept me from this banquet."

"*Lala* Mohammed *Pasha* will be further rewarded for his efforts."

"I could not have done it without the help of the *sipahis* led by Poiraz Osman *Bey*."

"Yes, and he will be awarded, too." The Grand Vizier turned to the *sipahi* leader. "In addition to the purse of money the treasurer brought for you, I am giving you one hundred prisoners to either sell or keep."

"Thank you, Grand Vizier," Poiraz Osman *Bey* said.

"And I have not forgotten the Khan," the Grand Vizier turned to *Ghazi* Giray II. "You will stay in the mansion of my treasurer. His large estate is in Petchevi across the Danube."

"Grand Vizier, those who work for you mirror your generosity." *Ghazi* Giray II acknowledged the treasurer.

The Grand Vizier smiled. The sooner word spread about his magnanimity, the better for him.

The afternoon turned to evening, yet no one mentioned the recent losses suffered by *Ghazi* Giray II's fierce warriors outside Targoviste in Wallachia. As servants brought out the next course on large platters, *Ghazi* Giray II turned to Poiraz Osman *Bey*, "The Austrians and Germans who fought against you?"

"They planted mines under the gate, but we vowed that Friday morning to defend Buda at all costs. If we did not succeed, we would die in the attempt."

Lala Mohammed *Pasha* nodded his agreement. "We routed them then the early rains came."

"Poiraz Osman was just one of many leaders of the *sipahis*," the Grand Vizier said. "Until I promoted him to become their *Bey*."

"You chose well," *Ghazi* Giray II said.

"I know."

"Tomorrow, I will ride back to *Stamboul*," Poiraz Osman *Bey* said.

"Are you unable to stay for tomorrow's banquet?" The Grand Vizier caught the *sipahi* leader's eye.

"I will be honored to attend your feast," Poiraz Osman *Bey* said.

The Grand Vizier appreciated the respect Poiraz Osman *Bey* gave him. He did not mind the *sipahi* leader's imminent return to *Stamboul*.

Nor did he question the able *sipahi* leader's loyalty.

Chapter 34 - London Bridge & Swan Theater

Upon this [London Bridge] is built a tower [Traitors' Gate], on whose top the heads of such as have been executed for High Treason are placed on iron spikes: we counted above thirty....Without the city [London] are some theaters, where English actors represent almost every day tragedies and comedies to very numerous audiences;...At these spectacles, and everywhere else, the English are constantly smoking tobacco; and in this manner . . . they draw the smoke into their mouths, which they puff out again through their nostrils like funnels, along with it plenty of phlegm and de-fluxion from the head.

Paul Hentzner, Travels in England [1598]
Translated from Latin by Richard Bentley

Traitors' Gate, London Bridge, England, Late Summer 1596

CROWDS THRONGED THE whole length of London Bridge. They stopped at the countless stores that lined both sides. Above those shops, apartments housed the owners and their families, as well as workers. When John Smith glanced up at one those buildings, he caught the eye of a young girl peering back down from her third-story balcony.

"John!" His friend Robert Bertie pulled him out of the way of an advancing carriage. Another carriage approached from behind, passing to the left of the other on the central roadway.

"I got distracted," John said.

Sir Robert Bertie had just finished telling the story of how he had been knighted at Cadiz.

"After the north wind pushed us out to sea, the two Generals called a War Council," Sir Robert Bertie continued. "Most naval officers wanted to pillage the coast, but others in the army complained that they were running low on provisions. Though the soldiers were being paid fourteen shillings a day, many had become ill, others weak."

"And the wounded?"

"The wounded were returned to England, but the Earl of Essex landed at Ferrol on the northern coast of Spain. He found very few Spanish ships there. Its citizens had abandoned the town, along with their belongings. Unable to pillage and plunder, the Earl of Essex burnt Ferrol and returned to England."

"Your shoulder?" John nudged his friend

Robert shrugged. "Hasn't hurt for weeks."

John elbowed Robert again. "You let an old woman knock you down with a stone?"

They walked past a man hung in stocks for public shaming.

Upriver, towards Westminster, flocks of swans swam near the shore.

"Many other soldiers were hit as they advanced down the narrow streets. The Spanish women climbed to the flat roofs of their houses and threw down the heavy stones."

"Where did they get those?"

"Likely from the rocky shores in the days since we arrived."

John remembered that the Spanish women were unharmed and allowed to leave Cadiz with their clothes and jewelry. "Well, Sir Robert, at least you survived."

"Unlike my uncle, Sir Thomas Wingfield." Robert's face saddened.

Between the buildings, on a clear section of the bridge, John looked down the Thames. The river beyond the Tower of London seemed even more crowded than it had when he had arrived from Orleans. "And the bounty?"

"Gold and silver, carpets and tapestries, wineskins and hides, and plate were all claimed. The arsenal held thirty crates of armor and another warehouse held tons of sugar." Robert added, "Everyone who fought on land received a share. After an accounting is made, her Majesty will receive her share to offset her cost of supplying the fleet."

They entered a huge building, the Southwark Gate and Tower. The five-story building extended far beyond both sides of the main bridge. As John's eyes adjusted to the darkness, a figure of a man drew near.

"But we haven't been paid back yet." A merchant stood in front of his shop. "We merchants outfitted several ships for the Queen."

"Perhaps her Majesty will compensate you after the accounting," Sir Robert Bertie said.

When John and Robert exited Southwark Tower they crossed over another open span. On the upstream side of the bridge, small boats brought corn to the mills built on platforms extending above the water. The corn would be sold or distributed to the citizens of London.

Robert pointed to the building straight ahead. "That's Traitors' Gate."

Circular towers anchored the four corners of the block structure, strong as a fort. Several human skulls had been attached to the end of pikes set atop the building.

"Traitors' Gate?" John asked.

"Recusant papists still plot against the Queen for High Treason. Ever since Henry VIII declared himself to be head of the Church of England." Robert paused. "Sometimes they are caught."

Skulls atop London Bridge

They walked through the building, below a heavy iron gate, and past a wagon waiting to pay the toll. When Robert stopped and turned, he gestured toward the notched top of the fortress gate. "After the bodies are drawn, quartered, and buried, the heads are put up there." Weathered human skulls had been fastened to the ends of thirty long pikes. "They replace older skulls, which are thrown into the Thames for the fish."

You can cross the bridge, John thought, but not the Crown.

Swan Theater, Bankside, London, England

WITHIN EARSHOT OF a noisy flock of swans, the two young men walked along the South Bank of the Thames towards a circular building. A large flag with a white swan waved above the river side of the wooden edifice, three stories tall.

John pointed to a playbill posted on the outer wall of the newly built summer theater. "Look, it's a comedy called *The Taming of the Shrew*."

"A new playwright named William Shakespeare of Stratford may have written it," Robert said.

"I've never heard of him. But it says his troop will perform."

"Someone told me about the play, some say it is about my grandmother, Catherine."

"Your grandmother?" John asked.

"Catherine, like the name of the shrew. The Lady Willoughby had a mind of her own and convinced my grandfather Richard Bertie to leave England during the reign of Bloody Mary," Robert said. "To be honest, in many ways, my own mother Mary *de* Vere has a quick tongue, too. About twenty years ago, her brother Edward *de* Vere, the Earl of Oxford, even produced a play called 'A Moral of the Marriage of Mind and Measure.' It might have inspired Shakespeare's play."

"Let's go watch." When they reached the gate, John asked the attendant. "How much?"

"If you stand, only one. And hurry if you are going in. It's starting."

"No, the best seats." Robert untied his purse and handed coins to the attendant.

Inside the arena, a large square wooden platform extended out from one side. Directly behind and over the stage, extra actors sat beneath a thatched roof. Two columns supported that overhanging balcony.

Play at a London Inn during the Reign of Queen Elizabeth

In front of the stage, spectators stood on the dirt and straw floor. In the early afternoon, they jostled for a view.

Three tiers of balconies circled along both sides of the open-air stage. Some spectators sat down, but many leaned against the rail. Off to the left, a small orchestra tuned their instruments. John and Robert found seats in the second tiered balcony towards the center and waited for the play to begin.

Set in the Italian city-state of Padua, two actors—the vagrant Sly and the hostess—appeared on the open stage. During the induction, when the hostess threatened to put Sly into stocks, the spectators grew attentive.

The crowds laughed at the actor who played the shrew, Katherine. Her father Baptista insisted Kate marry before her younger and quieter sister could marry another. Petruchio proposed to the eldest daughter, the dowry was agreed upon, and on the following Sunday, they married.

As the play unfolded, the spectators hissed, hollered, and laughed louder. When it was over, John asked, "Was Petruchio supposed to be like your father? After all, Petruchio and Peregrine sound somewhat similar."

"Perhaps." Robert laughed. "But neither my mother Mary nor my grandmother Catherine would have liked being called a shrew."

"At least no one threw vegetables this day." John had heard how bad performances were sometimes rewarded.

"No. It was a good play." Robert led John out of the Swan Theater. "Are you going back to Lincolnshire?"

"Yes, I must find the barrister in Lincoln overseeing my father's estate now that I'm almost of age."

"Before you go," Robert said, "we should see the running at the ring and joust tournament at Whitehall Palace."

John looked up at the sky. "It's getting late."

"Tomorrow."

On the way back to London Bridge, they walked toward another circular theatre. Like the nearby Bull House where dogs faced bulls, the Bear House promised a different type of spectacle.

John and Robert stopped outside the main entrance and peeked inside. Large bulldogs barked at and baited a bear. The loud taunts made the beast very angry. It swung its claw and threw the dog into the air.

Vendors sold fruit and nuts from trays, as well as ale made from barley and wine from the vine. Many of the male spectators smoked tobacco, packed in the bowls of clay pipes. Several spectators exited, blowing the smoke through their noses. They expunged not only the smoke, but also phlegm. One pale man wiped green mucous with his sleeve.

"If disease or the plague returns, the constables may once more shut down theatres and houses on Bankside." Robert led John away. "But on the other side of the Thames, there's a cockpit at Whitehall Palace."

"You know I don't like to gamble," John said. "It's a waste of money."

Near a white-washed building called a stew, prostitutes plied their trade. One took a man inside, while others bargained.

"I recognize some of those men." Robert shook his head. "Used to be good soldiers or sailors, but many seem to idle the time away, not only in the playhouses, but also in the taverns and inns."

Two sickly men overheard him and stared back. "Mind your own business. If they want to sell their commodity to us, it's up to them."

Robert and John walked on. "Didn't those two look ill?" Robert asked.

"Why the open sores on their skin?" John asked.

"Syphilis, dreaded disease," Robert said. "The Great Pox affects the mind, too."

Not wanting to dwell any longer in the area, John pointed. "Let's cross London Bridge. Perhaps we can see the joust."

"Yes, at Whitehall Palace."

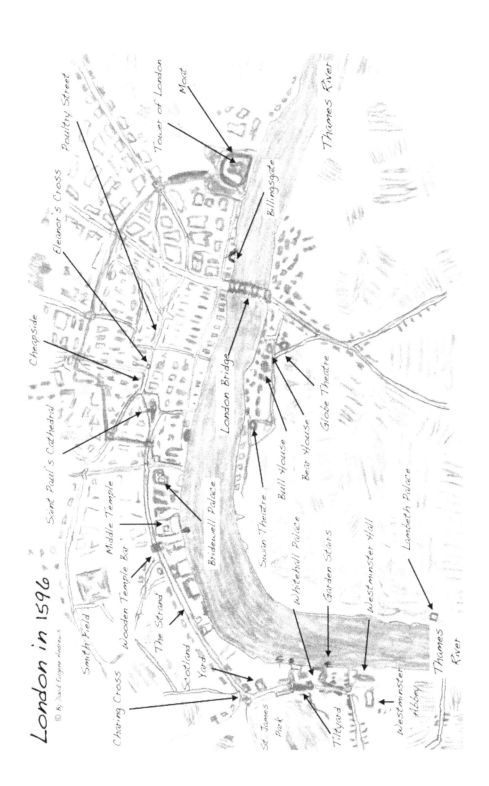

London in 1596

© By David Eugene Andrews

Saint Paul's Cathedral

Smith Field

Cheapside

Eleanor's Cross

Poultry Street

Tower of London

Moat

Billingsgate

Thames River

London Bridge

Middle Temple

Wooden Temple Bar

The Strand

Scotland Yard

Charing Cross

St. James Park

Bridewell Palace

Swan Theatre

Bull House

Bear House

Globe Theatre

Whitehall Palace

Garden Stairs

Westminster Hall

Tiltyard

Lambeth Palace

Westminster Abbey

Thames River

Chapter 35 - Cheapside and Bridewell

Afterwards when the King [Henry VIII] became enemy of the [Holy Roman] Emperor
[Charles V], he to disgrace the latter made it [Bridewell Palace] a place of confinement for
harlots and villains, who are kept there to the present day.

The men are forced to tread a mill, which is so constructed that as long as they tread it
flour is ground by it. The males as well as the females are whipped twice a week; besides,
the latter must work very hard until they have done penance for their evil doings (Most of
the females are prostitutes having been kept by men.)
Lupold von Wedel, Journey Through England and Scotland [1584]
Translated from German by Dr. Gottfried von Bulow

Poultry Street, London, England, Late Summer 1596

A HEN CLUCKED and flapped her wings. One of the vendors on Poultry
Street near Cheapside pushed the bird gently out of the way and retrieved her egg. He latched the wooden cage, turned, and shoved the
brown egg right in front of John Smith's face. "Fresh."

Smith swatted at a pestering fly and almost knocked the egg out of the
vendor's hand. "No." The sixteen year-old youth from Lincolnshire was
hungry, but had no place to cook it. "Not today."

At the end of Poultry Street, where Cheapside Street began, several
English women wore stylish hats. One talked to bare-headed young
maidens congregated around a stone building occupying the middle of
the street. Strong men, carrying empty jugs, waited for their chance to enter the one-story structure.

"What's inside?" John asked.

"A cistern," Sir Robert Bertie replied. "Water is piped through lead
pipes from outside London. We called it the Great Conduit."

Moments later, carriers retrieved the water from the lead-lined cistern
and carried the heavy containers to nearby houses. Some men delivered
jugs to the goldsmiths of the district, others to homes on Old Jewry Street,

named for Jews who had once lived there. The Jews had followed William the Conqueror from Rouen and Normandy into England. His descendent, King Edward I, known as "Longshanks" because he was so tall, persecuted the Jews. After banning the lending of money with interest, he confiscated their property and with his Edict of Expulsion expelled all of the Jews from England.

John and Robert followed one of the water carriers down Cheapside Street. John knew that 'cheap' meant 'trade' and understood why the area was called Cheapside: the street ahead was lined with shops. It was also easy to tell which shop sold what. Carved wooden signs extended from the front of each shop on poles six or seven feet long.

From the steeple of St. Mary's Bow Church on the south side of the street, melodic bells began to toll. Half-empty carts opposite the church displayed fruit and nuts, as well as a variety of vegetables.

"I've built up an appetite." Robert inspected a pear, but put it back down. Early shoppers on the main thoroughfare from the Tower District to Westminster must have chosen the best produce, for it was late in the day and the selection was sparse. At the apple cart, however, Robert untied his purse.

While his friend pulled out a coin, John noticed several boys down the block were not playing, but watching them. A little further away, a man wearing a plaid hat caught the boys' attention. Standing by a three-tiered stone structure in the center of the street, the man tipped his cap.

"I'll take two." Robert gave one apple to John and retied his purse to his belt.

John bit into the tart fruit and scowled.

"What is it, John? The apple?"

"No. I thought I saw someone by that cross." John gestured to the Great Cross of Cheapside. The nearly forty-foot-high monument, the eleventh of twelve crosses erected by King Edward I to commemorate the dozen overnight stops made during the funeral procession of his wife, Eleanor of Castile. The monument was topped by a small white cross.

John and Robert stopped to look more closely at Eleanor's Cross.

John again scoured the area for the man with the cap, but the man had slipped out of sight. The two boys, also, were gone.

Robert pointed to a depiction of a woman in one of the lower vestibules. "That's Diana, the Greek Goddess."

Eleanor Cross at Cheapside in 1500s

Suddenly, the two young boys reappeared. One chased the other around the cross and bumped into John. The younger boy stuck his hand into John's coat pocket, but John knew his pocket was empty.

The older boy nudged Robert.

"Robert!" John yelled.

Robert grabbed his belt. "Cut Purser!"

The second boy had severed Robert's purse from his belt. The two thieves ran. John and Robert chased them back past Mermaid Tavern and down Bread Street.

The small boys knocked over a tray of bread in front of a bakery. They turned a corner. One boy escaped down a rubbish-infested alley. Two fat rats scurried through the trash, but John would not be dissuaded from the pursuit.

The Cut Purser scaled a fence. Two more rats scurried up the wall and disappeared into the thatch of a roof.

John quickly scrambled over the fence. When the boy entered Watling Street, John tackled the thief.

"Let me go!" the boy yelled.

"What's going on here?" A well-dressed gentleman towered over them.

John looked up at the gentleman and his son. "A foister attempted to pick my pocket, and this boy cut the purse of Sir Robert Bertie, son of Lord Willoughby."

"A cut purser, you say?" The gentleman grabbed the boy's wrist.

"Let me go!" The boy twisted. "I didn't take anything."

"Don't lie to me." The gentleman leaned over the boy. "My name is Lord Richard Saltonstall and I used to be sheriff in the Tower District."

Robert scaled the fence and ran toward them. "John! You caught him."

While the boy struggled to escape the grip of the former sheriff, the stolen purse fell to the ground.

John picked it up and handed it to Robert.

Still gripping the boy, Lord Richard Saltonstall motioned for the young thief to stand still and turned to Robert. "You're the son of Lord Willoughby? I saw him at the Palace of Whitehall."

"My father is here in London?"

The boy twisted around but couldn't escape the former sheriff's hand.

"He arrived from Grimsthorpe earlier today," Lord Richard Saltonstall said. "Told me he had been delayed for weeks in Lower Saxony, but wanted to see the Queen's Secretary about the governorship of Berwick."

John recalled that Berwick was a castle on the Tweed River on the border with Scotland.

"What about the young vagrant?" Lord Richard Saltonsall's son asked, pointing to the squirming boy.

"Samuel, we'll take this thief to Bridewell Prison."

"Is it near?" John asked.

"Just past Blackfriar and the old city walls."

The man with the cap peeked over the fence and caught the lad's eye.

Lord Saltonstall turned to the boy. "Who's that man?"

"He'll hurt me, if I tell you," the boy confessed. "I ain't supposed to get caught."

When they looked back, the man had disappeared, too.

Lord Richard Saltonstall led the group past St. Paul's Church, the largest church in London. Its spire was gone, destroyed in a fire shortly after Queen Elizabeth acceded to the the Crown. Only a stub, the base of the steeple, remained.

Walking past Blackfriar, the group crossed at a small bridge over Fleet Creek, but they slowed when a cart pulling a woman passed them. People stopped and gawked at the woman trailing the cart.

"They're taking her to Bridewell," Lord Richard Saltonstall said.

"A thief?" John noticed the woman had a rash on her upper chest.

"No, a harlot. They always cart prostitutes. We'll follow them."

Bridewell Palace, London, England

THE CART REACHED the former palace of Bridewell first. Queen Elizabeth's father, King Henry VIII, had built the two-courtyard palace in just six weeks before the Holy Roman Emperor Charles V came to London for a visit.

Later, after a falling-out between the two monarchs, Bridewell was first converted into a hospital. Young King Edward VI, King Henry's son, bequeathed the stone structure on the banks of the Thames to the City of London. For the last four decades, Bridewell had been converted again to be used both as a prison and workhouse for wayward women and young vagrants.

Bridewell Palace Prison in 1666

After the prostitute entered Bridewell, the guard saluted. "Sheriff Saltonstall."

"Hold this boy until his trial. We caught the 'Cut Purser' when he attempted to escape."

"Straighten up, young man." The guard peered down at the boy. "You know vagrants can be hanged."

"Hanging's quicker than dying in prison," the boy snapped.

"Whipping you twice a week may change your attitude."

"I'm not scared."

The guard took the boy inside and up a wide staircase.

"Where's he going?" John asked.

"To tread a mill," Lord Richard Saltonstall said. "Along with runaways and vagabonds, he'll grind flour until his sentence is served. Other vagrants will pound hemp or pick oakum to caulk and seal leaks in ships."

"Will young vagrants ever change?"

Lord Richard Saltonstall shook his head. "Very few." He and his son crossed back over Fleet Creek Bridge and into the city.

John and Robert, meanwhile, walked in the opposite direction through Temple Bar and down the Strand toward Charing Cross. When they reached the inn, Robert ran to his father.

"Robert." Peregrine Bertie, Lord Willoughby smiled. Forgetting formalities, they gave each a huge hug. "It's been a long time. We need to go back to Lincolnshire soon. We have so much to catch up on."

"Your illness?" Robert asked.

"Venice and Vienna did not help that much, but I feel a little better now, especially after seeing you." Lord Willoughby turned to John. "I am sorry about the death of your father, but I've talked to the barrister."

"Is he here in London now?"

"If you both join me the Running of the Ring tournament tomorrow, you can see him," Lord Willoughby said. "The Queen's secretary has promised me excellent seats."

Later that evening at the inn, a nobleman was welcomed to join them at their table.

"Tomorrow," the nobleman said, "before the tournament, I will engage in falconry at Whitehall Palace. Would you like to join me?"

"We would be delighted to," Lord Willoughby said.

Chapter 36 - The Ring at Whitehall Palace

Having her Highness' [Queen Elizabeth's] presence, they rejoice, they triumph, they flourish, and they thrive, some by victualing, some by lodging courtiers, some by one means, some by another; they are all glad, and fare well. And no doubt but they could wish in their hearts that Whitehall were her Majesty's common abode . . .

John Norden, Notes on London and Westminster (1592)

Tis call'd the Evil:
A most miraculous work in this good king;
Which often, since my here-remain in England,
I have seen him do. How he solicits heaven,
Himself best knows; but strangely-visited people,
All swoll'n and ulcerous, pitiful to the eye,
The mere despair of surgery, he cures,

William Shakespeare, Macbeth, Act IV, Scene 3

Garden Stairs, Whitehall Palace, Westminster, Summer 1596

THE PEREGRINE FALCON'S high-pitched shriek pierced the air. On the Garden Steps leading down from Whitehall Palace to the Thames River, the falconer raised his gloved hand.

John Smith, Sir Robert Bertie, and Lord Willoughby watched as the falcon took off, flapped her strong wings, and soared to the sky.

With noble brown eyes as sharp as her talons, the falcon circled higher and higher; the great raptor knew who was friend and who was foe. When she soared to striking heights, larks in the formal gardens behind the steps replaced their morning greetings with warning cries.

The falconer signaled and his servants on the other side of the Thames flushed out waterfowl. Not far from the Swan Theatre in Lambeth Marsh, a skein of ducks took to the air. Forming a 'V', the ducks arched above the riverbanks and up the Thames.

High above, the Peregrine Falcon eyed its prey. She flapped her wings and started to plunge, straight down. Her wings tight by her side, she stooped. Traveling faster than the fastest fox, she banked. Adjusting her descent, she struck one of the wings of a duck flying in the middle of the V. Duck feathers flew and she banked again. Mere feet above the water, she caught the falling duck in her talons.

Whitehall Palace and Swans on the Thames

The falconer on the Garden Steps of Whitehall Palace once again raised his gloved arm. He whistled twice and moved his lure. Attached to a horseshoe at the end of a rope, the lure caught the falcon's sharp eye.

Prey in tow, the falcon rose higher and returned to her master with her capture. With leather jesses wrapped around her legs, the Peregrine dropped the duck at the falconer's feet and she landed on her master's glove.

Letting out a cry, she waited for her reward.

Taking meat from the lure, the falconer fed the bird with generous portions. "I must get ready." The falconer hooded his bird.

"For what?" John Smith asked.

"The Queen. She arrives back from Nonsuch Palace later this morning."

"Nonsuch Palace?" John Smith had heard of Nonsuch Palace, but was unsure where it was. "Is it far away?"

"In Surrey, south of London," Lord Willoughby said. "King Henry VIII built a beautiful palace and called it 'None Such,' because no palace had ever been built like it before."

"She'll arrive here? At the Garden Steps?" John knew the Queen rarely crossed via London Bridge, preferring to cross the Thames on her barge.

"No." The nobleman falconer pointed to the next landing, slightly downstream. "Her barge will land at the Privy Steps." The private entrance led to the older portions of Whitehall. He placed his falcon in its cage and handed it to his servant.

The group ascended the Garden stairs and walked through the formal gardens.

"The Dutch will be invited to join the alliance," the nobleman said.

"What alliance?" John asked.

"An offensive and defensive alliance between France and England." The nobleman led the others by a large sundial in the center of the garden. The long shadows confirmed that morning had barely begun. "Three months ago, before the Sack of Cadiz, King Henry IV sent the Calvinist Duke of Bouillon, Henri *de* La Tour d'Auvergne, to negotiate a treaty. After the terms were agreed to with the Queen, the Duke returned to France and gained King Henry IV's signature and seal. Formal ceremonies with the Duke and Queen were held at Nonsuch Palace at the end of August."

"And now the Queen returns to Whitehall," John said.

"Yes," the nobleman said, "because of the help the Dutch Republic gave her at Cadiz, the Dutch delegation no longer had to bow to her like English subjects." He led the others through the Garden Gate and into the Palace. "After arriving from Nonsuch, the Queen will administer the healing to the Scrofula."

A servant carried the dripping duck to the kitchens.

"Scrofula?" John asked.

"They called it 'The King's Evil.'" Lord Willoughby pointed his cane at a man on the opposite side of the courtyard. "Look."

The man's neck was swollen and ulcerous. He had just entered through the main gate, walked past the wooden Banqueting Hall, and stopped before the Great Hall.

Many of the buildings around the courtyard were decades old, built when Whitehall Palace was known as York Place. Cardinal Wosley, who was Archbishop of York, resided there when King Henry VIII ruled England. When the King insisted on divorcing Catherine of Aragon because she could not give him a male heir, Cardinal Wosley could not persuade the pope to grant an annulment. Later, the Cardinal fell out of favor and relinquished York Place to King Henry VIII. The King renamed his new palace Whitehall.

"After divorcing Catherine, the King secretly married a younger wife, Anne Boleyn, in a private part of this palace," Lord Willoughby informed the boys. "She gave birth to our Queen Elizabeth."

"The Queen arrives on her barge!" A crier rushed into the courtyard through the hidden door leading from the Privy Steps on the Thames. "Her Majesty arrives."

Guards moved into position, officers inspected uniforms. Servants rushed into lines to await her Majesty. Beneath stoic expressions, everyone was happy, for all flourished when Elizabeth stayed at Whitehall, perhaps her favorite abode.

Within minutes, Queen Elizabeth entered the courtyard. She walked past the chapel and entered the Great Hall on the courtyard side opposite the entrance to the garden. The healing ceremony would soon begin.

Great Hall, Whitehall Palace, Westminster, England

IN THE GREAT Hall, the aging Lord Treasurer, the staid Lord Chancellor, and the energetic Earl of Essex attended the Queen.

The first of ten men suffering scrofula approached her. The Queen prayed and touched him on the head.

Lord Willoughby leaned toward John and his son. "The Queen claims her right to administer the Royal Touch through her ancestry, the throne of France."

Queen Elizabeth touched each of other nine men, one by one. After the touching, she presented each with a gold coin.

At the end of ceremony, the Lord Chancellor poured water out of an ewer and into a basin held by the Lord Treasurer. Both Lords knelt down and the Queen washed her hands. Also on bended knee, Robert Devereaux, the Earl of Essex, handed her Majesty a cloth towel. She dried her hands and gave the napkin back to her favorite advisor, one of the two Generals responsible for the recent victory over the Spanish at Cadiz. The Earl and the two Lords remained on bended knee until the very end of the ceremony.

The ten, whom the Queen had touched, were all smiling when she sent them on their way.

As they exited the Great Hall, Lord Willoughby told John and Robert,

"Many attest to the healing power of God working through the Queen's hands."

If only the Queen could heal you, John thought. He knew the gout afflicting Lord Willoughby was painful.

"With the Queen's blessing, I hope to receive the Governorship of Berwick." Lord Willoughby added, "I will talk to her Secretary, Sir Robert Cecil later. In the meantime, we can have soup in a banqueting hall."

In a wood and canvas banqueting hall, John and Robert joined Lord Willoughby at a table.

The servant set a bowl in front of John. "Duck soup."

When John picked up his spoon, the young girl at the next table asked her mother, "Where did the duck come from?"

"Some questions should not be asked at meals," her mother said.

Holbein Gate, & Old Tiltyard at Whitehall Palace

Holbein Gate, Whitehall Palace, Westminster, England

LATER THAT AFTERNOON, with the joust set to begin, John Smith, Sir Robert Bertie, and Lord Willoughby ascended the steps leading to Holbein Gate. A long gallery contained dozens of paintings, including one of King Edward VI. Queen Elizabeth's half-brother had died young and the painting of him changed its appearance from side to front.

Four cylindrical towers anchored Holbein Gate over the public road leading from Charing Cross to Westminster. Further south, at the far end of the gardens, a second gate called King's Gate connected the two sides of Whitehall. Near St. James' Park, on the newer, or far, side of the public road, King Henry VIII had built tennis courts and bowling greens. An octagonal building stood several stories high.

"Sometimes they call Holbein Gate, the Cockpit Gate," Lord Willoughby said.

"Why?" John asked.

"Because of the cock pit over there."The octagonal wood building south of the far side of the gate could hold scores of spectators. "King Henry VIII even built balcony seats for himself above the gate, so he could watch the cockfights from there."

The trio crossed over the public road. In the distance, Charing Cross, the last of the twelve Eleanor Crosses, could be seen.

Platforms and a gallery attached to Holbein Gate overlooked the Tilt-yard. Lord Willoughby, John, and Robert settled into their seats and wait-ed for the Queen to arrive.

Tiltyard, Royal Palace at Whitehall, Westminster, England

MINUTES LATER, A coachman pulled four handsome horses to a stop at the southern end of the tiltyard where jousting was held. A knight, fully armored, exited the fancy coach at the bottom of the stairs leading up to Holbein Gate. His silver armor glistened in the noontime sun.

The silver knight retrieved a gift from his carriage and raised it with both hands. He glanced up to the balcony. Queen Elizabeth and her La-dies-in-Waiting had settled into their seats, but now they leaned forward and waited in anticipation of the day's pageantry.

The knight transferred the gift to his waiting servant, who bowed and bounded up the wide staircase.

The colorfully dressed servant walked past the section where John Smith, Sir Robert Bertie, and Lord Willoughby sat. He halted in the center of the platform and bowed to the Queen.

When her Majesty waved him forward, he presented his master's gift. Stepping back, he addressed the aging Queen in a loud voice, "In the whole kingdom, only your Majesty's own virtues exceed my master's." He motioned to the silver knight below and continued his short ha-rangue. "His virtues will certainly delight both you and the beautiful la-dies of your court."

"We accept your gift and give our permission for your master to fight." Queen Elizabeth conferred with her Secretary, Sir Robert Cecil. "Who will your master fight for?"

"The lady who gives her kerchief." The servant bowed and returned to his master below.

The silver knight mounted his powerful steed. Well armored, the horse trotted the length of the tiltyard, past hundreds of cheering fans. Built between St. James' Park and the road leading from Charing Cross to Westminster, the tiltyard was nearly one hundred fifty yards in length and about fifty yards wide. Wooden stands paralleled both sides of the tilt, the center divider or barrier that ran the length of the yard.

When the knight returned to the center section of the low wooden stands, he accepted a white kerchief from the prettiest of the English ladies. He stuffed the kerchief near his heart and spurred his horse to his page. The well-dressed page held a lance upright.

Everyone waited in anticipation. Guards peered down from the top of the four cylindrical towers of Holbein Gate. The silver knight grabbed his lance. More than a hundred yards away, a second knight dressed in black lowered his visor. The display of martial arts, the *au plaisance* tilt, was about to begin.

At the sound of the trumpet, the two knights charged each other. Faster and faster the horses galloped. Shields were raised. Lances raked, clanged, and shattered.

Both knights were struck, but neither was dislodged from his horse. Each raised his visor and returned to his respective starting point, at the near and far end of the tilt.

The silver knight grabbed a new lance from his page. Clad in steel plate from head to toe, the knights dropped their visors once more.

Again, the trumpet sounded.

Crowds rose in anticipation and shouted for their favorite.

The two knights charged once again. First one horse, then the other, trotted. Faster and faster, the two steeds galloped towards each other.

Blunted wooden lances came down, parallel to the ground. The silver knight crossed his lance over the low wooden fence. The black knight did likewise.The silver knight's lance smashed against the chest of his adversary. The black knight fell backwards before crowded stands. Simultaneously, a glancing blow hit the silver knight's shield. He, though hit, remained mounted.

The black knight suffered far worse for he was dismounted, knocked hard to the ground. The fallen rider slowly picked himself up from the grassy field. Visibly shaken from the fall, he pulled off his helmet and acknowledged his loss.

The silver champion, meanwhile, raised his fist. He rode the length and waved to the cheers and the applause. At the center of the stands, he pulled his reins and retrieved the white kerchief from his heart. Waving it for all to see, the silver knight leaned over and kissed the hand of the maiden who had given it to him.

After the silver knight rode to the end of the tiltyard, he received his reward from the Queen.

"Is it over?" John asked.

"No," Lord Willoughby replied. He pointed to a post about about forty yards north of the gallery. "A more challenging demonstration, the running at the ring, begins."

The perfectly square post was planted firmly in the ground. A thick crossbeam ran perpendicular to the sturdy post at its top. It extended straight out like a man's right arm stretching from his shoulder.

At the end of the crossbeam a small ring dangled about eight feet above the ground. Not much larger than an eye, that ring held steady in the pleasant summer breeze.

Lance in hand, the knight lowered his visor and spurred his horse. When it reached a fast trot, he lowered his lance and aimed its tip at the ring. Now riding at a gallop, he missed the target.

The crowd moaned in sympathy.

"It's harder than it looks," Robert said.

"The target's so small," John agreed. "You must have a steady arm and a better eye."

The second rider followed. He, too, missed the target. More riders tried their skill. All failed.

"It's impossible," Robert said.

"If I had the training," John said, "I could do that."

"It takes practice."

"When I get the rest of my inheritance, I'll hire the best trainer."

"What about your dream of going to sea?"

"That'll have to wait."

The last knight spurred his horse, lowered his lance, and charged the ring. To the cheers of hundreds, the tip of the lance pierced the ring. The victorious knight raised his lance and paraded slowly in front of the crowds. He rode to the end of the yard towards Holbein Gate.

John turned to Robert, "I want to do that.

"You would be good at it."

"I received word about your father's death," Lord Willoughby interjected. "The administrator of your father's estate is here at Whitehall."

"I should get a nice inheritance," John said. "I can use the money to train and ride."

"When can John meet with him?" Robert asked.

Lord Willoughby faced John. "The barrister from Lincoln is over there. He'll want to talk to you."

Smith saw the barrister receive some money from another gentleman. *Perhaps settling a wager*, he thought.

When they walked over to the barrister, Lord Willoughby reintroduced them. "Barrister, this is John Smith."

"John, it's good to see you again," the lawyer said. "Let us leave Whitehall and use an office in the Middle Temple. Are you free now?"

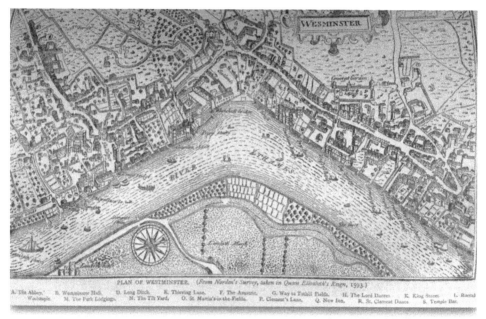

Whitehall Palace at Westminster, Charing Cross, and the Strand

"Certainly."

"John, I understand you and Robert learned some French," Lord Willoughby said. "Robert and I must return to Grimsthorpe. We must bid you *adieu*."

"Adieu."

John accompanied the barrister in a fancy carriage heading towards Charing Cross. They turned and continued down the Strand towards the wooden Temple Bar.

Along the way, John made plans for his inheritance.

Chapter 37 - Share of Fatherless Children

John Smith, my eldest son whom I charge and command to honor and love my aforesaid Lord Willoughby during his life.

Will of George Smith of Willoughby
Proved at Lincoln, England, 2nd April 1596

Who when he [John Smith] came from London, they liberally gave him (but out of his own estate) ten shillings to be rid of him; such oft is the share of fatherless children.

John Smith

Wooden Temple Bar, London, England, Summer 1596

AFTER PASSING through Temple Bar, the wooden gate spanning the street, they stepped out of the carriage. Further up a hill stood Ludgate Gate, the main land entrance into London, the inner town still surrounded by stone walls. John peered to his right, down a narrow lane extending down to the Thames River where Travelers disembarked from boats onto the bottom steps.

John accompanied the barrister through a brick courtyard, walking past a series of impressive structures. John stared up at an old church. "What is this?"

"Temple Church," the barrister said, "the former Church of the Knights Templar."

"The Knights Templar?" John asked.

"An order of knights who pro-

Wooden Temple Bar

tected Christian pilgrims from thieves and robbers lying-in-wait on the highways to Jerusalem. Within Jerusalem, these Christian soldiers kept their quarters near the place where the Temple of Solomon once stood, hence the name."

"But the knights themselves?"

"The Knights Templar was disbanded; it no longer exists. And here, at the site of the old temple, barristers now occupy these grounds. Now we are trained to practice law at the Inner Temple and the Middle Temple. Together, they are known as the Inns of the Court."

"They are schools for law?"

"Yes, and more."

Great Hall, Middle Temple, London, England, Summer 1596

Other courtyards, including one with a fountain, large trees, and green lawns, surrounded the Great Hall of Middle Temple. A cupola topped the red brick structure erected earlier in Queen Elizabeth's reign. John and the barrister followed several lawyers in long robes up the steps.

"What's going on?" John asked.

"The weekly lecture on geography. I had planned on attending." The Lincoln barrister hesitated. "Until I saw you."

"I don't mind listening."

An older lawyer intercepted the Lincoln barrister. "I thought you were going to join us."

The Lincoln barrister glanced at John. "I was delayed at Whitehall by Lord Willoughby and—"

John interrupted, "Maybe I should have gone with him to Grimsthorpe."

"We'll finish our business soon enough." The barrister turned back to the older man. "Is Richard Hakluyt speaking?"

"He's already begun along with a guest lecturer."

Inside the wood-paneled hall, younger barristers and their older mentors sat at long tables. Above the panels and windows, wooden beams shaped like double hammerheads arched to the ceiling, all the way to the cupola built high in the center. One of the older lawyers urged the newcomers to quiet.

John, standing next to the barrister by the door, turned his attention to a middle-aged man at the far end of the one-hundred-foot-long hall.

"Today," the middle-aged man began, "I have brought not only a friend of Sir Walter Raleigh, but also the man who managed Raleigh's estates while the Rear Admiral fought at Cadiz. Thomas Harriot will tell about the lost colony of Virginia."

"Thank you, Richard Hakluyt." Thomas Harriot began his talk. "As you most certainly know, Sir Walter Raleigh named Virginia in honor of our virgin Queen."

"God save Queen!" a nobleman interrupted.

"Hear him! Hear him!" other barristers joined the chorus.

"Our colony of over one hundred men stayed for almost a year in the New World on Roanoke Island." Thomas Harriot lit up his pipe. "You are familiar with how Indians smoke tobacco." He exhaled tobacco through his nose. "But they also believe that their gods are marvelously delighted with it. Sometimes they make hallowed fires and cast some of the tobacco powder for a sacrifice."

"They use it as a sacrifice," Richard Hakluyt repeated.

"Yes, and if a storm arises, they cast it up into the air and let it fall upon the waters to pacify the gods." Thomas Harriot breathed in more smoke. "After escaping danger, they do likewise, throwing it into the air with strange gestures. They sometimes dance, clap, and hold up their hands. They stomp and stare up into the heavens, all the time uttering strange words and chattering odd noises."

"Were the Indians friendly to the English?" Richard Hakluyt asked.

"We made friends with the Wiroans, who observed that whenever a neighboring village devised evil against us, we left those subtle practices unpunished. We did not seek revenge, yet God caused disease to fall upon those who had done us evil. Scores of men died in four or five of those villages."

"So they abandoned their idols?" Richard Hakluyt asked.

"The Wiroans talked as before, but when a drought plagued their corn, they came to us, asked us to pray to the God of England, and promised to share their harvest when the drought abated." Thomas Harriot continued, "Ten years ago, in August 1586, after Sir Francis Drake raided the Spanish Caribbean and their permanent colony at St. Augustine in Florida, he brought our whole colony, all one hundred and nine men, back to England."

"But didn't the original planters of the colony return to Virginia?"

"John White, who painted this map, returned with more settlers the following year. White brought along women, including his daughter and son-in-law."

"But wasn't that second colony lost?" Richard Hakluyt asked.

"Yes," Thomas Harriot said. "Ten days after Governor John White's daughter gave birth to the first English baby, he returned to England for supplies."

"And the baby?" Richard Hakluyt asked.

"Virginia Dare and her parents stayed on Roanoke Island," Thomas Harriot said. "John White scheduled a relief voyage the following year, but that had to be delayed because of the Spanish Armada. Six years ago, Sir Walter Raleigh finally was able to send White back with a relief voyage. By then, however, that second colony was lost."

"No trace?" a young lawyer asked. "Not of White's daughter or the baby?"

"None, except the letters C-R-O-A-T-O-A-N carved in a tree."

"What does Croatoan mean?" Richard Hakluyt asked.

"That's the name of one of the nearby tribes." Thomas Harriot pointed to an island on the map. "Towards the south, here. As many of you know, John White passed away three years ago. He never saw his daughter or granddaughter Virginia again."

While the lecture continued, rekindling John's interest in going to sea, a man quietly asked the Lincoln barrister, "Will you two be staying for dinner?"

"Not John." The Lincoln barrister motioned for John to exit the hall, before adding, "I'll be back shortly."

Office, Middle Temple, London, England

UPSTAIRS, INSIDE A barrister's office, the Lincoln lawyer motioned to John. "Have a seat."

John sat down on a hard chair.

"After your father died, we incurred some expenses, but now we need to close the estate of George Smith."

"Yes, my father saved money his whole life."

"Besides some woodland in Lincolnshire, there's nothing left for you."

"Nothing? What do you mean? What about my inheritance?"

"There is nothing left."

"Don't I get anything?"

"Do not pester me, John." The lawyer pushed ten small coins across the table. "Here's ten shillings."

"Only ten?"

"That is all that remains. You can do with it as you please."

"That's all? Out of my father's entire estate?"

"Expenses had to be paid for your victuals and the courts."

"And you!" John jumped to his feet, gripped the ten shillings tightly, and shoved them into his pocket. He slammed the door behind him and descended the stairs.

Outside, he stopped at the the Fountain Courtyard. "My father is gone." He shook his head and wandered past the Great Hall and toward Temple Landing on the Thames. "And I have nothing." John's dreams of riding and running at the ring would have to wait.

Temple Stairs in 1680

"You said something?" The captain of a small boat asked.

John reached for his passport and pulled out a shilling. "Take me to Gravesend." Gravesend was the most convenient port to depart to sea.

"I can't." The boatman paused. "The rules. Only the local ferry can transport passengers to and from Gravesend."

A young barrister John had seen at the lecture stepped forward. "I'm taking my own boat down towards Canterbury. You can ride with me."

John climbed into the boat, but before they reached the mouth of the Thames, the barrister stopped at Gravesend, where John found an English vessel sailing to France.

Mouth of the Thames, England, Late Summer 1596

ABOARD THE DECK of the English ship, the first mate shouted, "Then do all agree?"

"Aye, aye!" Every sailor and passenger, including John, nodded.

"If we are attacked, we will never surrender," a nobleman said.

"Before this ship will be captured," the first mate added, "we will set fire to it."

"And sink it," another sailor said.

No one dissented.

When the merchant ship reached the open sea, John joined a group of Englishmen listening to a young Venetian nobleman.

"Queen Elizabeth speaks Italian very well," the Venetian said.

"You met the Queen?" John asked.

"I had the honor to go on behalf of the Venetian ambassador to France. From Paris, King Henry IV sent the Queen letters of introduction for me, but I must tell you what impressed me most."

"What?" John asked.

"The fine wool." He pointed to a flock pasturing on a hillside overlooking the Thames. "It is the true Golden Fleece of England." The Venetian asked, "And you?"

"I'm going to Paris, too."

"To seek treasure?"

"If I wanted treasure I would have followed in the footsteps of Thomas Sendall."

"Who is he?"

"The greatest merchant in Lynn. He gave me this knife." John unsheathed the blade.

AROUND MIDNIGHT, ON the waters between France and England, bells clanged. "All hands on deck! All hands on deck!"

John swung out of his hammock, put on his cloak, and rushed past bundles of wool and up onto the deck. "What is it?"

"Seven ships!" The first mate pointed toward the north.

"Pirates from Dunkirk!" the captain shouted. "To arms!"

Gunners prepared the few cannons. Sailors grabbed muskets and swords.

"You're outnumbered," the Venetian nobleman said.

"We'll never surrender." The fully armed sailor turned to the young John Smith. "You know how to fight?"

"No." John touched his knife.

The sailor grabbed John's arm. "Never too soon to learn."

Chapter 38 - Compassion and Control

Which they [the translators] so honestly reported to her, [Aisha, Sister of the Sultan] took
(as it seemed) much compassion on him [Smith].

John Smith

Salon, Ibrahim *Pasha* Palace, *Jumada II*, AH 1011 (Dec. 1602)

"OUT OF MY own estate," Captain John Smith concluded, "they liberally gave me ten shillings."

Emine sat next to Aisha and continued to translate John's English into Turkish.

Aisha was shocked. "Ten shillings? Is that all?" How did he become so rich if it was not from his inheritance? And who holds his money to pay his ransom?

"But worst of all," John continued, "I hadn't really thought about what it was going to like without my father until then."

Aisha sympathized with John, for she knew what it was like to lose a father. After all, her father, Sultan Murad III, had died almost eight years earlier. "What about your mother?"

John looked away. "To be honest with you, I was no longer welcome in her home after she remarried. Her new husband did not want her oldest son to be in his house. And my mother respected his wishes."

Aisha stared at Emine as she translated.

"His mother removed John from her house?" At least Aisha had a home.

"Yes," Emine said, "that is what John said."

"Did that slow you from pursuing your adventure?"

John shook his head. "No. I became more determined."

"I am beginning to believe you," Aisha said. "Just like Queen Elizabeth could not be stopped by King Philip II."

"Aisha." Emine sprang off the sofa. "I didn't realize how late it was. I really must be getting back."

"You are right." Aisha, rising to her feet, reached for Emine's long

271

cloak. "Mother will be back shortly."

"Aren't you worried?"

"About talking to John? No, I'll just tell her I felt better after she left."

"And when I came by, I insisted on practicing my English."

"You are such a good friend." Aisha reached for her hand.

Emine peered over Aisha's shoulder.

"I hope to see you again," John said.

"We will see." Aisha motioned to the Overseer. "Take my English slave back to his quarters."

While servants straightened the reception room, making it as neat as it had been when her mother and sister had departed in the morning, Aisha escorted Emine through the garden and stopped beneath the covered archway leading to the First Courtyard. "My mother pressures me to ransom John, but I still do not know how he became so rich if he did not inherit it."

As the Overseer silently led the well-dressed Englishman through the far side of the garden, Emine waved goodbye.

After the departure of her guest, Aisha returned to her Vaulted Chamber. Alone at her desk, but still dressed in her favorite outfit, she wondered what had detained her mother from returning from the baths.

It must be important business.

Third Courtyard, New Palace, *Rajab*, AH 1011 (Dec. 1602)

SEVERAL DAYS AFTER being called away from the baths by the Chief Black Eunuch, the Sultan's Mother, Safiye *Valide Sultana*, crossed the

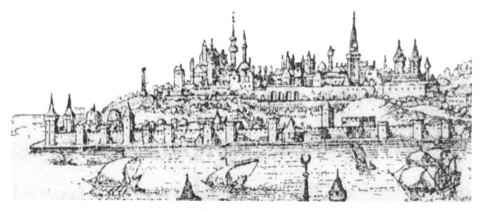

New (Topkapi) Palace in 1635

Third Courtyard of the New Palace accompanied by him. Only a few weeks earlier the kiosk windows had been shattered. After her son the Sultan received presents from the new ambassador from Venice inside the throne room, the Venetian ship *Martinella* fired its booming salute.

Under the direction of the Chief White Eunuch and his appointee, the *acemi oglan* had done their jobs, sweeping broken remains and installing new panes. The building housing the organ sent by Queen Elizabeth of England on the accession of her son appeared fully restored.

Osman *Agha*, known as the *Kizlar Agha* or the Chief Black Eunuch, pointed past the cadet dormitories to the Treasury on the far side side of the courtyard. "Revenues from Anatolia have fallen further. The rebels allow those who join their cause to keep the monies instead of paying us."

"The monies must come to the Treasury." The Sultan's Mother had already suspended building her New Mosque, the *Yeni Valide Camii*, because of the cost.

The Chief White Eunuch Gazanfer *Agha* stopped them outside the door of his apartment by the Gate of Felicity.

"What is it?" the Sultan's Mother asked.

"I did not want to upset your son, but I thought you should know."

"Know what? Sultan Mehmet III spends this afternoon with his harem favorite, listening to music and enjoying the dancing."

"I did not want to disturb him." The Chief White Eunuch, old and wise, spoke in a soft voice. "The Divan meets. Reports from Anatolia are not good. Everything is worse."

The Sultan's Mother, accompanied by her two closest advisors, the Chief White and Chief Black Eunuchs, went through the Gate into the Second Courtyard. "Join the Divan. I will watch the council meeting from behind the throne."

The two powerful eunuchs went into the open Divan, a low square building on the side of the grassy courtyard.

With the Grand Vizier in Belgrade, his Deputy, the *Kaimakam Saat-ci* Hasan *Pasha* sat on the throne. Soft light illuminated the white turbans of the other viziers who sat on long sofas on either side. The military judges from Anatolia and Rumelia were also in attendance.

"The latest commander is no more successful than the previous ones," a messenger said. "The troops from Aleppo and Mar'ash failed to stop *Deli* Hasan and his rebels."

"The rebellion grows?" the Deputy Grand Vizier asked.

"*Deli* Hasan reached Ankara," Gulzece Mahmud *Pasha*, a prominent *sipahi* leader said. "Ankara paid *Deli* Hasan a ransom so that he wouldn't destroy the city."

"Ankara is an important city in central Anatolia, but I'm certain Khosru *Pasha* can succeed in crushing the rebellion," the Chief White Eunuch said.

"How many times must we appoint a leader to fight in Anatolia?" the *sipahi* leader Gulzece Mahmud *Pasha* asked.

"Perhaps the Sultan should be told," the Deputy Grand Vizier said.

The Sultan's Mother opened the lattice shades behind the throne and captured the Chief White Eunuch's attention. She signaled 'no.'

"You must not tell him," the Chief White Eunuch said. "We do not want to upset Sultan Mehmet III again."

The Sultan's Mother rose and waited for the Chief Black Eunuch to reach her at the gate to the Imperial Harem. "Osman *Agha*, my son must not find out."

The Chief Black Eunuch nodded. "And he shall not."

Chapter 39 - Mischievous Purposes

"When I came to Constantinople [Stamboul], I perceived the sipahis going on with their mischievous purposes, but at first declined taking any share in them. Katib Jezami and others came running about me; and when I tried to escape them, they followed me, urging me to join them.

They used to tell me this and that; that the mufti [Sun'Ullah Effendi], all the viziers, the military judges, and other great men were in the plot; that they should without doubt accomplish their purpose; 'You're making yourself singular', they said, 'will not retard the execution of our plan, and your obstinacy will only serve to bring evil upon yourself'."

Poiraz Osman *Bey* [*Sipahi* Commander from Hungary]
Annals of the Turkish Empire by Mustafa Naima
Translated from Turkish by Charles Fraser

Kale-Megdan Citadel, Belgrade, *Rajab*, AH 1011 (Dec. 1602)

INSIDE KALE-MEGDAN, THE strong citadel of Belgrade overlooking the Danube, the Grand Vizier of the Ottoman Empire sat comfortably, cross-legged on the floor. He urged the Tartar Khan to complete the main course, fresh sturgeon from the river. The Grand Vizier once more wanted to honor *Ghazi* Giray II before the Khan and his warriors retired to their winter quarters.

The Khan donned a turban fancier than those worn by any Turk in the room. Unlike other Tartars or Mongols who maintained their ancient pagan beliefs, the Crimean Tartars had converted to Islam more than a century earlier.

Though smaller than the pair of feasts the two leaders held for each other when the Crimean Tartars arrived in Ottoman Hungary, the fare was no less scrumptious. As soon as the Khan finished the generous portions of fish, servants quickly removed the empty platters.

The Grand Vizier leaned towards his guest, a direct descendent of Genghis Khan. "Your Highness, tell me the details of the Battle in Wallachia. I must send a complete report to Gazanfer *Agha* at the New Palace."

"After we heard about the Christian army, we found them in the open, in a valley outside Targoviste." The Crimean Khan, as fierce as any of his warrior ancestors, gestured to the Lieutenant of the Grand Vizier. "Your own Lieutenant, Mustafa *Agha*, began the battle north of the capital of Wallachia."

"At midday, a little more than a month ago, our *janissaries* marched toward the enemy," Mustafa *Agha*, whose plumed hat reflected his importance, explained. "With our drums beating and our trumpets sounding, we advanced toward the Christian army of ten thousand. When two large squadrons of enemy horse counterattacked, my *janissaries* were forced to retire."

General *Beg-ogli*, the Khan's chief officer and eldest son, put down his drink. "When I gave the signal, thousands of my warriors advanced." He raised his arm. "They shot their arrows high and forced the enemy horse back. We cornered them against a mountainside, not far from a stream."

"By that time, we should have already won." The Crimean Khan *Ghazi* Giray II, whose nickname *Bora* meant 'storm,' grimaced. "I sent thousands more of my warriors against the Christian infidels. We lost many fine riders who became martyrs for Allah. By the end of the day, the battle was won. Very few of the enemy escaped over the stream and into the mountains."

"Your losses?"

"Nearly half of my brave army, but most of the survivors have recovered in Silistra and in other towns along the Danube."

The Grand Vizier had never heard of any Tartar army suffering such great losses. "Unlike any army you ever fought?" When the Khan did not respond, the Grand Vizier added, "You and your warriors can winter in Hungary."

The Khan looked at his general and other officers, including the one designated to transport captives back to Crimea. "We must make up the losses we suffered in Wallachia."

"You will be allowed to probe the frontiers beyond Kanizsa, but this Long War against Emperor Rudolph II has not ended. The infidel's tribute to the Sultan for both Hungary and Transylvania remains unpaid."

"But what about the rebellion in Anatolia?" the Khan asked.

"After the death of the rebel *Scrivano*, I had hoped that the Cecali rebellion would subside." The Grand Vizier referred to the name of the first Anatolian rebel. "Instead, *Scrivano's* brother, *Deli* Hasan, has increased his power. The rebellion has spread."

"My younger brothers joined them. I would have considered fighting them, but then our losses . . ."

"Two years ago, the *janissaries* talked of putting you on the throne," Mustafa *Agha* rejoined. "But now —"

"We need not speak about replacing the Sultan," the Grand Vizier interrupted. "Have you forgotten I shall marry Aisha, the Sister of the Sultan?"

"Does not that young widow still mourn?" the Khan asked.

"*Damat* Ibrahim *Pasha* died a year and a half ago," the Grand Vizier said. "Last spring, I sent the *Agha* of the *Janissaries* to negotiate the marriage contract with Aisha. The *kabin* or dowry was set at four thousand ducats. I look forward to the marriage."

"When do you plan to return to *Stamboul*?" the Khan asked.

"If winter proves as harsh as the last two years, I must delay, but as soon as the Sultan requests my presence. At least the current Grand Mufti does not insist I stay on the battlefront. After we put everything in perfect order, perhaps at the end of the next year's campaign."

"You remind me. With winter approaching, my warriors should go to their quarters."

"I have sent letters to the *sanjak*s throughout the *Vilayet* of Buda. Many can winter in Mohacs, the site of the famous battle." In the Christian Year 1525 the young Hungarian King Louis II had died at the Battle of Mohacs. Suleiman *the Magnificent* and the Ottoman army, four years after they conquered Belgrade, overpowered the Hungarian forces. "Further accommodations have also been readied in Pecs for you."

The Khan and his cohorts rose and followed the Grand Vizier out of the dining area and into the courtyard of the Upper Castle that the Turks called *Kale-Megdan*, fortress-field.

In the late autumn cold, an *orta* of janissaries stood in formation. On the far side of the courtyard, several hundred Tartar warriors, clothed in the traditional black sheepskin worn by their ancestors, mounted their short Tartarian horses. With bows and quivers filled with new arrows strapped to their back, they were ready, as always, for battle.

The Khan mounted his Arabian steed and acknowledged the Grand Vizier. "I will go to my quarters, too."

"I have written to the new *Sanjak* of Pecs. He broke the siege of Kanizsa and pursed the enemy, killing many."

"A warrior like me." *Ghazi* Giray II and both of his sons exited the courtyard.

After they rode through the gate, the Grand Vizier ascended the stairs to the top of the double castle walls. He wanted to see the strength of the Ottoman Empire's most loyal allies.

More than twenty thousand warriors broke camp and followed their leaders down to the banks of the Sava River. More than ten thousand had already encamped on the other side.

Besides weapons, each warrior had brought two or three extra horses, some to be used if his primary horse became maimed in battle. Other horses would be eaten, when provisions proved scarce. Each Tartar, in his turn, would supply a horse for meat, roasting it like others cooked beef or mutton.

Mounted next to the Khan, a strong warrior held his simple standard, a white mare's tail accented by smooth green taffeta. The number in his mounted guards swelled, reaching ten thousand.

The Grand Vizier walked along the walls and watched the remaining Tartar horsemen break camp in the meadows. Thousands more appeared. For more than two hours, the warriors on horseback forded the blue Sava. The fortress of Zuben, standing on a promontory on the opposite side of the Sava River, commanded the plains, where Ottoman armies advancing into Hungary would often gather for their summer campaigns.

After crossing the Sava and Drava Rivers and dispersing part of his Tartar army at Mohacz, the Khan would reach Pecs, one hundred fifty miles away from Belgrade. The remaining Tartar warriors would winter in Szigetvar or in Koppan, closer to Lake Balaton and the enemy.

With the sound of pounding hooves fading and the last of the Khan's army crossing the Sava, the Grand Vizier walked the upper castle walls. Beyond the Danube, high clouds streamed above the *Vilayet* of Timisoara. To the northeast, snowcapped mountains marked the border of Wallachia and Transylvania, provinces required to pay the Sultan yearly tributes.

When the Grand Vizier returned to the upper courtyard, he heard the neigh of a horse and he turned to the gate from *Stamboul*. He recognized the white eunuch from the New Palace. "What is it?"

"I rode as fast as I could." The eunuch handed him a letter and dismounted. "The rebel *Deli* Hasan has gained more ground."

"Against the new eunuch commander Khorsu *Pasha*?"

"Yes."

"Did you pass by my *sipahi* commander?"

"Between Edirne and Sophia. Poiraz Osman *Bey* should be in *Stamboul* by now."

Valens Aqueduct, *Stamboul*, *Rajab*, AH 1011 (Late Dec. 1602)

HOURS PAST SUNSET, Katib Jemazi, an important *sipahi* leader, kept his horse quiet beneath the Valens Aqueduct, the ancient waterway spanning the valley between the Third and Fourth Hills of *Stamboul*. Though no longer carrying fresh water from the city's outskirts to hidden cisterns, the remnants of the aqueduct stood more than five stories high. Below double arches, bricks above stone, the *sipahi* leader lifted his loose collar. A night breeze had replaced the afternoon warmth; he did not want to shiver.

Valens Aqueduct

Katib glanced at the other *sipahi* leaders present and turned to an important religious leader, a deputy of the former Grand Mufti Sun'Ullah *Effendi*. "I hope Poiraz Osman *Bey* accepts our invitation?"

"Do you know what his loyalties are since his return from Belgrade?" the member of the Ulema, the religious council asked.

"When he first arrived, Osman *Bey* declined to partake in our plan."

"Did you tell him that we want to purge the empire by blood?"

"I purposely left the details unsaid. He may need further persuasion."

"We should invite him to attend our feast."

"He must see everything is bad. Because the Grand Vizier assisted Sekul Murish to attack Transylvania, the armies of the Holy Roman Empire fought for Buda. The fight for Pest was most difficult."

"Osman *Bey* was there, but we must be careful here." The Deputy gestured to the religious school erected by the Chief White Eunuch. Small domes rose behind the plain walls of the single-story stone complex. "The headmaster of the medrese of Gazanfer *Agha* cannot find out."

"Yes, before Gazanfer *Agha*, only immediate members of the Sultan's family had ever been allowed to build a medrese inside *Stamboul*."

"All seems quiet." The last of the day's five prayers ended at nightfall and the students of Islam stayed inside.

"Perhaps Osman *Bey* should talk directly to Sun'Ullah *Effendi*?" Katib Jezami suggested.

"My mentor must be restored to his former position as Grand Mufti, the *Sheikh ul-Islam*."

"But Osman *Bey* must know that Sun'Ullah *Effendi* and the Grand Vizier do not get along."

"Remind me," Katib said.

"After *Damat* Ibrahim *Pasha* died and Hasan *the Fruiterer* became Grand Vizier, Sun'Ullah *Effendi* insisted the Grand Vizier immediately lead the war effort." The Deputy paused. "I was there when the Sun'Ullah *Effendi* who was the Grand Mufti went to the Sultan."

"The Mufti became angry?"

"Very much so. After that heated exchange, the Grand Vizier relented and went to the frontier."

"He has been in Europe ever since."

"For two years now, but before he reached Belgrade, the Grand Vizier appointed a new mufti in Edirne, even though he had no right."

"Later, Sultan Mehmet III replaced that Grand Mufti with another."

As a cloudy wisp swept past the quarter moon, the lunar brightness faded and the shadows on darkened streets deepened.

"Quiet," the deputy mufti said. "I hear riders."

Hasan Khalifeh and Poiraz Osman *Bey* drew closer.

The deputy mufti and the other riders led their horses into the moonlight. "We're glad you decided to join us," Katib Jezami said.

The *sipahi* leader Poiraz Osman *Bey* from Belgrade pulled his horse to a stop. "I have made no such decision."

"I have only told Poiraz Osman *Bey* the outlines of the plan," Hasan Khalifeh informed.

"I said I could not turn my back on the Grand Vizier. What is this is all about?" Poiraz Osman *Bey* asked. "The Grand Vizier has rewarded me with wealth, including slaves whom I've sold."

"Everyone agrees," Katib Jemazi said, "the Grand Mufti must be replaced."

"By whom?"

"Sun'Ullah *Effendi*."

"But what if the Sultan does not replace the Mufti?"

"We can discuss that matter at a feast."

"A feast? Tonight?"

"No, but soon."

Poiraz Osman *Bey*, the *sipahi* leader from Belgrade, remained silent.

"You must consider everything." Katib Jemazi led his horse back into the shadows.

Hasan Khalifeh, the deputy, and the other *sipahi* leaders slowly walked their horses. Passing beneath the walls of the Medrese of Gazanfer *Agha*, their steeds splashed though shallow puddles, while *janissaries*, carrying long sticks and patrolling dutifully on their evening rounds, paid scant attention.

Poiraz Osman *Bey* rode in the opposite direction, beneath the shifting shadows of the stone edifice. He glanced up at the reappearing moon and brightening clouds hovering over the sleeping city and shook his head.

Chapter 40 - Try the Truth

To try the truth, she [Aisha, Sister of the Sultan] found means to find out many [who] could speak English, French . . . to whom relating . . .

John Smith

Salon, Ibrahim *Pasha* Palace, *Rajab* AH 1011 (Dec. 1602)

THE DOOR OF the salon swung open and the Overseer of the Palace of Ibrahim *Pasha* announced, "Filiz, the French translator."

Aisha, Sister of the Sultan, warmly welcomed her friend. "I am so happy to see you."

"Please accept my apologies; I couldn't make it last week."

"Among friends there is no ceremony." Aisha offered a cushioned seat. "I am so happy you are here." After dismissing her servants and exchanging pleasantries, Aisha got to the point. "Your help in translating is invaluable. Last week, John told Emine and me how he saw Queen Elizabeth sailing on her barge on the Thames."

"Like your brother's barge?"

"Yes, the same one my father used."

Filiz laughed. "I remember seeing your father toss his court midgets into the air, overboard into the water."

"In good fun. They quickly swam back." Aisha paused. "But that is not why I wanted you to come. John is going back to France with his inheritance."

"Then he is rich?"

Aisha shook her head. "When his father's estate was settled in England, John learned he had no inheritance. His father worked hard for Lord Willoughby, but, save for ten shillings, the lawyers spent it all."

"That doesn't sound like much."

"It is not." A wave of sadness washed over Aisha. She had been her father's favorite. "I know how it feels to lose a father."

"Yes, you do." Filiz reached over and patted her friend's hand. "Are you going to tell your mother?"

"And have her send him a — ?" Aisha caught herself in mid-sentence. "Filiz, I must try to find the truth about his capture and how he met my fiancé the Grand Vizier, no matter how long it takes. Today, John can tell us about his journey to Paris."

Aisha strode to the door and caught the eye of the large black eunuch in the garden. "Overseer."

"Yes, Lady Aisha."

"Bring the *Capitano* to me."

"As you wish."

Minutes later, the Overseer brought John unbound into the salon. The morning sun, streaming through the tall windows, warmed the room. While Aisha served her guests fresh pastries, still warm from the palace kitchens, a servant poured coffee.

John accepted the petite cup. "*Merci beaucoup.*"

"*Bon jour, Jean,*" Filiz said. "Please tell us all about Paris. Aisha said you went back to France after only getting ten shillings from your father's estate."

"Yes, although I only received ten shillings from the lawyer, I still had my passport. That paper enabled me to travel out of England." John looked directly into Aisha's eyes. "I was sixteen years old when I sailed back to France."

"What happened to those seven ships at midnight?" Aisha asked. "Did they attack?"

"No. We sailed closer and saw they were not Dunkirk pirates like we thought, but merchantmen flying the English flag."

"Go on, please."

Filiz translated Aisha's words from Turkish. "*Continuez s'il vous plait.*"

"At Paris on the shores of the Seine, I met a Scotsman called David Hume of Godscroft."

Chapter 41 - David Hume of Godscroft

The poor throng into this city [Paris] in such numbers that it is impossible to move about the streets either on foot or on horseback. A census was taken, and they were found to amount to one hundred thousand some days ago; now there are many more. They have brought the plague— —the last calamity.

Piero Duodo, Venetian Ambassador in France

Paris, May 1596

Lord Hume, who in France, had the honor of seeing and discoursing with his Most Christian Majesty [King Henry IV].

Maximilian *de* Bethune, Baron *de* Rosny [Later, Duke of Sully]

Translated from French by Charlotte Lennox

It was the least thought of his [John Smith's] determination, for now being freely at liberty in Paris, growing acquainted with one Master David Hume [of Godscroft], who, making some use of his purse . . .

John Smith

Montmarte, Outside Paris, France, Early Autumn 1596

THE AROMA OF freshly baked bread wafted across John's path. At the foot of Montmarte, about a mile outside Paris, Smith spied the source through a window. Candlelight illuminated a baker taking the steaming loaves from his oven. Though dawn had not yet risen, the pleasant aroma whetted John's appetite. He walked up to the small bakery nestled among a small cluster of houses and knocked.

When the proprietor cracked the door open, John held up a coin. *"Je veux acheter du pain."*

The French proprietor eyed the coin. *"Anglais monnaie?"*

"Oui," John said.

"Je suppose." The owner snatched the shilling and retrieved a steamy loaf of bread.

French Baker

284

"Merci beaucoup." John stuffed the loaf into his satchel, slung the bag over his shoulder, and resumed his journey up the hill. He glanced at the lightening sky. The sun had not yet risen over the horizon. Few stars shone brightly, others quickly disappeared.

John continued his ascent and turned a corner. Ahead, at the top of a knoll, a wagon stopped in front of a mill attached to a four-bladed windmill. Two workers unloaded sacks of grain, grist to be ground into flour later in the day when the wind returned.

John looked toward Paris, now awakening. Distant torches outlined the city, but the torchlights soon disappeared. Paris remained a mystery: morning mist and low fog enveloped the city.

Further up the hill, John found a place to sit, not far from the walled abbey of St. Pierre, the church where Ignatius Loyola reportedly began the order of the Catholic Jesuits. John put down his knapsack and retrieved the warm bread. He unsheathed his knife and sliced the round block of cheese he had purchased the previous afternoon. He wanted to make his monies last: the meals at the inn were too expensive.

The evening before, the innkeeper had suggested that John go to Montmarte, informing him that it had been called the Mount of Mars: the Romans had once built a temple dedicated to the God of War when France was known as Gaul. The Romans also killed Saint Denis on Montmarte, giving the small mountain a second name, Mount of Martyrs.

To John's left, a plain chapel dedicated to Christian martyrs served to remind the faithful of the cost that the early Christians had paid. To his right, the four blades of the windmill stood silent in the first morning light. Directly in front of him, beyond the grain fields, Paris began to reveal herself. The Tower of the disbanded Order of the Knight's Templar stood behind the outer walls.

Montemarte and the Tower of the Temple in Paris

More of an oval than a pure circle, Paris had grown since Roman times, when the city known as Lutetia was built on the island in the Seine. That river, flowing from east to west, must have given life throughout the centuries, providing sustenance to the Parisians even in difficult times.

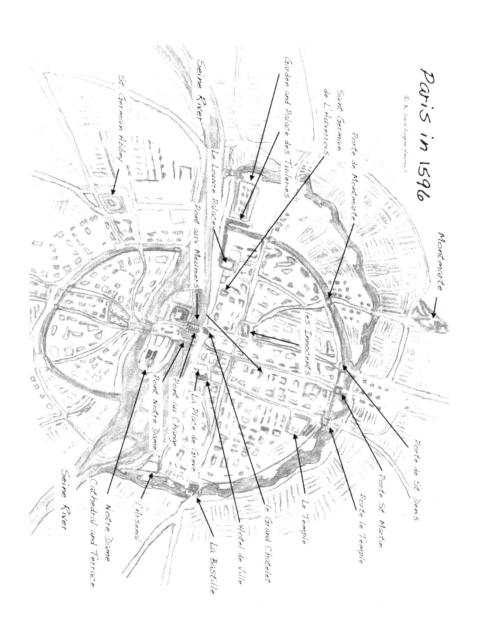

On the east end of *Ile de la Cite* in the middle of the Seine, the Notre Dame Cathedral dominated the skyline. Named "Our Lady" for the Virgin Mary, her center spire pierced the morning fog. Hiding and reappearing like a needle weaving in and out of cloth, that spire and two square towers pushed upward. The fog began to lift. Even as a woman is the heart of a home, Paris was clearly the heart of France.

A moat and walls encompassed the city that had grown on both sides of the Seine. Dirt roads from every direction converged on Paris. From East and West, North and South, all highways led to the nation's capital. At the eastern gate, the fortress Bastille stood mighty and strong, while to the west Louvre Castle butted against the remnants of the inner wall. To the south, on the left bank of the Seine, the universities in the Latin Quarter trained students. On the right bank, markets a mile away stirred to life.

John finished his breakfast and saved the rest of the bread and cheese for later in the day. He descended past Martyr Chapel and strolled through the harvested fields. Crossing over a moat, he entered through the *Porte de Montmarte,* one of the fortified gates. He walked past a hospital and glimpsed a fountain by the cemetery of *les Innocents,* where bodies from the recent plague were buried *en masse.* He soon walked

Le Grand Chatelet

past *le Grand Chatelet* and reached the Seine.

Just as John was about to cross *Le Pont Meuniers*, one of three bridges leading to the *Ile de la Cite,* he noticed fishermen downstream. When one pole bent, John decided to watch, stopping at the edge of the street and the top of a stone wall.

Below, the weathered fisherman landed the fish onto the muddy banks. He opened its mouth, and removed the hook.

Further down the riverbank, at the top of the steps near the Church of *St. Germain de L'Auxerrois,* one well-dressed nobleman waved to another.

Seine Riverbanks, Paris, France

"AU REVOIR!" THE nobleman waved to his younger friend again.

Standing by a boat tethered by the bottom step, the second nobleman held up several scrolls. He waved back. "I'll return in the spring."

"Write back soon." The nobleman spoke with a distinct Scottish accent.

"I'll secure the reply to the French proposal." The younger man placed the scroll into his bag and boarded the small skiff.

"I'll be at the *Hotel de Ville* all winter."

"And I'll catch a ship at *Havre de Grace.*" The departing gentleman sat down in the skiff.

The boatman untied the line and shoved off. The vessel drifted past the pilings of a new bridge. The *Pont Neuf* would connect Louvre Castle with another castle on the western tip of the *Ile de la Cite.*

The first nobleman watched the boat sail below a tower. Built at the corner of the outer city wall, that tower held iron chains that could be raised across the Seine, helping to protect Paris from any enemy siege.

The young John Smith approached him. "Are you Scottish?"

The Scotsman nodded and smiled. "I see you have an ear for accents."

"I worked for Master Thomas Sendall in Lynn. Scottish as well as Dutch and Flemish traders often visited our shop."

"What's your name?"

"John, John Smith. I just arrived from London. It's the first time I've been to Paris."

"First time in France?"

"No, I traveled to Orleans earlier in the year. And you?"

"David Hume of Godscroft." The Scotsman extended his hand. "Welcome to Paris."

After they shook hands, John pointed to the vessel sailing into a deep channel. "Who's that messenger?"

"He's not a messenger. He's a courtier for King James VI of Scotland."

"A courtier?"

"A prudent one with good judgment. A year ago, we Scots aided the

French, and recently, I had the opportunity to converse with King Henry IV. My friends will want to know everything. That trusted courtier will give my firsthand account."

"He's taking your letters back to your friends at the court?"

The boat disappeared in the river mist.

"Yes." David Hume of Godscroft turned to John. "And what brings you here?"

"I want see all Paris has to offer."

"Have you seen Notre Dame?"

"Only from a distance, when I climbed to Montmarte outside the walls at dawn." John added, "I need to change my shillings into French money."

"You can do that on the *Pont au Change.*"

"Is it nearby?"

"Just beyond *Le Pont aux Meuniers.*" David Hume of Godscroft pointed to the Bridge of Millers where water, channeled between wood pilings, powered large waterwheels. A half-dozen wheels turned grindstones inside the mills, directly above. Built side by side, the mills two-and-a-half stories tall lined the bridge from end to end.

John noticed some of wood pilings supporting the bridge needed repair. Rusty nails protruded out of the split planks. Ice, wind, and sun had taken their toll on the weathered wood. "Aren't they worried that winter rains might wash it away?"

"Paris has other worries," David Hume of Godscroft said. "During the warm spring, the plague hit the poorer sections. Even now officers send many who flocked from the country back to their homes." He pointed to *le Grand Chatelet,* a miniature castle and prison in front of the *Pont au Change* where an officer shooed away several French country boys.

Other travelers and coaches headed in the opposite direction, toward the Louvre Castle. David Hume of Godscroft and John Smith pushed through the crowds. They followed a man hunched over. He carried a huge stack of wood on his back. Probably to deliver to French homes, John thought.

Pont au Change, Paris, France

SMALLER THAN THE buildings on London Bridge, the quaint structures on the *Pont au Change* stood two stories tall.

"French kings wanted all the moneychangers in one place, so for hundreds of years, the kings have required they set up shop on the bridge," David Hume of Godscroft informed John. "With *le Grand Chatelet* on one side of the river, and the Palace of Justice on the island, the Provost of Paris will punish anyone who attempts to rob them."

Next to the goldsmith shop, John changed the last of his ten shillings

Notre Dame Cathedral

from his father's estate into French coins. Although it wasn't much money, John did not worry. He knew he could always find work and earn more.

David Hume of Godscroft also exchanged some Scottish coins into French crowns and ecus and the two crossed over to the island. They walked past the Palace of Justice. While a young couple strolled straight ahead over one of the two bridges connecting the island to the Latin Quarter of the Left bank, David Hume of Godscroft and John turned east.

The Scotsman pointed to the two towers rising high above a large square. "The *Notre Dame de Paris.*"

"*Magnificente.*" The gothic Cathedral appeared even more impressive than it had from distant Montmarte.

Plaza, Cathedral of Notre Dame, Paris, France

THOUGH IT WAS not Sunday, the large plaza, fed by the streets from the east, was filled with people. Two carriages, each pulled by four horses, stopped in front of the Cathedral. Two square towers framed the west façade and its three sets of doors. The massive doors in the center swung open.

When a white-haired Cardinal stopped at the top of the stairs, John asked David Hume of Godscroft, "Isn't that the *Legate de Latere?*"

"You know of Allesandro *de* Medici?"

"Only a little, I saw him in Chartres last spring."

"The Cardinal of Florence is a member of the powerful Medici family, who even now has close ties to the French throne."

"How so?"

"Catherine *de* Medici was the wife of the former French King Henry II. To celebrate the marriage of their eldest daughter Elizabeth *de* Valois to

King Philip II of Spain, King Henry II fought in a jousting match against the captain of his Scottish guard. The captain's lance pierced the King's visor and the tip

Lance Splinters inside King Henry II's Visor in 1559

splintered into pieces. King Henry II was mortally wounded and never recovered." David Hume of Godscroft added, "After Henry II died, Catherine *de* Medici's eldest son, Francois, became the French King at the age of fifteen and Catherine maintained power as regent. Upon his death, two other sons of Catherine *de* Medici later became Kings of France, and now her daughter Marguerite *de* Valois has become the French Queen."

"But I thought because of Salic law only sons can take control of the French throne."

"True. But before her next son King Charles IX's death, Catherine *de* Medici wanted him to consolidate power with other kingdoms through family alliances. That's why she arranged to have her daughter Marguerite *de* Valois marry a distant cousin Henry, King of Navarre, right here in this square in August 1572."

"Not inside the Cathedral?"

"No, on a stage by the *parvis* outside the main doors. Before his Catholic conversion, Henry was a Calvinist, so he was not allowed to marry inside Notre Dame."

"Where is Navarre?" John asked.

"The Calvinist Kingdom lies in the south of France, near Spain. "But how did Henry IV become the French King?" John asked.

"King Henry IV is King Henry of Navarre and he retains both titles. Marguerite *de* Valois's brother, King Henry III, inherited the throne from his brother King Charles IX, but King Henry III had no heirs. Upon King Henry III's death, King Henry of Navarre, who was the oldest direct male heir of a former French King, inherited the French crown and became known as King Henry IV, which makes his wife, Marguerite *de* Valois, the Queen of France. This is one way the Medici family maintains influence."

"I understand," John said.

"It was not so simple though. The marriage between Marguerite *de* Valois and King Henry of Navarre was arranged against her wishes."

"What do you mean?"

"At the marriage ceremony, when the priest asked King Henry of Navarre if he would take Marguerite *de* Valois to be his spouse, Henry quickly said, '*Oui.*' She on the other hand hesitated."

"Hesitated?"

"She was reluctant." David Hume of Godscroft paused. "When the priest asked whether she would marry King Henry of Navarre, Marguerite *de* Valois said nothing. The priest asked again. She kept mum. The priest repeated a third time, 'Will you marry King Henry of Navarre?' When Marguerite *de* Valois kept quiet, her brother, King Charles IX of France, pushed her head up and down."

After the *Legate de Latere* got into his carriage, John Smith and David Hume of Godscroft walked through the cloisters on the north side of the Cathedral to the Terrain on the eastern tip of the *Ile de la Cite*.

John commented, "The *Legate de Latere* appeared somewhat upset."

"Yes," David Hume of Godscroft said, "he must have seen the recent pronouncements by the Duke of Mercoeur."

"Pronouncements?"

"Clauses in many of the Duke's orders say 'until there is a Catholic King in France'."

"But I thought King Henry IV became a Roman Catholic."

"He did, but the Catholic League, including the Duke of Mercoeur, does not accept his conversion."

"And the Legate *de* Latere?"

"He writes the Duke of Mercoeur in Nantes, telling him that since the Pope has granted His Most Christian King Henry IV absolution, the Duke of Mercoeur should accept his conversion, too."

Terrain, Notre Dame Cathedral, Paris, France

BIRDS DARTED BACK and forth through trees already changing color. Though the sun felt warm, a mid-morning breeze carried some of the colorful foliage toward the Cathedral. The birds flew past the spire, rising high over the center of the nave.

On the other side of the terrace, a young girl chased an agile youngster around a tree. They ran through and kicked up one pile of the orange, red and brown leaves before the boy fell down. When the girl caught up with him, both laughed.

Further east, up the Seine, David Hume of Godscroft pointed out the Arsenal, not far from the Bastille. The *Hotel de Ville* stood directly across the river on the right bank. The impressive building fronted a large plaza.

Pont au Change Spanning the Seine

David Hume of Godscroft led John back through the Plaza and over the *Pont de Notre Dame*. Like the *Pont au Change*, the third bridge to the right bank of the Seine was lined with shops. But this bridge was sturdier, built on stone arches instead of wooden pillars. Two stonemasons worked below and made repairs.

After crossing, they turned right and soon reached the open plaza they had seen from the tip of the island. David Hume of Godscroft stopped in front a lone cross. "The authorities sometimes still execute criminals here in *le Place de Greve.*"

Like many other towns, John thought. He faced the huge hotel. "And that must be the *Hotel de Ville*?"

A fancy coach screeched to a halt in front of it.

"Many merchants come here to discuss business, sometimes with Italian bankers like Sebastian Zamet." Hume pointed out the important Italian financier. "Pensioners from throughout France also come here."

"What do you mean?"

"Under agreements made with previous French kings, many French noblemen in the capital collect pensions."

"Do they work?"

"No. They prefer the courts of Paris to their home estates but their demands on the central treasury are immense, especially when added to the cost of war."

"Shouldn't something be done?"

"The King must decide."

La Place de Greve, **Right Bank, Paris, France**

AFTER SPENDING SEVERAL days in Paris, John joined David Hume of Godscroft at *le Place de Greve*.

"You've been so generous to me," John said.

"I have a feeling you are destined for great things." David Hume of Godscroft asked, "Have you ever considered being a courtier?"

"A courtier?" John replied. "No."

The two men walked around a coach that had just pulled up. They followed the road leading north, towards the former Temple of the Knights Templar, the *Rue de Temple*.

Inside a restaurant, the two sat down at a simple wooden table.

A French maid with long black hair came over. *"Bon Soir."*

"Bon Soir," John replied. He remembered that he only had a few coins left from his inheritance. He again attempted to use some of the French he had learned at Orleans, *"Je survivrai sur le pain et le fromage."*

"Le pain et le fromage?" the proprietor's daughter repeated.

"Oui," John said.

"No," David Hume of Godscroft said, "I will pay. We'll start out with soup."

The young maid soon came back with the soup and fresh bread. *"Bon appetite."* She winked and smiled at John.

After sipping his soup, John tore off a piece from the warm loaf. "She's thin." He leaned toward David Hume of Godscroft. "Are all Parisian women thin?"

"Most. Queen Catherine *de* Medici did not allow any woman who did not have a thin waist into the courts at the Louvre. Many wore corsets."

"What are they eating?" John pointed to the next table.

"*Foie gras*," David Hume of Godscroft said. "Liver from a fatted goose."

"Would you like some?" the proprietor's daughter asked.

"Not tonight." John said.

They had almost finished the excellent meal, when John thought he heard a woman's cry.

"Ah!" a faint high voice shrieked again.

John turned toward the door. The shadow of a man ran past, pushing pedestrians aside. John blurted, "What's that commotion?"

"Let's see!" David Hume of Godscroft and John jumped from their seats and hurried to the door. They traced the sound of the crying voice. John peered into the darkened café next door. On the floor next to a table and an overturned chair, a young woman held a man's head in her lap.

"He stabbed him!" The woman screamed. "They stole our purse!"

John looked back up the street. The man with a cap turned a corner. John sprinted after him. "I can catch him!"

David Hume of Godscroft followed. Two policemen arrived at the scene and trailed a few steps further behind.

When John reached the end of the block, he ran down a dark passageway. The man with the cap looked back and disappeared again. Turning another two more corners, John hit a dead end. A huge building blocked his path. He looked left and right, no man in sight.

Within a minute the two French policemen and David Hume of Godscroft caught up with John.

"I chased him here, but he escaped!" John peered down the dark alley.

Frustrated, David Hume of Godscroft and John left the policemen to continue the search.

Reaching the *Rue de Saint Antoine*, David Hume of Godscroft pointed to a castle at the end of the street. "When he's caught, he'll end up there, the Bastille. That's if he's not executed in the public square, *le Place de Greve.* Let's go back to the hotel," David Hume of Godscroft suggested. "We can't do anything else here."

He and John returned to the place where the crime had occurred. The distraught woman in her bloodstained dress cried. "He's dead."

"We tried to catch the villain, but he escaped," John said.

"*Merci beaucoup.*" The French woman wiped her eyes. "They killed him for money he could not repay."

Chapter 42 - Letters to the Scottish Court

*It is therefore necessary that our Courtier act in every Respect with a great deal of
Circumspection, so that all his Words and Actions be agreeable to Prudence; and not only
to take care to have in himself excellent Qualities and Conditions, but to order and
dispose the whole course of his life in such manner, that it may in every respect be
correspondent thereto, and no ways disagreeable in itself, but make one Body of these
good Parts; so that every Action of his may result and be composed of all Virtues . . .*

Baldassarre Castiglione, The Courtier

Translated from Italian

*Master David Hume [of Godscroft] . . . gave him [John Smith] letters to his friends in
Scotland to prefer him to King James [VI of Scotland to become a courtier].*

Captain John Smith

Hotel de Ville, **Paris, France Early Autumn 1596**

"BON JOUR, MASTER Hume." A French courtier intercepted the Scotsman
at the front of the *Hotel de Ville.* "Are you ready to accompany me to Louvre Palace, so we can discuss the future relationship between Scotland
and France?"

"I know my young friend from England would like to come along,"
David Hume of Godscroft responded.

"Climb in." The courtier opened the door of the waiting carriage.

"Are you a courtier for King Henry IV?" John settled into his seat. "Do
you advise him?"

"Courtiers do more than just advise the King," the courtier replied.
"One time, a French King even disguised himself as a courtier."

An attendant loaded the last bag onto the back of the carriage. It circled around the white cross and exited *la Place de Greve.*

"I noticed that your French improves daily." David Hume of Godscroft asked, "How much Latin do you know?"

"Only what my teachers taught me at the free schools in England.
Why do you ask?"

The coach carried John, David Hume of Godscroft, and the French courtier along the road paralleling the Seine, passing *le Grand Chatelet* at the entrance of *Pont du Change.*

"If you are to be a courtier, you must know languages and history." David Hume of Godscroft said.

"And to know about Paris, you must understand about the St. Bartholomew's Day Massacre." The courtier leaned out the window and commanded the driver, "Take us to *Rue de Betisy!*"

Rue de Betisy, Paris, France

A FEW BLOCKS north of the Seine the carriage reached the street and the courtier again leaned out the window. "Stop the coach!"

The driver pulled the reins. The courtier pointed. "See that window?"

John peered up. "*Oui.*"

Balconies extended out of the three-story building.

"Admiral Gaspard *de* Coligny stayed in that room after an attempt to kill him."

"Who tried to kill him?" John asked.

"Catherine *de* Medici came up with a plan to assassinate the Admiral. She did not like the sway the Admiral had with her son, so just four days after the wedding of King Henry of Navarre to Marguerite *de* Valois, the mother of King Charles IX found someone from the House of Guise to carry out the plot."

"I do not understand," John said.

"At the time of the wedding," David Hume of Godscroft informed, "three main forces were at work in France: the Calvinist Reformers led by King Henry of Navarre; Catholic Loyalists of the French Crown of King Charles IX; and the House of Guise, ardent Catholics who supported Pope Gregory XIII in Rome."

"All three groups were in Paris at the same time as the wedding?"

"All three all vied for power, but the House of Guise called those who followed the Reformed Religion '*Huguenots*'. If the heretic *Huguenots* did not recant and give up their beliefs, the House of Guise thought they were worthy of death."

"It sounds explosive," John commented.

"It was. The Reformed leaders had come to Paris because of the wedding. They brought their weapons with them," David Hume of Godscroft said. "After the wedding, some leaders returned to their homes, but many others stayed. When the Calvinist Admiral Gaspard *de* Coligny walked back from the Louvre, someone tried to assassinate him. After the Calvinist Admiral *de* Coligny was shot twice on the street, the Reformers brought him back to this hotel to recover from wounds to his arm."

"Who did it?" John asked.

"No one was certain, but most believed the French King's mother Catherine *de* Medici played the Catholics against the Calvinists. The French King Charles IX wanted to find out who attempted to kill his friend, so he visited the Admiral here. Tensions remained high."

"The Reformers?" John asked. "Did they leave Paris?"

"A few. But most Reform leaders came to the Louvre to be under King Charles IX's protection."

The courtier signaled the driver.

The driver snapped his whip and the coach lurched forward.

Louvre Palace, Paris, France

TWO CONICAL-TOPPED TOWERS, the roofs made of lead, anchored the two eastern corners of Louvre Palace. Two other, smaller towers guarded the gates in the middle of the eastern wall. Royal guards stopped the carriage on the near side of the moat. After looking inside, they let the carriage cross over the drawbridge, through the gate, and into the Louvre.

The carriage stopped in the center of the square courtyard. Columns and statues graced one wall. A second wall also appeared only a few decades old, but the other two courtyard walls were much older.

Citizens representing many occupations walked to and fro. The Louvre was more than a castle, a prosperous enclave within a crowded city.

As soon as attendants opened the door, John stepped out. He immediately jumped back. Two horses and a carriage rushed by him.

When the moving carriage exited, the courtier stepped out. "Nobles must be going to Rouen."

"So fast?" John asked.

"Preparations for the King cannot wait," David Hume of Godscroft said. More horses and carriages lined one side of the courtyard. Other nobles and their attendants prepared to leave.

At the western end of Louvre Palace, John and the other two men climbed the steps. Down the halls, more citizens and courtiers mingled in the corners.

When John looked west out a window, David Hume of Godscroft pointed to the long palace on the other side of the city walls. "That's called the Tuileries Palace, because it was built on a tile pit. Catherine *de* Medici built that Palace because she did not like the coldness and austerity of the Louvre."

Tuileries was larger than the Louvre.

"What did Catherine *de* Medici do after the failed attempt to murder Admiral Gaspard *de* Coligny?" John asked.

"After Catherine *de* Medici realized that the assassination plot had failed, she went to the gardens of Tuileries beyond her palace. She came up with a list of *Huguenots* to kill."

"Would King Charles IX agree to such a scheme?" John asked.

"Not at first," David Hume of Godscroft said. "Five nights after the wedding of King Henry of Navarre to her daughter Marguerite *de* Valois, Catherine *de* Medici went to her son King Charles IX and gave him the list. She threatened to leave France if he did not carry out the plot. King Charles IX paced back and forth. He pondered for several hours."

"What did the King decide?" John asked.

"About midnight, King Charles IX gave his assent. He uttered those infamous words, 'Kill them all.'"

"Did he truly say, 'Kill them all'?" John asked.

"*Oui*," the courtier said.

"But the King may have meant only the Reformed leaders on the list," David Hume of Godscroft added. "His soldiers, however, thought it meant all of the Huguenots in France."

"What happened next?" John asked.

Saint Bartholomew's Day Massacre in Paris, August 24, 1572

"At two or three in the morning on St. Bartholomew's Day, the 24th of August 1572, the bells of *St. Germain de L'Auxerrois* tolled. Royal soldiers immediately began to slaughter the *Huguenots*."

"That's six days after Henry married Marguerite *de* Valois," John said.

"Yes. The St. Bartholomew Day's Massacre began right here in the

Louvre and at the hotel, where Admiral Gaspard *de* Coligny had been recuperating." David Hume of Godscroft informed, "King Charles IX's royal guards killed all of King Henry of Navarre's closest advisors."

"They had come to the Louvre for his protection." John asked, "Where was Marguerite *de* Valois?"

"She was in her chamber. When Royal guards chased one of her husband's advisors into her room, blood dripped on her bed."

John shook his head in disbelief. "What about Henry?"

"King Charles IX took King Henry of Navarre and his brother, the Prince of Conde, prisoner. The King gave Henry and Henry's brother three days to convert to Catholicism or die."

"Did they?"

"Both claimed to have converted," David Hume of Godscroft said, "but because of what Marguerite *de* Valois's mother had done, Henry could never fully trust his wife after that night. That's why she has been kept away in a castle for so long."

"What about all the other Reformed leaders in Paris?" John asked.

"The guards, who had been assigned to protect Admiral Gaspard, instead went up the stairs and killed him and his aides. Catherine *de* Medici had the police and soldiers kill every unsuspecting Reformed leader in hotels and inns across Paris, including men, women, and children."

"Including women and children?" John exclaimed, "That's wrong!"

"Not only that, but wherever *Huguenots* could be found across France, the killing continued unabated."

"No wonder the Reformers were so angry," John said.

"The next day King Henry of Navarre and his brother became Catholics to avoid being killed, but when Henry escaped more than a year later, he returned to Reformed Christianity," David Hume of Godscroft said.

After being handed a message, the courtier turned to the Scotsman. "David Hume of Godscroft, King Henry IV wishes to inform you that you can meet with him again after the Assembly in Rouen concludes."

"Excellent!" David Hume of Godscroft turned to the messenger. "I had just finished telling John about the St. Bartholomew Day's Massacre."

"Yes, that was a sad day," the courtier said. "But after King Henry escaped and all of the sons of Catherine *de* Medici died, he became King."

"As we already established, with the male line of the House of Valois extinct, Salic Law required that the throne go to Henry of Navarre and the House of Bourbon," David Hume of Godscroft elaborated. "But the ardent Catholic House of Guise would not accept Henry as the legitimate heir, since he still adhered to the Reformed Religion. The Wars of Religion continued, but the warrior King Henry of Navarre, now King Henry IV of France, gained ground in the French countryside. Two years ago, King Henry IV besieged Paris and thousands died. Henry, however, found an easier way to capture the city."

"What was that?" John asked.

"With the silent approval of his close Calvinist advisor Maximilian *de* Bethune, who is the Baron of Rosny, King Henry IV actually converted to Catholicism."

"Did the Parisians believe him?" John asked. "What about the Pope and the Catholic Jesuits?" John asked.

"Yes, the Parisians opened the city gates and Pope Clement VIII accepted the King a year ago." The French courtier was discreet and circumspect when men walked near them.

"John, would you like to become a courtier?" David Hume asked. "I have prepared letters of introduction to my friends in Edinburgh." David Hume of Godscroft handed John the letters. "Take them. They will introduce you to King James VI, the son of Mary, Queen of Scots."

"Merci beaucoup, Master Hume." John practiced bowing. Being a courtier to a king was preferential to being an indentured servant to a merchant, John thought.

"Au revoir." David Hume of Godscroft swept his arm in front.

With his letters in hand, John found a piece of cloth and rolled them up. He tied a string around them and put the package inside his cloak. Although happy to have seen Paris, John looked forward to joining the court of King James VI of Scotland.

John approached one of the drivers of a carriage in the courtyard. "Are you going toward *Havre de Grace?"*

"I can take you as far as Rouen, but you'll have to ride topside." The carriage driver grabbed his wide-brimmed hat and the reins.

When the last of the passengers settled themselves inside the carriage, they exited the Louvre and headed out the gates of Paris nearest the Gardens of Tuileries Palace. On the road to Pontoise, the wheels wobbled.

"It's been through much, but we'll get there," the carriage driver said. "It can handle the rain."

His hands wet and cold, John adjusted his hat. "So can I."

Chapter 43 - Carriage Ride at Pontoise

The women within, seeing a thousand abysses opened under their feet, apprehended the danger, and sent forth most lamentable cries. The coachman and muleteers endeavored in vain to stop the horses: they were already within fifty paces of the litter, when Madam Liancourt [Gabrielle d'Estrees], alarmed by the noise, looked out, and screamed aloud . . .
Maximillien *de* Bethune, Baron *de* Rosny [Later, Duke of Sully] AD 1596
translated from French by Charlotte Lennox

On the 14th day of October, the aldermen published to the whole city [Rouen] from the top of the tower of the Belfry of the Gros Horloge (a place traditionally used to make such pronouncements) that the entry [of King Henry IV] would take place the following morning.... And this publication was made by the Sergeant Ordinaire of the city, accompanied by six trumpeters on horseback, dressed in taffeta in the colors of His Majesty, with banners and similar materials, enriched by the Coat of Arms of France and of Navarre.
Discourse of the Joyous and Trimphant Entry, translated from French

Abbaye *de* Maubisson, Pontoise, France, Early October 1596

RAIN PELTED DOWN like beads cut from a string. Young John Smith lowered the wide flap of his hat. Another gust of wind whipped the carriage from side to side. John steadied himself and raised his collar, but to little avail: the spray hit his face anyway.

The carriage driver from Paris snapped the reins. With a second flip of his wrists, he encouraged the four horses forward on the road to Pontoise. "*Pardon*, John Smith. I hope you don't mind the rain, but I had no room inside."

"I don't mind," John replied. His French improved every day. "But your passengers?"

"They're dry inside." The driver chuckled. "Most are going to Rouen to prepare for the Assembly of Notables."

"Why the Assembly?"

"Simply put, King Henry IV needs money," the coachman said. "Last summer, his Majesty sent out letters and summoned nearly one hundred

302

nobles from throughout France to convene in an assembly next month. The King didn't want to risk calling an Estates General, since so many people have grievances. The last Estates General did not fare well, so he called an Assembly of Notables instead to address the problems of finances."

"Wars can be costly."

Burnt-out buildings, clearly pockmarked by cannon shells, probably from the Catholic League's siege of Pontoise six years earlier, stood alongside the road.

"But the King has made progress," the driver added. "Even though Calais fell earlier this year, the strong defensive actions of King Henry IV have checked the Spaniards. The Spanish Cardinal Albert has turned his attention to the north, attacking the Dutch Republic at Sluis and Hulst, where a Dutch cannonball killed Marshall Savigne *de* Rosne."

"Marshall Savigne *de* Rosne captured Calais, didn't he?" John remembered sailing past Calais earlier in the year.

"The Marshall was Cardinal Albert's best general." The driver paused. "But that is not the only bad news the Cardinal will receive."

"What do you mean?"

"The Ambassador from England has brought the Royal Scepter to Rouen. The Earl of Shrewsbury in England awaits the arrival of King Henry IV to finalize the Treaty between England and France, for both offense and defense."

"That should be a solemn occasion. And bad news for Spain."

"*Oui.* Who would have thought that within a year after being accepted as a true Catholic by the Pope that King Henry IV would enter into a treaty with the Queen of England?" the driver asked. "The King Henry IV's pregnant mistress, Gabrielle d'Estrees, the *Madam de* Liancourt, will also be present."

"A *madam*?"

"In name only. Earlier, her father arranged for her to marry a widower with forteen children, but Gabrielle d'Estrees moved to Paris to be near King Henry IV instead. She gave birth to King Henry IV's son about two years ago and the King declared Cesar legitimate last year." The driver added, "But King Henry IV and his son almost had a fatal accident at the start of the year."

"What happened?" John asked.

"Because his sister Catherine *de* Bourbon became ill last winter, King

Henry IV visited her in Picardy in January. While King Henry IV carried his son in her second floor bedroom apartment, the whole floor collapsed. King Henry IV leapt onto his sister's bed to save himself."

"And the boy?"

"Not a scratch. Cesar landed next to his aunt on the bed. All watched in amazement. The dust dissipated, they gazed into the big hole, and the debris settled on the ground floor." The coachman paused. "I used to drive for King Henry IV's mistress before another unfortunate incident."

"What incident?" John shook off his hat when the hard rain turned to drizzle. The carriage detoured off the main road.

"Last spring, Gabrielle d'Estrees visited her sister here at the *Abbaye de Maubuisson*." Half-barren trees lined the ponds on one side of the rich abbey.

"The sister of the French King's mistress is a nun?"

"Not just a nun, the Abbey Mother."

"Of the entire abbey?"

"King Henry IV's mistress was several months pregnant at the time when the mishap occurred."

"What happened?" John asked.

"Maximilian *de* Bethune, the Baron *de* Rosny, met Gabrielle d'Estrees at the abbey to escort her to King Henry IV at Clermont."

"Clermont?"

"To the northeast." The carriage driver pointed across the Oise River. Fortified walls and strong ramparts rose high on the hill on the opposite side. The road to Clermont split to the right and up the hill.

The carriage slowed on the stone bridge. The fortress gate with two parapet towers guarded the southern end.

After paying a small toll, the carriage driver continued, "Rosny rode ahead of the slow-moving train. I drove the carriage with Gabrielle d'Estrees, while a second carriage held the women of her court. Mules ladened with all of the baggage followed in single file. At the outskirts of Clermont, the road narrowed."

John's carriage exited the huge gatehouse and moved to the center of the bridge over the Oise River.

"Like the narrow road up there?" John asked.

"Only more so." The carriage driver kept a tight grip on the reins. "The road outside Clermont had a steep wall on one side and a deep valley on the other. The other driver stopped his four horses to check on the women and his carriage. When one of mules began to pass, however, it abruptly stopped."

"Mules can be stubborn," John said.

"The mule raised its head, brayed loudly, and shook its head. Its bell clanged loudly and frightened the four skittish horses. Before the driver had a chance to grab the reins, they took off. Two muleteers reached to catch the runaway carriage, but the horses pushed them both aside."

"On the narrow road?"

"*Oui*. The horses plowed ahead along the edge of the precipice. When the King's mistress Gabrielle d'Estrees heard the screams of her court and saw the runaway carriage heading towards us, she screamed, too. It was only fifty yards away."

"Gabrielle d'Estrees could have died."

"And so I could've, too," the carriage driver exclaimed. "When I gazed down the cliff, I saw no escape. Only a miracle could've saved us."

"What happened?"

"The wheels of the runaway carriage hit a rock. The pegs holding the wheels flew out. The wheels on both sides flew off. The two rear horses stumbled and fell and the litter plowed to a stop. The front two horses still ran, barely squeezing past my carriage. Gabrielle screamed aloud."

"If the wheels didn't fall off, you would have been pushed over the edge."

"*Oui*. A frightful thought."

John's carriage skirted beneath the ramparts of Pontoise.

"Rosny caught the runaway horses, but the women were still screaming. Rosny hit me and the other driver with his cane two or three times."

John cringed. "Sounds painful."

"Not much, but the punishment calmed the women down."

"And now?"

"I drive other carriages."

After spending the night in Pontoise, they resumed their journey to the northwest to Rouen. When the rain returned, John did not mind. He had letters from David Hume of Godscroft in his pocket. As soon as he could catch a ship at *Havre de Grace* at the mouth of the Seine, he would be sailing to Scotland.

Chapter 44 - Captain Joseph Duxbury

*At two o'clock in the afternoon the King, in royal robes, with his scepter in his hand,
entered the church accompanied by the English Ambassador and the scepter of England.
They heard vespers to most lovely music, and then they embraced and swore the League,
offensive and defensive . . . The Queen has named the captains of the levies of 3000 men.*

Peiro Duodo, Venetian Ambassador in France,
26th October 1596, Saint Maur, France

*Arriving at Rouen, he [John Smith] better bethinks himself, seeing his money near spent,
down the river [Seine] he went to [Le] Havre de Grace . . .*

John Smith

Palace of Justice, Rouen, Normandy, France, Oct. 18, 1596

JOHN SMITH FELT the meager weight of his purse and told himself, *I barely have enough francs to go to Scotland.* The English youth approached a well-dressed English officer. "Are you also from England?"

"Yes, I am." The English nobleman had a sword at his side. "What's your name?"

"John." He extended his hand. "John Smith."

"A pleasure to meet another Englishman. I'm Captain Joseph Duxbury. What brings you to Rouen?"

"I wanted to see France. Originally, I came here with Lord Willoughby's son and later, I returned to see Paris."

"Ah, Lord Willoughby. A brave and loyal soldier of the Queen."

"Yes, one day I hope to be like him. My father always urged me to serve him. That was before my father died."

"My condolences," Captain Duxbury said. "Did you come here to see the Rouen Pageantry? To welcome King Henry IV and for the signing of English-French Treaty?"

"No, I am on my way to the coast. I must find a ship sailing to Scotland."

"Scotland? What awaits you there?"

John pulled out the wrapped letters from Paris. "David Hume of Godscroft gave me these to present to the court of King James VI of Scotland. I want to be a courtier."

"King James may be the next king of England." Captain Duxbury placed a hand on John's shoulder. "Join me for a meal."

John checked the cloth purse tied to his belt. "To be honest, sir, I am running short of coin."

Captain Duxbury smiled. "That will not be a problem. I know the chefs for the ambassador. Come with me, John, to the old market square. Tell me more about yourself."

Hotel de Bourtheoulde, Rouen, France

INSIDE THE lavishly furnished *Hotel de Boutheoulde*, a large mansion facing *Place du Vieux Marche*, Captain Joseph Duxbury pointed out the English Ambassador, Gilbert Talbot. The Earl of Shrewsbury had a neatly trimmed mustache and a small beard.

"King Henry invited the Earl of Shrewsbury to dine with him," Captain Duxbury said. "This hotel serves the best duck in all of Rouen."

After eating, just outside the kitchen of the Hotel, Duxbury pointed out a bas-relief that depicted the meeting of the English King Henry VIII and the French King Francois I at the Field of the Cloth of Gold nearly seven decades earlier.

"Tomorrow," Captain Duxbury said, "English friendship with the French will be renewed. Why don't you stay another night to see that?"

Flattered that the impressive captain had offered, John agreed to stay.

Down the cobblestone street, the belfry of the *Gros Horloge* rang the day's closing tune. Captain Duxbury looked directly at John. "Meet me in front of the Abbey of St. Ouen tomorrow at noon. A new alliance will be formed."

Abbey of Saint Ouen, Rouen, France, Saturday, Oct. 19, 1596

THE NEXT AFTERNOON John Smith found Captain Joseph Duxbury in the plaza of the Church of Saint Ouen. Gilbert Talbot, the Earl of Shrewsbury, soon arrived from the *Hotel de Bourtheoulde* and exited his carriage. The English Ambassador carried the Scepter of England to the front doors of the gothic church. Dressed in full regalia and holding the scepter of

France, King Henry IV welcomed the representative from Queen Elizabeth. The French King and the English Ambassador entered the cathedral to formalize the agreement between the two realms.

After a short ceremony, music emanated from the Cathedral's open doors.

"It is official now," Captain Duxbury said. "The Treaty negotiated last May is finalized. We're allies with the French, both offensive and defensive."

King Henry IV and the Earl of Shrewsbury soon appeared on the steps and together acknowledged the crowds.

"Tomorrow, the Earl will invest the King into the most solemn Order of the Garter. In anticipation of the agreement, the Queen named me to be one of her captains." Captain Duxbury turned to John. "Would you like to join me?"

"To be a soldier? I was planning to become a courtier. Besides I don't know how to fight."

"I can teach you everything I know."

"That's kind of you, but I can't do both at the same time, can I? Be a Scottish courtier and an English soldier?"

"No, so you must ask yourself which path you prefer."

John thought of the sailing and adventures that he had dreamed about as a young boy. "By when do I need to let you know?"

"I must return to *Le Havre de Grace* by the end of next week."

Quay, Right Bank of the Seine, Rouen, France Oct. 24, 1596

IN THE FOUR days after the English Ambassador had invested King Henry IV into the Order of the Garter, the festivities continued with plays and songs. More delegations from all of France arrived in anticipation of the Assembly of Notables, scheduled for early November.

On the 24th, Captain Joseph Duxbury took John to the banks of the Seine River. "There's going to a naval demonstration today, the one the King delayed."

The King sat in stands near the bridge of Rouen. Cannons along the bank fired shots at several galleys near the bridge. Other ships fired, tacked and fired again in mock attacks.

"This is like a real battle," John said.

"Yes," Captain Duxbury said, "Have you given more thought about becoming a soldier?"

"Yes." John pulled out his papers from inside his cloak. "But I don't know if I should go to Scotland now."

"Only you can make that decision," Captain Duxbury answered. "If you join me to fight against the Spanish, I can't promise you much money, but I can promise you adventure."

The English Captain and John travelled together, downriver to the mouth of the Seine.

Le Havre de Grace, France, Late October 1596

SEAWATER SLAMMED AGAINST the ragged rocks at *Le Havre de Grace*. John Smith peered toward the western horizon.

"That's the ship to Scotland." Captain Joseph Duxbury pointed to a vessel in the tidal harbor.

The cold wind and salty spray stung John's face. Whitecaps broke over choppy waters. Gray clouds portended more rain.

"I can go to Scotland later." John rewrapped the papers David Hume of Godscroft had given to him and placed them back inside his cloak. "I want to be a soldier."

"Very well." Captain Duxbury led John away from the docks. "I'll teach you how to fight and how to ride, if you are willing, English recruit."

"Yes." John quickened his pace. "I am ready."

Glossary

Glossary of Terms

Acemi-Oglan   'Novice boys' who served in the under offices of the New Palace. Taken from the *devshirme* and trained in a craft or a trade, many later became *janissaries*.

Agha (Aga)   Leader or general; chief; master; commander as in *Agha* of the *Janissaries*.

AD   *Anno Domino*; Year of the Lord; Jesus Christ of Nazareth was born in Bethlehem

AH   Latin *Anno Higra,* signifying the year of the Pilgrimage, referring to the Prophet Mohammed's flight from Mecca to Medina in AD 622.

Allah   The name of god among those who profess the Muslim faith.

Apostles   The four large Spanish ships dEffending the Spanish fleet at Cadiz in 1596: the Admiral *Saint Philip; Saint Matthew; Saint Thomas;* and *Saint Andrew.*

Arc de Triumph   Ceremonial archway, often temporary, erected for celebrations or parades.

Baba   'Father' in Turkish.

Bailo   Title of senior Ambassador of Republic of Venice in *Stamboul*/Constantinople.

Bagnos   'Baths' in Italian.

Bedesten   Market' in Turkish. In *Stamboul,* pillars supported two covered markets: the Old *Bedesten* (now the center of the Grand Bazaar) and the New *Bedesten* (also called *Sandal)* outside which slaves were sold before a separate market was built.

Bohemian   Besides persons from the Kingdom of Bohemia, also used to identify Gypsies or *Roma.* (Later referred to artists and writers maintaining relaxed social standards).

Bey (Beg)   Turkish Governor (usually of a city); Lord.

Beylerbey   Governor of governors; head of an Ottoman province, i.e. *Beylerbey* of Cairo.

Beg-Ogli   Son of a governor. Title given (in 1602) to the son of the Crimean-Tartar Khan.

Bostangi Pasha   Chief Gardener. He oversees both the gardeners and the guards in the New Palace and reports directly to the Chief White Eunuch.

Buraya gel   'Come here' in Turkish.

Caliph   'Successor' to Mohammed. One of the titles of the Ottoman Sultan, acquired after the Ottomans conquered the Mamluk dynasty in Egypt in 1524.

Caliphate   Territory controlled by the Caliph.

Capitano   'Captain' in Italian.

Caravanserai   Caravan 'Palace.' Khan or inn where travelers stay with their camels or horses.

Catholic League   One of three groups vying for power in France in the late 1500s. Supported by King Philip II of Spain, the Duke of Guise led the Catholic League against the French *Huguenots* and the French royal families, both the Valois & Bourbons.

Celali (Rebellions)	Name of a rebel fighting against the Ottoman government in the early 16th century. After his death, term used to describe the ongoing rebellions in Anatolia.
Chiaus (Chiaux)	An Ottoman messenger who carries a truncheon with a knob at one end.
Coat of Arms	An emblem granted by a prince or monarch to knights showing valor in battle; Also granted to nobles, guilds and other organizations.
Concubine	A woman who lives with a man as if she were his lawful wife.
Cossacks	The name of an independent people from either the Dnieper River toward Poland or the Don River towards Moscow who raided Turkish lands in boats, or fought against the Crimean Tartars on horseback with bows, arrows, & firearms.
Council of Nicaea	Convened by Emperor Constantine in the town of Nicaea (present-day Iznik) in AD 325. More than 300 Christian bishops rejected Arianism, unanimously agreeing to the Nicene Creed, confirming God the Father and Jesus the Son are One.
Council of Trent	Convened in Trento, Italy by Catholic Church: a key to the Counter-Reformation.
Crenelated	Square or cubed battlements characterizing the tops of fortified walls.
Crimean-Tartars	The Ottoman Empire's most loyal allies. Descendants of one branch of the Mongols of Genghis Khan, the Crimean-Tartars converted to Islam and brought upwards to 100,000 warriors to the battlefield at the request of the sultan.
Damat	'Bridegroom' in Turkish. Title given to someone marrying into the Ottoman royal family, i.e. *Damat* Ibrahim *Pasha*, the first husband of Aisha, Sister of the Sultan.
Defterdar	Ottoman 'Treasurer.'
Dervish	A Muslim sect known for its swirling dances.
Devshirme	'Collection.' Refers to boys between the ages of nine and twelve taken from their Christian parents in Ottoman Europe, collected as tribute to the Sultan.
Dragoman	Translator.
Ducat	Official Venetian coin widely used in the Mediterranean from 1300s to 1700s.
Eighty Years War	Dutch War of Independence from Spain: began in 1568 and lasted until 1648.
Eski	'Old' in Turkish.
Eunuchs	Castrated while young boys, eunuchs did not grow facial hair during puberty. White eunuchs served in the Sultan's household, Black eunuchs in his Harem.
Fatwa (fetva)	An official decree or point of law signed by a mufti or *kadi*.
French War of Religion	Between the Catholic League and the French *Huguenots* from 1562 to 1598.
Galley	A ship, often with sails, but mainly manned by slaves pulling oars in calm seas.
Geneva Bible	Main English Bible translation used in England and Scotland during late 1500s.
Ghilman (-mun)	Young recruit(-s) who serve the Sultan (or serve the 'True Believers' in heaven).

Ghazi	Meaning warrior (*Jihadist*).
Grand Mufti	Leading religious authority (*Sheikh ul-Islam*) of the Ottoman Empire.
Haddith	Traditions of Islam, not part of the *Qur'an*.
Hajj	Pilgrimage to Mecca (one of the five pillars of Sunni Islam).
Hamam	Turkish bathhouse.
Harem	Hidden or forbidden, used to describe private quarters, i.e. Imperial Harem.
Hanseatic League	Merchant league controlling trade in Northern Europe and Baltic Sea during the Middle Ages and the early Renaissance period.
Haseki	Mother of an Ottoman Prince.
Ich-Oglans	'Interior Youths.' Forty select *devshirme* were raised and trained in the Third Courtyard of the New Palace, destined to take over the great Ottoman offices.
Imam	Muslim priest.
Indentured	Servant bound by contract for term of years: if contract broken, bound for life.
Janissary	*Yeni-ceri* meaning 'New Army,' the foot soldiers of the Ottoman Empire; started during the reign of Sultan Orhan through the collection of the *devshirme*.
Jesuits	Society of Jesus: Roman Catholic religious order founded by Ignatius Loyola.
Ghaza (Jihad)	Meaning 'struggle,' divided into Greater and Lesser *Ghaza (Jihad)*.
Ka'bah	Name of altar in Mecca originally claimed to be built by Abraham.
Kabin	Like a dowry, but paid by the man to formalize an Ottoman marriage contract.
Kadi (Cadi)	'Judge' in Ottoman Empire
Kadin	'Lady/woman' in Turkish. The Jewish kadin had access to the Imperial Harem.
Kaimakam	Governor of *Stamboul*, or Deputy Grand Vizier who rules the Empire while the Grand Vizier is leading the Ottoman army on the frontier.
Kapi Agha	'Captain of the Gate' of the *Seraglio* or New Palace; the Chief White Eunuch.
Khan	Compound or large home, usually with a large courtyard in the center; Also a title meaning leader, such as Khan of the Crimean-Tartars.
Kizlar Agha	'Captain of Girls' in the Imperial Harem of the New Palace; Chief Black Eunuch.
Knight's Templar	Military order charged with protecting Christian pilgrims going to Jerusalem from the early 1100s to 1312. Also called the Order of Solomon's Temple.
Köle(kul)	'Slave' in Turkish. The Köle of the Sultan served inside the New Palace.
Kulliye	'Complex' often consisting of a hospital, *medrese*, and a mosque.
Legate a Latere	Personal ambassador of the Pope, usually assigned to a specific mission.
Long War	Or 'Fifteen-Year War'; Ottoman Turkey vs. Holy Roman Empire, 1592 to 1606.

Man-of-War	Sailing ship outfitted for battle, often escorted Merchantmen.
Medrese	Islamic school, also known as *Madrasa* in Arabic
Merchantman	Ship carrying goods, often in convoys to the East or West Indies.
Mezes	Turkish appetizers.
Minaret	Cylindrical tower outside a mosque where muezzins issue call for prayer.
Minbar	Pulpit used by an imam inside a mosque.
Muezzin	Prayer callers.
Muslim	Follower of the Prophet Mohammed and the Islamic religion.
Nargile	Turkish water-pipe.
Oda	Chamber or school.
Odalisque	Virgins in the Imperial Harem.
Orthodox	Holding right opinions. Also refers to Eastern Christian Church after split Rome.
Orta	A *janissary* battalion or regiment.
Qibla	Direction of Mecca.
Papal Nuncio	Permanent ambassador or emissary of the Pope.
Pasha (Basha)	Important Ottoman official, often given a standard of two horsetails.
Patriarch	In a role similar to the Pope, the Patriarch of Constantinople led the Greek Orthodox Christians within the Ottoman Empire.
Pillager	Someone who pillages or loots. Pillagers scavenged the battlefield.
Pinnace	A small boat, usually with sails, used to shuttle between larger ships in a fleet.
Poop Deck	High deck behind the wheel on a ship, located towards the stern.
Qur'an (Koran)	Chief book of Islam, written in Arabic.
Reformation	Effort to "reform" Roman Catholic Church begun by the German Martin Luther and continued by the Frenchman John Calvin, and later by Scotsman John Knox.
Renegade	A person who abandons his upbringing. Used to describe those who abandoned the Christian faith and became Muslim, whether by force or persuasion.
Salic Law	French monarchy law whereby only male heirs can reign as king.
Sanjak	Ottoman leader of important towns, such as the *Sanjak* of Pecs in Ottoman Hungary. Each *sanjak* provided armed *sipahis* from *timars* in time of war.
Saray/ Seraglio	From the Persian, meaning 'Palace.'
Scimitar	Curved sword.
Shahadah	A Islamic pillar: "There is no god but Allah, and Mohammed is his Prophet."

Sharia	Strict Islamic law.
Shia Islam	One of two major divisions in Islam. These followers, called Shiites, believe that Ali, a nephew of and early successor to Mohammed, is the true Caliph.
Skiff	Small, flat-bottom boat.
Sipahi	Turkish horsemen provided by *Timariots* or *Ziamets*.
Standard	Symbol of Authority, normally flags on a pole. For the Turks, horsetails usually topped a pole about eight feet long. The Sultan's standard had four horsetails attached, while the Grand Vizier had three; important *Pashas* two; *sanjaks* one.
Sublime Porte	Originally inside the New Palace, name of the gate before the Ottoman throne.
Sunni Islam	Orthodox followers of Islam; Ottoman Turks and most Arabs follow the Sunni tradition and its Five Pillars. By contrast, most Persians are Shiites.
Tartaria	Land of the Tartars. Greater Tartaria included vast tracts of Siberia, from Muscovy to China. Petite Tartaria included the steppe of Southern Ukraine.
Tartars	A tribe originally conquered by and assimilated into the Mongol Empire. The Tartars (Mongols) had many sub-tribes including the Crimean-Tartars.
Tercio	Spanish fighting unit consisting of 3,000 pikemen, musketeers, & swordsmen.
Tiltyard	Jousting yard with a long rail in the middle of it; i.e., The white knight charges with his sharp lance and tilts at his foe.
Timar (Timariot)	Non-inheritable feudal Turkish land-holding; the leaseholder is required to provide and equip at least one *sipahi* rider to the Sultan.
Trinity (Triune)	The orthodox Christian belief that God the Father, God the Son, and God the Holy Spirit are one God, Three-in-One; a defining, essential tenet of Christianity.
Ulema	Muslim scholar.
Valide Sultana	The Sultan's Mother, the most powerful woman in the Ottoman Empire.
Valens Aqueduct	Roman Emperor Valens built it; carried fresh water to cisterns in Constantinople.
Veni, vidi, vici	'I came, I saw, I conquered' in Latin.
Vizier Azem	First Vizier or Grand Vizier.
Vilayet (Eyalet)	'Province' in the Ottoman Empire.
Voivode	Title of the leader of Moldavia or Wallachia, or other countries in Slavic Europe.
Walloons	A French speaking people of the Lowlands (present-day Belgium).
Waqf (Vakif)	Islamic charitable foundation.
Ziamet	Larger *timar* or land holding. Leaseholders of *ziamets* were required to provide five or more *sipahi* horsemen to the Sultan during the fighting season.

Glossary of People

Aisha,
Sister of Sultan
Betrothed to Grand Vizier *Yemisci* Hasan *Pasha* (Hasan *the Fruiterer*). Daughter of Sultan Murad III & Safiye *Valide Sultana. Widow of Damat* Ibrahim *Pasha.*

Albert of Austria
Cardinal and former Archbishop of Toledo; Promised in marriage to his cousin *Infanta* Isabella Clara Eugenia. Appointed General Governor of the Netherlands.

Alessandro
de **Medici**
Cardinal; The *Legate de Latere* sent to Paris by Pope Clement VIII to negotiate peace between King Henry IV of France and King Philip II of Spain.

Ali *Agha*
Agha of the Janissaries & married to Beatrice, sister of the Chief White Eunuch.

Alonso
de **Mendoza**
Leaders of a *tercio* at the Battle of Calais in April 1596.

Giorgio Basta
Able Albanian Catholic officer who fought in the Lowlands and in Transylvania.

Nicolo Basta
Brother of Giorgio Basta, a Catholic commander of horsemen in the Lowlands.

Sigismund
Bathory
Appointed Prince of Moldavia, Transylvania, and Wallachia by Emperor Rudolph II. Captain John Smith fought for Prince Sigismund Bathory in1602 and received his Coat of Arms from him.

Beatrice Michael
(Fatima Hatun)
Venetian sister of Chief White Eunuch Gazanfer *Agha.* She fled her failed second marriage in Venice and annulled it in *Stamboul.* She married Ali *Agha.*

Peregrine Bertie
Friend of John Smith. Younger son of Lord Peregrine Willoughby.

Robert Bertie
Friend of John Smith. Older son of Lord Willoughby. Robert fought at Cadiz.

Charles V
Holy Roman Emperor. Born in Brussels, Charles abdicated his throne, leaving the HRE to his brother Ferdinand; and the Lowlands and Spain to his son Philip.

Claude *la* Barlotte
Catholic Colonel of a Walloon regiment. Officer for Cardinal Albert in Lowlands.

Pope Clement VIII
Born Ippolito Aldobrandini. Pope of the Roman Catholic Church (1592 to 1605).

Cristobal
de **Moura**
Chief Domestic Minister to King Philip II of Spain.

Robert Devereaux
Earl of Essex. The Lord General of English land forces at Cadiz in 1596. Sailed at the lead of the second of five squadrons aboard the *Repulse* that summer.

Queen Elizabeth
Daughter of King Henry VIII and his second wife, Anne Boleyn. Sir Walter Raleigh founded Virginia and named it after his virgin Queen.

Francisco
de **Mendoza**
Admiral of Aragon, and Head of the Household for Cardinal Albert.

Gabrielle d'Estrees
Mistress of King Henry IV of France. Mother of two of his children.

Gazanfer *Agha*
Kapi-Agha, the Chief White Eunuch. Son of a Venetian official, Gazanfer and his siblings were captured at sea. He served Selim II, Murad III, and Mehmet III.

***Ghazi* Giray II**
Warrior Khan of the Crimean Tartars whose nickname *'Bora'* means storm.

Lewis Gunther
Of Nassau, Cousin of *Stadholder* Maurice of Nassau. Commander of Dutch forces who joined the fleet at the Sack of Cadiz in 1596.

Guzelce Mahmud
Pasha; Sipahi leader.

Richard Hakluyt
Compiled Principal Navigations, Voyages, & Discoveries of the English Nation.

Abdul Helim
(*Kara Yazici*)
Rebel leader in Anatolia. Known as *Kara Yazici* 'Black Scribe' in Turkish or '*Scrivano*' in Italian). Died in 1602, but his brother *Deli* Hasan succeeded him.

David Hume	Scotsman from Godscroft, who met John Smith in Paris and gave him letters of preference to his Scottish friends at the Court of King James VI of Scotland. Not to be confused with David Hume, the Scottish philosopher of the 18th century.
Hasan Khalifeh	Sipahi leader in Stamboul.
Deli Hasan Pasha	Hasan *the Fool.* Successor to his brother *Scrivano,* opposed to Ottoman throne.
Saatci Hasan Pasha	Hasan *the Clockmaker. Kaimakam* in *Stamboul,* Deputy Grand Vizier in 1602.
Yemisci Hasan Pasha	Hasan *the Fruiterer. Vizier Azem or* Grand Vizier of the Ottoman Empire. After the death of *Damat* Ibrahim Pasha, he's engaged to Aisha, Sister of the Sultan.
Henry IV	King of France, also warrior King of Navarre. Later known as Henry the Great.
House of Bourbon	Name of the royal family of France, starting with King Henry IV.
House of Fuggers	Influential family of German merchants and bankers, allies of the Habsburg.
House of Habsburg (House of Hapsburg)	Important dynastic family, providing many of whom served as Emperors of the Holy Roman Empire. They were Dukes of Austria and Styria since 1282. Its influence lasted until Archduke Franz Ferdinand was assassinated by a Serbian nationalist in Sarajevo, Bosnia, in 1914, triggering the outbreak of World War I.
House of Lorraine	Ruling family of the independent territory of Lorraine (now part of France).
House of Medici	Important Italian banking, political, & religious family from Florence, Tuscany.
House of Plantagenet	Royal family of England from 1145 to 1485.
House of Tudor	Royal family of England from 1485 to the death of Queen Elizabeth in 1603.
House of Valois	Royal family of France from 1328 to 1589 when King Henry III died.
Lord Charles Howard	Baron of Effingen, Grand Admiral of the English fleet to Cadiz in 1596. Sailed aboard his flagship, the *Ark Royal.*
Thomas Howard	Kinsman to Lord Charles Howard, commanded of the fourth of five English and Dutch squadrons aboard the *Mer-honour,* but transferred his flag to the *Nonpareil* before the final attack at Cadiz in 1596.
Huguenots	French Protestants. Name that the Catholics called those in France who followed the Calvinist doctrine. More accurately called members of the Reformed Church.
Damat Ibrahim Pasha	Aisha's first husband who died in 1601; not to be confused with Ibrahim *Pasha,* Grand Vizier of Suleiman *the Magnificent,* who built Palace of Ibrahim Pasha
Infanta Isabella	Daughter of King Philip III of Spain. Promised in marriage to her cousin, Cardinal Albert of Austria. Her full name is *Infanta* Isabella Clara Eugenia.
King James	King James VI of Scotland. In Paris, David Hume of Godcroft gave letters of introduction to John Smith to take to Scotland. Later, King James I England united Scotland with England into Great Britain. Believer in "Divine Rights of Kings" & unhappy with margin notes in the Geneva Bible, James 'authorized' new version.
Juan *de* Idiaquez	Foreign Minister of King Philip II of Spain.
Katib Jemazi	*Sipahi* leader.
Ferrante Loffredo III	*Marquis de* Trevico, the Catholic military leader of a Spanish *tercio.*
Marguerite *de* Valois	Queen of France. Queen Margot's husband King Henry IV kept her isolated at the Chateau d'Usson in the south of France and sought to annul their marriage.

Osman	*Kislar Agha*.Chief Black Eunuch. Oversaw Imperial Harem and imperial mosques.
Maurice of Nassau	*Stadholder* in Lowlands. 'His Excellency' commanded army against Spain.
Maximilian *de* Bethune	Baron *de* Rosny (later Duke of Sully). Advisor & confidant of King Henry IV. A member of the "Reformed" church; responsible for financial reforms in France.
Sultan Mehmet III	Ottoman Empire ruler, 1595-1603. Son of Murad III and Safiye *Valide Sultana.*
Sultan Murad III	Father of Aisha & Mehmet III. Ottoman Empire ruler who died in January 1595.
Mustafa *Agha*	A lieutenant to Grand Vizier Hasan *the Fruiterer.* Fought beside *Ghazi* Giray II.
Nur Banu	*Woman of Splendor.* Venetian Mother of Sultan Murad III, Aisha's grandmother.
Philip II	King of Spain and obedient Lowlands; son of Holy Roman Emperor Charles V.
Philippe Emmanuel	Duke of Mercoeur, Member of Catholic League and ruler of Brittany in Northwestern France. His full name was Philippe Emmanuel *de Lorraine.*
Philibert *de* Rye	Count *de* Varax, General of the Artillery for Cardinal Albert in the Netherlands
Philip William (of Nassau)	Prince of Orange. After his father Prince William of Orange was assassinated, Philip William was kidnapped & raised Catholic; also, half-brother of Maurice.
Poiraz Osman *Bey*	*Sipahi* leader promoted by the Grand Vizier Hasan *the Fruiterer*
Sir Walter Raleigh	Rear Admiral of the English Fleet to Cadiz aboard the *Warspite*
Jean Richardot	President of the Privy Council of Cardinal Albert in Brussels.
John Rolfe	From Heacham, Norfolk County, England; subsequently moved to Jamestown. As a widower, Rolfe (not John Smith) married Pocahontas and fathered a son.
Rudolph II	Emperor of the Holy Roman Empire and moved capital from Vienna to Prague.
Savigne *de* Rosne	Marshall of Catholic forces, the *Maestro de Campo* General of Cardinal Albert
Richard Saltonstall	Lord; former sheriff of the Tower District in London.
Scrivano	Meaning 'Black Scribe." See *Kara Yazici* Abdul Helim.
Safiye Valide Sultana	From Albania. Powerful and influential mother of Aisha and Sultan Mehmet III.
Sekul Murish	Former Prince of Turtzfeld, an independent kingdom in the mountainous border of Transylvania & Wallachia. Saw Grand Vizier Hasan *the Fruiterer* in Belgrade.
Thomas Sendall	Merchant of King's Lynn, for whom John Smith worked as indentured servant
Captain John Smith	Born in Louth, Lincolnshire, England *circa* 1580. Wounded while fighting for the Holy Roman Empire, John was sold into slavery and sent to Aisha, Sister of the Sultan, so she could ransom him. Captain John Smith was later elected at Jamestown as the first Colonial Governor of Virginia and became Admiral of New England. Referred to as "Father of America"(before George Washington)
Sun'Ullah *Effendi*	Former Grand Mufti, the *Sheikh ul-Islam.*
Gilbert Talbot	Earl of Shrewsbury. English ambassador sent to Rouen, France in 1596.
Sir Francis Vere	Lord Marshall of the English expedition to Cadiz; commander of the *Rainbow*
Sir Horace Vere	Brother of Sir Francis Vere, Lieutenant Colonel to Sir John Wingfield at Cadiz
Lord Willoughby	Peregrine Bertie; Former employer of George Smith, the father of John Smith; his two sons, Robert and Peregrine Bertie, were boyhood friends of John.
Sir John Wingfield	Brother-in-law of Lord Willoughby. Uncle of Robert Bertie. Commander of the *Vanguard* in the English fleet to Cadiz in 1596.

Glossary of Places

Alcazar	A Spanish royal palace, located in Toledo, Castile, Spain.
Anatolia	Asia Minor, Turkey in Asia.
Atmeidan	Turkish for 'Hippodrome,' the ancient 'horse' stadium in Constantinople.
Axiopolis	Old Roman fort on the Danube, near present-day Cernavodă, Romania.
Bakhchysarai	Name of Palace on the Crimean Peninsula. Capital of the Crimean-Tartars.
Barbary	Northern Coast of Africa, infested by pirates until U.S. Marines sent by Jefferson
Black Sea	Sea forming northern coast of Asia Minor & so. coast of present day Ukraine. The Danube & Dnieper Rivers empty into it. Crimean Peninsula extends out into it.
Bosphorus Strait	Connects the Black Sea to the Sea of Marmara and separates Europe from Asia.
Boston	Port town of Lincolnshire, England and namesake of Boston, Massachusetts.
Brabant	Province in the Lowlands, located in present-day Belgium.
Brittany	Duchy in northwestern France.
Brussels	Capital of the Obedient (Catholic) Provinces of the Netherlands.
Bursa	First capital of the Ottoman Empire in northwestern Anatolia.
Byzantium	Earlier name of Constantinople, present day Istanbul.
Cadiz	Port west of Gibraltar in Southern Spain.
Carpathian	Mountains dividing Transylvania from Wallachia in present day Romania.
Constantinople	Also called *Stamboul* meaning city. Present day Istanbul, Turkey.
Crimea	Peninsula jutting out into northern Black Sea. Old home of Crimean Tartars.
Danube River	Flows west to east, from the Alps to Black Sea. Europe's second longest river.
Divan	Meeting place of the Ottoman Council inside Second Courtyard of the New Palace; also (2) name of that Imperial Council; and (3) raised, cushion platform.
Edirne	Second Capital of the Ottoman Empire, Called Adrianople (in honor of Roman Emperor Hadrian, who also built the Hadrian Wall across northern England).
Edirnekapi	Gate leading to Edirne in the old, Theodosian land walls of Constantinople.
Eski Serai	The "Old Palace," where concubines of the deceased sultan were sent to live out their days. Located where the University of Istanbul now stands.
Hagia Sophia (Ayasofya)	The famous Byzantine Christian church built by Emperor Justinian around 537 and turned into the main imperial mosque after the Ottoman conquest in 1453.
Holy Roman Empire	Fashioned after the ancient Roman Empire, but comprised largely of Christian (both Catholic and Protestant) German states who elected Emperor Rudolph II.
Ibrahim Pasha Palace	Palace occupied by Aisha, Sister of the Sultan, Facing the Hippodrome. Parts of it are still existent and house the Museum of Turkish and Islamic Arts. Constructed by Ibrahim Pasha, Grand Vizier of Suleiman the Magnificent.
Iznik	Ancient Nicaea; Anatolian town outside Bursa renowned for its ceramic tiles
Kaffa (Caffa)	Important Ottoman slave town in Crimea. Present-day Feodosiya.
Kale-Megdan	Upper castle of Belgrade. Seat of Ottoman power in Europe. Overlooks Danube.

King's Lynn	Lynn. Town in Norfolk County, England where young John Smith worked as an indentured servant for Thomas Sendall. Formerly known as Bishop's Lynn.
Le Havre de Grace	Town at the mouth of the Seine River in northwestern France.
Louth	Town in Lincolnshire, England where John Smith learned Latin in school.
Magnesia	Also called Magnolia. Birthplace of Aisha in western Asia Minor.
Marmara	Sea between *Stamboul* and Asia Minor, named for the island by the same name.
Moldavia	Eastern province of present day Romania.
Montmarte	Mountain about a mile outside medieval Paris.
Navarre	Kingdom in Southern France, near Spain.
The Netherlands	Meaning Lowlands; 17 Provinces, including Holland, once controlled by Spain.
New Palace	Now known as Topkapi Palace, taking its name from *Top-Kapi*, Cannon-Gate
Normandy	William *the Conqueror* invaded England from this NW French region in 1066.
Ottoman Empire	Began in 1299 & lasted until 1922, when Ataturk founded Republic of Turkey.
Pecs	Town on Hungarian plain where Khan *Ghazi* Giray II wintered in 1602/03.
Picardy	Region in northwestern France.
Rouen	City on the Seine River in northwestern France.
Rumelia	Originally called Thrace, later, Land of the Romans, also Turkey in Europe.
San Lorenzo d'el Escorial	Stark palace built by King Philip II outside Madrid, Spain.
Sehzade Camii	The Prince's Mosque, located near the Valens Aqueduct in *Stamboul.*
Silistra	Seat of a *sanjak*, located upriver from Axiopolis in the lower Danube Valley.
Stamboul	Ottoman name for Constantinople, present-day Istanbul, Turkey.
Stara Planina	Old Mountains or the Balkan Mountains.
Targoviste	Former capital of Wallachia, north of Bucharest, not to be confused with Targoviste in Bulgaria, a city by the same name.
Temple Bar	A wooden gate (later made of stone) near Temple Church in London.
Transylvania	Northern province of present day Romania.
Wallachia	Ottoman Tributary. Southern province of present day Romania.
Whitehall Palace	Located just outside of London, England, in Westminster on the Thames River.

Timeline of Events

70	Destruction of The Second Temple in Jerusalem by the Romans; Start of Jewish Diaspora
323	Emperor Constantine the Great moves his capital from Rome to Byzantium
325	Emperor Constantine convenes 300 Christian bishops at Nicaea near Bursa in Anatolia
476	Fall of the (Western) Roman Empire; after Visigoths and Vandals had sacked Rome
622	Year of the Pilgrimage (AH), signifying Mohammed's flight from Mecca to Medina
800	Founding of the Holy Roman Empire by Charlemagne
1054	Schism splits the Roman Catholic Church and the Eastern Orthodox Church
1066	Battle of Hastings; William the Conqueror invaded England from Normandy
1204	Sack of Byzantine Constantinople by Venice and Latin West during Fourth Crusade
1215	Magna Carta signed by King John II granting liberties to barons in England.
1301	Osman I defeats Byzantines at Baphaeon and establishes Ottoman Empire in Anatolia
1326	Conquest of Bursa by Sultan Orhan *Ghazi*, son of Osman I, founder of Ottoman Empire
1352	Ottomans cross from Asia Minor into Thrace in Southeastern Europe
1369	Sultan Murad I, leaving Bursa, establishes second Ottoman capital at Edirne (Adrianople)
1453	Constantinople conquered by Sultan Mehmet *the Conqueror*
1492	Granada fell, completing *Reconquista* of Spain by King Ferdinand & Queen Isabella
1517	Mamluk Empire of Egypt fell to the Ottoman Empire
1521	Fall of Belgrade to the Ottoman Empire
1526	Battle of Mohacs, where the Hungarian King Louis II fled, dying in the marshes
1556	Philip II (House of Habsburg) becomes King of Spain
1558	Elizabeth (Last Monarch of the House of Tudor) becomes Queen of England
1562	Start of the French Wars of Religion: the Catholic League fought against the *Huguenots*
1566	Sultan Mehmet III born in Magnesia, inland from Izmir (Smyrna) in western Asia Minor
1568	Start of the Eighty Years War, also called the War for Dutch Independence from Spain
1571	Battle of Lepanto-*Don* Juan of Austria and Christian Holy League defeat Ottoman galleys
1577	Holy Roman Emperor Rudolph II selected by the Electors of independent German states
1580	John Smith born in Lincolnshire, England
1581	Levant Company chartered by Queen Elizabeth of England
1582	Circumcision of Mehmet III with festivals on the Hippodrome in *Stamboul*
1586	Marriage of young Aisha to *Damat* Ibrahim Pasha, Grand Vizier to Sultan Murad III
1588	Spanish Armada defeated by England
1590	Ottoman peace with Persia, ending a decade's long war started by Sultan Murad III.
1593	"Long War" between Ottoman and Holy Roman Empire begins. John's father George dies.
1595	Sultan Murad III, Father of Aisha, dies and her brother accedes to the Ottoman throneThe French-Spanish War between King Henry IV and Philip II begins.
1596	February - Cardinal Albert of Austria arrives in Brussels and becomes Governor General; April - Fall of the French Port of Calais on the coast to Cardinal Albert's commander; Summer - *Cecali* rebellion against the Ottoman throne spreads in northern Syria and Anatolia; July - Sack of Cadiz. English and Dutch fleet attack the Spanish relief fleet and the city; Autumn - Battle of Mezo-Keresztes: Sultan Mehmet III gains title of *Ghazi*; October - English-French Treaty signed in Rouen, France; Second Spanish Armada sails
1598	King James espouses "Divine Right of Kings" in his *True Laws of Free Monarchies*
1600	Ottoman conquest of Kanizsa in Hungary
1601	Aisha's first husband Grand Vizier *Damat* Ibrahim *Pasha* dies of natural causes. Hasan *the Fruiterer* becomes Grand Vizier, is promised in marriage to Aisha, goes to fight against Holy Roman Empire.
1602	November - Captain John Smith was sorely wounded in Wallachia, sold into slavery at Axiopolis on the Danube, and sent in chains to Aisha, Sister of the Sultan, in *Stamboul*.

English Slave Bibliography

Biographies and Memoirs of Captain John Smith

Arber, Edward, ed. *Capt. John Smith, of Willoughby by Alford, Lincolnshire; President of Virginia, and Admiral of New England. Works 1608-1631*. Birmingham: The English Scholar's Library 10 June 1884.

Barbour, Philip L. *The Three Worlds of Captain John Smith*. Boston: Houghton Mifflin Company, 1964.

Schmidt [Smith], Johanne [John]. "Vera desciptio Novae Angliae" in Johann-Theodor *de Bry's Americae pars Decima*. Oppenheimii: Hieronymi Galleri, 1619.

Smith, Bradford. *Captain John Smith; his Life & Legend*. Philadelphia: J.B. Lippincott Company, 1953.

Smith, John. *The True Travels, Adventures, and Observations of Captain John Smith*. London: 1629. Republished at Richmond: Franklin Press, 1819.

Wharton, Henry. *The Life of John Smith, English Soldier*. Edited by Laura Polanyi Striker. Translated from the Latin—Wharton used Smith's Latin name *Johannis Fabricius* and published his biography in 1680. Chapel Hill: University of North Carolina Press, 1957.

Woods, Katharine Pearson. *The True Story of Captain John Smith*. New York: Doubleday, Page, 1901.

England: Lincolnshire, London, and Shakespeare

Bertie, Peregrine. A Memoir of Peregrine Bertie, Eleventh Lord Willoughby de Eresby. London: John Murray, 1838.

Birch, Thomas. *Memoirs of the Reign of Queen Elizabeth, From the year 1581 till her Death, in which the Secret Intrigues of her Court, and the Conduct of her Favourite, Robert Earl of Essex, both at Home and Abroad are Particularly Illustrated, Vol ii [1596 to 1600]*. London: A. Millar, 1754.

Blythe, Ronald. *Akenfield: Portrait of an English Village*. New York: Dell Publishing, 1969.

Calendar of the Manuscripts of the Most Hon. The Marquis of Salisbury [Sir Robert Cecil] preserved at Hatfield House, Part VI [1596]. London: Eyre and Spottiswoode, 1895.

Brown, Horatio F., editor. *Calendar of State Papers and Manuscripts, Relating to English Affairs existing in the Archives and Collections of Venice, and in other libraries of Northern Italy, Vol. IX, 1592-1603 and Vol. X, 1603 to 1607*. London: Eyre and Spottiswood, 1897.

Burgess, William. *The Bible in Shakespeare*. Chicago: The Winona Publishing Company, 1903.

Camden, William. *History of the Most Renowned and Victorious Princess Elizabeth, Late Queen of England, Fourth Edition*. London: M. Flesher, R. Bentley, 1688.

Devereaux, Walter Bourchier. *Lives and Letters of the Devereux, Earls of Essex, in the Reigns of Elizabeth, James I, and Charles I, Vol. I 1540-1646*. London: John Murray, 1853.

Hume, Martin, editor. *Calendar of Letters and State Papers relating to English Affairs of the Reign of Elizabeth in the Archives of Simancas [Spain], Vol. IV, Elizabeth 1587-1603*. London: Eyre and Spottiswoode, 1899.

Greene, Mary Anne Everett. *Calendar of State Papers, Domestic Series, of the Reign of Elizabeth, 1595-1597*. London: Longmans, Green, Reader, and Dyer 1869.

Camden, William. *Annales or, the History of the Most Renowned Queen Elizabeth*. Translated from the Latin by R.N. London: Benjamin Fisher, 1635.

Collins, Arthur. *Letters and Memorials of State, in the Reigns of Queen Mary, Queen Elizabeth, King James, King Charles the First, Part of the Riegn of King Charles the Second, and Oliver's Usurpation, Vol. II [1596 to 1661]*. London: T, Osborne, 1746.

Daniel, Samuel. *Vision of Twelve Goddesses, Presented in a Mask, the Eighth of January, at Hampton Court*. London: Nicholas Okes, 1623.

De Lisle, Leand. *After Elizabeth*. New York: Ballantine Books, 2007.

Dickens, Charles. *The Adventures of Oliver Twist*. London: Chapman and Hall, 1585.

Early English Voyager, or the Adventures and Discoveries of Drake, Cavendish, and Dampier. London: T. Nelson and Sons, 1892.

Everett, A.L. "Shakespeare in 1596," in *The Shakespeare Association Bulletin*, Vol. 14, No. 3 (July 1939).

Fuller, Thomas. *Church History of Britain, From the Birth of Jesus Christ until the Year MDCXLVIII, Vol III*

[1580 to 1648]. London: Thomas Tegg and Sons, 1837.

Green, Mary Anne Everett, editor. *Calendar of State Papers, Domestic Series, Of the Reign of Elizabeth, 1595-1597.* London: Longmans, Green, Reader, and Dyer, 1869.

Gainsford, Thomas. *The Glory of England or a True Description of the Many Excellent Prerogatives, and Remarkable Blessings.* London: Edward Griffin, 1620.

Howell, Margaret. *Eleanor of Provence, Queenship in Thirteenth Century England.* Oxford: Wiley, Blackwell, 1998.

Hume, Martin A.S., editor. *Calendar of Letters and State Papers relating to English Affairs, Preserved in, or Originally Belonging to the Archives of Simancas [Spain], Vol IV, Elizabeth, 1587-1603.* London: Eyre and Spottiswood, 1899.

Hyamson, Albert M. *A History of the Jews in England.* London: Chatto & Windus, 1908.

Inwood, Stephen. *A History of London,* New York: Carroll & Graf Publishers, Inc., 1998.

Johnson, Paul. *Castles of England, Scotland and Wales.* London: Weinfield and Nicholson, 1989.

Lake, Peter, and Questier, Michael, editors. *Conformity and Orthodoxy in the English Church, C. 1550-1660.* Woodbridge: the Boydell Press, 200.

Laing, Lloyd and Laing, Jennifer. *Medieval Britain: The Age of Chivalry.* New York: St. Martins Press, 1996.

Law, Ernest. *The History of Hampton Court Palace in Stuart Times.* London, 1888.

Lee, Christopher. *1603,* New York: St. Martins Press, 2003.

Littletons Tenures in English, Lately perused and Amended. London: Charles Tetswiert, Esq., 1594.

MacCallum, M.W., editor. *Shakespeare's Roman Plays and their Background.* London, Melbource: Macmillan, 1910, 1967.

McManaway, James. *Studies in Shakespeare, Bibliography, and Theatre.* Richmond, Virginia: William Byrd Press, 1969

Markham, Clements R. *The Fighting Veres.* London: Sampson Low, Marston, Searle & Rivington, Ltd., 1888.

Noble, T. and Rose, T. *The Counties of Chester, Derby, Leicester, Lincoln, and Rutland, Illustrated.* Allom, Thomas, Illustrator. London, Paris, and New York: fisher, Son and Co.

Shakespeare, William. *The Living Shakespeare, Twenty-Two Pays & the Sonnets.* Campbell, Oscar James, editor. New York; The Macmillan Company, 1949.

Sheppard, Edgar. *The Old Royal Palace of Whitehall.* London, New York and Bombay: Longmans, Green, and Co., 1902.

Singman, Jeffrey L. *Daily Life in Elizabethan England,* Westport, Connecticut: Greenwood Press, 1995.

Strickland, Agnes. Lives of the Queens of England, From the Norman Conquest, Vol. 4 [Elizabeth]. London: George Bell and Sons, 1885.

Rosedale, Honyel Gough. Queen Elizabeth and the Levant Company: a Diplomatic and Literary Episode. Oxford, 1904.

Sheppard, Edgar. *The Old Royal Palace at Whitehall.* London, New York, and Bombay: Longmans, Green, and Co., 1902.

Sommerset, Anne. *Ladies in Waiting: From the Tudors to the Present Day.* London: Weidenfeld and Nicolson, 1984.

Strype, John. *Annals of the Reformation and Establishment of Religion, Vol IV.* Oxford: Clarendon Press, 1824.

Thornbury, Walter. *Old and New London: A Narrative of its History, its People, and its Places,* Volumes I-VI. Paris, London, and New York: Cassell, Petter and Galpin, circa 1880s.*

Turner, Sharon. *The History of the Reigns of Edward the Sixth, Mary, and Elizabeth.* London: Longman, Rees, Orme, Brown and Green, 1829.

Wedel, Lupold von. *Journey Through England and Scotland* [1584], translated from German by Dr. Gottfried von Bulow.

Wood, H. Jarvis. *Let the Great Story Told: The Truth about British Expansion.* London: Sampson Low, Marston, 1946.

France: Orleans, Paris, Rouen and King Henry IV

Adeline, J., Brunet-Debaine, Lalanne Max., and Toussaint, H. *Rouen Illustre*. Rouen: Chez l'Editeur, 1882.

Aguesse, Laurent. *Histoire de l'Etablissement du Protestantisme en France, Vol IV. [1589 to 1599],*. Paris: Libraire Fischbacher, 1886.

Allom, Thomas and Wright, G.N. *France Illustrated*. London: Fisher, Son, & Co. 1845.

Baird, Henry M. *The Huguenots and Henry of Navarre, Vol, II [1587-1610]*. New York: Charles Scribner's Sons, 1903.

Baumgartner, Frederic J. *France in the Sixteenth Century*. New York: St. Martins Press, 1995.

Bethune, Maximilian de. *Memoirs of Maximilian de Bethune, Duke of Sully, Prime Minister to Henry the Great, Vol ii [1594 to 1601]*. Translated from the French by Charlotte Lennox. London: J. Rivington & Sons, J. Dosley, S. Crowder, G. Robinson, T. Cadell, & T. Evans, 1778.

Browning, W.S. *A History of the Huguenots*. London: Whittaker and Co., 1840.

Bur, Girard de. *Histoire de la Vie de Henry IV, Vol III [1596 - 1605]*. Paris: Nyon. 1779.

Bussey, George, and Gaspey, Thomas. *Pictorial History of France, Vol. II [1461 to 1795]*. London: Wm. S. Orr and Co., 1843.

Capefigue, M. *Histoire de la Reforme, de la Ligue, et du Regne Henri IV., Vol. VII [1593-1598] and Vol. VIII [1597-1610]*. Paris: Dufey, Libraire, 1835.

Cayet, Pierre Victor. *Chronologie Septennaire*. Paris: 1606.

Cook, Sir Theodore Andrea. *The Story of Rouen*. London: J.M. Dent and Co., 1901.

Davila, H.C. *The History of the Civil Wars of France*. Translated out of the Italian. Savoy: By T.N. for Henry Herrigman, 1678.

Calvin, John. *Institutes of the Christian Religion by John Calvin, Vo. I & II*. Translated from the Latin and Collated with the Author's Last Edition in French by John Allen. Philadelphia: Presbyterian Board of Christian Education, 1936.

Cayet, Pierre-Victor. "Chronologie Novenaire, Contenant L'Histoire de La Gueer sour le Regne du Tres-Chrestian Roy de France et de Navarre Henry IV (1589 - 1598)" in *Nouvelle Collection de Memoire pour servir a L'Histoire de France*. Paris: Chex L'Editeur du Commentaire Analytique de Code Civil, 1838.

— — —. Chronologie Septenaire [1598-1604]. Paris: Jean Richer, 1609.

Charrier, E. *Negociations de la France dans Levant, ou Correspondances, Memoires et Actes Diplomatique, tome IV [1581-1589]*. Paris: Imprimerie Imperiale, 1860

Collinson, John. *The Life of Thuanus [de Thou]: With an account of Some of His Writings and a Translation of a Preface of History*. London: 1807.

Desclozeaux, Adrien. *Gabrielle d'Estrees*. London: Arthur L Humphreys, 1907.

Discourse of the Joyful and Triumphant Entry of the Very High, Very Powerful, and Very Magnanimous Prince Henry IV. Rouen, 1599.

Dumas, Alexandre. *Margaret de Valois [La Reine Margot], The Works of Alexandre Dumas in Thirty Volumes, Vol. 3*. New York: Collier, circa 1902.

— — — *The Three Musketeers [Les Trois Mousquetaires]* [New York: Nelson & Company, circa 1902.

Edwards, H. Sutherland. *Old and New Paris, Its History, its People, and its Places, Vol. I & II*. London, Paris, & Melbourne: Cassell and Company, Ltd., 1893.

L'Estoile, Pierre de. *Nouvelle Collection des Memoires relatifs a L'Histoire de France, Vol 15 [1589 to 1611]* Michaud. Paris: Didier et Ce,Libraires-Editeurs, 1856.

Freer, Martha Walker. *The History of the Reign of Henry IV, King of France and Navarre, Vol. I, Part ii [1594 to 1598]*. London: Hurst and Blackett, 1861.

Henri de Bourbon. *Memoirs of Henry the Great and of the Court of France during his Reign, vol. ii, [1590 to 1610]*. London: Harding, Triphook, and Lepard, 1824.

L'Histoire de Filipe Emanuel de Loraine, Duc de Mercoeur. Cologne: Pierre Marteau, 1689.

The History of Paris from the Earliest Period to Present Day, Three Volumes. London: Geo. B. Whittaker, 1825.

Horne, Alistair. *Seven Ages of Paris*. New York: Vintage Books, 2004.

Hussey, Andrew. *Paris: the Secret History.* New York: Bloomsbury, 2006.

LaCroix, Paul. *Les Arts u Moyen Age et a l'Epoque de la Renaissance.* Paris: de l'Institut de France, 1871.*

— — —*Moeurs, Usages et Costumes au Moyen Age et a L'Epoque de la Renaissance.* Paris: de l'Institut de France, 1871.*

— — —*Vie Militaire et Religieuse au Moyen-Age et à l'époque de la Renaissance.* Paris: de l'Institut de France, 1871.*

LeGrain, Jean Baptiste. *Decade Contenant la Vie et Gestes de Henry Le Grand.* Paris: Jean Laquehay, 1614.

Licquet, Theodore. *Rouen: Its History, Monuments, and Environs.* Translated from French by M.H. Barguet. Paris: 1869.

Matthieu, Pierre. *Histoire de France du Regne Henry IV [1598-1601]* Paris: J. Metayer, circa 1612.

— — — *Histoire de Henry IIII, Roy de France et de Naavarre, Tome Second.* Paris: Nicolas Buon, 1623.

Morice, Dom Hyacinthe. *Memoires pour Servir de Preuves a l'Histoire Ecclesiastique et Civlie de Bretagne, Tome iii. [1462 to 1600].* Paris: Charles Osmont, 1746.

Mornay, Phillippes de. *Memoires de Messire Philippes de Mornay, Seigneur du Plessis Marli. Vol I [1572-1589], Vol. II [1589 to 1599].* Chantilly: 1624.

Perefix, Haudouin de. *Histoire de Roy Henry le Grand.* Amsterdam: Chez Daniel Elzevier, 1664.

— — —*The Life of Henry the Fourth of France.* Translated by m. Le Moine. Paris: Didot l'Aine, 1785.

Perkins, *The Churches of Rouen.* London: George Bell & Sons, 1900.

Planta, Edward. *A New Picture of Paris; or, the Stranger's Guide to The French Metropolis, 15th Edition.* London: Samuel Leigh, 1827.

Thou, Jacques-Auguste de. *Histoire Universelle de Jacques-Augsuste de Thou, 1543-1607.*

Willert, P.F. *Henry of Navarre and the Huguenots in France.* New York G.P. Putman's Sons, 1893.

Wolnoth, William. *The Ancient Castles of England and Wales, Vol. 1.* London: Longman, Hurst, and Co., 1825.

The Sack of Cadiz, Spain in 1596

Abreu, Pedro de. *Historia Saqueo de Cadiz en 1596.* Cadiz: Revista Medica, 1866.

Bacon, Anthony and Birch, Thomas. *Memoirs of the Reign of Queen Elizabeth, Vol. II.* London: A. Millar, 1754.

Castro, Don Adolfo de, Historia *de* Cadiz y su Provincia. Cadiz: Imprenta *de* la Revista Medica, 1858.

Corbett, Juliann S. *The Successors of Drake.* London, New York, and Bombay: Longmans, Gree, and Co., 1900.

"Documentos Relativos a la toma y saco *de* Cadiz por los ingleses en julio *de* 1596," *Collecion de Documentos Ineditos para la Historia de Espana, Tomo XXXVI [Vol. 36].* Madrid: Imprenta *de* la Viuda *de* Calero, 1860.

Herrara, Antonio de, *Tercera Parte de la Historia General del Mundo, de XIIII anos del tiempo del senor Rey don Felipe II.* Madrid: Alonso Martin, 1612/

Hakluyt, Richard, ed."The Honourable Voyage to Cadiz, Anno 1596" in *The Principal Navigations, Voyages, Traffiques and Discoveries of the English Nation in Twelve Volumes, Vol. IV.* Glasgow: James MacLehose and Sons, 1904.

Orlers, Jean Jeanszoon and Haestens, Henry de. *Description & Representation de toutes les Victoires.* Leiden: 1612.

Raleigh, Sir Walter. *The Works of Sir Walter Raleigh, Vol. VIII: Miscellaneous Works.* Oxford: University Press, 1829.

Vere, Sir Francis. "The Commentaries of Sir Francis Vere" [originally published by William Dillingham ,1657] in *Stuart Tracts, 1603-1693.* New York: E.P. Dutton and Co., circa 1900.

Spain

Alberi, Eugenio, ed. *Relazion degli Ambasciatori Veniti, Serie I, Volume V [Spain, 1563 to 1598].* Firenze: A Spese dell' Editore, 1861.

Calvert, Albert Frederick. *The Escorial.* London: John Lane, 1907.

Campan, Cesare. *Della Vita del Catholico et Invittissimo Don Filippo Secondo, Parte Terza [1567 to 1580]*. Vicenza: Pietro Grecco, 1608.

Cervantes, Miguel de. *Don Quixote, Parts I and II*. Translated by Tom Lathrop. New York: New American Library, 2011. [Note: Cervantes fought at Battle of Lepanto and later captured, enslaved, and held by Barbary pirates.]

Crow, John A. *Spain: the Root and the Flower*. Berkeley and Los Angeles: University of California Press, 1963, 1985.

Documentos Ineditos para la Historia de Espana, Tomo 41 [Vol. 41] [including Cartas de Almirate de Aragon Francisco de Mendoza al Archduque Alberto (1596 to 1599)]. Madrid: La Viuda de Calero, 1862.

Feros, Antonio. *Kingship and Favoritism in the Spain of Philip III*. Cambridge: Cambridge University Press, 2000.

Gautier, Theophile. *The Works of Theophile Gautier in 24 Volumes, Vol. IV, Travels in Spain*. Translated and edited by F.C. de Sumichrast. Cambridge, MA: The Jenson Society, 1906.

Kaiser, David. *Politics & War: European Conflict from Philip II to Hitler*. Cambridge, Massachusetts: Harvard University Press, 1990.

Kamen, Philip. *Philip of Spain*. New Haven: Yale University Press, 1997.

Klingenstin, L. *The Great Infanta: Isabel, Sovereign of the Netherlands*. New York: G.P. Putnam's Sons, 1910.*

Mattingly, Garrett. *The Armada*. NY: Houghton Mifflin, 1959.

McCabe, Joseph. *A Candid History of the Jesuits*. New York: G.P. Putman's Sons, 1913.

Nani, Agostini, with Alberi, Eugenio, editor, "Sommario della Relazione," in *Le Relazioni degli Ambasaciatori al Senato Veneti, Series I, Vol. V, [Spain 1563 to 1598]*. Stati Europe. Firenze: 1861.

Parker, Geoffrey. *The Grand Strategy of Philip II*. New Haven and London: Yale University Press, 1998.

Pendrill, Colin. *Heinemann Advance History: Spain 1474-1700*. Oxford: Pearson Education, 2002.

Ranke, Leopold. *The Ottoman and the Spanish Empires in the 16th and 17th Centuries*. Translated from the German by Walter K. Kelly. London: Whittaker and Co, 1843.

Turkey and the Ottoman Empire: Constantinople and the Crimean-Tartars

A Compleat History of the Turks, vol ii [1595 to 1700]. London: Andr. Bell, 1701.

Amicis, Edmondo de. *Constantinople*. Translated by Maria Hornor Landsdale. Philadelphia: Henry T. Coates & Co., 1896.

Baker, Bernard Granville. *The Walls of Constantinople*. London: John Milne, 1910.

Baker, James. *Turkey in Europe*. London, Paris, and New York: Cassell, Petter, and Galpin, 1877.

Baratta, Cav. Avv. A. Compilata, *Costantinopoli Effigiata e Descritta*. Torino: Alesandro Fontana e Pomba e Gieuseepe Comp., 1840.

Batau, Lugduni. *Turcici Imperii Status seu discrusus varii de Rebus Turcarum*. 1630.

Baudier, Michel. *History of the Imperial Estate of Grand Seigneurs*. Translated from French by Edward Grimeston. London: William Stanley, 1635.

Beauvau, Henri. *Relation Journaliere du Voyage du Levant, Faict et Descrit [in 1604)*. Toul: Francis du Bois, 1608.

Becattini, Franceso. *Storia Ragionata del Tuchi, ae degl' Imperatori di Costaninopoli, di Germania, e di Russia, e d' altre Potenze Cristiane, Vol 2*. Venezia: Francesco Pitteri, e Francesco Sansoni, 1788.

Bernier, Tavernier. "A New Description of the Grand Seignior's Seraglio" in *Collections of Travels through Turky [Turkey] through Persia and the East Indies, Vol I*. London: Moses Pitt 1684.

Bertelli, Pietro. *Vite Degl' Imperatori de Turchi*. Vicenta: 1599

Biron, Theodore de Gontaut, *Ambassade en Turquie de Jean de Gontaut Biron, Baron de Salignac, 1605 a 1610*. Paris: Honor Champion, 1888.

Bisaha, Nancy. *Creating East and West: Renaissance Humanists and the Ottoman Turks*. Philadelphia: University of Pennsylvania Press, 2004.

Biddle, William [Guilielmus Biddulphus]. "The Description of the Famous City of Constantinople" in *Collection of Voyages and Travels*.

Blount, Henry. "A Voyage to the Levant" [Begun in AD 1634] in *Collection of Voyages and Travels, Volume I.*

Bomichen, M Georgium. *Historia Wee Grewlich der Grosse Mahomet/ Turctisher Keiser/de Namens der ander/di hoch berumbte Stadt Constantinopel.* Magdeburgf: Johan Francten, 1595.

Boyar, Ebru and Fleet, Kate. *A Social History of Ottoman Istanbul.* Cambridge: Cambridge University Press, 2010.

Broaquiere, Bertrandon *de* la. "Le Voyage d'Outremer" in *Recueil de Voyages et de Documents pour servir a l'Histoire de la Geographie.* Paris: Ernest Leroux Editeur, 1842.

Brown, Horatio F. "Marriage of Ibraim Pasha" in *Studies in the History of Venice, Vol. II.* London: John Murray, 1907.

Busbequius, M. *Ambassades et Voyages en Turquie et Amasie de Mr. Busbequius.* Traduitus en Francois par S.G. Paris: Pierre David, 1646.

Capponi, Niccolo. *Victory of the West: The Great Christian-Muslim Clash at the battle of Lepanto.* Cambridge, MA: Da Capo Books, 2006.

Chalkokondyles, the Athenian Loaonikos, and Thomas, Artus. *L'Histoire de la Decadence de L'Empire Grec et Establissement de Celvy des Turcs, Vol I [1352 to 1610].* Paris: Claude Sonnius, 1650.

Chishull, Edmund. *Travels in Turkey and Back to England.* London: W. Bowyer, 1701.

Colomb, Captain. *Slave-Catching in the Indian Ocean, A Record of Naval Experiences.* London: Longmans, Green, and Co., 1873.

Compagnoni, Dal Cav., "Comilata" *Storia Dell' Impero Ottomano, Vol. I & II.* Livorno: Glauco Masi, 1829.

Constantus of Constantinople. *Ancient and Modern Constantinople.* Translated by John P. Brown. London: Stevens Brothers, 1868.

Constellan, A.L. "History of the Turks" in *The World in Miniatures: Turkey, Six Volumes.* Translated from the French by Frederic Shoberl, ed. London: Ackerman, circa 1810.

Contarini, Francesco, and Nani, Agostino, Old and New Venetian Ambassadors in Constantinople, Valley of Pera, Istanbul, 2nd December 1602

Courmenin, Des Hayes de. *Voiage de Levant, Fait par le Commandement du Roy en l'annee 1621.* Paris: Adrian Taupinar, 1645.

Crawford, F. Marion. *Constantinople.* London: MacMillan and Co., 1895.

Davis, William Stearns. *A Short History of the Near East: From the Founding of Constantinople.* New York: the Macmillan Company, 1922.

D'Ohsson, M *de* M***. *Tableu General de l'Empire Othoman, 13 Volumes.* Paris: 1783.

Dursteler, Eric. *Venetians in Constantinople, Nation, Identity, and Coexistence in the Early Modern Mediterranean.* Baltimore: The Johns Hopkins University Press, 2006.

Dwight, Harry. *Constantinople, Old and New.* London: Longmans, Green and Co., 1915.

Eliot, Sir Charles. *Turkey in Europe.* London: Edward Arnold, 1908.

Eversley, Lord. *The Turkish Empire, Its Growth and Decay.* New York: Dodd, Mead, and Company, 1917.

Evliya *Effendi. Narrative of Travels in the 17th Century, Volume 1, Part i and ii; and Vol. 2.* Translated from Turkish by Ritter Joseph van Hammer. London: Oriental Translation Fund of Great Britain and Ireland, 1846, 1850.

Faroqhi, Suraiya. *The Ottoman Empire and the World Around It.* London: I.B. Tauris & Co. Ltd, 2004.

Fetvaci, Emine. *Picturing History at the Ottoman Court.* Bloomington, Indiana: Indiana University Press, 2013.

Finkel, Caroline. *Osman's Dream: The Story of the Ottoman Empire, 1300–1923.* London: John Murray, 2005.

Fisher, Alan. "The Sale of Slaves in the Ottoman Empire: Markets and State Taxes on Slave Sales, Some Preliminary Considerations," in *Bogazici Universitesi Dergisi,* Vol VI, 1978.

Flachat, Jean Claude. *Obervations sur Commerce et Arts, Vol. I & II.* Lyon: Jacquenod Pere & Rusand Libraires, 1766.

Frachetta, Girolamo. *Il Primo Libro dell Oration Nel Genere Deliberativo [Includes Sigismund Bathori oration Contra Turc].* Roma: Bernardino Beccari, 1598.

Frachetta, Girolamo. *Il Ragguaglio dell Marauigliose pompe con le quali Mehemet Settergi.* Venetia: Guido Martini, 1597.

Freres, Rouargue, Illustrator. *Constantinople et la Mer Noire.* Paris: Belin-LePrieur et Morizot, ed., 1855.

Garnett, Lucy M.J. *The Women of Turkey and their Folk-Lore.* London: David Nutt, 1890/

Gautier, Theophile. *The Works of Theophile Gautier, Vol X, Constantinople.* Translated from the French by F.C. *de* Sumichrast. New York: George D Sproul, 1901.

A General History of the Turks, Moguls, and Tatars, Vulgarly called Tartars. Translated from the French. London: J. and J Knapton, 1730.

Girardin, M. Amassades *de M. Le Comte de Guillaragues et de M. Girardin aupres du Grand Seigneur.* Paris: G. *de* Luines, 1687.

Gilles, Peter (Gyllius, Petrus). *The Antiquities of Constantinople.* Translated from Latin by John Ball. London: 1729.

Goodwin, Jason, *Lords of the Horizons: A History of the Ottoman Empire.* New York: Henry Holt and Company, 1998.

Grosvenor, Edwin. *Constantinople.* Volumes I and II. Boston: Robert Brothers, 1895.*

Hammer, Joseph. *Campaigns of the Osman Sultans, Two Volume [1389 to 1640].* Translated from the German by Thomas Aquila Dale. London: William Straker, 1835.

Hammer, J. de. *Histoire de L'Empire Ottoman.* Traduit *de* "Allemand par J.J Hellert, Tome Septieme 1574-1600. Paris: Bellizad, Barthes, Dufour et Lowell, 1837.

Hammer-Purgstall, J. *Geschicte der Chane der Krim unter Osmanischer Herrschaft aus Turkischen Quellen.* Wien: K.K. Hof- und Stattscruckerrei, 1856.

Hathaway, Jane. *Beshir Agha: Chief Eunuch of the Ottoman Imperial Harem.* Oxford: Oneworld Publications, 2005.

Hathaway, Jane. "Out of Africa and into the Palace: The Ottoman Chief Harem Eunuch," in *Living in the Ottoman Realm: Empire and Identity, 13th to 20th Centuries.* Edited by Christine Isom-Verhaaren and Kent F. Schull. Bloomington & Indianapolis: Indian University Press, 2016.

Hentzner, Paul [German Lawyer] and Naunton, Sir Robert. *Travels in England during the Reign of Queen Elizabeth with Fragmenta Regalia.* London, Paris, New York, & Melbourne: Cassell and Company, Ltd., 1901.

Heroltzberg, Jacobo Geudero ab. *Turca Kiketos: Hocest; de Imperio Ottamannico Bello Contra Turcas, Prospere Gerendo.* Francofurti [Frankfurt]: Wechelianis, 1601.

Hondius, Jodocus. "The Turkish Empire" in *Historia Mundi, Atlas Minor* by Gerardi Mercatoris Translated from Latin. 1634.

Howorth, Henry H. *History of the Mongols from the 9th to the 19th Century, Part II The So-called Tartars of Russia and Central Asia.* New York: Burt Franklin, 1880

Hughes, Charles. *Shakespeare's Europe: Unpublished Chapters of Fynes Moryson's Itinerary.* London: Sherratt & Hughes, 1903.

Hutton, William Hutton. *Constantinople: The Story of the Old Capitol of the Empire.* London: J.M. Dent & Sons, Ltd., 1921

Imber, Colin. *The Ottoman Empire, 1300-1650, The Structure of Power.* New York: Palgrave Macmillan, 2002.

Jacob, Samuel; Proctor, Colonel; Riddle, J.E.; and McConechy, James. *History of the Ottoman Empire, including a Survey of the Greek Empire and the Crusades.* London and Glasgow: Richard Griffen and Company, 1854.

Kinross, Patrick Balfour. *The Ottoman Centuries: The Rise and Fall of the Ottoman Empire.* New York: Morrow Quill Paperbacks, 1977.

Knolles, Richard. *General History the the Turks.* London: 1603, 1610, 1705.

Lamartine, Alpohonse de. *History of Turkey, Vol. III.* Translated from the French. New York: D. Appleton & Company, 1857.

Lithgow, William. *Total Discourse of Rare Adventures and Painful Pereginations, Of Long Nineteen Years Travel [1609-1638].* Glasgow: James MacLehose and Sons, 1906.

Lomartine, Monsieur de. "Slave-Market at Constantinople, " an account of a "Pilgrimage to the Holy Land and other Countries iin the East, in the years 1832 and 1833," in *Chambers' Edinburgh Jour-*

nal, No. 177 (20th June 1835), p. 168.

Lott, Emmeline. *Governess in Egypt, Harem Life in Egypt and Constantinople*. London: Richard Bentley, 1865.

Lybyer, Albert Howe. *Government of the Ottoman Empire in the Time of Suleiman the Magnificent*. Cambridge: Harvard University Press, 1913.

MacFarlane, Charles. *Turkey and Its Destiny, Vol. I & II*. London: John Murray, 1850.

MacLean, Gerald. *Rise of Orient Travel: English Visitors to the Ottoman Empire, 1580 to 1720*. New York: Palgrave Macmillan, 2004.

Mans, Peirre Belon du. *Les Observations de Plusieurs Signularitez et Choses Memorables, Trovvees en Grece, Asie, Judee, Egypte, Arabie & autres pays estranges [Including Constantinople], Trois Livres*. Paris: Hierosme *de* Marnef, 1638.

Mena, D. Manuel Antonio de. *Historia General del Imperio Otomano, Tomo I, Escritas en Arabigo Por Un Historiador Turco*. Traducidas en Frances por Monsieur *de* La Croix. Madrid: Manuel Fernandez, 1736.

Menzies, Sutherland [aka Elizabeth Stone]. *Turkey Old and New: Historical, Geographical and Statistical, Two Volumes*. London: Wm. H. Allen & Co, 1880.

Mignot, P. *The History of the Turkish or Ottoman Empire, From its Foundation in 1300, To the Peace of Belgrade in 1740, Vol I & II*. Translated from the French by A. Hawkins. Execter: R. Thorn, 1787.

Monroe, Will Seymour. *Turkey and the Turks Illustrated*. Boston: L.C. Page and Company, 1907.

Montagu, Lady Mary Wortley. *Letters of the Right Honorable Lady M___y W____y M____e, Written during her Travels of Europe, Asia and Africa to Persons of Distinction, Men of Letters & C. in different Parts of Europe, which contain among other curious relations, Accounts of the Policy and Manner of the Turks*. Paris: Didot the Eldest, 1779.

Moryson, Fynes. *Itinerary, Vol ii [1596 to 1601]*. Glasgow: James MacLehose and Sons, 1907.

Mour, Maler van. *Abbildung de Turkishcen Hoses nach den Gemalden*. Nurnberg: Christ. Weigel und Adam Gottlieb Schneider, 1789.

Mundy, Peter. *A Brief Relation of the Turks, their Kings, Emperors or Grand Seigneurs*. Istanbul: 1618.

Naima, Mustafa. *Annals of the Turkish Empire, Vol. 1*. Translated into English by Charles Fraser London: Oriental Translation Fund, 1832.

Neuwe Chronica, Turkischer Nacion, von Turcken Selbs beschrieben: volgendts gemehrt; undd in vier Bucher Adgetheit . [Four Books with history (Vol. I & II) from Osman I to 1589 ; (Vol. 3) Pandectes; Vol 4 (Incl. Siege of Vienna in 1529; Circumcision of Mehmet III in 1582; and Marriage of Aisha to Ibrahim Pasha in 1586). Franckfurt am Mayn: Andres Wechels, 1590.

Pardoe, Julie. *The City of the Sultan and Domestic Manners of the Turk*. London: G. Routledge & Co., 1854.

Parry, Vernon J. *A History of the Ottoman Empire to 1730*. Cambridge: Cambridge University Press, 1976.

Pedani, Maria Pedia. *Inventory of the Lettere e Scritture Turchesche in the Venetian State Archives*. Leiden: Koninklijke Brill NV, 2010

Pastpadi, Alexandre G. *Etudes sur les Tchinghianes [Gypsies or Romas] ou Bohemiens de L'Empire Ottoman*. Constantinople: Antoine Koromela, 1870.

Pierce, Leslie. *The Imperial Harem: Women and Sovereignty in the Ottoman Empire*. New York: Oxford University Press, 1993.

Pinkerton, John. *Turkey in Europe, A General Collection of the Best and Most Interesting Voyages and Travels in All Part of the World, Vol. 17*. London: Longman, Hurst, Rees, Orme, Brown, Paternoster-Row, and Cadell and Davies, 1814.

Poullet, Sr. *Nouvelles Relations du Levant*. Paris: Louis Billaine, 1668.

Purchas, Samuel. *Hakluytus Posthumus or Purchas His Pilgrims, Vol. VIII*. Glasgow: James MacLehose and Sons, 1905.

Reisebuchern, von Meyers. *Turkei, Rumanien, Serbien, Bulgarie.*, Leipzig und Wien: Bibliographische Institut. Circa 1898.

Reusner, Nikolaus, editor. *Selectissimae Orationes et Consultation Bello Turico, Vol. 2, Vol IV Lipsiae [Leipzig]*: 1596,1598.

Reston, James, Jr. *Defenders of the Faith: Charles V, Suleyman the Magnificent, and the Battle for Europe.* New York, NY: Penguin Press, 2009.

Ricaut, Paul. *The History of the Present State of the Ottoman Empire, In Three Book.*, London: Charles Brome, 1686.

Riley-Smith, Jonathan. *The Crusades, Christianity, and Islam.* New York, NY: Columbia University Press, 2008.

Rinieri, P. Ilario. *Clemente VIII e Sinan Bassa Cicala.* Roma: Civilta Cattolica, 1898.

Robinson, Francis. *Atlas of the Islamic World since 1500.* Oxford: Equinox, Ltd., 1982.

Safiye Valide Sultana, "Letters to Queen Elizabeth." in

Sagred, Giovanni. *Memorie Istoriche de Monarchi Ottomani.* Bologna: Geio: Recaldini., 1674

Said, Edward W. *Orientalism.* NY: Random House, 1978.

Sale, George. "History of the Othman Empire," *The Modern Part of Universal History, Vol. X.* London: C. Bathurst, J.F. and C. Rivington, 1781.

Sanderson, John. "Discourse of the Most Notable Things of the Famous City Constantinople" in *Hakluytus Posthumus* or *Purchas his Pilgrim, Vol IX.* Glasgow: University Press by Robert MacLehose & Company, Ltd., 1905

Sandys, George. "A Relation of a Journey Begun in Anno Domino 1610," in *Hakluytus Posthumus or Purchas His Pilgrimes in Twenty Volumes, Vol VIII.* Glasgow: University Press by Robert MacLehose & Company, Ltd., 1905

Sandys, George and Addison. *A General History of the Ottoman Empire, Illustrated.* London: Charles Marsh, 1711.

Sansovino, Francesco. *Historia Universale dell Origine Guerre, et Imperio de Turchi, Vol. II.* Venetia: 1654.

Sapiencia, Octavio. *Nuevo Tratado de Turquia con una Descripcion de Sitio, y Civdad de Constantiopla, costumbres del gran Turco, de su modo de govierno, de su Palacio, Consejo, Martyrios de algunos Martyres, y de ostras cosas notable.* Madr: Alonso Martin, 1622.

Scudery, Monsieur de. *Ibrahim or the Illustrious Bassa [Pasha], an Excellent New Romance, The Whole Work in Four Parts.* Translated from the French by Henry Cogan. London: Humphrey Moseley, 1652.

Skilliter, Susan A. "The Letters of the Venetian 'Sultana' Nûr Bânû and Her Kira to Venice". In *Studia turcologica memoriæ Alexii Bombaci dicata*, a cura di Gallotta, Aldo e Marazzi, Ugo. Napoli: Istituto Universitario Orientale, 1982: 515-536.

– – –. "Three Letters from the Ottoman Sultana Safiye to Queen Elizabeth I" in *Documents from Islamic Chanceries*. Stern, Samuel Miclos and Aubin, editor. Oxford: Cassirer, 1965.

Smith, Thomas. "Historical Observations Relating to Constantinople by the Reverend and learned Thomas Smith," in *Philosophical Transactions, Num. 152 (October 20, 1683).*

Soraznzii, Lazari. *Ottmannus sive de Imperio Trucico* in Abraham Bucholcero's *Catalogus Consulum Romanorum.* Ex Offincia Commenlinians, 1598.

Soranzo, Lazaro, *The Ottoman* [1597]. Translated from Italian by Abraham Hartwell in 1603

Spagni, Emilie. "Una Sultana Veneziana." in *Nuovo Archivio Veneto, Tomo. XIX, Parte 1.* Venezia: Prem. Tip Vesentini Cav. Dererico, 1900.

Spandounes, Theodore. *On the Origins of Ottoman Emperors.* Translated by Donald M. Nicol. Cambridge: Cambridge University, 1997.

Stoneman, Richard. *A Traveller's History of Turkey.* Brooklyn, NY: Interlink Books, 1993.

Tavernier, J.B. *Nouvelle Relation de L'Interieur du Serrail du Grand Seigneur.* Cologne: Coneille Egmon & ses Associez, 1675.

Turabi *Effendi*, Compiler. *Turkish Cookery Book, A Collection of Receipts [Recipes].* Circa 1864.

Thuani, Jacobi Augusti. *Historiarum Sui Temporis, Pars Quinta [1594 to 1607].* Francorfurti: Petri Kopssig, 1621.

Thornton, Thomas. *The Present State of Turkey or A Description of the Political, Civil, and Religious, Constitution, Government, and Laws of the Ottoman Empire, Two Volumes.* London: Joseph Mawman, 1809.

Tournefort, Jospeh Pitton. *A Voyage into Levant, 3 Volumes.* London: D. Midwinter, et. al., 1741

Vanel, M. *Abrege Nouveau Histoire Generale des Turcs, Tome Troisieme [1566 to 1648].* Paris: 1697.

Van Millingen. Alexander, *Byzantine Constantinople: The Walls and Adjoining Sights.* London: 1899.

Van Millingen. Alexander, *Constantinople, An Art History*. London: 1906.

Van Mour, Jean Baptiste, and Von Ferriol. *Abbildung des Turkischen Hoses nach den Gemaelden*. Nurnberg: Christ. Weigel und Adam Gottlieb Schneider, 1789.

Vignau, Sieur du. *L'Etat Present de la Puissance Ottomane, Avec les Causes de son Accroissement, & celles de sa Decadence*. La Haye: Abrahame *de* Hondt et Jacob van Ellinghuysen, 1688.

Wells, Charles. *The Literature of the Turks, A Turkish Chrestomathy*. London Bernard Quaritch, 1891.

Wheatcroft, Andrew. *The Ottomans*. (London: Viking, Penguin Books, 1993.

White, Sam. *Climate of Rebellion in the Early Modern Ottoman Empire*. New York: Cambridge University Press, 2011.

Wilson, Epiphanius, editor. *Turkish Literature, Comprising Fables; Belles-Lettres and Sacred Traditions*. Translated into English. New York: Colonial Press: 1901.

Withers, Master Robert. "A Description of the Grand Seignor's Seraglio Or Turkish Emperor's Court" in *Purchas His Pilgrims*. Circa 1620.

Wright, Clifford A. *A Mediterranean Feast: The Story of the Birth of the Celebrated Cuisinnes of the Mediterranean, From the Merchants of Venice to the Barbary Corsairs*. New York: William Morrow Cookbooks, 1999.

Zinfeisen, Johann Wilhem. *Geschicte Europaeischen Staaten, Geschichte des Osmanischen Reiches in Europa, Vol III [1574 to 1623]*. Gotha: Friedrich Andreas Perthes 1855.

* These sources were used for all photographs and drawings contained herein, with exception to the maps drawn by the author, David Eugene Andrews

Acknowledgements

THE PROCESS OF writing a book is rarely a singular work of the author. Families and loved ones often become sounding boards of ideas bounced their way. These ideas may deal with difficult passages or ideas needing to be reshaped. Using God-given talents, some artists may sculpt works perfectly the first time; others need to add water to hardening clumps of clay, to mold their work into recognizable forms. The wordsmith makes scenes, shapes characters, and gives substance to plot and story.

Besides loved ones who supported me along the way, I would like to thank all members of the Saddleback Writers Guild for their invaluable feedback. Specifically, I thank Jacquelyn Hanson, Jessica Danger, Mel Zimmerman, Richard Morgan, and Joy Young, now deceased. Listening to chapter after chapter, week after week, they made timely suggestions, clearing up misunderstandings. My appreciation extends to Amanda La-Pera for her editorial and stylistic suggestions. For any error not caught, the responsibility rests entirely with the author. My thanks also go to Adèle Franklin for exterior, background artwork and John Deguzman for cover graphic design, as well as to Eric Zuley, his father James Zuley, and EZWay Broadcasting, Inc. for their branding, marketing, and social media expertise.

Author's Note

This is a work of historical fiction. Dates of historical importance have not been changed. Major characters have not been placed in locations if they were known to be elsewhere. Memoirs, diaries, and first-hand accounts in different languages have been consulted, but translations can be imperfect. Anyone who has ever talked to a foreigner knows (and who isn't a sojourner who lives on this earth?), communicating is a process that can take both time and effort, even if it just learning to simply say, "Grazie."

About the Author

DAVID EUGENE ANDREWS earned two degrees in International Affairs, including a Master's Degree from Columbia University in New York City where he specialized in International Economics. He has edited and published numerous international economic forecasts for Fortune 500 companies. He loves languages and has studied German, Chinese, Italian, French, and Dutch. He enjoys travel, which has taken him to the Far East, the Middle East, and Europe.

Following the fall of Saigon, he worked at a Vietnamese refugee camp, setting up English as a Second Language classes across the state of Washington. While in Oregon, he co-chaired an International Affairs Symposium on the Middle East and the Oil Crisis. The first time he saw the Great Pyramids of Egypt, he was riding horseback with a friend.

At the height of the Cold War, an AP photographer captured him bearing an American flag, shaking hands with a Russian holding a Soviet flag. USA Today featured Andrews, a former ski instructor at Mt. Hood in Oregon, on its front page during its coverage of the Opening Ceremonies at the 1984 Winter Olympics in Sarajevo, Bosnia. More recently, he completed his Juris Doctor degree.

The English Slave is the first book in his historical fiction series *Empires and Kingdoms*. Throughout the *Empires and Kingdoms* series, readers find themselves immersed in the political, religious, and personal turmoil that characterizes the advent of the seventeenth century—a time when the Holy Roman and Ottoman Empires vie for territory and power in Southeastern Europe, and when kingdoms and dominions battle for influence and prestige in Western Europe and beyond.

CPSIA information can be obtained
at www.ICGtesting.com
Printed in the USA
LVHW091505111119
637000LV00007B/98/P